*I would like to dedicate this book to anyone out there who has
ever suffered or is suffering in an abusive or toxic relationship.
Please know that there is hope, there is help and
there is light at the end of the tunnel.*

For my true love and soulmate, David.

Oh! What a tangled web we weave, when first we practise to deceive.

Sir Walter Scott

PROLOGUE

Where the hell is Robert? The question repeats itself inside Laurie's mind on a loop as the woman's mouth opens and closes in front of her like a fish. She doesn't register what she's saying; she can't concentrate. Robert has gone AWOL and it's all she can focus on – that and trying not to drink any alcohol – and she has a bad feeling about both. Laurie wilts in the biting midday heat and looks past the woman into the crowd behind her with narrowed eyes. Where *is* he? He'd promised not to let her out of his sight today. He knew this was a big day for her – it was her first public outing to a social event in months, not to mention meeting the neighbours properly for the first time, and he'd sworn he'd be right by her side to help her through the ordeal.

The barbecue is already gearing up into full swing; men of various shapes and ages are gathered around a cluster of cylinder-shaped ovens, flames leaping from the sides, licking the grills and wafting blue smoke into the airless gazebo. Semi-naked children are playing in the heat, scurrying around after each other with water pistols, their shrieks punctuating the chatter and clatter of cutlery and chinking of glass as the women set the trestle tables and prepare to eat, drink and be merry. *Merry.* She's forgotten what that feels like. She can't remember the last time she felt the freedom of true happiness without something to help her along the way. Laurie hadn't wanted to come to today's barbecue – or the annual 'Cedar Summer Sizzler' as the residents of the close preferred to call it – but Robert had insisted. Besides, Monica was hosting it and she didn't want to let her friend down.

'You need to get out of the house, Law,' Robert had said. 'Socialise, start interacting with normal people; reintegrate yourself back into the world, into society. You know what your doctor said. You can't stay inside these four walls forever. It's not good for you.' *No, and neither had his affair been, or the terrible tragedy that had happened as a result of it.* Laurie tells herself to stop. She's getting morose and resentful again, dredging up negative thoughts, something she has been training herself hard not to do. Moving to 13 Cedar Close was supposed to be a new beginning for them, a fresh start, a chance to escape the painful memories of the past eighteen months. And things had been much better since they had moved here, hadn't they?

'It's just so lovely to finally meet you, in person anyway.' Laurie finally tunes into the conversation in front of her. 'Where have you been hiding all this time? It's got to have been six months since you moved in—'

'Five actually.'

In her left peripheral vision, Laurie spies a trestle table filled with bottles of wine and spirits and feels the pull of it like gravity.

'Gosh, five months – did you hear that, Graham? Laurie's lived here five months and this is the first time we've met her!'

Laurie glances at the man who has just joined them, bald and bespectacled. He looks as if he's had a lot of practice in zoning his wife out.

'Jessica, I said to myself, you *must* go round there, meet the new neighbours, but I didn't want to intrude, you know. I figured you'd be out and about when you were ready. I've met your husband though, a few times already. He's very… *friendly*…'

Laurie looks at the woman properly for the first time. Her dress is tight, too tight, like someone has poured her into it and forgotten to say 'when'; it exposes her ample cleavage with a thin divisive line.

'Where is Robert by the way?' The woman uses her husband's name in an overfamiliar way, or perhaps she's just being paranoid again. *He's very friendly…* 'I thought he was meant to be DJing today? You know, that's quite an accolade, being in charge of the music – for a newcomer anyway.'

'I'm sorry, what did you say your name was again?'

'Jessica.' The woman's forced smile looks more like the prelude to a scream. 'Jessica Bartlett, and this is my husband, Graham. We live next door to you!' she says with a touch of incredulity.

'Yes. Yes, of course. I know that. I'm sorry, I'm terrible with names,' Laurie apologises. And lies. She's actually exceptionally good at remembering names. Well, she was, once upon a time, before the accident. *Before the accident.* That's how her life is measured now, before the accident and after the accident. God, she could murder a drink, just to cool off. It's so damned hot.

'Well, I suppose that's understandable…' Jessica says, cocking her head to one side and casting Laurie a pitying glance, one she recognises only too well. *Has Robert said something?* He'd promised not to say anything to anyone – both he and Monica had sworn that they wouldn't. Instead, they'd come up with a cover story between them about Laurie having had an operation and needing to convalesce in case anyone questioned them about her being housebound. It wasn't a complete lie. But Jessica's expression unnerves her. She needs to find Robert.

A flutter of panic rises up through her diaphragm. Where is her husband? Laurie feels the eyes of her neighbours upon her like a bug trapped in amber. She couldn't blame their natural curiosity about the fragile-looking, elusive woman from number 13 who had barely left the house since she'd moved in. They probably thought she was a right snooty cow who thought she was above everyone else, though that couldn't have been further from the truth. But Jessica was right about one thing: the residents of Cedar Close were close. It was almost impossible to be anonymous and for others not to know, or want to know, your business.

'We're a real community here,' Jessica continues as though reading Laurie's thoughts. 'We look out for each other. A problem aired is a problem shared…' she says, pausing, her voice dropping an octave. 'You know you can always talk to me… if you ever need to.' Her head is cocked again and now Laurie is convinced that she knows something. 'Anyway, I'm dying to see what you've done to the house. Monica said you were in the interior-design business before the— Oh look, there's Karin. Hi, darling!' Jessica begins waving, bingo wings wobbling furiously.

Out of the corner of Laurie's eye she sees Monica making her way towards them with a tray of food and feels a rush of relief.

'Amuse bouche anyone? Lolly darling, go and get that husband of yours, will you?' Monica instructs her from the corner of her mouth. 'He's supposed to be sorting out the music and he's buggered off back home.'

'Back home? What's he doing there?'

'Yes, saw him go about half an hour ago. God knows what he's doing… go and chivvy him along, will you, darling? We need him on the decks, get the party started.' Monica holds out the tray. 'Mrs Foster made these blinis – amazing really, considering she's blind. Look at how perfect they are – almost the same amount of caviar on each one. Incredible.'

Jessica pops one into her mouth, a mouth that appears to be permanently open, and Laurie wonders if her husband has been inside that mouth and hates herself for thinking such horrible, disgusting thoughts. *She can't help it.*

'I'll go and get him,' Laurie says. She's relieved to make her excuses.

'Lovely to meet you, Laurie,' Jessica calls out to her with a mouthful of caviar, adding, 'finally.'

*

Why does Robert always do this, slip away on his own? Laurie thinks as she makes her way across the close. He knows it irritates her, upsets her. Is that why he does it? She tells herself to calm down, not to upset herself. She needs to give him a break. He's really been trying so hard lately, especially since the move, showing her more affection and attention than he had for a long time.

Putting her key in the door, Laurie goes to call out his name but something stops her. Instead, she takes her sandals off and treads lightly through the house into the kitchen. Robert's not there, nor in the living room. She hears a muffled voice, faint. He's upstairs, and it sounds as if he's talking to someone on the phone.

She takes the stairs tentatively one by one until she reaches the bedroom. The door is slightly ajar and through the crack she sees him standing by the bed, facing the window. She hovers behind the door, her breathing heavy and a little laboured.

'Baby, listen to me.' His voice is low, hushed. 'I swear to you I will be there soon… just a few more days…'

Laurie's heartbeat is pulsing loudly in her ears. *He's talking to a woman.* No. No! It was probably just a client, his mother maybe… He wouldn't, not after everything… But she'd just heard him use the word 'baby', hadn't she?

'I'll tell her I've got a gig somewhere up north or something, make an excuse… Yes… yes, baby, I know… Look, it's not going to be like this forever… Trust me, I promise you… I promise you both… She's improving day by day. The medication is keeping her on an even keel. I just need to get her to integrate more… No… no… Claire, please don't cry…'

Laurie feels the breath leave her body like someone has taken a lump hammer to her chest. *Robert is talking to Claire*. Her instinctive reaction is to burst through the door but she can't physically move – it's as if her feet have been soldered to the carpet. *Not Claire*. It can't be… Please no… Panic grips her and she steadies herself against the wall.

'Listen to me, Claire.' Robert's voice sounds more authoritative now – there's gravitas to it. 'I love you. I love you and Matilda more than life itself and we *will* be together, a proper family. You just have to trust me. You do trust me, don't you? Please say you trust me, baby. I want you, and our daughter; I want us all to be a family together. I just need a little more time… She's still unhinged and I – we – don't want her suicide on our conscience…' Robert pauses. 'How is my little girl doing anyway? Is she sleeping okay?'

Laurie watches him listening attentively.

'A tooth! Oh wow! Her first tooth!' He laughs softly, and she hears the tenderness in his voice, a sound that is like a chainsaw to her heart.

Rigid, Laurie covers her mouth with a shaking hand. A silent scream rages inside her head, the noise reverberating off the walls and ceilings. It feels like a scene from a horror film, her worse nightmare realised, and it's all she can do not to slide down the wall into a heap on the carpet. Instead, she takes a few deep breaths and forces a smile as she gathers the momentum to walk through the door.

'Robert?' Laurie says, swinging the door open and watching as he spins round in surprise, almost dropping the phone. 'What are you doing up here? You're wanted outside.'

CHAPTER ONE

Three months later

The scallops or the prawns? Laurie is undecided as she peruses the fish counter, carefully studying the shellfish nestled on their beds of crushed ice, mentally weighing up which ones are likely to please him most. *Please him.* Even now, after everything, she is still conditioned to put his feelings first. A familiar ache rises up inside her chest cavity and pulls at her, triggering a rush of oxytocin. She feels the flutter of adrenaline as the chemicals rush through her body and she puts her hand up to her chest in a bid to regulate her heart's increasing thud.

It's an addiction, Laurie. She hears the clipped, matter-of-fact voice of her therapist. *Trauma has bonded you to him by a chemical addiction. You're an addict…*

Now she thinks of it, hadn't they served scallops as a starter for their wedding breakfast? That's right – scallops in a lemon-and-herb butter sauce. She thinks she might even still have the shells somewhere that she kept as mementos. Perhaps scallops would remind him, jerk his memory back to that day when they had been so happy and hopeful, *so in love*.

The scallops it is then. She orders half a dozen from the red-faced, awkward-looking teenager behind the counter and hopes that Robert will appreciate them; she's always been a great cook, when she used to cook that is, *before the accident*. She wonders if Claire is as adept in the kitchen as she is. Claire looks like the type of woman oven chips were designed for. She was probably too busy with the baby now to prepare extravagant meals – no doubt she orders in most nights. Laurie visualises Claire pushing a pram around Iceland, hot and harassed, haplessly throwing ready meals into a basket and gives a ghost of a smile.

She makes her way towards the checkout – only she has to go past the booze section on the way, past the rows of shiny green and brown bottles of wine and spirits. She tries not to look at them but it's too tempting. One bottle wouldn't hurt, would it? After all, this was going to be their last supper together. *But oh look – the vodka is on special!* Without thinking she is already holding it in her shaking hand, placing it in the basket along with an expensive bottle of Château Margaux. Robert likes red with a meal. Hang on though: she's serving a fish starter, so perhaps some Prosecco as well then… The bottles make a familiar clank together in the basket, a sound that fills Laurie with a mix of anticipation and shame. She hears her therapist's words again. *Many addicts swap one addiction for another, Laurie. And some people develop another addiction while trying to anesthetise themselves from the first.*

She wills her mind to be silent, to stop the relentless voice inside it. She doesn't look at the bottles, pretends they're not there as she makes a mental run-through of her shopping list. That's when she spots one of her neighbours, someone she met at the BBQ whose name now escapes her.

'Hello,' she says instinctively. She's sure she's noticed her putting the alcohol into her basket. *Ah well, after tonight it won't matter. Nothing will.*

Laurie smiles and nods at the woman; she feels compelled to acknowledge her out of politeness. But the woman's presence mentally pulls her back to the day of the street barbecue, that beautiful, hot, fateful summer's day. Oddly, she remembers how she had accidentally trodden on a woman's foot, the blind lady who lives next door to Monica – the one who made the canapés – as she'd fled back into her house, tears streaming down her cheeks. She supposes it's something of a blessing that the old lady couldn't have seen the events of that dreadful day. It was more than three months ago now and people were *still* talking about it. She could tell by the hushed whispers and disparaging looks that were cast her way whenever she passed her neighbours on the street.

The woman walks past Laurie without saying a word and her rejection elicits a stab of misery within her as she makes a hasty retreat to the tills, her effervescent mood all but diminished in the few seconds it's taken to get there. She stares at the produce as she places it onto the conveyor belt, her heart beating rapidly. Has she remembered everything? This meal has to be her most spectacular. It will be her final parting gift to Robert. He is coming over to 'talk about the next step'. She knows what this means. He wants a divorce. He wants to *talk it over* with her, check that she won't go 'off the rails' again and appease what little conscience, if any, he possesses. He no doubt wants to finalise the details, discuss the finances and who gets what, a conversation she has been dreading and one she is going to make sure will never take place. He wants a divorce so he can marry Claire, so they can be a proper family unit. Robert, Claire and Matilda together. The family *they* should've had. Tonight, she's going to make sure that this will never happen.

The house is spotless and smells fresh as Laurie enters the hallway, yet it still feels as cold and empty as she does inside. This place is far too big for her now. It was probably too big for them both to be fair, but the plan was always that they would fill it, that there would eventually be the four of them. She is painfully reminded of her solitude once more.

And then there were none…

Laurie's nerves are in ribbons so she decides on a leveller. Just one to steady herself because she needs a clear head tonight. She reaches for the vodka inside the carrier bag, empties it into a glass and swallows it back neat like lemonade. She pours another almost instantly, savouring the burning sensation as the clear liquid slips down her throat and hits her empty stomach. *Anaesthetised.*

Screwing the lid back on the bottle purposefully, she sets about prepping the meal: washing, chopping, seasoning. She makes a beurre blanc sauce like a professional and rolls the pastry around the beef with effortless skill before placing it in the oven on a low temperature. Then she turns to herself. She's already been to the salon today for a blow-dry. Her Chloé maxi dress, the one he likes, is hanging on the back of the kitchen door, freshly dry-cleaned. It felt good to have a sense of purpose again, someone to buy and cook a meal for, to look beautiful for, *one last time*. She takes a quick shower, careful not to get her hair wet, dresses herself in the walk-in closet cum 'powder room' that he'd let her design – she'd always wanted one – and observes herself in the full-length mirror: her glossy blow-dry and subtle make-up, the fluidity of the dress attaching itself to her skinny frame. She's too thin and knows it. The accident had re-triggered her eating disorder, a legacy from her early teenage years when she had been consumed by low self-esteem and helplessness. Her breasts are almost non-existent, but she doesn't care. What good were they to her now?

She spritzes herself with Thierry Mugler's Angel perfume, a signature scent she'd been wearing the day of their wedding. He said it reminded him of her.

It's 7.30 p.m. and the table is beautifully laid, the candelabra lit, emanating a warm, rich glow in the homely yet chic kitchen she'd spent painstaking hours designing to his taste. The Wellington is cooked, keeping warm in foil; the dauphinoise is gently bubbling;

seasonal veg is ready to be blanched. The scallops could be flash cooked upon his arrival. She takes the apple strudel from the oven, the comforting smell of freshly cooked filo pasty and fruit filling her nostrils.

Laurie checks the chilled wine, thinks about opening it and pouring herself a glass in a bid to kill the butterflies inside her belly that are dancing like they're on ecstasy. *Butterflies.* Only she knows they aren't real, that they're simply *a potent cocktail of chemical triggers* that she has become a slave to. So her therapist says.

At 7.48 p.m. she pours herself another vodka. She'd prefer a glass of wine but doesn't want Robert to see that she's already opened the bottle, so vodka will suffice. She throws it back and pours another, hoping the beef Wellington will keep warm. At 8 p.m. the flutters of anticipation dancing inside her guts have slowly morphed into spiteful jabs of fear. Robert is late. He's probably stuck in traffic she consoles herself and checks her phone, but there's only a message from Monica that says, '*Good luck tonight, hon.*' She manages a thin smile, touched by her friend's support. Tonight will mark the first time she's seen Robert since the barbecue, an event she would rather forget, a day she wished had never happened, one which changed the course of everything, *again.*

By 8.38 p.m. she's opened the Prosecco and is three quarters of the way into the bottle. She feels light-headed, drunk, defeated. The darkness in her mind is creeping in like the night outside, the dim light of hope within her fading almost simultaneously. *Where the hell is Robert?*

She checks her phone again but there are no messages. Rage suddenly rises up in her like blood rushing to the surface of a fresh wound; all the effort she's made, all the trouble and expense she's gone to! *That evil bastard!* Perhaps he was never really coming at all and it had simply been another of his wicked games.

And then the thought enters her head: what if he really *has* had an accident? *Oh God, a car crash*! Panic grips her. She slumps over the kitchen table, stretching her thin arms out in front of her and closes her eyes. 'Til death us do part,' she says quietly, over and over again.

CHAPTER TWO

Laurie wakes with a start some time later. Her head is spinning; her mouth is as dry as a sandpit. Her lips are stuck to her teeth through dehydration. She struggles to focus in the pitch dark and groans. She's lying on the bed; she thinks she's in her own bedroom though she cannot be completely sure. How did she get there? She exhales heavily. Has she blacked out? It wouldn't be the first time. Shame creeps in and threatens to engulf her as she attempts to prop herself up on her elbows and her fingers touch something cold on the bed next to her. It feels like metal. *What is it?* She feels for it again but can't find it in the darkness. It's a struggle to pull herself up into a seated position, but when she does she realises she is wet, that her dress is sticking to her thighs and her hands feel slippery.

She reaches out in the dark, arms outstretched like a zombie, feeling her way through the room. She needs to find the light switch on the wall. Her eyes are starting to adjust a little now but it is too dark to fully focus. Her fingers meet the wall and she whispers 'thank God' as she locates the light switch. Only nothing happens, so she presses it again. *Jesus Christ.*

Feeling for the handle, she opens the door. The entire house is in darkness. Carefully, she makes her way across the landing. Familiarity, like muscle memory, tells her there's a lamp on the table at the end near the stairs and she feels for it, attempts to switch it on, almost pulling it over in her haste. It doesn't work. She curses. She needs water, to rehydrate, and to get out of her wet dress. It's sticking to her legs… cold and uncomfortable. She tries to remember the last thing she did before she blacked out. She was in the kitchen, waiting for Robert, the dinner ruined, her heart destroyed.

Disorientated, she navigates her descent downstairs, hitching her dress up with one hand, the other steadying her against the wall. The staircase is winding and wooden so she is careful – she's fallen down them before. Panic swells inside of her as she concentrates on keeping herself upright. She promises herself once more that she will never touch another drop of alcohol again in her life.

Practically blinded by adrenaline, she locates the understairs cupboard in the darkness and is hit by a rush of cold, musty air as she opens it. She's on her hands and knees now, frantically scrabbling around for a torch, but it's too dark and her fingers can only find shoes and wellington boots, an umbrella and other unidentifiable objects that she casts aside in haste and panic. She starts to wail with sheer frustration. Her phone! There's a flashlight on her phone! She races into the kitchen and begins to search the table in the darkness, knocking the empty vodka bottle onto the floor in her haste. It smashes loudly, causing her to gasp and curse but at least she's found her phone. Laurie's relief is almost palpable as she presses it with shaking fingers. Flooded with emotion she starts to cry as it comes on. She has just 7% left on the battery. It will be enough.

Switching the flashlight on she races back to the understairs cupboard and locates the electric box. As she suspected, the switch looks like it has tripped out and she flicks it back up. Light violently floods her vision, causing her to cover her eyes with her hand. She stands back against the wall, exhaling deeply, her head pounding, her whole body visibly sagging with exhaustion and relief. And that's when she realises, as she looks down at herself, that she is completely covered in blood.

CHAPTER THREE

'Afternoon, boss. Did I wake you?'

Davis's voice is almost irritatingly chirpy. I've been awake for a while but I don't let her know this.

'What time is it?' I roll over, check my watch. It's 11.06 p.m. I pull the duvet back and roll my feet onto the carpet, thinking it could do with a clean, or a good vacuum at least. It's cream, the carpet, and shows every speck of dirt, but it was what Rachel wanted. 'Wooden floors everywhere else but the bedroom,' she'd said. There are still some of her feminine touches left: the chandelier and the ornate mirror above the dressing table; the fluffy sheepskin rug at the end of the bed; the floral duvet that I haven't washed in weeks and the curtains that match it. But gradually she has disappeared, bit by bit, and I can feel the place becoming more and more of a bachelor pad, growing shabbier and more unkempt. Like most women, she held the place together. I have neither the time, nor the inclination for home decor now she's gone.

'Late,' Davis says. I groan inwardly. I don't sleep well these days, and even when I do manage some shut-eye I'm plagued by dreams – vivid and colourful dreams, practically psychedelic – that leave me feeling exhausted when I wake up.

I yawn, scratch my head, get a whiff of my own sour breath. I'm anticipating what Davis is about to tell me, simultaneously wondering whether I'll have the chance to treat myself to a shower.

'Go on…'

'Homicide, boss. Body up on Cedar Close, number 13, male victim. Robert Mills, thirty-nine. The call's just come in.'

'From who?'

'The wife.'

'The wife found him?'

'She made the call. We're on our way down there now.'

'You said homicide…'

'His throat's been cut, boss, sliced open at the neck, and he's got multiple stab wounds. The wife was hysterical. Looks like a domestic. You need to get down there. Woods has requested that you—'

'Who's already on the scene?' I cut her off mid-sentence.

Davis pauses, which fills me with dread as I think I already know what she's going to say next.

'Martin, boss.'

I close my eyes and silently curse. *Delaney*. It would have to be Delaney. I haven't seen him since the 'Goldilocks' case that we worked on together, finding a female serial killer. It still plagues my dreams sometimes, and it almost cost me my job, forcing me to take a sabbatical. When I returned to the nick, he'd been posted somewhere else and I felt all the better for it if I'm honest, and I always try to be. I didn't like Delaney instinctively on sight, and there's not many people I can say that about on the force, or in any other area of my life. I usually get to know someone a little first before I decide not to like them. He was an exception to that rule. I picture his smug, self-satisfied, handsome face and feel deflated that I'll soon be reacquainted with it.

'Right you are. Number 13 you say?'

'Yes, Gov. Unlucky for some.'

Unlucky for Robert Mills by the sounds of things.

CHAPTER FOUR

Kiki

'It wasn't me. I didn't do it!' Kiki looks up at her mother's face bearing down on her. It's contorted in anger, red with rage.

'Thou shall not lie! Do you hear me, girl?' She smacks her daughter hard across her cheek, causing Kiki to whimper. 'It's a sin to lie! And it's a sin to steal! You've brought shame to this family – do you know that? We're good people, well respected in this community, and now we have a thief for a daughter – nothing but a common thief!'

Kiki rubs the sting on her cheek. She wants to object; she wants to say again that it wasn't her, that she didn't take anything, that it was Bertie who'd stolen the bag of pick 'n' mix sweets from Mr Patel's, but she knows it's no good. Her mother won't believe her – she never does.

'We took you in in good faith, Kiki.' Her mother's rage doesn't appear to be abating. 'We gave you a home, a family, and look how you've repaid us. The shame…' She's shaking her head, opening the kitchen cupboards, pulling pots and pans out and crashing them down onto the cooker. 'You were a bad seed, born out of sin to become a sinner yourself! You need to get down on your knees and pray, you hear me? On your knees!'

Kiki does as she is told and drops to the floor; she begins reciting her prayers in a low whisper.

'Faster!' her mother says. 'Louder! Beg for forgiveness... Tell Him what a sinner you are and that you renounce the devil inside you. Tell Him!'

Kiki shuts her eyes tightly though it doesn't prevent her tears from coming. She didn't take the sweets from Mr Patel's shop. She didn't. God sees all, that's what her mother and father tell her and what they say at Bible study. So how come he didn't see that it was Bertie who had stolen the sweets? Why was God punishing her? She'd get the belt for this.

'You just wait until your father gets home.' Her mother's warning tone confirms her fears and Kiki begins to cry louder. 'Stop whining!' Her mother slaps her again, across the top of her head this time, sending her sideways. 'You're no good, Kiki. Your own flesh and blood knew it and got rid as soon as they could. That tramp who gave birth to you never even knew who your father was...'

Kiki wants to cover her ears but doesn't dare. Instead she lets the hopelessness she feels inside claim her once more. She'd always known she was adopted from as far back as she could remember. Her mother had told her four years ago, when she was just five years old. She's nine now, 'going on seventeen' as her mother has said to her derisively, although she didn't really understand what she meant by it, not fully. In fact, she didn't understand anything at all and certainly not why her mother seemed to hate her so much. She had always tried so hard to be good, to please her and Daddy. Daddy didn't pay her much attention, except when he was giving her the belt, but Mummy seemed to reserve all her anger for her daughter, though only ever in private. In public, and always at church, she would even cuddle and kiss Kiki, show her a little affection, which felt good.

Mummy did most things in secret, like drinking alcohol. Kiki knew where she kept her secret stash of it, in the back of the cupboard underneath the stairs. She had seen her take the bottles and drink straight from them sometimes, though her mother knew nothing of this and, of course, she hadn't dared to breathe a word to anyone, except her brother Bertie. He was three years older than her and her best friend. In fact, Bertie was her only friend. Sometimes though, like today, he would betray her, make her shoulder the blame for his misdemeanours. But she would never dream of telling tales on him. Bertie had a temper on him too, like Mummy, and could be quite mean. But for the most part he was her only ally, her one source of comfort.

'Get to your room now, you little bitch! I don't want to see your face until tomorrow morning. You'll get no dinner tonight, not after stuffing your greedy face with all those stolen sweets!'

Kiki runs from the kitchen and up the stairs, two at a time. Bertie is already waiting for her in her bedroom.

'Nice one, kiddo, thanks for not snitching. Here, I saved you some Fruit Pastilles and look' – he pulls something out of his pocket – 'a Creme Egg, your favourite.'

Kiki manages a smile, even though her face is still stinging and her head feels sore. She throws herself down onto the bed and begins to cry.

'Mummy hates me. She says I'm evil, that no one wanted me... Not even my own mother.'

'Don't listen to her.' Bertie lies down next to Kiki on the bed and hugs her. 'She's just a drunken witch who knows nothing. I think you're the best thing since sliced bread.'

'You do,' she says. 'I think you're the best thing since sliced bread.'

He laughs, holds her tighter.

'Why does she hit me? Why does Daddy hurt me? Daddy's going to give me the belt when he gets home. I'm scared—'

Bertie sighs. 'I won't let them hurt you, Kiki.' He holds her tighter. 'It's my fault you got caught. I'll take the punishment like a man. We must stick together, yeah, you and me?'

'I love you, Bertie.'

'I love you too, Kiki.'

She's smiling again now, though he can't see her face from the spooning position they're lying in.

'You're my Kiki. And they may not love you but I do.'

She snuggles into him some more and feels a hardness pressing against the small of her back, but she doesn't mind. Bertie loves her and that's all that matters.

CHAPTER FIVE

I'm still singing along to Boston's 'More Than a Feeling' as I pull up outside. Rachel always used to say, *You murdered that track, Danny*, every time she heard me sing. I can't help but smile at the irony as I switch off the engine.

Number 13 is a smart-looking house – a very smart-looking house on a very smart-looking close. It's what the old man would classify as 'suburban chic', I think as I pull up the driveway. It's a cherry-tree-lined, pretty address tucked away on the outskirts of Barnet, where those who've made it come to live and child-rear. It's non-London London, a slice of suburbia in the city – the outskirts really, if you're going to be pedantic. With its detached houses and perfectly mowed lawns, it reminds me of one of those upmarket neighbourhoods in LA, attractive, but lacking soul somehow. The houses on Cedar Close are pretty similar-looking in as much as they're all huge. There's money here for sure, and it seems the residents don't mind letting their neighbours know about it with their Jaguars, Range Rovers, top-of-the-range soft-top Minis and even a couple of Porsches on their gravelled and gated drives. I imagine the residents here all know one another; it's secluded, private, a *close* close. I also imagine they're all secretly in competition with each other too: who has the biggest driveway, the best car, the prettiest wife and the highest-achieving kids? It's an assumption of course, but those are the thoughts running through my mind as I step out of my car.

Blue lights are flashing outside number 13, giving the atmosphere a familiar inky glow and filling me with anticipation. I see the yellow-and-black tape, two police vans and three cars. Forensics are marching in and out of the front door with a sense of purpose; they look like giant green ants. I take a deep breath. I didn't manage to shower but I did brush my teeth; I suppose one out of two ain't bad.

I walk towards the house, mentally assessing the scene. This doesn't look like the typical place where someone gets their throat savagely cut. But looks can be very deceiving so I'm making no assumptions. Yet. I notice the shutters in the large sash windows, those expensive-looking white ones that Rach always talked about getting for our apartment – until I'd seen the price of them! 'We're on the third floor – no one will see them anyway!' was my take on it at the time, if I recall.

'Yes, but we will see them, Danny – that's the whole point!' she'd replied.

I smile at the memory. I'm sure I acquiesced in the end.

But we never did get round to it.

Lucy Davis makes her way over to me. 'Good evening, boss.' She's even chirpier in the flesh. I like the fact that Davis is not yet tarnished by the job; in the best way possible, she's actually thrilled to be working on homicide.

A lot of people back at the nick think I've got the hots for Davis. She's young and pretty in a girl-next-door kind of way with a friendly yet firm disposition, so it's not altogether surprising. I don't fancy Davis, but I do like her. I like her work ethic, her quiet determination and almost militant meticulousness, her attention to detail. She thinks outside the box and she's loyal too, unlike Delaney, who I have a nagging suspicion is going to be a real ball-ache on this one.

'Is it, DS Davis?' I say. 'I'd never have guessed.'

She gives me a wry smile. 'I picked you up a Costa.' She hands me a hot cardboard cup. 'Skinny latte with a shot of hazelnut.'

'I'd marry you if you weren't already taken, Davis.' I flash her a grateful smile as I take it and she looks away, a little uncomfortably.

'So, hit me with it.'

'It ain't pretty.'

I had a sneaking suspicion she was going to say that.

'The deceased: Robert Mills, thirty-nine, due to turn forty in a few weeks. His throat has been cut – looks deep, boss, almost severed his head. And he's been stabbed. Multiple times.'

Nice.

'You mentioned a wife.'

She nods, looks down at her notepad.

'Laurie Mills. She made the call. She was covered in blood when we got here, blathering, incoherent. She was intoxicated. It looks like a domestic, Gov. Probably an argument that got out of hand.'

I stare at the house as Davis talks. There's something odd about it that I can't put my finger on. I get a bad feeling from it, like it's an unhappy house.

'Delaney is with the wife. Baylis, Murray and some of the team are out doing door to door, talking to the neighbours – the ones who're still up that is.'

I glance at the street. There are people standing at their front doors and looking through their windows, observing the scene unfolding, their faces illuminated by the flashing lights. Some are in their dressing gowns – the curtain twitchers. Hopefully they'll have some information to share. They look the type.

'Good. Secure the road. Make sure no one comes in or out. Deal with any press. This is the Golden Hour, Davis.'

The Golden Hour is a term homicide gives to the first sixty minutes on the scene. This is when we need to garner as much evidence as possible, forensic mainly, but also circumstantial. My job is to make sense of both and put them together so that you see the full picture. Some coppers are all about the forensics, but for me the two go hand in hand. One doesn't really work well without the other – you know, a bit like Lennon and McCartney.

I duck underneath the yellow-and-black tape and enter number 13 with a strange feeling. *More than a feeling*.

CHAPTER SIX

The first thing I see is Delaney. He's standing in the large, open-plan kitchen, which is off the main living area and attached to some sort of conservatory. He's talking to someone: the wife, I'm assuming. I can't see her face, just a mass of long brown hair as she's bent over the table with her head in her hands. As I enter the kitchen, I notice there's blood on them and on her – a lot of it.

'Dan,' Delaney acknowledges me in that irritatingly familiar way of his, like he's known me all my life. He approaches me, turns his head towards mine in a clandestine fashion. 'We're looking at a domestic here… She's hysterical, doesn't know what's happened, says she can't remember, isn't making much sense… She's intoxicated… and she has injuries to her wrists. Self-inflicted by the looks of things.'

He makes to continue but I cut him off by physically passing him as I move towards the table, towards Mrs Mills.

'Mrs Mills… Laurie, I'm DI Riley – Daniel Riley…'

The woman raises her head from the kitchen table. Her face looks like a crime scene in itself, a red mass of mucus and swollen eyes. Her lips are trembling and every muscle looks as if it's screaming out in agony. She tries to speak but only a small rasp escapes her lips. Her hands are bloodied and shaking, her dress heavily stained. She's a proper mess.

'I… I… Oh God… Robert… Robert… I don't know what happened… don't… I can't remember… I was asleep… I thought he was… He stood me up…' She collapses onto the table, her head thudding against the wood.

'It's okay,' I reassure her, 'it's okay. Can you tell me what's happened, Laurie?' I ask.

She's shaking her head, lifting it a few inches off the table and then banging it back down again repeatedly.

'Get her out of here,' I say sharply, turning to Delaney. 'Take her down the station. We'll speak to her there.'

Delaney nods reluctantly.

'We're not going to arrest her, boss?'

'For what?' I snap back. 'We don't know what's happened yet. She needs to be checked over first. Send two of the team down there with her. We'll interview her once she's been seen by the quacks.'

'Any sign of a break-in?'

'Nope.' Davis is keeping pace behind me as I make my way up the stairs. 'And nothing has been taken.'

Except for a life, I think, but I don't say it. *DI Obvious*.

'The en suite, boss,' Davis says. 'He's in the guest en suite.'

This strikes me as a little odd. Why is Robert Mills in the guest en suite of his own house?

'They were estranged, he and the wife,' Davis says, pre-empting my next question. 'She was expecting him for dinner around 7.30 p.m. but apparently he never showed up. She said something about falling asleep, waking up in the dark… a switch tripped or a power cut? Then she sees she's covered in blood and panics. She calls his number, her husband's, and says she heard his phone ring upstairs, went to take a look and… well… you'll see for yourself.'

The guest bedroom is busy, as I would expect. Forensics are all over it, dusting for prints, taking samples, bagging up evidence, taking measurements and photographs. It's a large double room, which holds a king-sized bed comfortably and is decorated to a very high standard in tonal creams and beiges. The furniture is white and has that distressed look that's popular now. Shabby chic, I think they call it. There's a dressing table with an ornate oval mirror above it that houses perfume bottles and a box of tissues. There's a sheepskin rug, expensive looking, on the floor in front of it. Large and rather sumptuous-looking cushions in various sizes and fabrics are scattered across the bed. The bedspread looks antique, in keeping with the style, and appears untouched. The bed looks inviting, probably because I haven't slept well and feel exhausted. I resist the urge to throw myself on it.

It's a nice guest room, clean and feminine-looking – lots of attention to detail. The walls are adorned with black-and-white photography, well-lit, soft-focus images of a woman in various boudoir poses, sexy yet subtle, almost ethereal images. In some she is posing naked, though it's suggested nakedness rather than obvious, and in others she's wearing lingerie. I can't tell if it's the wife or not. The shutters are white, matching the ones downstairs, and they're closed. A flashlight goes off next to my ear, startling me a little – I'm edgy through lack of sleep – and I wince. The sound of a camera popping always makes me think of death now, which is a bit of a shame really, as I'm quite keen on photography. Perhaps I'll pick up a camera more often when I retire, if I ever manage to retire that is, because according to Woods, 'You never stop being a copper, Riley, even when you're asleep or in your dotage.' He's such a comfort, is Woods. I give myself a wry smile. Not that I'm getting much of that lately, sleep or comfort.

On first glance there's nothing out of place in the bedroom. It looks pristine, like a showroom; there are no scattered clothes, no messy spots, no signs of it being lived in. I spot Vic Leyton among the throng of green-covered bodies, recognise the back of her head as I make my way towards the en suite. She turns as she hears me approach.

'Ah, Detective Inspector Riley.' She smiles at me; even her smile seems efficient somehow. It's oddly nice to see her again, though the circumstances in which we always meet never are.

'Ms Leyton.' I bow my head by way of acknowledgement.

'This is a particularly nasty one.'

She cuts to it, no pun intended. Good ol' Vic, she never sugar-coats stuff and I respect that.

'Savage really,' she muses.

Vic stands back as I crouch down next to the body. Robert Mills is lying on his side with his back towards the door. He's fully clothed in a pair of smart blue jeans and is wearing a white – well, formerly white – T-shirt underneath a leather jacket. I catch a faint smell of aftershave, something soapy and fresh. I'm guessing he's a tall man, or was, because his frame seems to cover quite a distance along the tiled floor even with his legs bent up towards his chest in a sort of half-foetal position. From the back he looks as though he could be sleeping, passed out drunk on the floor, his dark hair fanning out underneath him like a woman's.

It's only when I lean over him and see the blood that I'm confronted with the horrific truth. Robert Mills' eyes are wide open, piercing and icy blue; they're staring straight ahead of him, almost in surprise, or shock I imagine. Blood has collected in a pool around his throat, staining the whole front of his T-shirt, soaking it through. The wound to his neck is deep, exposing sebaceous fat – ugly yellow bubbles of it protrude from his open flesh and I think I can see bone, or cartilage or something. The cut is long, jagged, almost from ear to ear in distance, making a gaping, bloody mess of his neck; it looks like someone's taken an axe to him.

I stand and move around the body, then crouch down over him again at another angle. My knee makes a nasty click as I bend, reminding me that I'm getting old – well, older anyway. I have a birthday next week, one I'd rather forget about, one I will be spending alone, or rather alone down at the nick, unless the old man insists on taking me out for a drink like he has every year since Rachel died.

There's blood on the walls, splashes of it on the shower glass and sink, and that's when I see the mirror. The words *Lying, cheating scumbag* have been written on it in what I'm assuming is Robert Mills' blood. I think it's fairly safe to conclude that it's been written by whoever murdered our friend here. My stomach does a little flip, which is unlike me – I'm pretty well acquainted with blood and gore, having seen more than my fair share of abattoir-style slaughters, gory road accidents, and broken and bloodied bodies, but this attack is truly stomach-churning in its brutality. It looks as if considerable force has been used – frenzied, aggressive, violent force: *savagery*. Someone was very clearly pissed off with Mr Mills here.

I look at his face. Even with his neck sliced open you can tell he was a handsome bloke, kind of hipster-looking, like one of those types who frequents trendy bars in Shoreditch.

'I'm afraid that's not everything,' Vic says in that dispassionate way of hers that makes me wonder if she might be passionate in *other ways* to counterbalance it.

'Hit me up,' I reply, which sounds kind of blasé, but I don't mean it to. There's nothing mundane about murder.

'He's been stabbed, multiple times by the looks of things. Looks like a few major arteries were hit in the process, and the lungs. He would have been extremely short of breath, sprayed blood with every exhalation,' she explains. 'That's assuming, of course, that the wounds were inflicted before his throat was cut. I'll need to get him on the slab for further examination before I can give you anything conclusive, but judging simply by looking, my money's on his throat being cut first, followed by a somewhat frenzied stabbing attack.'

I nod sagely. 'How long?' I ask. 'How long has he been dead?'

'Not so long, actually,' Vic says, 'judging by his temperature. It's just gone 11.45 p.m. now.' She checks her watch. 'Anywhere between two to three hours I'd hazard a guess.'

I do the maths.

'So we're looking at TOD somewhere around 8–10 p.m.?'

Vic tilts her head to the right. 'Give or take.'

I stare at Robert Mills' body a little longer. It's a grim picture of a man literally cut down in his prime, slaughtered like an animal.

'Looks like we've got the weapon, boss.' Davis appears at the bathroom door. She's holding a large, bloody kitchen knife in a plastic zip-lock bag.

I nod, thinking it's safe to assume so – either that or Mills here likes a very close shave. I take it from her with a gloved hand and inspect it through the plastic. It's one of those chopping knives you see in wooden blocks in the kitchen, a chef's knife, similar to the ones Rachel used in the restaurant where she worked, large and razor-sharp with a thick black handle. It's heavy in my hand, weighty, and I feel guilty that it reminds me of her. I imagine the force that must've been used to slice right through the deceased's flesh; it would have been considerable by the looks of the damage done.

'It was on the bed. Forensics bagged it up after taking pictures.'

So there was no attempt to hide the weapon or dispose of it. Interesting.

'And the phone? You said something about the wife calling his phone.'

'We found it next to the sink,' Davis explains.

I turn back to Vic.

'It's definitely in keeping with the wounds,' she says, pre-empting my question. 'The knife.'

'You know you've always got a viable secondary career as a clairvoyant, Vic, if this game doesn't work out for you,' I say.

She smiles thinly. 'What are the hours?'

It makes me wonder what Vic does in her spare time for pleasure when she's not cutting up the dead and putting the pieces, literally, back together.

'Long,' I say, 'and the pay is rubbish.'

'Hmm, not much in the way of a change then,' she muses.

I want to add, 'Yeah, and you'd still be dealing with stiffs in one way or another!' but I reckon that may be overstepping the mark, so I don't.

'Give me the low-down on the neck wound,' I say, thinking about Laurie Mills, the state she was in and how Delaney appeared to be handling her when I arrived, leaning over her almost menacingly. 'Shouldn't there be more blood, given the severity?' There's not exactly a shortage of claret on Robert Mills' body and T-shirt thanks to the stab wounds – in fact, there's a river of the stuff surrounding him, splashed up the tiles of the bathroom and, of course, on the mirror – but I can't help thinking that there should be more of it around his upper body, around the neck area.

'Perceptive of you, Detective,' Vic says, almost looking half-impressed. 'You're learning.'

'From the best,' I say, but I can tell she's done with the banter now and has switched back to being purely professional.

'There's a misconception about the cutting of the throat. I blame TV shows and films… People expect blood and gore on a level that doesn't correlate with science, at least not always—'

I nod. Vic has started with the riddles.

'It all depends on how it's done, you see,' she continues. 'Cutting the front of the throat simply severs the windpipe. If it's done with enough precision, the combination of the swelling and partial collapse due to cartilage severance will cause the victim to choke. This would be slow and not especially bloody; it wouldn't guarantee an efficient death. Actually, people have been known to have picked themselves up after a few minutes and walked to get help.'

'Looks pretty efficient to me!' I can't imagine what it would feel like to slash the throat of another human being, but I reckon it's safe to assume that the intent to cause severe harm is pretty much a given.

'Severing the major veins however, well, that would be messy, very unpleasant, and also slow and rather noisy…' She glances at me and pushes her glasses a little further up her small nose. 'Gurgling, choking, that sort of thing.'

'I get the picture.'

'A large volume of the person's blood would have to drain before they die with this method, so, like I say, messy and slow.'

I glance at Mills' body then back up at Vic. She's in the zone now, concentrating, drawing her conclusions in real time as she inspects the wound in detail.

'Cutting the carotid artery is the most efficient way to guarantee a fast death,' she explains. 'It basically cuts off blood flow to the brain and because it's so fast, it can be pretty neat. There would be some blood loss, pretty much in keeping with our man here, until the heart stops beating anyhow, but it wouldn't be the horror show it would be if the veins had been severed. If that had been the case, then we'd probably need waders.' Vic says this without a hint of irony. 'Still, it's a noticeable amount. Of course, if the trachea had been severed as well then it all might just drain straight into the lungs. But then of course if he'd also been stabbed…'

I inwardly wince at the horror Robert Mills must've experienced in those final moments, unable to breathe, choking on his own blood. Simultaneously, I think I'm a little bit in love with Vic Leyton. She talks about death as though she's reciting a recipe. Almost makes it sound palatable.

'So,' I ask, 'to summarise, you think the suspect cut the artery, and they knew what they were doing to make a clean, or *cleaner*, job of it?'

'Yes to the first, but I couldn't possibly comment on the last, I'm afraid. That would be speculative.'

I nod. I suspect 'speculative' isn't a prevalent word in Vic's vocabulary.

'There are no visible defence wounds to the hands, no cuts, abrasions, bruising, although a proper PM will reveal any nuances… It looks as if he didn't put up a fight, which suggests the knife wounds occurred after his throat was severed. Maybe even as he lay dying, or already dead.'

I stare at the corpse in front of me, viewing it from different angles. I spot something. 'There's something underneath him,' I say, bending down once more. It's sticking out, just visible beneath his chest, under his ribcage, a piece of paper…

Vic raises her eyes as I gently push Robert Mills' body with my fingers, grateful for the thin layer of protection that my rubber gloves offer. 'Looks like a letter,' I say as I slide it from underneath him. It's an envelope, the corner of which is blood-soaked, but the rest is intact, unblemished. I feel a rush of excitement, adrenaline gathering a pace as it fizzes through my lower abdomen and up through my guts. It's addressed to 'Mrs Laurie Mills' in typed letters, looks official. It's open.

My breathing is shallow as I gently remove the contents from the envelope. Even Vic Leyton looks intrigued as I very carefully and gently unfold the A4 piece of paper.

'Dear Mrs Mills,
    I am writing to inform you that your husband, Robert Mills, has instructed us to act on his behalf with regards to divorce proceedings…'

'It's from his solicitors.' I turn to Davis. 'It's telling the wife that he's begun divorce proceedings. Dated three days ago… Get this to forensics.' I put the letter back into the envelope as carefully as

I took it out. 'And get onto the solicitor, a Michael James at James, Stannard and Co., based in Soho by the looks of the headed paper.'

Davis nods efficiently, taking it from me.

I see the ambulance guys coming through the guest room now with a body bag ready to take Robert Mills to the mortuary, a venue I'm pretty sure wasn't on his bucket list of places to go before he turned forty, and I glance at Vic Leyton.

'Perhaps you'll need to talk to the wife,' she says dryly, glancing briefly at the murderer's message on the mirror.

'Perhaps I do,' I remark.

Jesus, I can't wait.

CHAPTER SEVEN

Laurie Mills has never been in a police car before and sheer naked terror runs down her spine as she sits in the back seat next to a female police officer whose silence is only adding to her burgeoning fear. She stares out of the window at the passing cars but takes nothing in. Every few minutes a rush of reality hits her like a sledgehammer to her chest: *Robert is dead! Robert is actually dead!*

She sees him on the floor of the guest en suite, replays the moment over in her mind on a diabolical loop: how his familiar frame seems almost alien as she enters the bathroom, like it isn't really Robert at all, but someone else collapsed and bent up out of shape. Nothing could have prepared her for what she had seen, and her mind had been frantic in an attempt to rationalise the irrational. It had occurred to her for the briefest moment that this was some kind of bizarre joke – a sick, tasteless prank – until she'd seen the blood that is, and the wound where it had come from.

Laurie gasps again as the images torment her; she squeezes her eyes tightly shut. She hadn't seen the message on the mirror at first. She had been so preoccupied with her dead husband's corpse that she'd not noticed it. *Lying, cheating scumbag…* She had stared at the letters like they were Greek. She didn't understand. Who had written it?

'He… he was supposed to come for dinner…' she says, suddenly feeling the urge to speak.

The policewoman nods, takes a notepad from her jacket.

'He didn't show up. I thought… I thought he'd stood me up… I was furious… He'd hurt me so much… with the baby and everything, with Claire… after the accident… I rang his phone… I heard it ringing upstairs—'

The policewoman is scribbling in her notepad, simultaneously nodding up at her and murmuring soothing words like, 'It's okay, Laurie—'

'Oh God… Oh God, Robert, my Bobby… oh God.' She buries her face in her hands. 'I… I'd made him beef Wellington…' Laurie thinks of Claire suddenly and looks down at her hands. They're covered in blood; it's drying into the grooves and lines of her skin, underneath her fingernails. She begins to shake. 'No… no… NO!'

'It's okay,' the policewoman reassures her again. 'We're almost at the station now. You'll be seen by a doctor; we'll get you cleaned up. It's okay.' Her voice is soft but authoritative, and Laurie finds it strangely comforting to let someone else take control. She's used to others being in control and telling her what to do now, ever since the accident.

'We'll need to take some samples from you, Laurie. DNA, fingerprints, bloodstain samples – it's standard procedure, okay? Is that okay, Laurie? Do you understand what I'm saying? Then we can get you cleaned up, have a cup of tea and talk, okay?'

Laurie's staring at her hands, at the bloodstains on them.

'Laurie? Laurie, is there anyone you want us to call for you?'

She's still staring at her hands as she answers. 'Yes… yes, I understand…'

The PC nods. 'Okay… it's okay,' she says, but they both know it isn't. 'You're not under arrest.'

This sends a jolt through her solar plexus. Arrest? Why would she be under arrest? Why are they talking about arresting me? *Oh my God, they think I've killed Robert.* A slither of self-preservation begins to penetrate through her shock and terror, marginally sobering her thoughts, bringing her back to herself.

'I… I want to speak to my mum,' she stammers. 'My mum…'

The police officer pats her arm again but it feels robotic, emotionless, and she wants to pull away; she doesn't want to be touched. Laurie feels sick, nausea rising up into her guts. She thinks of the message written in blood on the mirror again. The killer's message. *Jesus Christ*. Panic and fear is arriving now in full force, seizing her throat and tightening like a vice round it, shortening her breath.

'Did I kill him?' she says the words aloud, without realising, without thinking about them too much. 'Did I kill Robert?'

The policewoman, she suddenly realises, is wearing gloves.

'I don't know, Laurie,' she asks gently. 'Did you?'

CHAPTER EIGHT

The press have already arrived as I leave the house. A group of them has congregated at the end of the close, straining to find a way through the police barriers, like vultures circling a fresh carcass. Good news always travels fast. I spot Fi in among the throng and pretend I haven't seen her. We've been out for a few drinks in recent months, me and Fi. I suppose you could call them dates. On our last 'date' she stayed over and we ended up in bed together. I think we both knew it was on the cards. I wouldn't go as far as to say we made love, but it was nice sex, good sex even, and it had felt comfortable and natural. I'm glad my first time since Rachel was with Fiona Li. We're friends first and foremost, and I like her a lot. I trust her and respect her, even if she is a hack. Plus, she's beautiful and funny. She's a good woman. And yeah, I fancy her. Or maybe it's something else. Anyway, it just sort of happened after a few drinks.

There was no awkwardness the next morning. In fact, it was kind of nice waking up next to a warm body and having a makeshift breakfast of tea and stale toast. But there were no butterflies, not like there had been with Rachel, and I didn't get that same ache when she left, the ache I used to get whenever my girl walked out of the door. In some unspoken way it was as if we both needed each other for that one night. For different reasons maybe, but there was no bad feeling. She left on good terms. I think we both knew it wouldn't happen again. I haven't called her since that night and I feel bad about that; things just got in the way. Now it's been a couple of weeks and it might be a bit awkward…

'Dan!' She spots me and calls out to me as I make my way down the driveway and like a complete coward I pretend I haven't heard her, which makes me feel even shittier.

'Forensics are rushing through the phone and the prints on the knife,' Davis says as she follows me down the driveway.

I nod, trying to squash the sense of unease that has misted over me like November fog. On the surface this looks like a straight-up domestic, a spurned wife taking revenge on her cheating husband. The attack has all the hallmarks of a crime of passion. It very possibly is, only my intuition is telling me there's something more, that it's not as cut and dried as that and to reserve my judgement before jumping to any obvious conclusions.

'Anything from the neighbours?'

Davis nods. 'Quite a bit actually.'

'Oh?'

'It's fair to say that it was common knowledge that the Millses' marriage was in big trouble,' she says. 'Allegedly, Robert Mills had been having an affair and it turns out he had a child with another woman. They were giving things another go it seemed, he and the wife, though according to the neighbour I spoke to he hadn't been at the marital home much recently, making her think that he'd left to be with his mistress. Seems they kept themselves to themselves when they first moved in, which was back in February, especially Laurie Mills, bit of a recluse according to' – Davis checks her notebook – 'a Mrs Jessica Bartlett at number 15, to the left.' She points at the property next to the Millses' house. 'She says she often heard them arguing when the deceased lived there – shouting and slamming doors and what not – and that the deceased was always coming and going. He was friendly enough though, apparently, chatty – made more of an effort to integrate into their little community than the wife.'

'Doesn't make her a murderer,' I say quietly, almost to myself. 'And…?'

'The team are out doing more door to door now,' Davis replies. 'Some of the neighbours weren't in or didn't answer. Jessica Bartlett suggested we talk to' – she leafs through her notebook again – 'a Mrs Monica Lewis, lives at number 25, opposite the Millses. Apparently she and Laurie were best friends, known each other for years, went to school or college together.'

'Right. Well, we need to speak to her.'

'Bartlett said something about an incident that happened back in July.'

'An incident?'

'A very public argument between Laurie and Robert Mills. Apparently, Mrs Mills publically outed her husband's affair and the fact that he'd fathered a love child to everyone at a street barbecue before fleeing to her house in floods of tears. Made a right drunken show of herself, as Bartlett put it, *and*… now this *is* quite interesting.' Davis raises her eyebrows.

'Go on…' Davis loves to do cliffhangers, but I indulge her. It's a small price to pay for her tenacity.

'*And*, the neighbour recalls how Mrs Mills threatened to kill her husband, screamed how much she wanted him dead in front of the whole street.'

'I see,' I say. 'Well I guess that is pretty interesting. But it's hardly a confession, is it? I mean, I imagine it's what a lot of wives say to their cheating husbands in the heat of the moment.'

Davis looks down at the floor suddenly, like I've struck a nerve.

'I want everyone spoken to, a list of names of everyone who lives here. I want to find out who the Millses were, what their life was like, what *they* were like. Someone might've seen something tonight; they all look like a bunch of curtain twitchers so I'm pretty convinced something will come up. And that Monica woman, the friend you mentioned, talk to her. I want her interviewed first, then everyone else on this street.'

Davis nods. 'Technically, it's a close, boss,' she grins at me and I mock frown at her in response.

'So, do we know who the other woman is yet? A name for the mistress?'

'Claire someone, no surname yet, no address. Maybe Laurie Mills can shed some light.'

'Send someone down there as soon as we've got an address, okay?'

From the corner of my eye I can see Fi again. She's standing off to the left of the crowd of vultures, looking at her phone. I turn back to Davis. 'What's your take on this, Davis?' I ask her because I know how it looks. The message on the mirror, the murder weapon, no forced entry and an acrimonious break-up fuelled by infidelity. Some might say the writing, in this case quite literally, is on the wall. And yet I just don't think so…

'There was no break-in, boss, no one else at the scene, the suspect is claiming temporary amnesia during the time the murder happened, there's a weapon and a motive, and by the wounds inflicted, I'd say it was done with some degree of frenzy, fuelled by passion, hate, revenge. It's not looking good for Mrs Mills.' Davis hesitates. 'Yet… I don't know… She's such a tiny person,' she says, mirroring my own thoughts. Her intuition is speaking to her, just like mine is.

Laurie Mills is – from what I have briefly seen, and from what Davis has clearly noted too – tiny. She's a diminutive woman with limbs like a bird, and a broken one at that. That's the image that popped into my head when I first saw her, *a broken bird*. To kill a man twice, maybe three times her size just seems so… unlikely, though admittedly not impossible. Human strength cannot be underestimated in extreme circumstances, no less extreme emotions, but there was, *is*, a fragility to Laurie Mills that made me feel she could barely pick up a knife and fork, let alone practically decapitate her strapping 6ft-plus husband and plunge a knife repeatedly into him.

'People can have the most incredible strength when they want to,' Davis says, reading my thoughts once more. 'Rage, protecting their children, fear—'

'Yes.' I agree with her because I know it's true.

'Hate,' Davis says with a tinge of sadness. 'It does terrible things to people.'

I think of Craig Mathers then, the man responsible for ploughing into my Rachel on her motorbike, killing her, and our tiny unborn child inside her, outright, and his face flashes up in my mind.

'Doesn't it just,' I say.

CHAPTER NINE

Laurie – Spring 2015

'You're going away again?' Laurie blinks at her husband, the disappointment in her voice matching her expression.

'C'mon now, Law, you know it's my job. That's what I do, what I've always done. Please don't start.'

'I'm not starting,' she says, careful not to sound defensive. She doesn't want to upset him, but she wants to address the issue of them spending so much time apart. 'We've hardly spent more than a whole week together in three months. We'll never start a family like that.'

She hears him sigh, watches him roll his eyes.

'Here we go again… You sound just like Martha did, and Tammy and the others. I thought you understood, Law; I thought you were different.'

Laurie feels herself bristle, stuck somewhere between protestation and acquiescence. She resents it whenever he compares her to his coterie of 'crazy controlling exes' – it always managed to shut the argument down, lest she be lumped into the same category. But it wasn't too much to ask, wanting to see your new husband more than a few days a month, was it?

'Besides, you're going to be away yourself in a couple of weeks; the big hotel contract… Deborah and Jack will want you with them when they go to Italy – you're the best designer they've got on the team and they know it.'

She turns away from him but can't help smiling. She knows what he's doing, softening her up with compliments.

'It's just that you've been away so much lately. We've hardly had any time for… us.' Laurie pouts a little to take the edge off her obvious discontent. She doesn't want to sound needy; Robert said that Martha was the biggest whinger he'd ever met and she's nothing like Martha, or the others who'd tried to hold him back and clip his wings, women who had attempted to 'own him', as he'd put it. Women who did not understand his need for creative freedom and his wanderlust; women who were jealous, needy and questioning of his myriad female friends. That's why he'd married her, he'd said. 'You're nothing like any of the others – you get me, you allow me to express myself, to be myself. That's what a true soulmate is, Law; that's why I want to take my last dying breath with you…'

Robert lifts her up by the waist onto the kitchen work surface and pulls her skirt up in one seamless move, causing her to gasp with excitement. She loved his spontaneity, particularly his sexual spontaneity. It turned her on.

'Mmm.' He kisses her hard on the mouth, pulling her underwear to the side and slipping his fingers inside of her. 'I'm sorry I've been neglecting you, baby… You know I want us to be together more than ever. But my job,' he says between kissing her mouth. 'You know what the industry is like. You've got to take the gigs as and when and where they come.' He covers her neck in scattergun kisses. 'You know how much I love you, Law – you're the best thing that ever happened to me. I want you to be the mother of my child, of my children…'

'Uh-huh…' she says, letting her head fall back. Her husband turned her on so much more than any man she'd ever known. There was something in his touch, something elusive that she found irresistible, like a half-remembered song. Much as she hated them spending so much time apart, she did understand. Bobby was a sensational photographer and had worked hard to accrue an impressive portfolio of clients. Her man could work a room like no one else

she'd ever known. People, women in particular, were drawn to him; she understood this more than anyone. Robert had a way of making a woman feel like she was the only girl alive in that very moment.

When Monica had introduced him to Laurie seven years previously she had been captivated within minutes; the way his eyes seemed to see right through to her very soul, like he could read her thoughts and knew all her secrets. She enjoyed watching the way he engaged with people and effortlessly brought them out of themselves; it was nothing short of a gift that had gained him many admirers.

'You're like the Pied Piper, do you know that?' she had said to him on more than one occasion. When Robert played a tune it seemed to cast a spell on people, enchanting them and enticing them to follow him, like the Lord of the Dance. She was proud of her husband and trusted him implicitly. So what if he sometimes worked with beautiful models! She was beautiful too, and he'd chosen her; they'd chosen each other.

Besides, Laurie was also making something of a name for herself in the design world. She had sparked the interest of various high-end clients, including celebrities and politicians, and was currently working with her bosses on the theme of a brand new luxury five-star hotel in Lake Como, Italy. Her career was taking off alongside her charismatic husband's, and she knew they had the dual potential to become something of a celebrity couple. But what she really wanted was a baby, to give her husband what she knew deep down he craved the most: a family.

'Let's get as much practice in as we possibly can,' he said, entering her roughly and burying himself deep inside her on the kitchen work surface, causing her to gasp aloud in pleasure as she arched her back to receive him. His phone began buzzing on the surface next to Laurie, and despite her ecstasy she automatically glanced down at it.

'Where are you? I miss you. X'

Robert's eyes followed suit. 'Some stupid menopausal client,' he said, dismissing the text. He slowed down a pace but did not stop, pushing himself deeper into Laurie as he looked her directly in the eye. 'She's got a thing for me apparently.'

'Oh yeah?' Laurie smiled, raising an eyebrow. 'Haven't they all?'

'You've no competition, Law. There is no competition. Anyway, she's in her late fifties, early sixties, and is the size of a small planet.'

'And if she wasn't?'

'Well then, I'd be fucking her.'

She slapped his bare backside playfully, though niggling doubts lingered in her mind. No. She trusted him implicitly…

'Bastard!'

He pushed himself deep inside her again, taking long, hard strokes, causing her moans to crescendo.

'Your bastard,' he said as she came hard in his arms. 'Only yours, Laurie. Always only yours.'

CHAPTER TEN

'Ah, Riley.' Chief Superintendent Woods looks pleased with himself as I enter his office. 'Looks like we've got an open-and-shut number with the Mills case. Laurie Mills has asked for a solicitor, so we're waiting for Michaels or one of the other duties to show up. Shouldn't be long now. Then we can get in there and have this all wrapped up within a few hours.'

I blink at him. Woods appears disinterested in discussing the case any further, as though he's already moved on mentally.

'I'd say she needs psychiatric assessment before we think about making an arrest.'

'Delaney reckons she's sound enough of mind,' he replies, rooting around for something on his untidy desk. 'Ah, there it is.' He locates the stapler triumphantly underneath a pile of files and, I note, a copy of *Fishing Times*.

'*Doctor* Delaney, you mean?' I say facetiously.

Woods glances up at me and continues, 'She's having her prints and photos done now, then all the forensics. After that she'll be looked over by a doctor and assessed. The wounds inflicted on her wrists were superficial. We'll do it by the book as always, Riley. Once the doctor gives the all-clear, you can read her her rights.'

'On what grounds should we arrest her, exactly?'

Woods looks back up at me then, indignant. I knew *that* would get his attention.

'On the grounds, Riley, that it appears she brutally murdered her bloody husband! Then made a half-hearted attempt at killing herself.'

'We don't know that, sir,' I say, standing straight, almost to attention. 'We don't know that for definite.'

'Well it's certainly looking that way, wouldn't you agree?'

I go to speak but he cuts me off. 'She was covered in her husband's blood; she was the only person at the scene; there was no sign of an intruder or a break-in; the murder weapon was a kitchen knife that she'd been using to chop onions a few hours before his death. Somewhat conveniently she says that she can't remember a damn thing; she appears to have a motive – by all accounts she'd been mouthing off to the neighbours about wanting him dead for months; lastly, she seems to have attempted to take her own life. Will that suffice?' He certainly doesn't bother to hide *his* irritation. 'Oh, and the fact it also appears she wrote her husband a final farewell on the mirror telling him exactly what she thought of him. In the poor bastard's own blood.'

'We don't know that *she* wrote that message on the mirror. Forensics haven't come back with anything conclusive yet – no fingerprints, no analysis. At the moment all we have is circum-stantial.'

Woods shakes his head, releasing a few flecks of dandruff into the air and I think, perhaps unfairly, what a TV cliché he has gradually turned into over the years.

'Do you do this deliberately, Riley?' he says, standing now. It appears he's been seated a while because his trousers are crumpled while the top half of him remains impeccable.

'Do what, sir?'

He's gripping the stapler. 'Be deliberately obtuse.'

'Obtuse? No, sir,' I say calmly, which I know will aggravate him even more. 'I'm just saying that we have no evidence – no concrete evidence – yet.'

'You know as well as I do that we don't bloody well *need* concrete evidence to arrest her, to detain her.'

'I'm well aware of that, sir. But I don't think this is as open-and-shut as Delaney might th—'

'Ah, so that's what's bothering you, is it?' Woods interjects. 'Delaney. What is it with you two?' he mutters like a jaded parent.

I avoid answering his question but this remark makes me wonder if Delaney has been saying things about me too.

'What *bothers* me, sir, is that…' I pause. 'What bothers me is that we may be jumping the gun in having this one all sewn up.'

Woods sighs heavily. 'And what makes you say that, Riley? This is about as open-and-shut as they come and yet here you are…' He sighs again and scratches his receding hairline once more, releasing a few more flakes of skin into the ether.

I have to agree with Woods about how this looks, but something is niggling at me. Something, but I'm not sure what it is yet. 'Intuition, sir,' I say after a moment's pause.

Woods blinks at me but his appearance seems to have slightly shifted. He looks less angry and more… nervous. He doesn't speak for a moment.

'Has it ever been wrong, sir?' I ask, admittedly quite arrogantly, but I can't help myself. It's how I truly feel in my guts. 'Have you seen the suspect? Have you *seen* Laurie Mills?' I ask the question knowing full well that he hasn't, because there's no need for him to. Most people only ever get to see the top half of Woods from behind his desk. His role is largely sedentary these days. Some of the lads joke that he could be wearing stockings and suspenders underneath that desk and no one would know. Seeing his full stature today is a rare honour. 'She's like a child, probably weighs around 90lbs,' I hazard a guess. 'She looks emaciated, anorexic, like she doesn't have the strength to lift her own eyelids, let alone ambush a man almost twice, possibly three times her size, stab him repeatedly and almost decapitate him.'

Woods' narrowed eyes meet mine.

'There's no one else in the picture, Riley. It appears she executed him in a fit of jealous rage over his serial cheating, a woman on the edge by all accounts. And you know how the saying about hell hath no fury goes. I've had a look at the reports from the neighbours. Laurie Mills is an unhinged alcoholic, suffering from depression. The letter you found on the body was informing her of Robert Mills' intentions to divorce her and it pushed the woman over the cliff by the looks of it. *And* you and I both know that size, when it comes down to it, is irrelevant.'

I raise an eyebrow. I imagine this is a conversation he has with Mrs Woods. I feel a touch saddened by Woods' blatant assumptions. Whatever happened to being innocent until proven guilty? Has Woods forgotten about the nuances in this job even after all his years in it, how things aren't always simply how they appear? And what about the small matter of evidence and witnesses? As yet we've got nothing concrete at all. It *appears* Woods has decided what's what on conjecture and assumptions alone and that he wants this one to be simple and sewn up so he can get on with reading about his tackle.

'If,' I say, 'Laurie Mills flipped out and almost severed her husband's neck in a fit of rage and stabbed him multiple times, then why didn't she abscond? Why go to the bother of writing the message on the mirror? Why didn't she stage a robbery, flee the scene of the crime, or make a better job of slicing her own wrists open? We both know that's the usual state of play in crimes like this.'

Woods looks irritated again. 'Maybe she *wanted* to be caught – maybe this wasn't just a crime of passion but cold-blooded, premeditated murder. Maybe she lured him to the house with a plan to butcher him and plead temporary insanity, then staged a half-arsed suicide attempt, claiming amnesia. Oh Jesus, Dan, I don't know… It's your bloody job to find out.'

Uh-oh, Woods has used my Christian name. This does not bode well.

'Look, just don't be difficult for the sake of it, okay?' He says this with a resignation that somehow gives me a sense of victory. 'We could have this one wrapped up quickly with the CPS if you don't go all Columbo on it.'

'Perhaps,' I say, non-committal. I'm mildly offended by the Columbo reference; I'm decades younger, and I dress better. 'But I'd like to see what forensics come back with first.'

'So would I!' he bellows. 'If only to shut you up.'

Woods rubs his temples with his forefingers. I tend to have that effect on him and I can't say I don't get a small kick out of it.

'I mean, come on, Dan!' He cocks his head to one side. 'If she sprung him from behind with a knife it wouldn't make the blindest bit of difference what the woman weighs, would it?'

I stifle a smile. He's questioning himself now. I've got to him, planted the seed of doubt.

'Probably not, sir, but I'm telling you there's more to this than meets the eye.'

Woods buries his head in his hands. There's a long pause.

I finally break it. 'Let me interview her. Let me and Davis talk to her.'

Woods gets up from his desk again, I assume as some kind of statement.

'Delaney's prepped for it,' he says. 'He wants this one, Dan.'

I'm sure he does, I think, imagining the power trip it would give him. That's what men like Martin Delaney, I suspect, got into the job for: power.

I say nothing. I let my silence speak instead.

'Okay… *Okay*,' he says eventually. 'You *and* Delaney do it, but get this one in the bag as soon as possible, Riley. Don't make any more work for yourself or the team simply because of one of your bloody hunches, do you understand?'

I nod. 'Have they ever been wrong, sir? Any of my "bloody hunches"?'

Woods inhales, makes to speak, but seems to think better of it and waves me out the door instead.

'Thank you, sir,' I say, and smile to myself as I shut the door behind me.

CHAPTER ELEVEN

Laurie Mills has been sitting inside the cell for what feels like days yet she knows, realistically, that it can only be a few hours at best. She's wearing a pair of grey joggers and a matching sweatshirt that they have given her, both of which are at least three sizes too big for her minuscule frame. 'Smallest we've got,' the woman had said, expressionless, as she'd handed them over. The Chloé summer dress that Robert liked and she had been wearing has been taken from her, for, she assumes, analysis. She was shocked by the amount of blood on her clothes, her hands shaking as she'd handed them over in some kind of twilight reality. They have taken DNA samples from her, the blood on her hands, her fingerprints and nail clippings, strands of hair and her photograph. She'd sat in stunned silence as the uniformed female officer instructed her to 'turn to the left', 'turn to the right', and 'look straight ahead'.

The woman had been professional but almost jovial, attempting, at one point, to engage her in conversation as she moaned about the camera being 'temperamental'. But Laurie had been unable to speak. Her larynx felt compounded by shock, like it had seized up and locked itself shut. She felt paralysed by fear, by the thousands of questions sprinting through her mind at breakneck speed, her brain unable to process one before the next presented itself. She feels trapped, exposed, *humiliated*. Her mind is exhausted yet still, somewhere, something tells her she should keep her wits about her. She must hold it together to prove that she did not, *could not*, have killed her husband. Because she didn't, did she? She has nothing to be frightened of. The truth is non-negotiable, right? It will come out. It always does, in the end, just like his sordid love affair. She has trust in the truth, in justice, in the system.

But she doesn't really understand the system, does she? She sees those programmes on telly, those cases where the wrong person is convicted for something they didn't do. Is this what's going to happen to her?

Panic and doubt are creeping in around Laurie like fog. Her memory of last night feels the same, *foggy*. Could it be that she blacked out, or is it because there isn't anything to remember? She isn't sure and it's scaring her. Her whole life has seemed like a blur for so long, a dark cloud of depression. *Time*: she had lost all concept of it after she discovered the affair; the days had become seamless, all rolling into one somehow. Sometimes, particularly in the immediate aftermath of the accident, she had slept right through whole days, waking in a disorientated sweat, not knowing if it was day or night, or which day of the week it was. Robert had taken her life gradually. Slowly, insidiously, he had stripped her of everything, of her very joy for existence, of her essence. Over the years, Laurie realises, little by little he had been taking a piece of her day by day, killing her softly.

She looks around the cell. It reminds her of a public toilet, like the ones you see in train stations, cold and clinical. The tiles are white, shiny, uniform ones and she notices the walls are smooth – there are no sharp lines on which to self-harm. Angled to the left there is a metal toilet that can be viewed from the door. If you were sitting on it, someone could actually see you, not full frontal, but definitely a side glimpse. She needs to pee but can't for this reason. She is crying but it doesn't register with her: it hasn't for a long time now.

The bed she's lying on has a thin blue mattress made of slim foam and is covered with a blue, waxy, plastic-type material. It smells of the sweat and anguish of a thousand men and no doubt a few women too. She can barely lie on it but has to every now and again, when exhaustion forces her to. She pulls the grey blanket they have given her over it to stop the smell reaching her nostrils but it's of little comfort.

Laurie folds her tiny frame in half as she lies down but she can't rest. She is inside a police cell. And Robert is dead.

Someone looks in on her, pulls the small shutter down, but she can't see if they're male or female and she pulls the blanket tighter up around her chest to hide her face. She feels like an animal in a cage. How can they just do this, lock her up like this, treating her like a murderer. Is she a murderer? She wonders when or if they will let her out and resists rushing to the door and pounding it with her small fists. She doesn't have the strength anyway and this makes her angry. It's all been taken from her. She has been robbed of everything.

The duty solicitor should be on their way now, surely? They told her they would come and get her when the solicitor arrived and that she would be interviewed and assessed by a doctor. She has never had to use a solicitor before, not unless she includes the one she and Robert used when they bought the house. She thinks of her house then. How will she ever be able to go back there, to the place Robert died, where she found him lying in a pool of his own blood, his throat severed almost in two?

Panic returns again as the image of his body flashes up in her mind. Suddenly Laurie remembers the phone call. They allow you one, just like on the telly. She had thought of calling her mother, as a child does when they're in trouble. But her mother lives in California, the time difference makes things difficult and there wouldn't be much she could do from there except make a fuss. So she had called Monica instead, her best friend. Monica would know what to do. She always did.

The sound of the iron door opening startles Laurie back to the present and she bolts upright.

'Laurie Mills?' a uniformed man with a gruff voice addresses her.

'Yes?'

'They're ready to see you now.'

CHAPTER TWELVE

Kiki – 1986

'Stop it, Bertie, you're hurting me.' Kiki's half-laughing as she says it, although it's true, he *is* hurting her. Sometimes she thinks he doesn't know his own strength and at other times she thinks he hurts her deliberately.

'Wuss,' he says, dropping her wrist. 'Oh, come on, don't tell me those are tears I see?'

'No!' she says, spinning round, putting her back to him so he can't see her face and the fact that she's welling up. Bertie has a habit of making her feel opposing emotions in quick succession, sometimes even simultaneously: happiness, sadness, laughter, tears, pleasure, pain… but that's what made spending time with him so thrilling and exciting.

'Ah, c'mon, Ki, I was only playing. I've been giving you Chinese burns since you were two years old.'

'It's called child abuse,' she replies, flashing him an ironic smile. It's something they both know about. 'So, did they get you the car?'

His face reveals the answer. 'Look out of the window.'

Bertie grins as she opens the curtains and peers out, rubbing away the condensation to get a better look at the shiny red Ford Escort.

'You lucky sod!' Kiki breathes, making more condensation on the windowpane. 'That's brand fucking new!'

'Wanna go for a spin in her?'

'Do I!' Her excitement wanes almost instantly. 'But Mum will never let me go out in it with you though. That would be too much like having a good time, even on Christmas morning – in fact especially on Christmas morning, when I should be on my hands and knees praying for my sins and singing happy-bastard-fucking-birthday to Jesus Christ.'

He laughs. 'I love the fire in you, Kiki. One day, we'll be away from here, from them. One day soon, I promise. I'm going to study hard and get a job, get us the fuck out of this mental institution they call a home.'

She looks at him lovingly. 'You will? You promise? I think I'll go mad if I have to stay here without you. I couldn't bear it if you left me here alone with them. I'd rather be dead.'

Bertie stares at Kiki, suddenly struck by how much she has grown recently, how tall she's getting, how she's turning into a woman. His eyes travel the length of her as she stands awkwardly in front of him, somehow uncomfortable in her own skin yet defiant at the same time. She has done a good job of hiding her emotional scars, he thinks, but the ones on her arms, where she cuts herself, are just visible beneath the cuff of her nightshirt.

'Fuck her *and* him. Anyway she's downstairs prepping the spuds and Brussels sprouts you spent last night peeling, no doubt already been at the brandy. I'll sneak you in the boot.'

'No you bloody won't! I'm not getting in the boot. I'm claustro-whatsit called?'

'Claustrophobic. Santa *Claus-trophobic*.'

'Ha ha, idiot. I'll get dressed.' She turns round and pulls her nightshirt up over her head. 'No looking!' But she knows that he will, and secretly she wants him to.

'Wrap up though, because *baby, it's cold outside*.' He breaks into song and she starts to laugh. He has a good voice but she doesn't want to tell him that. His head is big enough already.

'Looks like Santa forgot about me again this year.' Kiki looks down at the end of the bed and sighs. 'A hand-engraved Bible again, oh and extra piano lessons. *Thank you, Mummy; thank you, Daddy.*' She mimics a sickly, childlike voice.

He watches her as she pulls a sweater on over some jeans. 'What would you have really liked for Christmas then?'

Kiki taps her lip. 'Hmmm, roller skates, some Giorgio Beverly Hills perfume and a Madonna album...'

In fact, a bra is what she had truly hoped for. Her breasts were visible now beneath her clothes. All the girls at school wore them. Except for her, of course, and she'd not got the courage to ask her drunken old bitch of a mother – it wasn't worth the aggro and lecture on sins of the flesh that would inevitably follow. 'Anything but a bloody Bible. I mean, how come you get a car and I get a Bible? How it that fair?'

'Because I'm old enough to drive. I'm sure they'll get you a car too when you're old enough.'

But they both know he's saying that just to make her feel better.

'Yeah, right.' Kiki pulls her jeans up over her slim legs.

'Close your eyes,' he says.

'What for?'

'I have a surprise for you.'

She giggles. 'What is it?'

'If I tell you it wouldn't be a surprise, would it, dopey?'

She complies, squeezing her eyes shut.

'No cheating,' he says, placing a wrapped package in her hands. 'Happy Christmas, Kiki. Santa may have forgotten you, but I never will.'

She opens her eyes and stares at the wrapped present for a few seconds before tearing it open with excitement. Inside is a plain, simple white bra with the tiniest yellow flowers on it. For a second she thinks she might burst into tears.

'You can try it on if you like. I promise not to peek. Scout's honour.' He crosses his fingers and they both laugh.

Almost tearing her sweater off in haste, she turns her back to him and puts the bra on, savouring the soft cotton fabric and the way it makes her feel.

'Let's see if it fits you,' he says and she turns to face him, her cheeks burning; love, embarrassment and warmth spread through her adolescent body. 'I love it,' he says softly.

'I love you, Bertie,' she replies. 'It's the best Christmas present ever.' Kiki hugs him then, wraps her arms around his neck and kisses his cheek. She feels his hands on her back, the tips of his fingers lightly touching her skin, gently running over the soft cotton fabric.

'How about that ride then?' she says. 'Take your new toy for a spin—'

But he pulls back from her and she senses the change in his mood instantly. 'Another time,' he says sharply. 'I said I'd take Becky from up the road in it first anyway. Best you get dressed and get downstairs before it becomes a Christmas to remember for all the wrong reasons.'

'Okay,' she says, feeling crushed as he shuts the door behind him.

CHAPTER THIRTEEN

If Delaney were the kind of copper worth his boots, one who was able to read people better, then it would be clear to him, like it is to me, that Laurie Mills is in an emotionally fragile condition right now and the best way forward is to treat her with extreme caution. Despite getting the all-clear from the doctor, she has 'suicide case' written through her like a stick of Blackpool rock. Instead, however, Delaney appears to be taking the bull-in-a-china-shop approach, or perhaps *bully* would be more appropriate.

'For the benefit of the tape, today's date is Saturday, 14 October 2017. Myself, DS Martin Delaney, and DI Daniel Riley are both present, as is David Michaels, duty solicitor. Could you please clearly state your name, address and date of birth?' He addresses Laurie coldly, with an air of superiority.

Laurie Mills looks at him, then me, nervously. Then she turns to Michaels. I think I know Michaels. We've met once before. If I remember correctly his looks are quite deceiving. He's a weasel-faced man with particularly bad taste in suits – today he has opted for a grey shiny number circa 1985 and a purple tie – like he's just stepped out of some dubious 80s nightclub with a name like 'Bon Bonnies'. But actually, he was one of the more astute duties I've come across, and he seems to actually care about his clients. I'm secretly glad he's here for Laurie Mills today. Right now, she looks like a rabbit caught in headlights and I feel a pang of empathy for her. I know, I know – I just can't help it.

'Yes… um… my name is Laurie Ann Mills, my address is 13 Cedar Close, London N21…' She rubs her temples with her thumb and forefinger. 'Oh God, my mind's gone blank… er, 6GX… yes, 6GX. My date of birth is 21 July 1979.' Her voice is shaky, almost a warble. She's panicking, of course. Most people do when they find themselves arrested for suspected murder.

I nod at the cup of water on the table in front of her and she reaches for it as though she has been waiting for permission to take a sip.

'For the benefit of the tape once more,' Delaney says, 'I have to caution you again, okay. You do not have to say anything, but it may harm your defence if you do not mention when questioned something which you later rely on in court. Anything you do say may be given in evidence.'

Laurie nods.

'Do you understand why you're here, Mrs Mills?' Delaney is seated next to me now. I can smell his aftershave. It's a little overbearing, a bit like him.

'Yes,' she says, wringing her hands as she chews her bottom lip. 'Yes, you think I killed Robert. You think I killed my husband.'

I stay silent and observe, let Delaney work what he believes to be his magic first.

'According to Constable Rawlins, who accompanied you from your home address to the station, you said, when asked if you killed Robert Mills, that you didn't know. That you didn't remember. Is that correct?'

Michaels whispers something in her ear and Laurie's expression doesn't change, like she hasn't heard him.

'No. No, I don't remember,' she says. 'I don't think I killed him.'

I see Michaels visibly flinch.

'You don't *think*?' Delaney says. 'Well, you need to *think*, Mrs Mills. Your husband is dead. Someone slit his throat with a knife and watched the blood drain from him, then they stabbed him a total of eighteen times, even going as far as writing him a final farewell on the mirror in your guest bedroom. Were those your parting words to your husband, Mrs Mills? We know he was having an affair and that he fathered a child with his mistress. That's correct, isn't it?'

Laurie Mills almost melts in her chair, like the Wicked Witch of the West who's just had a bucket of water thrown over her.

'He was stabbed? *Stabbed*?' She looks genuinely surprised by this information. I watch her expression carefully.

'Yes, eighteen times in the chest and stomach.'

Her eyes widen. 'Oh God…' She buries her face in her hands. 'Stabbed—'

'Is it possible, Mrs Mills,' Delaney continues apace, 'that you killed your husband in a fit of jealous rage? You recently found out about the child, didn't you? The fact your husband had fathered his mistress's child. Did it push you over the edge? Your husband was coming over that night to serve you with divorce papers, wasn't he?'

I think I see another flicker of surprise, or perhaps it's shock, on her face as she finally looks up. She's shaking her head.

'No… No…' She's crying. 'I don't remember… I blacked out… I… I… fell asleep. I must've… I was waiting for him… The beef Wellington… He… he didn't come…' Her face is screwed up with anguish and emotion. Delaney is pushing her too hard too quickly and I don't like it. She obviously can't think straight and thinking straight is what I need Laurie Mills to do right now.

'It's okay, Laurie,' I say before Delaney can go at her again. 'Just tell us what you *do* remember.'

Delaney gives me a sharp sideways glance and I pretend not to have noticed it. *Prick*. 'Tell us, from the beginning, everything you remember about that day, about yesterday. Start from when you woke up in the morning until the moment you discovered your husband in the bathroom. Take your time, Laurie. As much detail as you can.' I nod at her reassuringly and keep my voice low and calm, the antithesis of Delaney, who is leaning forward on the table, chomping at the bit like a lion circling a wounded antelope.

Laurie hugs herself as she sits in the chair. She's so tiny she can almost wrap her arms around her entire frame. I study her closely. She's a pretty woman, despite the puffiness of her eyes and the redness of her skin from crying. Perhaps she's even beautiful, and I'm suddenly reminded of the photographs, the black-and-white artistic nude shots that were hanging on the wall in the guest bedroom where Robert Mills was found.

'It's okay,' I say again. 'Whenever you're ready. You've faced a terrible shock and I know this must be difficult for you.'

Her big brown eyes look up at me, grateful. I see something in them that I have recognised in my own many times before: grief and pain.

She takes an intake of breath, blinks back the tears. 'I went shopping,' she says. 'Robert... well, he... he was due to come over, to come to the house. He said he wanted to talk. He sent me a message in the morning, that morning, asking if he could come to the house.'

Her phone is with forensics and they should be back to us with something very soon to corroborate this.

'Do you know what he wanted to talk to you about, Laurie?' I'm being gentle with her, trying to coax her into opening up. I don't want to let Delaney loose on her. Not yet anyway. I want the measure of her first. If he's not careful with her, I suspect Mrs Mills here will clam up like a shell.

'No... he just said he needed to talk. I hadn't seen him in a while—'

'How long?'

'A few weeks, maybe a couple of months... Not since the...' She stalls, looks at me. 'Not since the day of the barbecue.'

'Ahh yes,' Delaney chips in. 'The street barbecue. We spoke to some of your neighbours. There was an altercation that day, wasn't there, between you and your husband? Back in' – he looks down at his notes – 'early August, 10 August.'

'Yes,' she replies quietly, dropping her chin. 'There was.'

'You threatened to kill him, your husband, at the barbecue, is that right? In front of your neighbours and friends?'

She makes to speak but Michaels stops her, talks quietly in her ear again.

'We'll get to the barbecue,' I say. 'Keep telling us about yesterday, Laurie. Robert texted you and told you he was coming over to the house to see you. What time was that?'

'He texted me in the morning, around 9.30 a.m. I think,' she replies, her voice just above a whisper, hoarse from crying. 'When he said he wanted to talk, wanted to come to the house I hoped… well, part of me hoped he was coming to…' She stops. 'He said he'd be over around 7.30 p.m. I decided to make him a meal. We usually ate around that time, when we were together.'

'He agreed to come to dinner?'

She shifts in her seat, looks agitated. 'No, not exactly. I just decided I would make him dinner – surprise him, I suppose. I went to the hairdressers—'

'What time?'

'About 1.30 p.m. Then I picked up my dress from the dry-cleaners.'

'The dress you were wearing last night?' We'll hear back from forensics about that soon, too.

'Yes. It was Robert's favourite. Well, he always said he liked it on me…' Her voice dissipates into sadness and she tries to smile, though it looks more like a lid on a scream.

'Go on, Laurie. You went to the hairdressers, picked up your dress from the dry-cleaners. Then where did you go?'

'Home, I think… Yes, I went home. Hung the dress up. I… I pottered around the house for a bit…' Laurie screws her eyes tightly together as if this will somehow make her thoughts clearer.

'My friend, she popped in to see me.'

'Your friend?'

'Yes, my friend Monica. Monica Lewis. She lives opposite me.'

'What time was this, Laurie?'

She exhales, her agitation returning.

'Come on, Mrs Mills, think!' Delaney butts in and I imagine what a good-cop bad-cop cliché we must be coming across as. I don't think there can be any ambiguity over who is who. I can see she's struggling, poor woman, that even the smallest amount of pressure is causing her distress. Like I said, Delaney is handling her all wrong.

'I… I don't know… Maybe 3 p.m. – 3.30 p.m.? I didn't look at the time…'

We'll need to get the neighbour in, this Monica Lewis, get her to corroborate Laurie's story. I write her name down on the notepad in front of me and suddenly think about that American woman, Monica Lewinsky. 'That woman' who led to Bill Clinton's impeachment and the speech he gave where he lied to his country on public television, claiming that he'd never had 'sexual relations' with her. He was convincing though; I'll give him that.

'We had coffee I think, chatted a bit. Then she left and I went to the supermarket to buy the groceries for dinner, for Robert.' Laurie's face crumples a little as she says his name.

'Which supermarket?' Delaney snaps.

'Waitrose, the one just off the high street.'

'What did you buy?'

'Look, is this relevant?' Michaels chips in. 'Mrs Mills' shopping list bears no relevance to her husband's death, does it?'

'I was going to… I *did* make him scallops in their shells with a beurre blanc sauce and beef Wellington. He… Robert, loved my cooking.'

'What time did you return from the supermarket, Laurie?' This is actually the question Delaney *should've* asked.

'I can't remember the exact time but—'

'Roughly?' Delaney chips in.

'Oh God…' She's getting visibly more distressed as he presses her, tapping her feet nervously on the floor.

'I don't know… It was just getting dark, maybe around 4.30 p.m.? I don't know… I'm sorry.'

'It's okay.' I give her what I hope is a reassuring nod. 'Did you see anyone while you were out – a friend, a neighbour, anyone who would recognise you?'

She runs her hands down her face, clawing at her skin as if this would somehow help her think. 'No, no one… Well, actually, I saw one of the neighbours – I'm sorry, I can't remember her name. She lives a few doors down from Monica.'

'What did you do when you returned home?'

'I had a shower, got ready and dressed. Then I started preparing the food, cooking the meal I had planned.'

'Did he stand you up, Laurie? Did he turn up late? Was dinner ruined and did that make you angry?'

She looks at Delaney nervously. 'I was angry, yes… when he didn't show up at 7.30 p.m. I felt… I felt let down.'

'Let down and angry. That's understandable, Mrs Mills,' Delaney says. 'He'd been unfaithful hadn't he, your husband? Had an affair with a…' He flips through his notepad. 'With Claire. That's right, isn't it?'

She visibly flinches at the sound of Claire's name. 'Yes. He did.' Her voice is a low, hoarse whisper of a thousand emotions.

'He left you, didn't he, to be with Claire, his mistress?'

I can see that this line of questioning is excruciatingly painful for Laurie Mills and I struggle not to reach out and comfort her.

'Yes,' she says. 'Physically. But he never left me, not in the true sense of the word…' She says this with such melancholy that it resonates in the interview room. And I understand. Rachel. She's never really left me.

'But you weren't living together?'

She swallows. Draws breath.

'He came round that night to serve you with divorce papers, didn't he? And that was too much, wasn't it, Mrs Mills? That was the final straw, the final insult. You knew your marriage couldn't be saved and that your husband was going to start a new life with his lover and their child so you—'

'NO!' she says, with much more conviction this time.

'But we found the papers, the solicitor's letter. It was underneath his body in the bedroom, still in the envelope, unopened.'

Laurie looks at me as if for confirmation of this, like she thinks Delaney is bluffing. So I nod at her and she starts to cry.

'I… I thought… I thought that maybe… It crossed my mind he may want a divorce, but I didn't think he'd ever go through with it. I didn't see any papers, no solicitor's letter.'

Delaney sits back in his chair, pleased with himself.

'What *did* you see, Laurie?' I ask her gently.

She pauses for a short moment that feels longer than it is. 'I drank some vodka,' she says, her head low. 'I had a couple of drinks while I was preparing the meal. Then a couple more as I sat and waited for him and watched it all spoil. I thought he'd stood me up. That he'd changed his mind… Robert liked playing games… mind games—'

'And you were rightly pissed off that you'd gone to so much trouble, yes?' Delaney begins with the leading questions again.

'Yes,' she admits. 'Yes I was.'

'So, what did you do, Laurie?' I cut in again. *Softly, softly catchee monkey.*

'I drank some more,' she answers, obviously ashamed as she drags her hand across her forehead, pulling at the skin on her cheeks once more. 'The vodka… then the wine, the Prosecco. I… I think I fell asleep.'

'That's a fair bit of alcohol,' Delaney remarks. 'Do you drink like that a lot, Mrs Mills?'

Michaels shifts in his chair, the fabric of his shiny suit catching the light. It really is a bad suit and I wonder if I should ask him where he got it so I can avoid that particular shop.

'I drink more now,' she says quietly. 'Since the accident.'

'The accident?' Delaney asks.

'Look, I feel like we're getting off track here,' Michaels pipes up. I'm inclined to agree with him but the accident comment intrigues me. I make a mental note of it; we'll get back to it later.

'What time did you wake up, Laurie?'

She looks at me; her lips are quivering and her hands are shaking uncontrollably. 'I don't know. It was dark. It was pitch black and I was lying upstairs on the bed,' she says. 'I don't know how I got there—'

'And what did you do next?' I ask.

Her brow is furrowed as she strains to recall the details.

'I felt groggy,' Laurie continues. 'The lights weren't working... I tried to turn them on but... I thought maybe there had been a power cut so I decided to go downstairs and look for—'

'Look for what, Mrs Mills?' Delaney keeps interjecting, won't let her finish. He hasn't learned the art of staying quiet and waiting for people to fill the silence.

'Look for a torch. I felt wet, like my dress was wet. I was so disorientated. It was dark. I was upstairs and I didn't know why. Robert had stood me up and—'

'Was Robert already in the house then? Did you see him? Did he show up late and you had some kind of argument? Did things get out of hand?' Delaney is pushing again. This is more like round-three questioning. This is not how I like to do things and I've half a mind to cut the interview there and then. Instead I shoot Delaney a look. One that says *ease the fuck up* in no uncertain terms. It seems to work because he sits back from the table.

'In the house already? No... no... Well, I guess he must have been. But I didn't know... I swear I didn't know he was there

until— And there was no argument because I didn't see him.'
Her eyes are pleading with mine. 'I didn't know he was there. I
thought he'd stood me up. I – I…'

She's babbling, distress coming off her in waves. Her eyes dart
around the room before they rest on mine and I look directly into
them. I know a thing or two about lying, and about liars too.
Inevitably you learn in this game. You sure as shit hear enough
of them and meet enough of them. They're not always easy to
spot without a trained eye though. Some liars, the psychos and
seasoned manipulators, are so exceptionally adept at pulling the
wool over everyone's eyes that they can convince almost anyone:
police, judges, therapists, their families and friends and co-workers.
Psychopaths are such consummate liars because they believe their
own lies. They lie to themselves first and foremost. And if you've
convinced yourself that you're telling the truth, well then, it's not
really a lie is it? I've even known some to pass polygraphs with
flying colours. But as some clever sod once said, *You can fool all
of the people some of the time, and some of the people all of the time,
but you cannot fool all of the people all of the time…* Jesus, now who
was it who said that?

Anyway, sometimes, even with the most skilful and practised
psychopaths and liars, little things often give them away. It's in the
minutiae, in the ever-so-subtle details, if you know what to look for.
Body language is key. A tilt of the head, the flicker of an eyelid, a brief
downward turn of the mouth, the slightest shrug of a shoulder… All
of us believe we are in control of our bodies, but they can betray us
in subconscious ways. Guilty people often overcompensate; they
mimic a reaction that they feel they *should* display. But you can't
mimic truth. It exists in itself and it has a way of exposing itself.

Don't listen to what people tell you, Riley, an old-school DCI
I worked under once told me. *Look at what they show you.* And
right now, Laurie Mills is showing me that she hasn't really got a
clue what Delaney is talking about.

'I looked for the torch but it was too dark. I couldn't see a thing, so I went to the kitchen to find my phone and used the torch app on that. I saw that the switch had tripped so I flicked it up and the lights came on. That's when I saw… that's when I saw the blood.' She starts whimpering again, shaking her head violently as if trying to erase the image, like an Etch A Sketch. 'So much blood…' she whispers. She's pulling at her hair now, twisting it between her fingers until strands of it fall onto the table.

'Did you know where the blood had come from, Laurie, the source?' I ask the question tentatively because she's talking now, opening up a little, remembering things, and I silently pray that Delaney doesn't mess up and say anything that will shut her down. She's as fragile as fine china, like she could break at any moment. And I'm concerned that if she does she won't be able to put herself back together again.

'I was in shock, to see that much blood… God…' She exhales and inhales in a bid to regulate her breathing. 'I thought it must have come from me. That I'd hurt myself somehow.'

'So you don't remember cutting your wrists, Laurie?' Delaney chips in.

Where is Lucy Davis when you need her? I swear Woods has done this on purpose, put me with Delaney on this case to deliberately antagonise me. But I do need to find a way to work cohesively with him. And by cohesively, I mean without wanting to knock his teeth down his throat.

'No! No I don't.' She looks at me and Delaney, then down at her tiny bandaged wrists. 'I swear I don't remember cutting my own wrists at all. I just… I just don't think I would do that… I wouldn't—'

Delaney looks at his notes. 'You suffer from depression – that's right, isn't it, Laurie?'

Laurie is staring at her wrists now. There's a pause. 'Yes. Since… Yes, I do.' Her voice is laced with so much sadness I can almost taste it. 'If I was ever going to commit suicide it would have been then, after the accident,' she adds quietly. I think about asking her about the accident but Delaney cuts in before the question reaches my lips.

'Were you stalking your husband, Mrs Mills?'

I catch the look on Michaels' face; I can see he's trying to stop himself from burying his head in his hands.

'Stalking him? No! No, not stalking… I wasn't… Oh God, look, you don't understand what he was like, what the relationship was like—'

'What was it like?' Delaney pushes further.

'So you called his phone?' I say, cutting in over Delaney. I need to establish the events of that day and night, get the interview back on track. 'When you saw the blood, you called your husband's phone. Why did you do that, Laurie?'

Her decision to phone Robert strikes me as odd. Why would Laurie Mills, having just committed a vicious and brutal murder, call her husband's phone knowing he was dead? Agreed, she could've wanted it to look like some kind of alibi, throw us off the scent; make it look like she didn't know he was dead at that point. It could have been a careful, calculated move on her part, but I'm not getting that from her at all, not from the poor bewildered wretch sat shivering with fear in front of me. If Laurie Mills is lying, then she's one of the best I've ever come across – Oscar-worthy in fact.

Laurie wipes her nose with a tissue that she takes from the box on the table. Her face looks red raw from crying. 'Yes. I rang his phone. I wanted to know why he hadn't shown up. I was scared… confused—'

'Can you remember what time this was?' Delaney is back, leaning forward on the table now. It's like he's been taking lessons in police work by watching old episodes of *The Sweeney*.

Laurie rubs her forehead again. She looks drained and exhausted. I know the feeling.

'Really, I have no idea. I didn't look at the time. I didn't think to. The blood, the dark… I was panicking – nothing made sense. It rang out I think, his phone. I tried it again. That's when I heard the noise – the ring—'

'You heard the phone ringing?' A rush of adrenaline causes my pulse to quicken.

'Yes,' she says, 'I realised a phone was ringing… I was calling Robert's number and I could hear a phone ringing. I didn't understand, didn't know what was going on, so I followed it. It sounded like it was coming from upstairs—'

Delaney opens his mouth to speak and I have to stop myself from physically pulling him backwards. I am in charge here. Best Delaney knows it. I suddenly think of Fi again. The press will be all over this by now of course. A man dead in his own home, found by his estranged wife – who attempted to cut her own wrists, albeit superficially. It's got all the elements of a front-pager: passion, jealousy, betrayal, rejection, attempted suicide… So far so good, and yet I'm unconvinced.

'I heard the phone ring,' she says, again. 'And then I went upstairs.'

CHAPTER FOURTEEN

Laurie holds her head in her hands and feels her fingernails digging into her forehead. The full reality of the situation she finds herself in has not yet fully penetrated her rational brain. It's as if she's having an out-of-body experience; as if she's a spectator in her own life, watching herself as though she were the audience in some tense stage drama, or having a particularly vivid nightmare from which she's sure she will wake. Her cortisol levels are off the scale as her fight-or-flight instincts propel her into a heightened state of alert. She's used to this feeling: it's familiar, comforting almost.

The detective sitting opposite her, the one with the cold eyes and expressionless face, frightens her. He *believes* that she's killed Robert. It's evident in his body language, in the directness of his speech and its delivery. He's trying to push her into making a confession. She needs to be stronger. She always needed to be stronger, didn't she? She *should* have been stronger. None of this would've happened if only she hadn't been so weak, so filled with self-loathing, guilt and shame.

She's trying to answer the detective's questions as best she can through the pea-soup-like fog in her mind. The antidepressants she's been on don't help her memory too much. It's as though there's a thin layer of dust that has blanketed it, like looking through a smeared windowpane.

Laurie attempts to comfort herself, to 'show up' for herself as her therapist would say, by focusing on her breathing, regulating it, stemming the panic rising up through her small diaphragm.

Forensics will prove that she didn't kill Robert, won't they? She must put faith in the system. *Faith. Hope.* She had never given up hoping. Hoping that he would change, hoping that he would see how much he was hurting her, hoping that if she hung on just this one last time then things might be right again…

Laurie knows she will have to talk about the accident. They have already touched on it. And she will be obliged to answer them. Even at the thought of this she can feel the fresh, flimsy stitches of those gaping emotional wounds begin to unpick.

'You followed the sound of the phone, Laurie? You went to locate it?'

The other detective is speaking now, the nice one. *Nicer*, anyway. She suspects this is their modus operandi: good cop, bad cop, a cliché reserved for those TV police shows she sometimes used to watch back when she could concentrate on anything long enough. His eyes are definitely kinder than the other man's, and she is naturally more easily drawn to them. She thinks she can see empathy in them, perhaps even sadness itself. It's a small reassurance. He's just another human being. She wonders if Monica has arrived yet.

'Yes. I kept calling his number and it kept ringing out, going to voicemail. I could hear that it was coming from somewhere upstairs and—'

'Was it not a little odd that you could hear your husband's phone ringing inside your house? Did he still have a key to the property?' The not-so-nice detective doesn't let her finish.

'Yes… yes I think he still had a key. It is – *was* – still his home. *Our* home. But he'd never just let himself in before, not since… I thought— Well, I initially thought that he'd turned up while I was sleeping, though I'm sure he would've woken me. He hated me drinki—' She stops herself short.

'He didn't like you drinking?'

Laurie shakes her head. She doesn't want to elaborate; she feels so much shame already.

'I thought that he'd probably gone upstairs for some reason – to lie down, take a shower or something… I don't know. I thought maybe he must've fallen asleep. I didn't know what was going on… I was covered in blood, it was dark—'

'Seems a bit odd, don't you think? That your ex-husband would just turn up, not wake you when you were supposed to be having dinner together, and then decide to go upstairs and lie down?'

'No, no… I mean yes… and he's not my ex-husband. And he didn't know I was preparing dinner. But yes, I was confused… I didn't understand it myself.' She's shivering. It's cold in this room, or perhaps it's just her shredded nerves. She has trouble keeping warm these days. She always feels cold. Her mother says it's because she's too thin and there's not enough meat on her bones. But she thinks it's because she feels dead inside.

'Just tell us what happened next, Laurie.' The nice detective speaks again and his voice is soothing.

'I looked in the bedroom… I was still calling his number and it was ringing, but I couldn't locate it immediately. I was searching, frantic, but he wasn't there, in the bedroom. I kept calling… and then I stopped on the landing and listened, and it sounded like the ring was coming from the guest room so I went in. I saw he wasn't on the bed but the noise was closer so I looked in the en suite and that's when…' Laurie feels horror crash into her as the image of her husband, of Robert, lying on the bathroom floor, confronts her again.

'What was the first thing you noticed, Laurie?' Nice Detective says, almost too quickly, like he's trying to ask the question before Bad Detective gets a chance to.

In spite of Laurie's predicament she still senses tension between the two men. She's an expert on picking up tension. Her therapist told her this was because of her own state of hypersensitivity, part of her PTSD.

'Aside from your husband, what was the first thing you noticed about the scene?'

'His shoes,' she replies. 'He was wearing new shoes. I could still see the remains of the labels on the soles where he'd tried to peel them off.'

'So you didn't notice the blood, Mrs Mills, or that your husband's throat had been severed? Or the message on the mirror…?'

Bad Detective's tone is accusatory, as though somehow this observation about Robert's shoes makes her guilty. This is when she begins to doubt herself and her recollection of events. Is it possible she really did finally flip and has blanked it all out in a bid to manage the psychological damage? She has read about this kind of thing happening to people who suffer with extreme anxiety and depression before. Happening to other people – that's what she had thought about fatal car accidents too. But she knows, guiltily, that she has experienced alcoholic blackouts before, times where she has drunk herself into a dark abyss of oblivion in a bid to obliterate the searing agony inside her shattered soul. She wonders if they will find this out. Will they speak to her therapist? Obtain her GP records? Should she just come clean now? Laurie wants to ask the advice of the funny little man sitting next to her who smells faintly of TCP, a smell which reminds her of being in hospital, triggering yet more anxiety, but she thinks this will make her look like she has something to hide so she doesn't. She doesn't want to mention the blackouts because of how damning it might look.

'I… I was in total shock. I… How could I possibly have been expected to…? I was hysterical – I couldn't take it in. I thought it was a sick joke, that Robert was maybe playing some kind of sick joke on me. Or that he was drunk and had fallen over, or that he'd hurt himself, knocked himself out. I – I just wasn't expecting to see him there, not like that—'

'Of course not – that's understandable,' Nice Detective says. He's on her side, isn't he? He seems to be.

The knock on the door startles Laurie and she visibly jumps in her seat. Her heart is racing again, galloping frantically, almost painfully, inside of her chest. She can feel the onset of an anxiety attack; her mouth is as dry as sandpaper and she sips some water. It brings no relief.

'For the benefit of the tape, DS Davis has just entered the room. Interview terminated at…'

Laurie looks over at the female officer and tries to read her expression as she begins to speak to the good cop in hushed tones.

'Will you excuse me for a moment?' he says. 'I think now might be a good time to take a break.' He glances at Bad Detective who's still looking at her with a hint of menace and suspicion in his dark eyes as he stands and they all leave her alone with the odd-smelling solicitor. Dread begins to trickle on top of her anxiety and fear; something tells her things are not looking good.

CHAPTER FIFTEEN

Davis's expression puts me immediately on high alert. Clearly she has news.

'The court order was rushed through… phone records.'

She hands me a sheet, a list of calls made from Laurie Mills' phone. I am about to enter the incident room but stop short of the door and read it there. My eyes scan it as Delaney comes up behind me and attempts to look over my shoulder. I know I somehow need to work with this guy so I resist the childish impulse to turn it to such an angle that he can't see. It's rude to read over people's shoulders. *And irritating*.

Even if Laurie Mills is a killer, she is a vulnerable one. This may sound like a ridiculous statement but it doesn't make it untrue. I've seen emotionally abused and battered women throughout my career, some of whom have turned on their perpetrators and done them in, usually in a frenzied, spur-of-the moment defensive attack, or simply because they couldn't take any more and caved the bastard's head in. It still makes them murderers of course, I'm not disputing this fact, but when you dig deeper, when you listen to the stories these women tell, the years of horrific and unrelenting abuse of their minds, hearts and bodies, and the living hell they've endured at the hands of monsters who were supposed to love them then it makes a lot more sense.

Does it justify what they did? No, not in the eyes of the law, although there have been times when I've felt these women had *every* justification to extinguish such malignant, cruel punishers from their lives and I've secretly high-fived them in my head. Human beings have limits, and some of the abused women I have encountered had had theirs pushed beyond the realms of what could be considered human. The law is the law of course, and sadly in these cases it doesn't always distinguish. But I don't like abusers. Jesus, who does?

'She's telling the truth,' I say, 'about the calls she made to his phone. And the times add up.' I scan through the records. The last activity recorded on Laurie Mills' phone, aside from calling her dead husband's number, is a text message sent to an as-yet-unidentified number at 3.12 p.m.

Davis is hovering by the door next to me. She looks a little uncomfortable. The body language between her and Delaney is brittle as she keeps her eyes focused on me. Something is not quite right, and like an animal I sense it.

'That close must be CCTV'd up to the hilt, all that money there. See what the neighbours have got, what the Millses have got, if any. Laurie Mills claims there was some kind of power shortage. Find out if it was just number 13's electric that tripped out or if the whole street was plunged into darkness. And get hold of anything from yesterday of Laurie at the hairdressers and at the dry-cleaners. See if there's footage we can recover from the supermarket. We can cross-reference it all. Make sure the timings add up.'

'What about the mistress? Claire someone?'

Davis nods. 'Claire Wright. Lives in Luton.'

'We need to get round there,' I say. 'You and me, ASAP.'

Davis nods again.

Delaney holds his hands up. 'Shall we just finish this? Can we? Let's just get this wrapped up. Maybe then we can all go home and' – he shoots a look at Davis – 'go to bed.'

I watch the exchange between them. Davis gives nothing away in her expression, but I think I see a slight bristle. *Jesus Christ, have they slept together?* I concentrate on the matter at hand and push such an unsavoury thought to the back of my mind. I like Davis – she's a good copper and I trust her judgement – but if she's been doing the dirty with Delaney then this puts my whole opinion of her in jeopardy.

'It's possible someone could've already been in the house,' I say.

'No sign of a break-in though,' Delaney reminds me. 'No sign of any intruder. No classic signs of a robbery.'

'She could've left the back door open, a window… Someone could've walked right into the house either before she blacked out or while she did. It's not enough to keep her, Martin, let alone present anything to the CPS at this stage and you know it. We need forensics, hard facts, and we need to look into Robert Mills' life a whole lot more. This is a man with secrets. A man who cheats on his wife, has affairs. I suspect, by looking and listening to Laurie, that he was possibly an abuser.' I've said what I think now and I can see the agreement in Davis's eyes.

'There's no evidence of that,' Delaney says measuredly. 'The neighbours heard them arguing but he's got no previous, never been pulled in for DV.'

'Sometimes the bruises are on the inside,' I snap back, shutting him down. 'She isn't lying about timings,' I continue. 'She did call her husband when she said she did. We need witnesses. Let's piece together Laurie Mills' day yesterday, get the timing down pat.'

'The team are on it, Gov. Sending people down tomorrow to the hairdressers, the dry-cleaners, the supermarket to corroborate—'

'And the witnesses who say she threatened to kill her husband at the barbecue?' Delaney adds smoothly. 'What about them?'

'She said something about an accident,' I address Davis, trying not to think of her and that schmuck Delaney in bed together. I thought she was married? 'We need to find out about this accident. We need to talk to Laurie Mills some more. The clock's ticking.'

'We can always apply for an extension,' Delaney says. 'Wait and see what comes back from forensics.'

He's clearly relishing the idea of prolonging Laurie Mills' agony. Hell, maybe she *is* the killer. Maybe she *did* slit her husband's throat and stab him in a frenzied attack and then slit her own wrists in a bid to end it all. But we need to prove it – we need to make a watertight case before we charge her and we've got less than twenty-four hours to do so. If we don't have enough evidence to charge her and she's still our prime suspect, then we'll release her on bail and keep tabs on her. That's the protocol and Delaney knows it.

Laurie Mills doesn't look like the type to abscond. I'd bet my bones she isn't a danger to anyone, with the exception of herself maybe. Right now, she doesn't look like she could put one foot in front of the other.

Harding pops her head round the door just as I'm about to walk through it.

'Gov.'

'Harding—'

'There's a Monica Lewis downstairs. She's asking to speak to you. Reckons she was with the suspect around the TOD.'

I turn to Delaney and I'm unable to prevent a small smile from escaping my lips.

'Well, perhaps we might not need that extension after all.'

CHAPTER SIXTEEN

'Oh thank God!' Monica Lewis stops pacing as I enter the room and for a moment I think she might throw her arms around me. 'Is she okay? Is Laurie okay? I came as soon as I heard.' Her face is a picture of concern. She looks like she might have been crying, or is about to. 'This is just awful. God… just *so* awful.'

I nod, extend my hand. She's still holding her car keys and places them on the table. 'Detective Riley. Dan Riley.' She shakes my hand solidly. 'Please, sit down.'

'I've been absolutely frantic,' she says, 'out of my mind with worry when I got the call. I was in bed when all the commotion happened. Slept right through it. When I got the call from Laurie I thought I must be dreaming.' She gives a little absurd laugh. 'I just… I just can't believe this has happened. Is she okay? Where's Laurie? Is she alright?'

'She's okay. She's in the interview room, helping us with our enquiries,' I say calmly in a bid not to alarm her any further.

'But you've arrested her?' She shrieks the words in disbelief, puts her forehead in her hands. 'You've arrested Laurie. You know that's ridiculous! She'd never harm Robert. God help her, she loved that man more than life itself, even after everything he— Look, she's not stable, you do know that, don't you, Detective? Laurie is vulnerable, *very* vulnerable. I can't imagine what must be going through her mind right now! Oh God,' she says again, 'poor Laurie. She's had so much tragedy in her life already. This will push her over the edge.'

'She's just helping us piece everything together at this point.' I don't mention the cuts on Laurie's wrists. *Not yet*. Let's see what she has to say first.

I watch Monica Lewis as she fights back tears, chewing on her bottom lip. I'd say she was around the mid-thirties mark, a similar age to Laurie, possibly a little older, or maybe that's down to what she's wearing – a roll-neck jumper and plain leggings, like she's thrown them on in the dark, which, to be fair to her, she probably has. Her blonde hair is scraped back into a loose low ponytail. I suspect she hasn't brushed it, and her face is free of make-up. She's probably just got out of bed.

'How do you know Laurie Mills, Mrs Lewis? It is Mrs, isn't it?'

'Yes,' she says, adding, 'I'm a widow,' by way of explanation. 'My husband, Dougie. He died suddenly of a heart attack last year. He wasn't even forty years old.'

'I'm sorry,' I say genuinely. This job is a constant reminder to me that I'm not the only one who has lost someone so young in tragic circumstances. Yet somehow it still doesn't make it any easier.

'We… well, just me now, live directly opposite the Millses. I've known Laurie since I was a teenager and Robert, well' – she pauses, as if thinking – 'most of my life. We're like sisters, Laurie and I. After the accident she moved opposite to be close to me, so I could help look after her. She doesn't really have any family, no one close anyway. She's practically a recluse. We're like sisters…' Monica repeats. Tears well up in her eyes. I push a box of tissues towards her across the table but she doesn't take one.

'What she's had to endure, what she's been through, and now this! She's a shell of who she used to be because of Robert and what he did. I wish I'd never introduced them to one another.'

'The affair you mean?'

'Oh God, and the rest of it.' She shakes her head as if this is the tip of the iceberg. 'What happened, Detective? What happened to Robert? Laurie said that he was dead. That he'd been *murdered*. Is… is that true? Has Robert been murdered?'

'Yes. I'm afraid he has. I can't give too many details at this point, Mrs Lewis, other than to tell you that Robert Mills was, we believe, killed sometime between 8 and 10 p.m. last night.'

Monica Lewis gasps and says something incoherent. Then she starts to cry. She says what feels like a hundred 'oh Gods'.

'There's press swarming the entire close you know.' She sniffs, wiping away tears with her fingertips. 'It was mayhem down there when I left, reporters everywhere.'

I'm reminded of Fi. I need to call her. I'm surprised she hasn't been on the phone fishing for info already to be honest and this makes me feel bad. Perhaps she feels as awkward as I do.

'I don't advise you to talk to the press, Mrs Lewis, but of course it is your prerogative to do so if you wish. You said Mrs Mills – Laurie – doesn't like to go out much?'

'Yes, she's practically agoraphobic. It's part of her condition I think.'

'Her condition?'

Monica shakes her head again and sighs. 'Depression. Severe depression. She suffers from PTSD, that's post-traumatic str—'

'I know what it is,' I cut her off gently and she smiles apologetically.

'Yes, of course. It was after the barbecue, the annual summer street barbecue, that's when it started up again, after she found out— Well, like I said, I really felt for her and all she'd been through.'

'What did you find out?'

I keep my questions open. Fi told me it's one of the first rules of good journalism to always ask an open question. It keeps people talking.

'Well he was still cheating on her, wasn't he? Had been for years, only she was completely unaware of it for a long time. Unaware that Robert had been leading a double, maybe even treble life. Who knows how many others there were—'

'When did she find out about his infidelity, Monica?' I start making notes.

'Last year. She discovered a second phone, saw some messages… some woman he'd met at a studio he worked at, apparently – Robert's a photographer. She was the receptionist or something… I mean, Laurie is an intelligent woman, Detective. She once had a good career you know, in interior design. She's very talented. Used to do up famous people's houses and everything. He stole that from her too,' she says, sighing. 'Then he threw her, and their marriage, overboard, for some nobody, some overweight little tart with—'

'Right,' I interrupt her. She's heading off-track. There's a reason she's here and I need her to tell me what that reason is.

'She was pregnant at the time,' she says, 'when she found out about the affair I mean – Laurie was pregnant.'

Surprise must register on my face because she says, 'Oh, she hasn't told you about the twins?'

'Twins? No,' I say. 'She's hasn't mentioned them. Not yet.'

Her left eyebrow arches ever so slightly. 'Well,' she says, almost bristling, 'Laurie was eight months pregnant with twins when she found out about Robert's secret life. She was happier than she'd ever been before, suspected nothing. She was looking forward to becoming a mother, and then she discovered the truth about the affair.'

'What happened to the twins?' Laurie hasn't mentioned any children and there were no children at the address.

Monica's face registers surprise this time. 'Jesus, she hasn't told you anything, has she? Well, the day she found out about Robert's double life with this Claire woman, she was beyond distraught, as you can imagine. I mean, beside-herself distraught, as any wife would be, but she was heavily pregnant on top of it, you know, full of hormones, emotional, and the lies, the betrayal, such terrible,

terrible deceit… well, her life fell apart in that moment – *she* fell apart, basically.' Monica's voice is loaded with gravitas. 'She'd been driving down to where he was working when it happened, to confront him about the affair.'

'When what happened?'

'The accident,' Monica says, as though I should already know this. 'She was driving down the M25 in a terrible state, crying, hysterical, hormonal, heavily pregnant… in total despair and devastation – that's how she described it anyway. She wasn't concentrating properly, couldn't see through the crying, driving a little faster than usual. I think she said it was raining too. Anyway, she clipped another car as she changed lanes, or something like that – I forget the exact details now – but anyway, she lost control and careened off the motorway, went straight through the barriers and rolled the car at around 75 miles an hour. Total write-off. It took them nearly six hours to pull her out of the wreck. She was barely alive when they finally got her free.' Monica looks away, as if it's too painful for her to recount the details. 'She suffered such atrocious injuries: a collapsed lung, broken ribs, a shattered collarbone, internal bleeding and God, I can't even remember what else now… A catalogue of horrific injuries; she's only just functioning again now really. It was a miracle that she came out of it alive.'

My heartbeat increases and the broken-bird image flutters into my mind again. I think I know what's coming next.

'They couldn't save the twins. Both of them died inside her – her torso took a lot of the impact. They had to be cut out of her at the hospital. A girl and a boy. She called them Milo and Nancy.'

An icy shiver runs through me. *Car accident. Dead babies. Rachel.*

'She never recovered fully. I mean, physically yes, more or less, but mentally, emotionally…' She shakes her head. 'I mean, who could recover from that?'

I swallow hard and nod. Who indeed?

'And after?'

Monica shakes her head again, her expression pained. 'She spiralled into depression, as you might expect, poor girl. The death of those unborn babies… I think it sent her…' She pauses, choosing her words carefully. 'The psychological impact on her was huge. I know – I witnessed what it did to her, the complete and utter devastation. She unravelled completely. She was under medical supervision, put on antidepressants, sedatives and a cocktail of prescription drugs, all sorts. She had severe post-traumatic stress disorder and became suicidal. She also began self-medicating' – Monica glances up at me from across the table with lowered eyes – 'with alcohol. She developed a bit of a dependency, though I wouldn't say she was a full-blown alcoholic, just someone… someone who couldn't cope with the pain. Laurie had a lot of therapy, and grief counselling too. She still sees a therapist, I think. She couldn't go back to work, obviously, and Robert had to take time out to look after her, to help her get back on her feet, literally, because she couldn't walk for a few months.'

She snorts, a little contemptuously. 'He was cut up about the accident, so he says, although he rarely mentioned it, not to me anyway. I found him rather cold and callous after it all happened. Laurie swore me to secrecy about it when they arrived at Cedar Close. She didn't want the neighbours to know, couldn't bear being pitied. She just wanted to disappear. I understood that… I *do* understand that.' Monica says this with a hint of melancholy, as though she has reasons of her own to be invisible. 'It's a horrible, tragic story, Detective. How she suffered, it was—'

'But they began to rebuild their marriage? Laurie and Robert? They moved to the close and started afresh? Was that the idea?' I'm trying to piece it all together, make sense of their sad and tragic story.

Monica gives a sarcastic laugh. 'Hmm, yes, well, that was the *idea*. Or so she thought. I suggested they move nearer to me, so that I could help take care of her, help her convalesce. Like I said, we're practically sisters and she really was there for me after Dougie died; the least I could do was to return the favour. So when the house opposite came up for sale they decided to buy it. He'd told her, Robert that is, that it would be a new beginning and promised her, *again*, that things would be better. Only what he hadn't told her was that he was *still* seeing his mistress, Claire. Must have skin like a rhino whoever she is, and no bloody conscience, *bitch*.' She spits the last word venomously. 'Seems he was just biding his time until Laurie's mental and physical well-being had improved, and that once she was up on her feet properly and off most of the medication, he was going to leave her. Just couldn't seem to keep away from that little tart—'

'But he had already left, hadn't he? He was no longer living at the house… he was initiating a divorce.'

Monica looks surprised by this statement – she smiles in fact. 'Oh, *was* he now? Callous bastard,' she hisses. 'Yes, well, he had to bring his nasty little plan forward somewhat because Laurie discovered he was still involved with Claire and that, worst of all – and this absolutely crushed her – Claire and Robert had had a baby together. A secret love child. A girl: Matilda. That's the little bastard's name.'

Monica's rage and disgust is evident, and she's not bothering to hide it. 'She thought he was probably planning to divorce her in the end, and ultimately leave her the house as a parting gift: a kind of guilty trade-off, in my opinion, so he could go and begin a new life with Claire and the bas— and the baby.'

'How did Laurie find out?' I ask. 'When did she discover this?' My guts are churning because I know that everything Monica is telling me is enough for a very clear motive. Some might go as far as to say Laurie Mills had good reason.

'The day of the barbecue in August, just gone.' Monica crosses and uncrosses her legs almost provocatively, even in sloppy leggings and flip-flops. I notice she has a small tattoo of a lizard on her foot. 'We have an annual barbecue every summer,' she explains, animated as she speaks. 'The whole close gets together and we have this big cook-up – food, drinks, music, games for the kids, dancing… It's really good fun. Each year a different household gets to organise it, to host it. This year it was mine and my Dougie's turn. Only he wasn't around for it, obviously, so I organised it by myself.'

'So what happened at the barbecue? There was some kind of altercation between Laurie and Robert, wasn't there?'

Monica's green eyes widen and she leans forward across the table. She's stopped crying now. 'It was pretty awful,' she says. 'Robert was DJing at the party. He was pretty good actually,' she remarks, as though this is relevant. 'Anyway, Laurie had made it to the barbecue. For some people on the close, it was the first time they'd properly met her in six months, maybe even *seen* her. Like I say, she was practically agoraphobic. She seemed in good spirits that day though – chatty, happy. At some point Robert disappeared; he'd gone back to the house. Laurie went looking for him.'

I nod. 'And then?'

'So, back in the house she hears him talking on the phone to someone upstairs, so she hides behind the door and listens. It's her. *Claire.* And they're talking about Matilda, about a first tooth or something, and the penny drops. She confronted him, so she says, and he confesses, you know, that the baby is his, and they have this major stand-off in the house. Anyway, he comes back out to the party. Gets straight back on the decks like nothing's happened, all smiles for the crowd. Laurie starts drinking, hits the Prosecco hard. She's visibly drunk the next time I see her. You've seen how tiny she is, Detective. Well, she was knocking them back like no one's business, started dancing and making a bit of a show of herself. I tried to stop her. Kept asking her what was wrong, what had happened. But she was only interested in throwing alcohol down her neck. Next thing, she's gone behind the decks where Robert is and grabs the microphone off him, pulls the plug on the music and starts giving this drunken speech to the whole street about how it's so wonderful to be part of the neighbourhood, how she's grateful to us all for being so welcoming. She starts talking about Robert, saying stuff like, "I suppose you've all met my wonderful husband here, especially the *female* fraternity," or words to that affect. Well, that remark certainly got everyone's attention because she said it in a snarky way, you know, and that's when she starts telling everyone about the affair. About Claire and how he'd been cheating on her when she was pregnant with their twins. Called him a lying, cheating scumbag and a—' She pauses, looks at me a little awkwardly. 'A cunt. Actually says it in front of everyone, kids and all. This caused a few gasps let me tell you. The couple at number 56, the Phillipses, started ushering some of the children inside…'

Lying, cheating scumbag. The exact words that had been written in the mirror. I imagine the scene in my mind. The hushed silences of the neighbours as they look on in intrigue and horror at the drunken spectacle Laurie's making of herself.

'Go on…'

Monica, raises her eyebrows, coughs into her fist. 'He – Robert – he tries to wrestle the mic out of her hands but she's having none of it. And they're grappling with it. He looks furious. She's upset, crying, drunk. That's when everyone starts to think, uh-oh, big domestic about to blow up. But it was also, well, you know how it is, gossip, other people's business… you don't want to watch but you can't help yourself.'

I raise my eyebrows. 'And?'

'And *then* Laurie starts telling everyone about the accident, telling us all about the twins… how this was supposed to be a fresh beginning for them but that she'd just heard him on the phone to his mistress again and that, in fact, they had a child together… It just all came tumbling out in a drunken rant, this horrible, horrible story. I was shocked – I mean, dumbfounded. I knew all about the affair of course, but *a child, a baby*? It was news to us both. Shocking news. She was crying, swearing, calling him names, hysterical, and said she—' Monica pauses again, looks at me earnestly. 'She said she was going to kill him, that she wished he was dead, or would die, or something like that.'

'Okay—'

'But she said it in the heat of the moment,' Monica quickly adds. 'She was beside herself. Drunk. Really obviously very, very upset as you can imagine. I mean, who wouldn't be? I twice attempted to get her off the stage but she's stronger than she looks and she pushed me away. I think it was Reg from number 19 who eventually gently took the mic off her. Then she fled back to her house. Robert went after her. Everyone was just standing there in a hushed silence, open-mouthed. It totally killed the buzz for a bit. Everyone was horrified you know, by the story, and by the showdown.'

She pauses for a moment, stares off a little as though replaying the scene in her head. 'I felt sorry, so, so sorry for her, I really did. That's why I went over there later, after the party had wound down, to see if she was okay. I'd seen Robert get in his car and drive off, but as I was hosting the party I couldn't really abandon everyone and go to her. I can only imagine how it must've kicked off inside that house.'

'So, she never said anything to you about any previous violence, domestic violence? Did their arguments ever turn physical, do you know?'

Monica shakes her head. 'Not that she ever told me, no, and I'm pretty sure she would've. I never saw any bruises or anything. I think it was more psychological abuse…' She shifts a little uncomfortably in her chair. Uncrosses her legs again.

'Monica, do you think your friend – do you think Laurie – is capable of murdering her husband, of killing Robert?'

She lowers her eyes a little then looks up at me uneasily. 'I suppose it's possible,' she says eventually, sighing. 'Lord knows I'd want to kill the bastard if he did to me what he did to her! Metaphorically speaking,' she adds, realising who she's talking to.

She suddenly lunges forward across the table. 'You've got to understand what she's been through, Detective Riley – the accident, the depression and drugs, and the alcohol. No one comes through what she's been through unscathed. Worst thing is that I know she deeply loved him, Robert – even though he'd deceived her so badly throughout their marriage, she still wanted him back. It was a toxic relationship. I think it has sent her over the edge a couple of times. So sad—'

'Okay, I see,' I say. I feel a little deflated. Perhaps Woods is right and this is an open-and-shut case after all. Yet despite everything I've heard I just can't convince myself that Laurie Mills is a killer. I don't feel it in my guts. And I trust those guts of mine, even if they are currently grumbling to be fed.

'But that's why I'm here, actually,' she adds. 'That's why I came to see you in the first place.' Monica Lewis is looking directly at me, earnestly. 'Because Laurie *couldn't* have killed Robert.'

'Why's that?' I ask.

'Because she was with me at the time,' she says. 'I saw what happened.'

CHAPTER SEVENTEEN

She's in a car with Monica. They've let her go. No more time in a police cell. No more questions, for now. Everything is silent. Something Monica said has stopped the madness. The words the solicitor said to her, the words the detectives said to her as she left the police station, she cannot remember them; they are impervious, jumbled conversations lost in a river of relief. Doesn't matter, they have let her go and she is in the car, next to her friend. She is safe now. But then she remembers that Robert is still dead. *Robert is dead.* And she still can't remember what happened.

'He was nice,' Monica says.

'Who was?' Laurie answers on autopilot, still shell-shocked.

'The detective. Dan something... Dan Riley. He was nice... good-looking too, for a copper.' Monica giggles a little.

Laurie can't process what Monica's saying. 'I just want to go home, but not *home* home—' Not to the place where she had found him butchered.

'It's okay,' Monica says, 'you're coming home with me. They've said you can stay with me, that it's okay.' She touches Laurie's knee, gives it a squeeze.

Thank God Monica is here. 'What did you say? What did you tell them?' She can't remember being released. Her recollection of leaving the police station is blurred at best, not quite real.

'You need some rest, hon, you really do. You've had a terrible shock. You need to sleep, then we'll get you seen by your doctor as soon as possible. Maybe you need some pills or something.'

Pills. More pills? She rattles with enough of them already. Pills, the answer to everything apparently.

'They let me go—'

Monica is bent over the steering wheel, straining to view the junction ahead. 'Yes, well they had to really.'

'Why? Why did they have to?'

Laurie feels sleepy, exhausted, like her head is about to topple from her neck. Her mind feels woozy, like it's taking longer for the messages in her brain to compute into words.

'That'll be the Valium,' Monica observes, watching Laurie struggle to stay alert.

Valium? She doesn't remember taking a Valium.

'I had a couple in my bag,' Monica explains. 'Emergency supplies. Thank God for jellies, eh? You'll sleep better now.'

She hasn't got the strength to reply. It's like she's been lobotomised. She thinks of her mother then. How is she going to tell her that Robert is dead? That someone murdered him in their home. And that someone might even have been her own daughter. Why can't she remember?

'The police said they'll be in touch. They'll no doubt come round to ask you more questions, interview you again, and me no doubt. They'll talk to the neighbours, fish for stuff. But you mustn't worry.' Monica pats her knee again. 'I'll take care of it all, okay? Just let me take care of it all, take care of you too.'

Laurie manages a small smile. She doesn't know what she'd do without Monica. She's all she has. 'Robert...' His name evaporates into the air as she whispers it from dry lips. She feels light-headed.

'I know, darling, I know. But it's going to be okay.'

'I'll need to organise a funeral... tell Stan and Agnes, his parents. Oh God, maybe they'll think that I did it. Maybe they won't let me come to the funeral! They'll think I killed their son and they'll hate me.'

'Fuck Stan and Agnes!' Monica's shriek startles her. She's hypersensitive to loud noises. 'We need to get you home. Get you tucked up in bed. There will probably be reporters buzzing around – you should've seen them earlier, bloody vultures. I'll get rid of them all, I promise. Let's just get you home for now. We'll worry about it all in the morning, after you've had some proper sleep… and you really must eat something.'

The thought of food gives Laurie a nauseous, watery feeling in her stomach. She wonders if she'll ever be able to keep anything down ever again. But she would like to sleep. She can't fight it any longer. She hasn't slept properly since the day she discovered her husband's infidelity and her insomnia had progressively worsened since the accident. Night terrors tormented her religiously and she hadn't managed more than a shallow state of semi-consciousness in over a year and a half. It had been pure never-ending torture.

Suddenly she thinks of Claire. *Claire*. Does she know that Robert is dead? Will the police have told her by now? *Poor Claire. No more baby daddy for her. No more Robert for anyone*. Panic engulfs her once more as Monica turns the car into Cedar Close. Her house is sealed off by yellow tape. It's no longer her house, *their* home. Now it's a crime scene, unfamiliar and frightening, a house of horrors. She will never be able to go inside her home again. There are people still milling around. She thinks she sees them in the shadows or perhaps it's her imagination. Who are they? Are they forensics? Press? Police?

'Oh God, I don't think I—'

'It's okay. We'll go straight in the garage and through the back way. No one will see, I promise.'

Laurie nods. She has faith in Monica. Her eyes close as the tyres crunch over Monica's gravel driveway; the electric gates click and hum as they shut behind them. She thinks she can see people, shadows of dark figures, through squinted eyes and camera flashes, their bright lights popping like fireworks illuminating the darkness.

'Mrs Mills! Laurie! Have you been charged with your husband's murder? Did you kill your husband, Mrs Mills? Was it because of the affair, Laurie? Mrs Mills! Laurie…' She can hear their voices all around her and shields her face with her hands as they pull inside Monica's garage.

'Thank heavens for mod cons, eh?' Monica remarks as the door automatically closes behind them, shutting out the intrusive din. She's safe. For now.

Laurie is practically a zombie, the walking dead, as Monica leads her into her guest bedroom. It's clean and fresh-smelling – Buckingham Palace compared to where she's just come from. The white king-sized bed looks grand and inviting. She just wants to sleep. Sleep and not wake up. Or wake up to find it was all just another one of her night terrors. She almost convinces herself of it as Monica peels back the duvet for her to climb in.

'I'll get you some PJs, get you out of those awful prison clothes, and bring you a cup of tea,' Monica says efficiently. But she isn't worried about either of those things right now. She's just glad to be free, that they let her go, and to be able to sleep, finally. Yet deep inside her, past the mental and physical exhaustion, she knows, *fears*, that this is simply the beginning, the start of a horror show in which she has been cast in the starring role. Robert has been killed – murdered – and someone is responsible. Perhaps that someone is her, in which case they will discover this and she will go to prison for the rest of her life. She thinks about the cell she has just come from and its clinical coldness, the claustrophobia and the smell, and she thinks she's crying again because her face feels wet.

'I think that maybe I killed Robert,' she hears the slur in her own voice as Monica is turning to leave the room to fetch her tea and PJs. 'I think that maybe I just snapped and killed him but I can't remember because I was so drunk… and the pills… the alcohol mixed with the pills. They'll know – they tested my blood.

I let them test my blood. I wasn't thinking straight but I just thought… I couldn't have killed him, could I? My own husband – *my Bobby*? I loved him, even after everything he'd done… I still *loved* him, Mon.'

Laurie hears herself speaking but it's like she's already asleep and has slipped into a dream – a foggy, fuzzy, altered state. 'I thought he didn't come to the house… but did he? He must've. The police say he had a letter from his solicitor, telling me he wanted a divorce and maybe I just… lost it. I… I just can't remember. Oh God help me, *I just can't remember*!' Laurie feels herself losing consciousness, slipping between light and dark, thoughts looping through her mind on repeat, like a computer glitch.

'I just want to die,' she says. Is she speaking, or dreaming? Which is it? She isn't sure. 'I wish it had been *me*.' Her voice is high-pitched, wracked with anguish and emotion, and it doesn't resemble her own, like it's coming from far away. 'There was no break-in they said – that detective said there was no forced entry… nothing taken, nothing stolen… so I just, I just…' Her head falls back onto the pillow; she's awake but asleep, trapped in a diabolical twilight somewhere in-between.

Monica comes to Laurie, sits down on the bed beside her. Takes hold of her gently by the arms and eases her into a full recline. 'Look, you really need to rest, Lolly.'

Lolly is her old nickname from when they were young. She hasn't heard Monica call her that in ages.

'Come on, darling. There, that's it, just close your eyes, let yourself fall into it… relax… That's it, just relax… It's all going to be okay…'

CHAPTER EIGHTEEN

Laurie – Winter 2016

'She's just a colleague, a friend, Laurie; will you give it a rest? I've told you at least twice before: we worked together on the Chardonnay shoot, that two-day thing down in Kent. She kept in touch because this business is all about contacts – you know that yourself.' Robert's tone is dismissive, which only serves to irritate her more.

'So why is she calling you at 11 p.m. then, Robert? Surely not to discuss business?' Laurie is standing in the kitchen of their apartment. She's got a client meeting, an important one, in less than two hours and her nerves are shot to pieces.

'I don't fucking know!' he snaps back, 'ask her! I didn't take the call, remember?'

They had been enjoying a rare moment of downtime together the previous evening, cuddled up on the sofa watching crap TV and sipping wine, when his phone had rung around 11 p.m. He'd declined the call. It rang again and he repeated the action, this time switching his phone off.

'Who is that?' she'd asked, feeling she had a right to know. He was her husband after all, and she was curious.

'Melanie Jones.'

'Who's Melanie Jones?'

'A colleague I worked with a while back, on some wine shoot for a trade mag—'

'Why would she be ringing you at 11 p.m.?' She sees a flicker of irritation cross his features as she lightly enquires.

'Don't know, Law, search me.'

'Why didn't you answer it and find out?'

'Because it's late, like you said.'

'But isn't that all the more reason to answer the call?'

'Please, Laurie. I'm not in the mood for the Spanish Inquisition.'

She'd sat upright. She hated it when he tried to shut her down like this. What was he trying to hide? 'I'm not giving you the Spanish Inquisition. I'm just asking why a female colleague would be calling you at 11 p.m. and why you wouldn't answer.'

He doesn't take his eyes away from the TV screen. 'Yes, and I've answered both questions. Do you want me to repeat myself?'

'Don't be so defensive. Why are you being defensive? It's a perfectly legitimate question.'

'I'm not being defensive. With you it's always questions, questions, questions. I don't question you, do I? I don't grill you every time Jack Dempster dials your number.'

'Yes, but Jack's my boss. He's married to Deborah and he doesn't call me at 11 p.m.'

'That I know of—'

'What does that mean? Don't be ridiculous!'

'Well, you spend a lot of time with him…'

She looked at Robert, incredulous. 'That's because he's my boss – I work for him, Robert! Jesus, you've known Deb and Jack since… since I got the job, practically.'

'I've always thought he had the hots for you myself.'

She shakes her head, snorts a little. 'Now you really are being ridiculous.'

'Well, so are you—'

'No I'm not. Jack hasn't called my phone at 11 p.m., and if he did it would clearly be to discuss work. This... this Melanie woman, you shot with her a few weeks ago for all of two days—'

'I'm tired, Laurie. I'm not doing this. I'm going to bed.'

She felt anger rise up inside her. 'Doing what? Talking to me? Your wife? Offering me some kind of explanation as to why a female associate is blowing up your phone late on a Thursday evening?'

'What is it you want me to say, Laurie?' He sighs wearily, like the conversation is the biggest drag for him. 'That I've been fucking the life out of her since we met behind your back?'

She had jumped up then, enraged, hurt, upset. 'Why are you saying that, Robert?' She'd felt tears coming, the beginning of them pricking her eyes.

'It's what you're thinking, clearly,' he says.

'No.' She shakes her head. 'It's not what I'm thinking. Why do you always try to tell me what I'm thinking?'

'Because I know what you're thinking.'

'You don't!'

'Yes I do, Laurie. It's written all over you. You don't trust me, do you? You never really have.'

'That's not true! I... I just wanted to know why a female colleague was—'

'Yes, yes, I know – why she was calling and I've told you I don't know! I'm going to bed.'

'So why switch your phone off?' Laurie doesn't want to ask any more questions but she can't help herself. Her intuition is forcing her to. She does trust Robert, doesn't she? But she hates the way he is so dismissive of her, how he manages to turn the conversation round so that she feels guilty for asking a question. And she's still reeling about the ridiculous notion of Jack Dempster, her boss, having the hots for her.

'Because I didn't want to speak to her, whatever it was she bloody wanted... You're being paranoid, Laurie, and I'm not into it, okay?'

'Into it? I'm your wife, Robert. I've got a right to ask, haven't I?'

'Yes, and I've told you over and over again. What part of I don't know why she called *don't you understand? Look, I'm tired. Good night.'*

Robert had gone to-bed, their rare cosy evening together cut short and ruined. Laurie had sat on the sofa for a while after he'd gone to bed, mulling over the conversation in her mind. Had she been unreasonable? Was she being paranoid? Maybe she shouldn't have asked any questions, just left it alone. They so infrequently got to spend the evening snuggled up on the sofa together and now she'd gone and ruined it by grilling him about some old client. She'd slipped into bed next to him a little time later, hoping they would make love, but he was already asleep.

Come the morning, Laurie's thoughts had shifted somewhat. She couldn't get the niggling feeling out of her head that something was amiss. Robert's reaction, his defensiveness when she had asked a perfectly innocent question had set off alarm bells. But she was confused; Robert had a way of twisting things around so as to make her doubt herself. Her main objective was not to upset him. Upsetting Robert meant days of sulking, of the silent treatment, and she couldn't bear that. But sometimes she just couldn't stay silent herself, even though she knew that by voicing her concerns, she would be in line for such punishment.

'Look, are we going to ruin the morning as well as a perfectly good evening discussing Melanie Jones?' Robert pours himself a coffee. He doesn't ask her if she wants one. 'Because if we are then I'm out of here.'

'Out of here?'

Robert rolls his eyes. 'Jesus Christ, Laurie, you don't know when to stop, do you? On and on and on and on… Haven't you got a job to do, something better than standing around all day arguing about some phone conversation that never even took place?'

Laurie swallows hard, feels the emotion rising within her, stress swelling like yeast, but she stays silent. 'I've got a big meeting with *the Italian hoteliers this morning,' she says quietly, holding back the need to burst into tears.*

'With Jack?' he asks sarcastically.

'Yes, with Jack. And Deborah too, his wife—'

'Good luck,' he says dryly, turning to look at her now. 'I'm going to be away for a few days. On a shoot in Newcastle, some men's mag thing.'

Laurie looks at him in surprise. 'You didn't say!'

'Didn't I? Well, I'm saying now. I'll be gone before lunchtime – just got to throw a few things in a case and then I'll be off.'

She feels her guts twist. 'All a bit last-minute isn't it?' She knows it's the wrong thing to say, that it'll annoy him, but she can't help herself, her and her big mouth.

'Don't start again,' Robert says with a warning tone in his voice. 'A lot of my job is last-minute, Laurie, and you damn well know it is.'

'I wasn't saying anything, I just…' She stops herself short. 'When will you be back?'

'Thursday, Friday maybe, depending on how the shoot goes.'

Laurie nods. She wants to ask him who he'll be shooting, about the crew and the magazine – normal questions that would come up in conversation – but she knows it will come across as her grilling him so she stays silent instead.

'Well,' she says evenly, 'I hope the shoot goes well.'

'Thanks,' he says, turning his back to her as he pours more coffee. 'Hope your thingy with the hotel lot goes well too.'

He sounds disingenuous and now she really feels like crying. 'I've got to go,' she says, hovering. She at least wants a small hug and a kiss before he goes. 'I'm sorry,' Laurie says and he turns round and looks at her.

'What for?'

'For doubting you last night, for the questions—'

Robert smiles then, places his cup down and wraps his arms around her. 'It's okay,' he says, kissing the top of her head. 'Look, I love you,

Laurie. You're my wife, my life, my everything… You have nothing to be jealous about – you know that, don't you?'

She buries her head into his neck, inhales the scent of his skin, the remnants of his soapy Tom Ford cologne, and nods, trying not to break down.

'Just stop with the paranoia and questions, yeah, then everything will be golden.'

Laurie nods silently again, not trusting herself to speak.

'I'll call, okay?' Robert says as he turns to leave.

Only she knows that he probably won't, like the last time they'd had words before he'd gone away. He'd switched his phone off for three days while he'd been out in Paris and she had driven herself crazy trying to reach him, her calls and texts becoming more frantic, more fevered, more emotional. He had sworn it was an issue with his phone provider but deep inside Laurie knew it was something more: punishment. It was Robert's way of telling her that if she dared assert herself too much then she would be cut off, shut down and dismissed.

'Okay,' she says. 'I love you.'

CHAPTER NINETEEN

'So,' I address the incident room. It's buzzing with that strange sort of electricity that generates whenever there's a new case, the kind of energy that's difficult to put into words. Adrenaline is your best friend on homicide – it's what keeps you going, and it's basically what's holding me together right now because I haven't had much shut-eye and I'm starting to hallucinate about pillows turning into Big Macs.

'We've had to let Laurie Mills go,' I say to a room full of groans. 'I know, I know, it's not ideal but it appears she has an alibi around the TOD and as yet there's nothing solid to seal the deal. We'll just have to wait for forensics.'

More groans. They're disappointed, naturally. Circumstantial evidence puts Laurie Mills at the top of the suspect list, a list which currently only has her name on it. To the naked eye, most would say it's a foregone conclusion that forensics will come back with the evidence we need to put Mrs Mills behind bars for a long time. Only mine is telling me to look a little closer and that the picture isn't quite all it seems. I know that Woods wants a quiet word with me because I saw him beckoning me into his office through my peripheral vision as I walked past, but I pretended not to notice. Woods can wait. I'm getting good at dodging people lately, which reminds me I haven't called Fi yet. I silently tut at myself. Still, I'm hoping I'll be able to give Woods the slip before I head home for some desperately needed sleep. Fi, however, is a slightly different story.

I glance at Martin Delaney. He's looking over at Davis as I begin to speak, as if he's trying to catch her attention. His look reinforces my suspicion that something has gone on between them and it unsettles me. Sex, affairs and all of that business is rife in every workplace and the nick is no exception. It's not encouraged of course; like the old man always told me, *Never crap where you eat, Daniel,* but people are people at the end of the day and even coppers are human – some of them anyway. I don't particularly like it on my watch though. It complicates things, and I don't like *Delaney* being on my watch at all.

I continue. 'Laurie Mills is still our prime suspect, but I also think we need to start looking beyond the obvious right now. Robert Mills was a man with a chequered past, a man who indulged in extra-marital affairs. Someone with secrets. We need to dig around deeper, cast the net a little wider. Laurie Mills might not be the only one out there with a grudge to bear.' I try not to look at Delaney. 'Just because Laurie Mills has a motive and found the body doesn't automatically mean she's the killer, okay? Let's keep an open mind for now. Wait for forensics.'

'It looks pretty clear-cut to me,' a voice pipes up from the back. A voice I don't recognise. 'Annie Mitchell, sir.' She announces herself with an air of confidence.

I look over to see a pretty, mixed-race woman – well, she looks more like a girl to be honest, fresh-faced with hungry, bright green eyes. Just lately I've begun noticing how young everyone looks. *Wait til you get to my age, Danny boy!* was my dad's response to this observation.

'Where you from, Annie?'

'Central, boss. Woods brought me in. Wanted me to have the "Dan Riley experience", apparently.' She raises an eyebrow.

There are titters from the team, although I swear I can hear Delaney laughing above everyone else.

'Well, welcome aboard, Annie. Hit me up,' I say, knowing this is trendy speak and that I probably sound just like my father.

'Okay.' Mitchell looks chuffed to be kicking things off and I inwardly smile. I remember what it was like being new to homicide. The thrill of the clock ticking; the exhilaration and sense of urgency and purpose; the excitement of being part of a team of people united by the same agenda – catching killers.

'Well, we have the weapon, boss, the motive, and the PS at the scene of crime covered in the victim's blood. No break-in, nothing taken… looks pretty open-and-shut to me.'

I look over at Mitchell. I'm slightly disappointed and I think it shows. 'We don't know it's the victim's blood yet, Mitchell,' I gently remind her.

'Who else's could it be?'

'Her own, perhaps. Laurie Mills appears to have attempted suicide by slashing her wrists, though the wounds were fairly superficial. It's also likely that there was a transfer of blood onto her clothes when she discovered the body. Just so you know, Mitchell, jumping to conclusions is *not* part of the "Dan Riley experience".'

Mitchell looks embarrassed and I feel like a bit of a shit.

'So… the good news is, as Mitchell has kindly pointed out, that we have the murder weapon. We know what was *used* to kill Robert Mills and we know *how* he was killed.' I tap the picture of the 8-inch kitchen knife that's displayed on the board behind me next to the gruesome images of Robert Mills' mutilated corpse. 'There was no attempt by the killer to hide the murder weapon and it appears to have come from the Millses' kitchen. We believe it was used by Mrs Mills some hours earlier to prepare dinner.'

'The last supper,' Harding says, deadpan.

I raise my eyebrows. 'Quite. It's currently with forensics, so we'll see what they throw up.'

'I'm not a gambling man,' Delaney remarks, 'but if I was, I'd say it's pretty much a given that the wife's will be the only dabs all over that knife.'

I nod and swallow back a smart-arse, sarcastic reply. 'Well, she doesn't *deny* using the knife earlier that evening to prepare dinner, but let's see what they've got, yes? We know the TOD was somewhere around the 8–10 p.m. mark; the body was still warm, still fresh, when we got there and we know there was no forced entry to the property. So, no, no sign of a break-in or any intruder.' I nod at Mitchell and pause for a moment. The noises my stomach is making are reaching a crescendo and I wonder if the team can hear them. I could murder a bacon sarnie, no pun intended. It's difficult to eat healthily in this job sometimes and Rach's voice suddenly comes to me. *A good breakfast sets you up for the day, Danny*. Her speciality was this omelette-type thing with eggs and chorizo and peppers. I can almost taste it now and my mouth begins to water just thinking about it, *about her.*

'Monica Lewis, a close friend and neighbour of both Laurie Mills and the deceased, who lives opposite the Millses' place, claims that Laurie came over to her house around 8.15 p.m. She was in a distressed state, but Mrs Lewis claims that this was pretty standard by all accounts and there was nothing to trigger any alarm bells, no blood on Laurie's clothes, nothing to indicate anything sinister had taken place. She'd been drinking, though again, this was nothing unusual apparently, and she was upset that her husband had stood her up. Laurie Mills expressed some concern that her husband might've been involved in an accident and maybe that's why he hadn't shown up—'

'That's an understatement,' Delaney remarks dryly.

'Car accident, specifically,' I continue.

'So, how come Laurie Mills didn't mention the fact that she went over to her neighbour's house around the TOD in interview? Seems a little odd she wouldn't want to exonerate herself, or give herself the best alibi she could.'

'I agree, Martin,' I say, 'but that's just it. Laurie Mills doesn't seem to remember very much past 7.30 p.m. at all. Visiting her friend, cutting her wrists, passing out upstairs—'

'Selective memory, if you want my opinion.'

I don't. 'Perhaps,' I say.

'So why didn't she just call him when he didn't show up – the husband – check he was alright?' Murray asks. 'That would be the obvious thing to do, no?'

I open my hands. If there's one thing I have learned about both murder and the human condition, it's that nothing is ever obvious. 'Well in ordinary circumstances it would be, but the dynamics of the Millses' relationship were pretty tricky by all accounts. Seems that Robert Mills was something of an emotional abuser, liked to play mind games, screw around with his wife's head. Laurie Mills felt, so she told Monica Lewis, that he'd not shown on purpose, that he'd deliberately stood her up, that he was on some kind of power trip maybe. Monica Lewis advised her not to call him, thought it would be playing into his hands. She says they talked for a while, drank some wine together and at around 10.40 p.m. Laurie Mills returned to her house; Lewis claims she watched her walk through her front door.'

'Can anyone corroborate this?' Delaney says.

'No.' I say plainly. *But I believe it.*

'She could have already killed him at this point though,' Mitchell speculates. 'She could've committed the murder, changed her clothes, washed up a bit, then gone over to her friend's to ensure she had an alibi.'

'But the estimated time of death was around or after 8 p.m., according to the coroner. Monica Lewis says Laurie Mills arrived at her house at around 8.15 p.m. It's unlikely, given Laurie Mills' disposition, though admittedly not impossible, that she could've killed her husband in such a frenzied and brutal attack, washed and cleaned herself up and then just nipped across the road to see her friend for a few drinks and a chat in the space of around fifteen minutes. Plus, Monica claims that Laurie was wearing the same dress she had on when we brought her in, and there wasn't a speck of blood on it at that time.'

'So it's possible that someone snuck into the Millses' house while Laurie was at her neighbour's place, murdered Robert Mills and then left,' Davis says rhetorically. 'So how did they get into the property?'

'Yes, it's possible and that, well, we don't know yet.'

'She was drunk, right?' Mitchell says. 'She could've forgotten to close the door properly. Or left the back door unlocked.'

'All possible,' I agree. 'So let's not rule out an outsider. Someone could've been watching the place, staking it out. They could have seen Laurie leave and taken their chance. Mills was a womaniser by all accounts, so let's not rule out a jealous husband or boyfriend, or even a spurned lover.'

Delaney, I note, is shaking his head.

'Any thoughts you want to share, Martin?' I mock-smile at him.

'No,' he says, pausing before adding, snidely, 'Gov.'

I turn my attention back to the team. 'Rawlins, I want you and Harding to get on to that solicitors as soon possible. Find out when that letter advising Laurie Mills that Robert was planning to divorce her was drafted. Find out what was discussed, okay?'

Harding holds her pen up as if to say *got it*.

'Murray?' I look over at Jill. 'What have you got?'

'Um, yes, Gov. CCTV. Most of the residents at Cedar Close have it, including number 13, so we're collating it, then we'll go through it and see what turns up.'

'What about the power cut?' Delaney asks. 'Laurie Mills said something about there being no power when she switched on the lights.'

I nod.

'Bit convenient, don't you think?' he continues. 'I mean, she wakes up to a dark house, can't see anything, no power, no memory... seems like a strange coincidence to me.'

'Possibly,' I say dryly. 'So get on to the rest of the neighbours. Find out if anyone else's electric was down around the same time. And get an electrician down there, check nothing's been tampered with, yes?'

I think I see Delaney's face fall a touch and I struggle not to feel smug. Well, seeing as he brought it up, he can deal with it, although I sense he deems this kind of detective work beneath him. 'And I want *all* the neighbours questioned, even the ones you've already spoken to. What they saw, what they heard, any background on the Millses. Oh, and ask about the summer barbecue. Allegedly Laurie Mills had a very public meltdown in front of the whole street when she discovered that her husband was still cheating on her with his mistress, so get the low-down on that.'

'Doesn't warrant her killing the poor bastard though, does it?' Delaney says.

I notice that he's looking at Davis again and a knot forms in my stomach. I'm hoping it's just hunger.

'No, Martin, it doesn't,' I agree. 'But it might go some way as to explaining *why* she did, *if* she did. Which brings me on to another bit of info. Laurie was eight months pregnant with twins when she discovered her husband's infidelity, and she was involved in a serious car accident the day she found out. She had to be cut out of the wreck, and the babies had to be cut out of her. Both of them died.'

The room falls silent. That shuts everyone up. I knew it would because it had a similar effect on me when Monica Lewis told me.

'Understandably, Laurie suffered from depression and some sort of mental breakdown following the accident and the death of her babies, developing an alcohol and prescription-drug dependency, so we need to get in touch with her GP and therapist to see if they can or will tell us anything. Find out what meds she was taking, any side effects, that sort of thing. Oh, and put a rush on the CCTV. Monica Lewis says she has it, or did, but it recently broke and she hadn't got round to replacing it. We know that Robert Mills entered his house at some point and never came out again. We need times… we need factual, hard evidence, people, not hearsay. Footage, forensics, witnesses… you know the drill.'

'What about the mistress, Gov? Claire somebody,' Davis asks.

'Claire Wright,' I say. 'Yes, Claire Wright, Robert Mills' mistress and the mother of his eight-month-old baby girl. They live in Luton. We need to pay Miss Wright a visit, give her the good news, if she hasn't already heard by now.'

'Don't tell me, boss – you want me to do that?' Davis looks at me, her eyes slightly raised in expectation.

'You *and* me, Davis,' I say, smiling at her as I catch a well-disguised but just about visible look of annoyance on Delaney's face.

CHAPTER TWENTY

Kiki – aged 13

'So, what do you think?'

'What do I think of what?'

'Of the dress, stupid?' She does a little twirl, eager to see his reaction. It's a grown-up dress; one of those ra-ra ones that all the cool, older girls at school wear.

'Where did you get it from?'

She taps her nose with her finger. 'Never you mind where it came from. What do you think of it?' She twirls round again. The dress has made her happy. She feels sexy in it, alluring and trendy. It will turn heads at the disco tonight. She's heard that Steve Thornton wants to dance with her and she's excited, not because she particularly fancies Steve Thornton but because he's shown an interest in her and this makes her feel powerful. He's in the year above her at school and has a reputation for being a bit of a bad boy. Apparently he nicked his dad's car once and drove it all the way down to the shopping centre before the police caught him. This alone is reason enough to like him.

'Where are you going in it?'

'To the school disco tonight. It's at the youth centre. There's going to be alcohol there and everything.'

He pulls his headphones off his ears. 'Can't you piss off? I'm supposed to be studying. One of us has got to work towards getting us out of this shit pit.'

She feels her bubble burst instantly. 'What's the matter with you? Don't you like the dress? It's the dress, isn't it?'

'You'll never be allowed out the front door dressed like that,' he says, looking her up and down.

'Dressed like what?'

'A little slut.'

'Go fuck yourself!' she says, placing a hand on her hip. 'And the old bag can get stuffed. Anyway, I was hoping you'd distract her while I sneaked out.'

He turns away from her, lies back down on the bed. 'And why should I help you?'

'Oh c'mon, what's your problem? Why are you being so moody?'

'I'm not moody. Just got shit to do, that's all. Like I said, one of us has got to work towards getting us out of here. If I study hard and get a decent job then we'll have enough money to run away together. That is what you want, isn't it, Kiki?'

'You know it's what I want, what I've always wanted.' She goes over to him, touches his arm. His bruises are fading now, almost gone. Her own are hidden by her dress. They're far too careful to leave marks that would be visible. 'But I want to go to the disco too. Are you going to help me or not?'

'What's in it for me?' he asks.

'Name your price.'

His small, almost Machiavellian grin develops slowly. 'Who you going to the disco with?'

'Tina and the others,' she says, propping herself up on her elbow as she joins him on the bed.

'And Steve Thornton? Is he going too?'

She sits up. 'How do you know about Steve Thornton?'

He taps his nose this time. 'I know everything, Kiki.'

There's a moment before the realisation dawns. 'Oh my God! You've been reading my diary!'

He shrugs but doesn't deny it.

'You bastard! That's my private stuff!'

'There are no secrets between us, remember that. It's just me a you, Kiki.'

She looks down at the duvet cover, her face reddening. He's read her diary, and now he knows everything about how she feels – about life, about love, about sex and Steve Thornton and about him too. She feels violated, exposed and ashamed.

'Do you really think those things about me, Kiki?' he asks, lightly teasing her. 'Those things you wrote in your diary, those feelings you have, those sensations and tingles you sometimes get in private places—'

She wants the ground to swallow her whole. She can't bring herself to look at him. 'You shouldn't have read it,' she manages to say, but she feels like crying and begins to.

'Hey, why are you upset?' He puts an arm around her, a protective arm. 'You'll mess up your make-up.' He pulls her down next to him and holds her, just like they'd always done since they were small, when she would creep into his room in the dark of night and they would comfort each other, the warmth of their respective bodies like reassuring blankets. Despite his mean streak, he was the only one she trusted, her only source of affection.

'Because it's wrong to think those things.' Her voice is tiny, barely audible. She buries herself into the nook of his armpit so that he can't see her face. 'Maybe Mum is right and I am a dirty sinner, just like my real mother.'

'Hey.' He pulls her head up towards him by her chin. 'Stop with the shit talk. That's crap and you know it. You're not a sinner, Kiki; you're a young woman, a human being – a normal, living, breathing human being. If anyone's the sinner then it's those bastard hypocrites downstairs—'

'I feel ashamed.'

'Well I don't,' he says, defiant. 'I feel those things too.'

'You do?'

'Yes.'

'About me?' she can't help asking.

'Yes, about you, Kiki, only you. I only ever think about you.'

'Just me?'

He squeezes her waist playfully; she's ticklish there, as he knows only too well.

'Have you kissed him yet, this Steve Thornton guy?'

'No!' she says, a little too loudly. 'I've never kissed anyone before, I swear.'

'But you were planning to tonight, weren't you?'

'No!' she says. 'I wasn't! I'm not!'

'Liar!' He laughs. 'You were planning to lose your cherry to Steve Thornton because he drives a Ford Capri!'

'Fuck off!' she says, half laughing with him now, though she can't get his words out of her head. *You, Kiki, only you. I only ever think about you.*

'Anyway, you must've kissed loads of girls, and done it with them too,' Kiki teases him back.

'A few maybe,' he says elusively. 'Girls like me. I turn them on.'

'Big-head.'

'Big something…' He smirks and she slaps him on the arm.

'So, are you going to cover for me tonight or what?' She brings the conversation full circle, their moment of awkwardness dissipating.

'Yes, but first you need some practice.'

'Practice?'

'Yes. If you're going to kiss Steve Thornton with the Capri tonight then you need to know what you're doing. No one likes a sloppy kisser.' He's leaning over her now, his lips touching hers, and she closes her eyes, feels her heartbeat quicken. His tongue feels soft and warm as it enters her mouth and she sighs as it begins to play with her own.

'Relax… gently,' he whispers into her mouth and she sighs again as a thousand sensations rush through her, alien endorphins singing throughout her body.

'I will cover for you tonight, Kiki,' he says between kisses, 'on one condition.'

'Name it,' she says, squirming beneath him, her mind and body struggling to process the pleasurable feelings she's experiencing for the first time.

'Lay with me tonight.'

She has laid with Bertie since they were children, creeping in and out of one another's bedrooms, timing down pat so as never to get caught. This time though she understands from his voice that he means something different, *something else.*

'Yes,' she says, 'tonight.'

CHAPTER TWENTY-ONE

By the time Davis and I reach Claire Wright's Luton apartment, the chicken and bacon sandwich I'd thrown down my neck on the journey has started to repeat on me. Davis had run into the service station for me after I'd told her to 'grab the first thing off the shelf'. And she had, literally. It hasn't gone down well.

I wanted to ask Davis about Delaney on the drive down but I held myself in check. It's not really my business at the end of the day, but it was a struggle not to fish for information. Instead I was a bit tricky and asked her what she and 'the husband' had planned for Christmas, which was a bit lame given that it's only October. She gave me an odd look, like I'd lost the plot or something, and said, 'Don't know, Gov. Haven't thought about it yet. Probably spend it at Mum's like I always do, like we do most years.'

Oddly though, she didn't ask me why I had asked, which I found more telling than any answer she gave me.

Anyway, Davis rings the bell to flat C and we wait.

I'm not looking forward to this. And I don't need to explain why. On its own, telling someone their loved one is dead, murdered no less, is not something any normal person would or could ever relish, unless they were a sadist. And now that I've been on the receiving end of such life-shattering news I find it harder to deal with than most. My guts are churning as Davis rings the bell again. I blame the sandwich.

'Who is it?' a harassed voice says over the intercom and I hear a baby grumbling in the background. It reminds me of my new neighbour and her offspring with impressive lungs, and I remember I've got that to look forward to when I get home. *The joy never ends*.

'DI Dan Riley and DS Davis from CID. Is that Claire Wright? Miss Claire Wright?'

There's a pause.

'Yes… Yes, I'm Claire Wright. What's this about?'

I can hear the mix of fear and confusion in her voice. I imagine, like most people who are paid an unexpected visit from the plod, a thousand thoughts have just sprinted through her mind, none of them good.

'Can we come up please, Claire?' Davis says gently. 'We need to speak to you.'

I'm really hoping she's not going to say, 'What about?' and I'm relieved when she presses the buzzer to let us in.

Claire Wright is a very pretty, short, kind of plump girl in, I would guess, her late twenties, although I am spectacularly bad at guessing a woman's age and always go into a sweaty panic if I'm ever asked to. Women seem to like to trip you up like that, don't they? Aesthetically, Claire's very different to Laurie Mills. Blonde hair in contrast to Laurie's dark, blue eyes to her brown, pale skin to her olive complexion, and, compared with poor Laurie, appears like she enjoys a good meal every now and again. Claire looks like the type of girl who scrubs up well yet, when all the decoration comes off, is just a pretty girl-next-door type. But she has a nice smiley face and twinkly blue eyes, which only compounds the misery I feel at having to say what I'm about to.

'Is everything okay?' she asks, a little nervously. 'I'm sorry about the state of the place. This little madam here…' She looks down at the baby in her arms. I'd say she is around eight months old but I could be wildly off the mark. What do I know about babies? Other than that they make a hell of a racket when you're trying to sleep. Oh, and that mine was killed before I ever got to meet him or her. 'She's teething,' Claire sighs. 'Had me up most of the night. I haven't had the energy to clean up and look at the state of me, I—'

I look around the modest apartment. It's a little messy, baby paraphernalia everywhere, but it looks clean and cosy enough.

'No need to apologise,' Davis says. 'Listen, Claire, can we sit down?'

Her face drops then, but the light hasn't gone from her eyes completely. Not yet. But it will. Believe me, it will.

'Has something bad happened?' Her voice is edgy now, filled with fear. I can almost see the panic as it creeps onto her face like poison ivy. She throws a baby blanket off the sofa and moves a few cushions out of the way with one hand. I wonder if I should ask her to put the baby down, if it would be safer to. Luckily however, the little thing looks as if she's fallen asleep and so she places her in a fancy, frilly pink Moses basket that's next to the sofa. We all sit down tentatively. I feel like time is moving in slo-mo, every action amplified and magnified. I detest this part of the job.

'I believe you are in a relationship with Robert Mills. Robert Mills of 13 Cedar Close. Is that right, Claire?'

She looks caught off guard, as if his name was the last she had expected to hear.

'Rob… Yes, Robert's my… well, he's my boyfriend.' She looks to the side as she says this, a little awkwardly, but she's still smiling. 'He's the father… he's my daughter's father. What's happened? Is Rob okay? He's not been hurt, has he?' Confusion cuts through her voice like glass. And I'm about to shatter it.

'Listen, Claire, I'm so very sorry; we're very sorry to tell you this, but Robert Mills was found dead at his address in Cedar Close last night. I'm afraid he was murdered.'

In my experience it's best to say it all in one go. No ripping the plaster off gently. It only hurts more. I watch, my heart filled with familiar pity, as the expression on her face changes as the words register. It's amazing how expressive the face can be. I read shock, horror, disbelief and anguish across hers in less than a second.

'Rob… Rob's dead?' Instinctively she looks over at the basket where the baby is sleeping, as if somehow she might have heard the news and she needs to protect her from it. 'Oh my God!' Her hands go straight up to her face and she folds herself in half. 'OH MY GODDDDDDD!' And then she starts to scream.

Davis goes to her and puts her arm around her, but she's still screaming and the noise wakes the baby, who starts screaming in sympathy. So now they're both screaming. And I *feel* like screaming with them because it's a horrible thing to witness, to see another human being so distraught, especially as I've been the bearer of such bad news and there's nothing I can do about it. I nod to Davis to pick the baby up because Claire Wright is in no fit state to. She's in pieces. She goes to the basket and I take a seat next to Claire.

'Listen, Claire, love, I'm so sorry. I know it's a terrible shock; please trust me, *I know*. Is there anyone who can be here with you? A friend, a family member or a neighbour perhaps? You see, we need to ask you some questions.'

But she's still wailing. Her hands are shaking. 'Rob… Oh God, not Rob! It can't be true! He can't be dead! What about me and Matilda? What about Matty?'

Davis and I make eye contact. She's got the little one in her arms now and is jiggling her up and down to try to quieten her down. I can't exactly follow suit with Claire, so I say, 'Claire, I need you to be strong for a moment. I need to ask you some questions. We really need your help.'

'How was he killed? How did Rob die?' Her knees are trembling. She's jiggling *herself* up and down now.

'His throat was cut,' I say evenly, trying to keep the emotion from my voice. 'And he'd been stabbed. It would've been very quick,' I add, although I don't actually know this for a fact; I'm simply guessing, because hey, I don't actually know what it feels like to have your throat cut open and a knife plunged into your flesh repeatedly. But from what Vic Leyton said, it's highly probable that the killer took him by surprise, most likely from behind. So the best-case scenario is that he was caught unawares and didn't have too much time to think about it.

'Claire, did you know Robert was going to see his wife last night, at the marital home in Cedar Close?'

'She's only his wife on paper. He was trying to leave but because she's a psycho she wouldn't let him go. Used all sorts of emotional blackmail on him… You do know she's an alcoholic? She's mental, unhinged… she'll have killed him! Oh God, Laurie killed him! He told me that she had threatened to kill him, or kill herself—'

Davis is looking at me. The baby has settled a bit now, wrapping her little fist tightly around Davis's hair, attempting to put it in her mouth. She's a sweet little thing – the baby I mean, not Davis – and I feel a wave of sadness wash over me for that little girl who'll never know or remember her father.

'Claire, can you tell me where you were last night? It's a routine question, okay?'

She looks startled but it's a natural reaction and I don't read anything into it.

'I was… God, I was here… with Matty. I'm always here with Matty.'

As I'm pretty sure Matty can't speak, I ask her if anyone else can corroborate this.

'Well, no… Oh, actually yes! I called my mum around 7ish. I speak to her most nights. I can give you her number. You can check the phone records or whatever. I was watching some ITV drama thing on telly and we'd been discussing it. Rob told me he was going over to see Laurie. They'd been separated for a while and he said he was finally going to ask her for a divorce. You see, Laurie didn't know about Matty... not until recently. I'd been begging Rob to tell her that she was his, that we were still together, but you see she'd been in an accident and—'

'Yes,' I cut in. 'Yes, I know about the accident.'

She looks a little sheepish. 'Don't think I'm a horrible, heartless person. I'm not, really... I know she – I know Laurie went through a lot. But I'm telling you it sent her off her rocker. He couldn't leave her after that because she was suicidal. He was planning to be here with us, to start a new life as a family but then she... well, then she found out about us and then she had her accident and he felt he couldn't just leave her, you know? She was too unstable. Plus, she needed care for some time after the accident...' Claire is rambling, spewing it all up like a dodgy kebab after one too many.

'When did you and Robert meet, Claire? When did you begin a relationship?'

She's slightly more composed now, though she's still crying and visibly shaking. She wipes her face with a muslin cloth that's over her shoulder. Presumably it's something to do with the baby and not some kind of fashion statement I'm not aware of.

'We met a little over four years ago. I was working as a temp at a photography studio, answering the phones and stuff. Rob's a photographer. He works at the studio regularly, shot a lot of stuff there for his clients, different magazines and stuff. We just got talking—'

'Did you know he was married?' Davis asks. 'Did you tell he had a wife?'

Claire looks over at her. Her mascara is clearly not the water-proof kind as it's stained her face; she looks like a bad version of Alice Cooper.

'Yes. Eventually. We started hanging out, you know, going for a few drinks after his shoots. We started off as friends really, although it was obvious there was an attraction between us. He told me he was unhappy…'

I resist the urge to emit a little grunt and roll my eyes.

'He told me that he didn't love her anymore. We began an affair about three weeks later…'

I'm sure I see Davis raise an eyebrow, though I could be imagining it.

'It got serious pretty quickly. We fell in love!' Claire starts to cry harder now and I squeeze her arm. I need her to keep talking. 'It just happened… *we fell in love.*'

'It's okay,' I say. 'We're not here to judge anyone. We just need to know a bit of background. Anything that might help.'

She nods, sniffs deeply and exhales in a bid to calm herself.

'Did Robert have any enemies that you know of? Anyone he upset at work, owed money to, anyone you can think of who may have had a grudge against him for any reason? A jealous ex-boyfriend of yours, a disgruntled client…?'

She shakes her head vehemently. 'No. None. None that I know of anyway, and I would've known. Rob and I, we talked about everything. We had no secrets. That's what he used to say to me, "no secrets between us". Everyone loved Robbie. He was the life and soul. No one had a bad word to say about him – well, except for Laurie. I threatened to tell her, Laurie I mean, about us a few times. Rob kept saying he would leave her and I waited… but there was always some reason, some excuse, why he couldn't. And then… and then she got pregnant, and I was out of my mind when he told me it was twins. *Twins!* And he said he didn't want the babies, that he didn't want *her*. That he wanted me. And I know he did. I *know.*'

I imagine the scenario in my mind: classic textbook 'my wife doesn't understand me… we haven't had sex in years'. And all of a sudden she's pregnant with his child, or, in this case, children.

And I can't help thinking that Robert Mills was a liar and that somehow this has led to his untimely demise.

'I carried on seeing him,' Claire continues. She's clearly in shock now, struggling to make sense of everything as she rocks herself back and forth in her seat, hugging herself tightly. 'He wouldn't let me end it. I did try, but every time, you know, he reeled me back in. All these promises… promises that we'd be together, that we had a future together. That I was the love of his life – the one he *really* loved. And then she found out about us, messages on a phone or something… pictures,' Claire says coyly. 'Rob was furious. He couldn't understand how she'd found out. He was always so careful—'

I bet he was. 'I see. Okay…'

'And so he came clean.'

Sounds to me like he didn't have much of a choice, I think, though I don't say it, of course. I see Davis out of the corner of my eye, placing the little girl back in the basket. She's managed to get her back off to sleep. Davis is clearly something of a natural.

'He was angry at first, you know,' she says, her voice tremulous, 'when I told him about the baby. I was six months gone already. I couldn't bring myself to tell him. He didn't want her to find out – Laurie, I mean. Said that she wasn't stable enough after she lost – after what happened. So I kept on waiting, went through the pregnancy alone. When Matty was born he totally fell in love with her. I'd never see him like that before – besotted by her he was. He swore to me that once they were settled in the new house he would leave Laurie and come to be with us, as soon as he felt she was stable enough. I mean, she'd really lost the plot, pills and booze and depression, a real mess—'

I want to say, *You can hardly blame her*. But I don't. Robert Mills was clearly a very convincing character. And by convincing, I really mean manipulative.

'And then the barbecue happened,' Claire says. 'Laurie over-heard us talking on the phone or something. Realised that we were still together. That we'd never stopped being together. And she gathered, from what she'd heard, that Matty was his… *ours*.'

Davis is seated opposite us now, leaning forward as she takes notes.

'Did he tell you what happened at the barbecue?'

Claire shrugs. 'Only that she lost the plot in front of the whole street. Called him a liar and a cheat in front of all the neighbours… told them about us, about Matty, in a drunken showdown. Humiliated herself, made herself look like a right psycho bitch from hell – that's what he said.'

I hold my tongue and remember I'm not here to pass any judgements. Not audibly anyway.

'I was glad really, that she'd overheard that conversation. Because not long afterwards he said he was leaving her. That he desperately wanted to get away from that close—'

'Was he here yesterday, Claire, with you and—'

'Matty. Yes. He took a few days off to be with us, to get the divorce proceedings going and spend some time with Matty. He'd been to see a solicitor and everything. I was so happy… Finally, *finally* he was going to commit to us properly. Get rid of that albatross around his neck – that's what he used to call her, his wife: "The Albatross".'

Seems like our victim was all heart.

'What time did he leave the apartment, Claire? This is very important. Try to think exactly.'

She shakes her head and I imagine her painful, jumbled thoughts crashing into each other. 'It wasn't long after lunch, I suppose. Around 1ish. Not much later than that. I put Matty down after feeding her around 1ish; she sleeps for a couple of hours. He kissed us both goodbye. Told me he loved me. That he loved us both.' Her voice cracks with emotion as it dawns on her that those were her lover's last words to her. She's lucky in a way. Some people never get to say goodbye, or 'I love you' to their loved ones. Their parting words are often hurried and mundane 'see you laters' or sometimes, painfully, even cross words.

'Did she kill him?' Claire asks. She has a trail of mucus running from her nose that she wipes away with the muslin cloth. 'Did Laurie kill Rob?'

'We don't know yet,' Davis informs her gently. 'She's a person of interest. We're making enquiries.'

Claire nods. 'She did it… Laurie… I know she did. It couldn't possibly be anyone else. Everyone loved Robbie.'

Well, he certainly didn't mind sharing the love around from what I'm learning.

'Is she… Have you arrested Laurie? Is she going to go to prison?' We stand to leave.

'She's helping us with enquiries,' Davis says gently. 'We'll keep you informed.'

'We'll need to talk to you again, Claire,' I say. 'We may need you to come to the station and give a statement. Would that be okay?'

She nods, the tears still streaking her face. I feel dreadful, leaving a young mother like this, distraught with a small baby in a basket next to her.

'Can you call someone, Claire? Your mum perhaps? Someone to sit with you.'

She nods again.

'I'll call Mum,' she says quietly. 'My mum will come.'

I nod agreeably and gently touch her arm.

'You will get them, won't you? Whoever did this. Laurie… you will get her—'

'Yes,' I say, 'I promise you, Claire. We will get whoever did this.' *And I mean it. I mean every word.*

CHAPTER TWENTY-TWO

I'm driving on autopilot on the way back to Davis's house, almost sick with exhaustion. My brain is no good to anyone like this, worn down like a battery. I need a few hours' kip to recharge, a shower to wake me up and a decent breakfast to get me started again, but I know I'll be lucky to achieve even one out of three. Through the fog of exhaustion however, there are a couple of questions that keep cycling like Bradley Wiggins around my battered brain.

'Why do you think he left to go to Laurie's house so early?' I say aloud to Davis, who, incidentally, appears as knackered as I do and even looks a little peaky. *Peaky.* It's an old-fashioned word favoured by my old man, which reminds me I should call him. I should probably call Fi too, and I feel a stab of self-loathing for having ignored her at the crime scene last night. What the hell's the matter with me? I deal with hardened criminals for a living yet run away from a kind and beautiful woman with whom I've shared an intimate night. I need to man up.

'Claire says he left the apartment after lunch, around 1ish. So where did he go? We've got Laurie Mills at the hairdressers around that time, shopping, picking up dry-cleaning… even in traffic it would take less than an hour to drive to Cedar Close from here.'

Davis shakes her head. 'Ran some errands? Stopped off in the pub for a drink? Met up with a friend? Another lover? Who knows? Maybe he went straight to the house. Maybe he was already there and when she came home, she killed him and then prepared dinner and concocted the amnesia story after the event.'

I chew my bottom lip. I'm starving as well as tired; it's a lethal combination. In wars they use sleep and food depravation as torture techniques to break a person down. Even the chicken dinner for one I have in the freezer back at our, sorry, my apartment is beginning to sound appetising. I think about eating it in bed.

'It's possible.' Possible. Yet my gut is telling me it's unlikely. 'Hopefully the CCTV will clarify,' I say.

I glance at Davis. She's almost puce in colour, or maybe it's the light. It looks like a storm is brewing and the sky has turned a deathly shade of grey.

'You okay?'

She nods, covers her mouth with her hand. 'Just tired, Gov.'

'Tell me about it,' I say. 'I'm starting to hallucinate about duvets… and frozen meals for one.'

She manages a small smile. 'Can't be easy, on your own,' she says, pausing.

My instincts are telling me that Davis wants to get something off her chest, but I don't push. Instead, I change the topic back to business.

'There's something Claire said, something she said that Robert Mills had said to her… something like, "I can't wait to be away from that close, or to get away from that close…"'

'What about it, Gov?' Davis is yawning and I catch it.

'Why did he say "close" and not, "I can't wait to get away from Laurie" or "the wife"? Struck me as odd.'

Davis shrugs. 'Maybe he didn't like the place. Maybe it meant the same thing, the close, the wife… all of it.'

'Maybe,' I say, unconvinced.

Davis takes a slug of water from a bottle and makes a guttural noise.

'You sure you're okay, Davis?' I frown at her as we pull up outside her apartment block. It's modest, but nice enough. *Modest.* Bloody hell, I'm turning into my father by the hour. 'Get some shut-eye – you look like you need it as much as I do. Let's reconvene in' – I check my watch – 'approximately four hours and fifty-two minutes.'

Davis nods. She's still covering her mouth and as she opens the car door she immediately throws up onto the pavement.

'Bloody hell, Davis, are you sure you're okay?' I lean across the passenger seat as she retches on the kerb.

'I hope it wasn't that sandwich,' I say, trying to inject a little humour into things.

Davis wipes her mouth and slumps back into the passenger seat. I blink at her silently for a few moments.

'Sorry, Gov,' she apologises, dabbing at the mess on the passenger seat.

'Just had the bloody thing valeted as well.'

A light in her apartment comes on and we both watch as her husband peers through the curtains. 'You should go,' I say. 'Looks like the old man is waiting for you.'

She nods. But she doesn't budge.

'Look, Lucy…' I use her Christian name like Woods uses mine when he wants to say something earnest. 'Do you want to tell me what's going on? I mean, tell me to mind my own business if it's personal, but—'

'I think I'm pregnant, Gov,' she says quickly, like the quicker she says it, the less real it is.

I blink at her, stunned for a moment. 'Well, that's great,' I say, because that's what you're supposed to say, isn't it? 'Should I say congratulations?' I'm sensing from her face that it might not be the right word.

Davis nods. Looks down into her lap and we sit in silence for a moment longer.

'If I am pregnant, then I'm not sure who the father is,' she says eventually.

It's my turn to sigh then, as thoughts of sleep and a chicken dinner for one rapidly disappear.

CHAPTER TWENTY-THREE

So, turns out I was on the money after all and my worst suspicions have been proven correct. Something *has* been going on between Davis and Delaney, and now Davis thinks she might be joining a club she had no intention of becoming a member of. Very rarely, I find myself wishing I wasn't always right.

I feel a mix of sympathy and irritation as Davis pours her heart out to me. It's clear from the way she's speaking – fast and candid – that she's been desperate to talk to someone. And while I'm somewhat flattered that person is me, part of me wishes it wasn't. Turns out that schmuck Delaney had been making a play for her for months and finally struck gold one night after a few too many in the White Hart, a local establishment close to the nick that's frequented by our kind.

'It was a drunken mistake,' she tells me sheepishly. 'And now I think I'm in the shit. I don't want to lose John…' We both looked over to the window of Davis's apartment but John was no longer standing there. I wonder if he suspects anything and it suddenly strikes me that perhaps he thinks it's *me* she's been off doing the dirty with.

'It's not me you need to apologise to,' I say gently, and she screws her eyes shut and groans. 'But Delaney, Davis? Of all people. I thought you had more sense than that.' I know I shouldn't say it but I do. I can't stop myself.

'You don't need to tell me, Gov,' she says, self-loathing evident in her voice. 'It's just… well, me and John… things haven't been great lately. We hardly see each other, and when we do we're always knackered or distracted and so, you know' – she lowers her eyes again – 'things haven't been good in *that* department… and Martin, well, he'd been putting it on me for weeks – months even. The innuendos and flirting, buying me coffee, being overly friendly… I took it in good humour initially, didn't think too much of it, brushed it off as banter. I suppose I've been feeling a bit…' She stops. 'Oh I don't know, lonely maybe. Then that night, in the Hart, we got talking, me and Martin. He was asking me about John, you know, if I was happy, all of that. And at the end of the night he came on to me and I… I'd had too much to drink and…' She buries her head in her hands. 'And it just happened.'

I'd carried on looking at her in silence. Unsure exactly what to say.

'I can't believe I fell for it,' she says, and I think she's crying but it's dark and I can't be sure. 'It was just the once. I mean, I can hardly remember because I was so—'

'Spare me the details, Davis,' I say. 'Unless you want that sandwich to make a reappearance.' I laugh gently in a bid to lighten the conversation but actually I'm a little cross with Davis, although not as cross as I am with that piece of shit Delaney. He knows Davis is married. Or perhaps that's the whole point. I know for a fact Davis isn't the first female copper, or married one for that, to have fallen foul of Delaney's 'charms'. And no doubt she won't be the last. I'm fond of Lucy. Genuinely. I don't want her to have been another of his conquests, another notch on his bedpost to fuel that insatiable ego of his. I feel like she's let me, and herself, down – not that I need to say it, judging by the look of her.

'Does he know?' I ask her. 'Does Martin know about the pregnancy scare?'

'No!' she says. 'And I won't be telling him.'

I glance sideways at her. 'Good,' I reply. 'I'd think twice about telling that smug bastard the time.'

Davis laughs a little, but it sounds desperate – more like a prelude to a scream. 'Thing is, Gov, now he won't leave me alone, Delaney. Ever since it happened he keeps making all these snide comments, sly little digs, like he's got something on me, you know… I just can't believe it… It was only the once.'

'We all know once is all it takes, Lucy.'

She looks away, embarrassed, and stares out of the car window. 'I can't believe I've been so stupid.'

'Neither can I. Look…' I soften my tone because she's self-flagellating enough. 'It was a mistake. Don't beat yourself up too much. If you are, you know, in the "family" way then I can't tell you what to do. But what I do know is that I need you on this case. You're the best DS I've got. And don't ask me why but I've got a nasty feeling that all isn't as it seems on this one.'

She smiles at me then. Seems genuinely touched by my compliment and instinctively I put my arm around her, pulling away quickly when I remember that John might be looking out of the window. I don't want to be held accountable for *all* of Delaney's cock-ups, no tasteless pun intended.

I watch as Davis disappears into her apartment, cutting a forlorn figure. I could be wrong, and maybe I'm reading too much into it, but I can't help wondering if Delaney has gone after Davis to somehow get one over on me. Frankly, I wouldn't put it past him.

CHAPTER TWENTY-FOUR

I trip over a pair of trainers as I walk into my apartment and I curse. The place is a mess where I'd left it in haste. It feels like I haven't been home in weeks. I shuffle into the small kitchen and open the fridge. It's practically empty as usual, though there's always a few beers knocking around, so I grab one, take a deep slug and search the freezer compartment for that gourmet chicken dinner for one, only Davis's news has all but killed my appetite so I give it a miss and opt for a mini pork pie instead. Hey, don't say I don't know how to live.

After my nutritious dinner I strip off and grab a quick shower before throwing on some bed clothes, namely a pair of ancient Superdry joggers that Rachel bought me and I can't bear to be parted from, and a clean white tee. She liked me best in my 'comfies' as she used to call them. Thinking of Rach reminds me that I still haven't called Fi. It's nagging at my conscience but I'm exhausted and I don't feel up to having *that* conversation just now. I text her instead. *'Hi Fi, how are you? Drink in the Hart this Friday? D x'*

Yes, I know, cop out. Literally.

I let my head fall back onto the pillow and wonder if I've been a little hasty writing off anything more with Fiona. It's at moments like this that I wish I had the comfort of a body next to me; someone to hold on to, to fall asleep with, our limbs intertwined, our heartbeats synching. It would be nice to have someone to come home to; someone to chat to about our respective days; someone to relax and unwind in front of the TV with, to share dinner and a bottle of wine. I find myself thinking about all the lonely people in the world, all the Eleanor Rigbys and Father McKenzies. Widows and widowers, like my old man, single mums, abandoned kids, and those who haven't found someone to share their existence with. And I wonder then, if there's no one to witness your life, do you even exist at all?

It's in these moments that I miss Rachel the most and crave a human touch, a smile or a kiss. That night with Fi, it had felt natural, easy, comfortable. But it had not felt the same. And it makes my heart feel heavy because I know, no matter how good the sex is, no matter how beautiful a woman is or how much we have in common, I will never again feel the same with someone else as I did with Rachel.

As I'm drifting off into the land of Nod it starts: *the baby upstairs*. It's like it somehow instinctively knows and has decided to open its airways. Loudly. I groan and roll over, grit my teeth and pull a pillow over my head, willing it to stop. Only the little shit seems to know this and ramps up into high-pitched screaming – you know, how babies do when they're seriously pissed off. I imagine its little face, all purple and screwed up as it continues to exercise its lungs like it's just discovered what they're for.

I lie in the dark listening to this small human being crying in peaks and troughs that seem to reach an ear-splitting crescendo every five minutes or so. After about an hour, I've reached breaking point and fuelled by a severe lack of sleep, I throw back the duvet and stomp up the staircase to the apartment above, and thump loudly on the door. A good few seconds later, a young woman answers it. She's holding the source of the noise over her shoulder and her long dark hair is piled in a messy bun on top of her head. I go to speak, give her a piece of my frazzled mind, but before I can get the words out, her face goes all crumpled and screwed up like the baby's and she starts to cry.

CHAPTER TWENTY-FIVE

'I think the police are still outside, parked across the road, outside that nosy bitch Bartlett's house. I've never liked her, that Jessica, full of her own piss and importance. Anyone would think she's the only woman in the world who owns an Aga and has Sanderson wallpaper in her lounge. There are still a few journos hanging around too by the looks of things. They've been ringing the doorbell all morning, since 6 a.m., bloody parasites. Can you even imagine what it must be like to be famous, have them outside your door 24/7, having your every move watched and dissected? What a pain in the arse, even with all that money. Anyway, how are you feeling, hon?'

Monica drops the curtain, moves away from the window and sits on the edge of Laurie's bed. 'I've made a fresh pot of coffee and some scrambled egg,' she says in a sing-song voice that mothers usually reserve for their sick children. 'I'll bring it up. Do you think you could eat something?' She cocks her head to one side, placing her fingers on her arm.

Laurie's eyelids are heavy and she struggles to open them. She feels like she's been drugged. When she finally blinks her eyes open, the realisation hits her full force like a hatchet to the skull. *Robert is dead*. It isn't a nightmare after all. 'I don't think I can, Mon,' she says, sitting up and rubbing her gritty eyes. 'I'm not hungry.'

'But you've got to eat, love. There's hardly anything of you as it is. I'll bring it up anyway, hmm?' Monica runs her hands down her skinny jeans as if to smooth them, making sure the curtains are closed before she goes. 'Just try a few mouthfuls – for me, yeah?'

Laurie nods and tries to feel grateful. Monica has been good enough to her already. 'Thanks, Mon. Look, I really appreciate this, everything you've done for me, for looking after me. I'm sorry. I know you don't need this. I—'

'Shhh,' Monica cuts her off. 'Listen, what are friends for? You were there for me after Dougie went, weren't you? I wouldn't have got through that terrible ordeal if it hadn't been for you.'

'Oh, Mon… the pair of us…' Laurie feels a stab of despair in her chest. Monica has suffered too, losing Dougie like that. It had happened the year before the accident, when she'd been happy and everything had been normal. Dougie's sudden fatal heart attack had devastated and shocked them all. With hindsight, Laurie was glad that such a tragedy had happened when it had, if it had to happen at all, because back then she had the strength to be there for her friend, to help her, comfort her and take care of her, just like Monica was doing for her now. God forbid it had happened after the accident. She would have been useless. *Good to no one*. Just like Robert used to tell her. Poor Dougie. She thought of him then, pictured his familiar happy-go-lucky, smiling face, his sunny disposition. It had been almost incomprehensible to think that he could just suddenly drop down dead like that at thirty-seven. It was no age at all.

God only takes the good young, Laurie remembered saying to someone at the funeral, though she can't recall who now. Only now she's not so sure. He took Robert too. Well, someone did anyway. And the police think it was her. Maybe it was her? She needs to try to wrap her head around this notion, the idea that maybe she's a murderer. She wonders if she'll end up on one of those low-budget TV shows, like *Women Who Kill*, and if they will depict her as a cold, callous, jealous harridan and take the angle that it's no wonder her husband went off with another woman.

She thinks about that prison cell. If it wasn't for Monica, she'd still be rotting in that awful place now, locked up like an animal in a cage. The memory resurrects naked fear within her, sending it crashing through her solar plexus and causing her body to tremble. She tries hard to collect her thoughts but her mind is jumbled and confused, and she cannot concentrate on one thought long enough to process it before another appears. The frustration makes her want to cry. It's like her soul has been sucked right out of her and she feels dead inside, like she's slipped into a black hole inside herself and can see only a pinprick of light at the top. *There's no coming back from this, Laurie*, she tells herself. She'd told herself that after the accident too. *No coming back*. But she had, hadn't she? She had tried. She had fought so hard. She couldn't imagine ever in this lifetime or the next feeling more despair, rage, guilt, shame, terror, pain and anguish than she had following the loss of her babies, the loss of Milo and Nancy, and yet now… *now this*. She can't understand how all of this has happened.

Laurie looks at the window and dreads what is waiting for her on the other side of it. *This is all a terrible mistake. They will see that, won't they?* The police… the press… Robert's parents? Can she make them see – understand?

Less than two years ago she was the happiest she'd ever been in her lifetime. Pregnant and happy, due to have twins – *twins*! Her mind rewinds back to the moment she'd discovered she was carrying two babies. 'I've got something to tell you, Bobby,' she'd said, returning home from her twelve-week scan, light-footed and high on pregnancy endorphins and the momentum of such wonderful news. 'I think you had better sit down.' She smiles then, involuntarily, as she remembers his face. The look of shock, surprise and then… well, it was elation she saw wasn't it?

'Twins! Oh my God, Law.' He'd put his hand up to his mouth before throwing his arms around her, enveloping her in his embrace. Her Bobby. Her husband. He could be so gentle and loving, so caring and affectionate. No one pretends to be happy, do they? No one pretends to love someone, do they? Not for all those years…

He had *seemed* so genuinely ecstatic. It had felt so real, his arms around her, holding her. How delighted he had been. How he had kissed her cheeks, told her he loved her. How he couldn't wait to meet his two – *two* – children.

'The look on your face!' she had said and laughed, over the moon with his reaction. 'Well, it's nothing to what my face must've looked like when the sonographer told me there were two! I almost passed out with shock! Did you know there were twins in your family! It comes from your side, you know!'

'How would I know?' he'd said, the mention of his family clearly taking the sheen off the moment. She feels the elation of the memory passing as the realisation hits her that Robert had never really told her *anything*. Not one moment of truth in all their years together, not least the vows they had made on their wedding day.

It was all lies, Laurie. Her therapist's voice suddenly appears in her mind. *All of it. You have to try and accept that.* Accept. How could she accept? How can anyone accept that their entire relationship was built on deception and lies? How does someone come to terms with that? They can tell you that you *must* accept it all they like, but *how*? How do you begin to try to emotionally process something like that? How do you accept that every moment, every memory, every intimate detail you have shared with another person was not based in any truth or reality? That behind the mask of love and respectability they were duping you, lying to you, using you… and for reasons you cannot understand, that make no sense to a rational mind.

Laurie feels the sharp stab of betrayal once more. That hopeless, all-encompassing feeling that renders everything she has ever experienced and felt in her entire life defunct and meaningless. How could it all have been so *meaningless*? Every word, every action, every deed and touch… it all meant nothing. *Nothing at all.* She'd explained to her therapist that it was impossible for her to accept this.

'It did mean something to him, Laurie. Just not the same as it meant to you. He cannot feel the same as you feel, as normal people do. He has a personality disorder. He's not hardwired in the same ways as you… or I. The things you feel… you've felt, they were real – all of them. But he's unable to feel those things, not in the same way. He only pretends he can. He knows he has to pretend to be part of society, to fly under the radar undetected, to have a wife, a life… He mimics emotions. He was, is, your mirror. He mirrors you back to yourself. All that love, all that devotion, all the care and forgiveness and generosity… it's not his, Laurie, it's yours. He's showing you who you are. But really he's empty, like a shell, a bucket with holes in it, nothing but a reflection. No matter how much you try to fill that bucket, it will keep leaking and leaking, and you'll keep giving and giving, until there's no more Laurie left. And he walks away with your skin, your essence, your soul, to fool yet another giving person, another empath or co-dependent. He sniffs them out, like a predator, like a shark smelling blood. And it will be the same story, Laurie, every single time. The pattern will repeat itself, like a cycle, just as the sun rises and sets. It's not you, Laurie. Do you understand this? It is not you. It's his condition and there is nothing you can do to change it.'

Death by a thousand cuts.

Laurie knows now of course that the memory she has, that precious, intimate and beautiful memory she has of telling Robert that they were expecting twins, is worth nothing now. Zilch. Nada. Zero. She knows now that he had been seeing *her* at the time she had imparted their happy news. His lips were kissing another woman's, his mouth and tongue and body inside another woman's, telling her he loved her and wanted her, claiming that Laurie was a 'psycho', someone he couldn't leave, who wouldn't let him leave her, and that she was to blame.

She had later discovered that only a few hours after telling Robert that she was carrying both his babies and they had celebrated together by making love, he had gone to Claire and spent the night with her. Still, to this day, she cannot understand how her husband, the man she had loved her entire adult life, could be so heartless. How could he somehow compartmentalise parts of his life so seamlessly and without conscience?

Monica re-enters the bedroom some moments later carrying a tray with purpose. She has the overly jovial demeanour of someone who is trying hard to make light of what they know is a dire situation. She places the tray on the bed next to Laurie and nods at the plate of food. 'You really must eat, Lolly. I insist. You'll be good for nothing, good to no one if you don't.'

Good to no one. Laurie stares at the plate of scrambled eggs and wonders if she can muster up a forkful just to appease her friend. She can manage a coffee at least.

'The police are going to want to speak to you again,' Monica says, buttering herself some toast from a side plate. Laurie watches as she slathers on some strawberry jam; she feels sick. 'But the good news is that I've been onto Marcus Wainwright, my solicitor, and he's agreed to represent you, if needs be. He's good – very good. He'll give you the best advice on how to proceed with the police.' Her voice is efficient, reassuring.

'Thanks, Mon,' Laurie says, although it's an effort to speak. 'What do you think is going to happen? Do you think they'll charge me?'

Monica sighs, takes a large bite of her toast and jam. 'Well, I guess it all depends on what evidence they have. But I can't see how they can now. Not now I've given you an alibi.' She smiles triumphantly, tucking strands of her platinum hair behind her ears.

'Drink some coffee, darling,' Monica instructs her. 'It'll wake you up.' She pours Laurie a cup. 'If you do exactly as I say then things will be okay.' She pours the milk efficiently. 'You need to get the story straight.'

'Story? What story?'

Monica waves a dismissive hand and gestures to the plate of food in front of Laurie. 'Eat,' she says. 'You're going to need your strength to get you through this. You're going to need your wits about you.'

The coffee tastes burnt in Laurie's throat as she swallows it.

'With my alibi and a decent lawyer, it should be enough for them to back off, for now anyway,' Monica says, like she deals with this kind of thing as a matter of course.

'What did you tell them? The police.' Reluctantly, Laurie cuts into the egg under her friend's watchful eye. 'What did you say to them, Mon?'

Monica pauses, putting the remainder of her toast down purposefully and looks straight at her. 'I lied to them,' she replies.

Laurie attempts to swallow some scrambled egg but it gets lodged somewhere between her tongue and oesophagus. 'You lied? To the police? What about? *Why?*' Her mind is coming back into focus now. But it's a struggle and she vows never to take another Valium in her life. She can't think straight. It's like her brain hasn't booted up properly and keeps misfiring and restarting itself.

'I had to.' Monica seizes Laurie's hand suddenly, catches her off guard and she drops her fork. 'You'd still bloody well be there in that cell if I hadn't. And you don't want to be back there, do you?'

She shakes her head. *Hot fear.*

Monica pushes the tray aside. Slides closer to her on the bed. She's holding Laurie's hand tightly and it's making her feel nervous. 'I lied and said that you'd come over to my place around 8 p.m. That you were in a state, upset, a little... drunk. I had to make it sound convincing,' she says apologetically. 'You were upset that

Robert hadn't turned up for dinner, that he'd been up to his usual tricks.' Her voice sounds sour and she scowls. 'I said we chatted and we'd had a few glasses of wine, put the world to rights, and then I'd seen you off home. Watched you walk into your house.'

Laurie stares at her friend, her heart knocking violently against her ribs. 'But… but which part is the lie?' she manages to ask. Suddenly she wishes that her mother were here. That stupid, selfish mother of hers who'd all but abandoned her her entire life but who would tell her – *force her* – to snap out of it and get a grip.

'All of it,' Monica says. 'None of it bloody well happened. You didn't come to the house. We didn't chat. Or drink together. Or put the world to rights. None of it.'

Laurie feels an icy chill run through her body. She needs explanations but things are becoming more and more confusing, and the fug in her brain won't clear for long enough to allow her to get a grasp on what her friend is saying, something, she suspects, which shows on her face because Monica is pleading with her now. 'I *had* to lie, Laurie. I had to.'

CHAPTER TWENTY-SIX

Laurie feels like someone has dredged her empty stomach. 'Why did you have to lie to the police, Mon?' She knows she must ask the question but she's fearful of the answer.

Monica looks at her intensely with steely eyes. 'Listen to me, Laurie.' Her voice is authoritative but still genial as she tucks a piece of hair behind her ear, habitually. 'We need to get every single moment of this story correct. Those coppers, that bloke, Dan whatshisname, he's nobody's fool. If we haven't got our story straight, they'll annihilate you and you'll see yourself through the menopause in prison.'

Laurie feels paralysed as she watches her friend speaking in slow, measured words. 'They'll question you, grill you on every little detail and I mean, *everything*, about that night. The timings, the clothes you were wearing, what we drank, what we talked about, if there was TV on in the background, if you had your fucking period, *everything*. And then they're going to look into your life. Leave no stone unturned. They'll dig up dirt, invade your privacy, uncover any secrets, any skeletons… They'll want to know everything about you and Robert, your marriage, the accident…'

Laurie swallows back the bile that has risen into her throat. Just thinking about it makes her feel sick and exhausted. The image of Robert lying on the bathroom floor flashes up in her mind yet again like a still frame. The look on his face, one of shock and surprise, she thought, like he couldn't quite believe what had happened. It gives her chills. She needs a stiff drink and thinks of asking Monica if she has anything in. If she's not sober then none of this is really happening.

'Why did you have to lie?' Laurie's voice is shaky and tight in her throat as she repeats the question.

'Look, Laurie. There's something I need to tell you.'

Monica's grave tone and expression is really scaring Laurie now and a fresh release of cortisol ignites the familiar sensation of fight or flight in her.

'I don't want you to panic, okay?'

'Tell me what?' Laurie's voice sounds squeaky and laboured. 'Please, Mon. Just tell me. No secrets, remember?' *Sisters don't have secrets*: that's what Monica had always said since they'd met in their late teens at a mutual university friend's party. They had always told each other everything. She could rely on Monica to tell her the truth.

Like most young women, they had shared their innermost thoughts as they navigated their way through adulthood together: the failed relationships and career struggles; and, in Laurie's case, the tempestuous relationship with her mother that had plagued her childhood and young-adult life until she'd moved away to California. It had been Monica who'd told her straight that the dress she'd chosen for her and Robert's wedding day made her look a little 'frou-frou' and helped her pick something much more chic. There was nothing they couldn't tell each other, no lip service, just the truth.

'Sisters…' Laurie says, feeling sleepy again. The drugs she's been taking are zombifying her, making her feel spaced out. She would stop taking them; go to her GP and get an alternative. She couldn't function on these bastard things.

'Oh God, Lolls.'

Monica's pained expression is freaking her out and she squeezes her friend's hand tightly as though to brace herself for what she's about to say.

'That night… the night Robert was… well, I came by to check on you… I'd been worried about you all day, you know, what with seeing him for the first time since the barbecue, with him coming to the house and everything… I just had this bad feeling about it, you know, some weird kind of sixth sense. So, I thought I would drop in on you, make sure it was all going okay. I think I rang the doorbell, but there was no answer, so I looked through the window, through the shutters and…' Monica looks away, unable to finish the sentence.

Laurie's heart is smashing against her ribs as she hangs on to every word. She has to consciously remind herself to breathe. 'And what? What did you see? Mon… tell me! What did you see?'

'I saw you both in the kitchen. You and Robert. You were arguing. I couldn't hear your voices clearly, or what you were saying, but you were shouting in Robert's face, waving your arms about manically. And he looked pretty angry too. I think he was trying to calm you down. He had hold of your shoulders at one point… and that's when I saw you pick up the knife—'

'The knife,' Laurie repeats the word. '*The knife*?'

'Yes.' Monica blinks at her almost nervously, chewing her bottom lip.

'I had a *knife*?'

Monica nods slowly. 'You started wrestling with each other and that's when I banged on the window. But you didn't hear me. Neither of you did. I panicked, thought of calling the police. But… but I knew… well, I figured, being as Robert is – *was* – three times the size of you that he'd have disarmed you. I mean, I know you two had your fair share of fights. I know they sometimes got out of hand, but I never thought… never believed in a million years—'

'What? You never thought what?' Laurie can't believe what Monica is saying. So Robert *had* come to the house. She *had* seen him. And they *had* fought. Dread claws its way through her body, tugging at her vital organs as it rages through her. Perhaps it has happened again. Perhaps she'd had one of her blackouts. She'd suffered a couple of similar episodes following the accident where she had acted out and had no recollection of it the following day. She had always put them down to too much alcohol, but what if it was something else? Robert had liked to describe these forgotten moments to her in graphic detail the following day. He'd enjoyed watching her squirm as he recounted what he called her *psychotic episodes*, how she had screamed and wailed like a banshee, throwing herself on the floor, pounding him with her fists, and the time he claimed she had gone for him with a pair of sewing scissors. He'd dined out on that one for weeks, the eternal victim of her 'abuse'. *You could've killed me, Laurie. I had to restrain you, prise them from your grip before you did me, or yourself, any harm. You're insane, do you know that, Laurie? In-fucking-sane. You need to be locked up in a secure hospital.* His words still sting her now as she thinks of them. The burn of humiliation, the look of contempt on his face and the subsequent shame she had felt.

'Robert… he was there, in the house? Are you sure? Are you sure it was him, Mon? I… I don't remember. Not a thing. I don't remember seeing him, or speaking to him or—'

'You're going to need to tell them, the police I mean, that your memory is returning and that you recall coming over to my house, wearing that dress you had on.' Monica's voice has resumed some authority. 'We talked about Robert not showing up and you were upset and drunk. I comforted you. Advised you not to call him because I felt it was another of his sick little mind games and that he'd stood you up in a bid to deliberately hurt you, because that's just the sort of thing Robert does… or did. Laurie, are you listening to me? You need to listen to me. You need to repeat it all back to me like a mantra, okay? This is important, Laurie. Your liberty is at stake here – we're talking about the rest of your life…'

Fear and exhaustion have consumed her. She's not sure she has the emotional or physical strength to fight anymore, to deal with an intrusive police investigation, with the past being dredged up, her life dissected and discussed, painful memories she has worked so hard to push to the bottom resurfacing like rubber balls in water. It has taken everything she'd had left, these past few months, to regain some semblance of a normal life. *A normal life.* That's all she'd ever wanted. Not this. None of this.

Laurie is shaking uncontrollably. She's a murderer.

'Marcus will prepare the best defence for you. You're the victim of domestic violence, of psychological abuse, years of deception, infidelity and cruelty, the mental torture and the effects of the accident, of losing Milo and Nancy.' Monica devours the remainder of her toast and butters another piece animatedly. Laurie can't understand how she can eat anything, or why she is so calm, so together. Monica was always the together one.

'The accident, that'll be your coup de grâce. How you discovered he was still with that fat bitch and that they'd had a baby together while you had lost both of yours in the worst way possible. How it sent you spiralling into a deep, dark, debilitating depression. You weren't in your right mind. The alcohol... the pills... the eating disorder and psychotic episodes... and then, the final nail in the coffin, Robert coming over to serve you with divorce papers after promising you a fresh new start together, his final act of betrayal. I mean, really, when you say it all out loud it's little wonder you—'

Laurie stares at the congealing plate of food beside her. 'Little wonder I what?'

'That you killed him,' Monica whispers. 'And then tried to kill yourself. With Marcus working his magic you may well get a reduced sentence, or even let off on the grounds of diminished responsibility. I see it all the time on TV. It's the best we can hope for.'

Laurie is in a place past horrified. *Reduced sentence.* 'But I... I don't think... I didn't kill him... No! I don't remember him even being there, at the house. I was waiting for him… he didn't show up. God, no… Tell me you're wrong! I couldn't have done that. I wouldn't. Surely I'd remember if I killed my own husband and then tried to kill myself? Surely something would've come back to me, a flashback, *anything*.' Laurie thinks about coming clean about the arsenic, how she had thought about poisoning Robert, but she decides against it. She would never have gone through with it.

Monica takes her hand again. 'You've suffered a dreadful shock. And it's not like this hasn't happened before, is it – you blacking out and not being able to remember anything? It's the mind's way of protecting itself from deep trauma. And you've certainly suffered your fair share of that. A jury will see that. They will, I promise you.'

Laurie can't focus, can't *think*. All she feels is sheer naked, hot fear searing through her body. 'Do *you* think I killed Robert? Is that what you're saying?' She knows how it looks, how it seems. Despite her fragile emotional state, she is not missing her faculties. She is not mad like Robert used to tell her she was, almost convincing her sometimes. She is sure she did not kill her husband, or cut her own wrists, though how either of these things has happened she can't explain. She doesn't understand it, any of it.

Monica is still holding her hand tightly. And she doesn't like the way her oldest friend is looking at her.

'I don't think you killed Robert, my darling,' Monica says gently. 'I *know* you did.'

CHAPTER TWENTY-SEVEN

I'm juggling my phone and a flat white with a shot of vanilla as I enter the incident room; I need caffeine and sugar, as I'm feeling less than refreshed after my night of broken sleep. Fi has replied to my text message: '*That would be lovely. 1 p.m.? Fi x*' I go to take a sip of my coffee but don't quite make it. *Shit.* I'd forgotten about arranging to meet up. I fire off a quick response – '*Great. See you then*' – and immediately feel conflicted.

'Morning, boss. You look knackered.' Murray doesn't sugar-coat it.

'No, please, say what you really mean, Murray, and yes, well-observed.'

'So, we'll let Murray kick things off,' I address the team. 'Bring me up to speed.'

'The Millses' phone and email logs from the techs,' Murray explains, 'they make for insightful reading.' She raises an eyebrow. 'Lots of heartfelt outpourings to the deceased from his wife, going back a long way. They may have been Mills, but their marriage certainly wasn't Mills and *Boon*.'

I give a little head tilt in appreciation of the pun and I hear someone say, 'Boom, boom.'

'It's pretty depressing reading actually, Gov, but there's nothing there. No direct threats made against his life, nothing that would raise any alarm bells. But it's clear that Laurie Mills was one heartbroken lady, tormented by her husband's affair, or should I say affairs.'

If Murray expects me to register surprise she'll be waiting a while because this is far from a revelation. Everything I have learned about Robert Mills thus far suggests he had 'womaniser' written all over him.

'The deceased, however, well, let's just say he wasn't exactly contrite. In fact, I'd say he wasn't in the least bit sorry about his indiscretions, judging by some of his replies. A right callous bastard if you want my opinion.' She shoots me a derisive look. 'It's clear he held Laurie Mills in contempt most of the time, despite what she'd been through. Although occasionally he threw her a few crumbs of hope for reconciliation; the odd lifeline here and there, which is probably why she hung on. Pretty cruel really, promising her a fresh start when he had zero intention of it, telling her he still loved her… stringing her along with a load of bullshit and false promises. Not surprised it sent her off her head. If that had been my old man, I'd have kicked him to the kerb the moment I found out he'd been doing the dirty. But it appears Laurie Mills was the forgiving sort. *Very* forgiving. She still wanted the marriage to work, even after all the lies and deception and that terrible accident.'

'Trauma bonding,' I say. 'Stockholm syndrome. It's not uncommon in abusive relationships.'

Murray sighs and places the folders on my desk. 'Most of the texts sent from Laurie Mills' phone have been traced back to Robert or the friend – Monica Lewis, is it? And there's a few to a Sarah Wells – seems to be her therapist. Well, anyway, she deactivated all her social-media accounts around eighteen months ago, following the accident it looks like. There were a couple of home-video clips on her PC that might be worth you having a look at though. Some wedding footage, and a fairly recent clip at what looks like a house party with the deceased, when she was obviously pregnant.'

I nod. 'Has Robert Mills' PC thrown anything up?'

'Ah well, slightly different story there, Gov.'

I had a feeling it might be.

'Countless emails, phone and text exchanges between himself and the mistress, Claire Wright… although it appears she wasn't the only lucky lady on the scene. Our Mr Mills was something of a player by all accounts: lots of flirty emails with women he associated with through his job, models and stylists and the like, women he kept in touch with on social media, exes he 'met up' with occasionally. He certainly liked to keep his options open where women were concerned. There's one in particular, Leanna George. Looks like something went on between them and got rather nasty.'

I scribble the name down on my notepad. 'Where can we find her?'

'Her number's on the file, sir.'

'Good. Call her. Ask her to come in for a chat.'

Murray nods. 'Search history is nothing unexpected; mostly relates to work, a couple of porn sites, nothing too sinister. The techs are trying to retrieve his trash folder now. Maybe we'll find a few gems in there. His social media is very much active though. Posted almost daily right up until the day of the murder, mainly images of stuff he was shooting for work, although there were some personal images too, lots of images of *himself*, lots of banter and flirtatious comments to women. Interestingly, his relationship status reads "single".'

We exchange knowing glances.

'Well, let's keep an eye on it if it's still active, check the sympathy posts for any leads.'

'Yes, Gov. Notably, there are no photos of him and Laurie anywhere on his Facebook or Instagram accounts, not one, not even going way back. It's like she didn't exist, like she never existed in his life at all.'

'And the pièce de résistance, Murray?' I ask. She looks at me a little blankly. I roll my eyes. 'The text messages, on the day of the murder?'

'Yes, Gov, of course.' She flushes. 'Well, there's one the day before the murder.' She locates the page in the folder with one hand, placing her pen between her teeth. 'Robert Mills texted his wife at 9.37 a.m. She replied a few minutes later. That was the last exchange between them. But' – Murray's eyes light up and she's smiling now – 'later on that day he sent two messages and made one phone call. The texts were to Claire, the mistress, and to his mother, and the phone call was to an unknown recipient.'

'An unknown recipient?'

'Yup.' Murray looks pleased with herself. 'The number isn't listed in his contacts list. But, get this: in the space of the last three months this unknown number shows up at least twenty-eight times.'

'Great stuff. Let's get onto the phone company and trace it.'

Murray nods efficiently. 'Times check out on Laurie Mills' phone on the night of the murder. She called his number at 10.38, 10.39, 10.40, 10.42 and 10.45 p.m. All of which went unanswered, like she said.'

I pause thoughtfully. Woods isn't going to like this. We've not got enough to present to the CPS, not yet – certainly not now that she's got an alibi and that her timings check out.

'Any word on forensics yet, the knife?'

'Nothing yet, Gov, chasing them up,' Harding says. 'We're going through the CCTV that we collected from the neighbours. And we've got hold of the CCTV from the supermarket and the camera along the parade of shops where the hair salon is, where Laurie Mills had her hair done.'

'And?'

'Nothing from the neighbours' houses yet, boss, sorry. There's a fair bit still to go through though. But the supermarket and hair-salon footage show her arriving and leaving at the times she claims.'

I go to pick up my desk phone but it rings before I get to it. It's Vic Leyton. She needs me to come down to the pathology lab. Apparently, she's got some 'interesting' news.

CHAPTER TWENTY-EIGHT

The sound of the intercom buzzer makes Claire jump and she curses. It's after 11 p.m. She hurriedly peeks at Matilda in her Moses basket. The noise has caused her to stir. She's only just got her off to sleep as well. She stomps towards the intercom.

'Who is it?' she hisses. If it's one of those bloody reporters again… like vultures circling a carcass they were – Robert hadn't been dead for twenty-four hours before they'd starting blowing up her intercom and phone.

There's a slight pause.

'Is this Claire Wright's apartment?'

She doesn't recognise the voice. 'Who wants to know?'

Another pause.

'Is that you, Claire?'

She wraps her dressing gown around her chunky frame, the one she's been wearing for three days solid. She doesn't want any visitors. She doesn't want to see anyone. She's too distraught, too tired, *too everything*. She has hardly slept since the police visit and she still can't take it in. Her Rob: *murdered*. None of it felt real. It *couldn't* be real, could it? Other people get murdered, people off the telly. Not people you know. Not people you *love*.

Claire had never experienced death of any kind in all her twenty-nine years so far, except for when her dog had died when she was nineteen, and that had been traumatic enough. She'd needed a week off work to cope with the grief. Now, however, she had a small human being to care for and she had no choice but to force herself to get out of her bed and carry on. But she was barely functioning and had gone into a state of denial. It was easier to deal with if she could pretend it wasn't really happening. So far she hadn't done a bad job of convincing herself, but when her mum had switched on the TV and Robert's murder had been reported in the local news yesterday, she had spiralled into complete meltdown.

The reporter, a middle-aged woman with a severe haircut who reminded her of an old school teacher she'd once had – and never liked – had addressed the camera with a grim expression. She was standing in Cedar Close, outside Robert's house, she presumed. Rob had never taken her there. She supposed it had made it easier for her to completely disassociate herself from that part of his life, from Laurie and the house. She had never seen or been near either of them and hadn't wanted to. That way they weren't really real.

In fact, she didn't even know what Robert's estranged wife looked like – she'd never even seen a photograph. Initially she supposed she'd been a little intrigued but Laurie Mills wasn't on any social media so there was no way of looking her up. Apparently she'd got rid of it after the accident because she couldn't deal with the outpouring of sympathy, or something like that. Although this struck Claire as odd, since Rob had always told her how much Laurie loved to play the victim card; she would've thought the mad cow would welcome all that sympathy and pity.

She had a mental picture of what Laurie might look like, largely gleaned from the derogatory comments Robert had made about her over time. Apparently, she had long dark hair, 'like a witch', and was 'anorexic skinny', which had kind of bothered her a bit at the time when he'd said it, because she battled with her yo-yoing weight and was always trying to shift a few extra pounds, not least since she'd given birth. Rob had always assured her that he found her attractive though, referring to her voluptuous figure as 'delicious'. She supposed that because Rob had always spoken so negatively about Laurie, 'his psycho ex-wife', she'd never had cause to feel threatened by her and, as such, the need to see what she looked like had never become overwhelming. Fact is, whatever that nutjob looked like, he didn't want Laurie. He wanted *her*. And Matty. And that's all that had mattered.

Her mum had tried to switch Claire's TV off so she wouldn't have to watch the case unfolding but she had snatched the remote from her and increased the volume.

'A man was found brutally murdered in his own home in North London last night,' the reporter's clipped voice rang out through the TV. 'Mr Mills, who had worked as an interiors and fashion photographer for the likes of John Lewis, was about to turn forty in two weeks' time. He was pronounced dead at the scene. A thirty-seven-year-old woman, believed to be the victim's wife, was taken into custody for questioning and later released without charge.'

'Released without charge!' she'd screamed at the TV. 'She murders him and they've let her go!

Her mum had tried to calm her down.

'Claire, love, come on, turn it off. You'll only upset yourself more.'

But Claire had sobbed herself into an inconsolable mucusy stupor until her mother had been forced to physically put her to bed.

She leans against the wall next to the intercom; she's so exhausted that it's a struggle to stand. 'It's late. Who is this? I've got a baby sleeping, you know… Just go away. I don't want to see anyone or speak to anyone.'

'I know it's late and I'm sorry.' The woman's voice sounds apologetic. 'My name's Abby King. I'm from the *North London Enquirer*. Please, Claire, can I come up and speak to you? It won't take five minutes. I want to talk to you about Robert, your partner.'

Just as she'd thought, another reporter sniffing around, like flies to shit they were. But the woman's use of the word 'partner' stops her in her tracks for a second. *Yes, she was his partner, wasn't she?* The fact that this has been recognised, and by the press no less, feels good. She had been Robert's secret for so long.

'Look, you knew Robert better than anyone,' the voice continues. 'You're the mother of his only child. I know you probably don't feel like talking right now but I just need a bit of background on him, on the pair of you. I know this must be a dreadful time for you and I'm so sorry, truly. But I was passing by on my way home and thought… Look, you can *help*, Claire. You knew him best. Help us to draw a picture of Robert, what he was like, the kind of father he was. This is a terrible, awful tragedy and a brutal killing of the man you loved. We want you to be able to express to readers just how this has affected you, and your daughter. We know his wife was questioned… that she blames you for the demise of their marriage—'

The comment inflames her. 'Blames me!' Claire gasps in outrage. 'She's a freaking psycho-murdering bitch! Blames *me*! Rob couldn't stand her. He couldn't get away from her. She stalked him, you know, wouldn't leave him alone, couldn't get over the fact that he wanted me and us, and…' Claire realises she's shouting into the intercom and stops herself. 'Look… okay, come up. But five minutes is all you're getting.'

'Believe me,' the voice says, 'five minutes is all I need.'

CHAPTER TWENTY-NINE

The woman at the door looks weirdly familiar, like Claire's seen her somewhere before but she knows this can't be possible. She's just tired. Her brain isn't at its sharpest right now. It's a struggle to think beyond the next few seconds.

'Suppose you'd better come in,' she says, ushering the woman inside. 'Get this over with.'

The woman flashes her a grateful smile.

'Abby, you say your name is?'

'Yes, King – Abby King from the *North London Enquirer*. I'm a crime reporter. I promise this won't take up too much of your time – and thank you, Claire. I know how difficult this must be for you.'

'Do you? Why? Has the love of your life been murdered by his ex-wife too then?' Claire hears how horrible she sounds but she can't help it. She's angry and in pain and exhausted.

'But she wasn't his ex-wife though, was she? They were still married.'

'Only on paper.' Claire directs her to sit down on the sofa, irritated by her remark. 'If we can speak quietly I'd be grateful. I don't want to wake Matty up. She knows something is wrong and hasn't been sleeping well ever since we found out about…' A sob catches in her throat and she comes a little undone. 'Every time I look at her I see his face.'

Abby nods sympathetically at the crib. 'Can I have a little peek?'

'Okay, but please don't wake her. I've only just got her off.'

Claire watches as the woman peers into the Moses basket.

'She's gorgeous,' she whispers, cooing softly at the sleeping baby as she picks up a photograph next to the crib of the three of them together, Robert, Claire and Matty. 'She has her daddy's eyes.'

'Look, I'm sorry to be rude but can we hurry this up?' The woman's presence is already beginning to irritate her jangling nerves. She just wants to go to bed, to sleep and wake up in the morning and find out it's all been one great big nightmare.

'Yes, of course. Like I said, I'm a reporter and I just need a bit of background on the deceased, your relationship to him, how you met, what he was like, stuff like that – as much as you can give me. Obviously, it's a terrible tragedy, a young, first-time father being so savagely, senselessly murdered. Our readers will want to know what he was like, who could've done such a thing to him and why. We're working with the police on this, if that makes you feel any better – well, you know what I mean, more *reassured*. Sometimes we share information, the press and the police, and they feed us things we can print in the hope that we'll trigger something, jog a memory perhaps…'

Claire sighs. Suddenly she realises how she must look, dressed in a dirty dressing gown, unwashed and puffy-eyed from all the relentless crying she's been doing. She hopes the reporter doesn't want a photograph too. 'Please excuse the way I look. The past couple of days have been the worst of my entire life. Rob, he is – he *was* – the love of my life. I can't believe… I just can't believe he's gone.' Claire falters as the pain rises up through her chest once more. 'And to have died in such a horrible, *horrible* way… it's unbearable.'

The reporter is staring at her, nodding earnestly as if she understands her pain. 'I can only imagine. Tell me about him, the love of your life—'

'Rob? Oh God…' She shakes her messy hair. It hasn't had a brush through it for days. 'He was… just so loving, so caring… so romantic.'

'Romantic?' The reporter gives something of a wry smile. 'Really?'

'Yes. He was always buying me gifts. Little things, thoughtful things… things he knew I would love. He once surprised me with a trip to Venice too, before Matty came along – that was pretty amazing, completely unexpected. Just told me to pack a bag one day and whisked us both off…' She loses herself in the memory for a moment, adding, 'I think that was the weekend we conceived her actually.'

'Was it really?' the reporter asks rhetorically, as if she's thinking about something else.

'He was just so… *alive*, you know? Everyone loved him; he walked into a room and lit it up with his smile, his banter, his jokes. You couldn't not love Rob. He was so talented too, such a brilliant photographer. He took pictures of me all the time, said I was perfect model material.'

She thinks she hears the reporter snort, but she must be imagining it. 'I need a coffee; do you want one?' Claire is already halfway to the kitchenette, which is integrated on the other side of the small living room.

'Um, yes, please, if you don't mind. Milk and two sugars, thanks.'

Claire nods wearily as she shuffles around opening cupboards. It's a struggle to even boil the kettle.

'Did he pursue you, or did you pursue him?' the reporter calls out to her from the sofa. 'You knew he was married, after all?'

The coffee jar is empty and she exhales. She has some of those sachet ones somewhere. They'll have to do. She's not in a place to care much.

'Um… well, he pursed me, actually – pretty relentlessly in fact.' Claire's a little taken aback by the direct line of questioning. But she guesses that's reporters for you. *Skin like rhinos, that lot*, as her mum would say.

'It was love at first sight, for both of us. We were destined to be together right from the word go. *Soulmates*, that's what he said.

He wanted to take his last breath with me, die in my arms, old and happy.' The words choke in her larynx.

Now she could have sworn she heard the reporter snigger, but that couldn't possibly have happened, could it? She's sleep-deprived. She's hearing things, imagining them. 'He wanted us to go and live in Cannes, in France. He said he's always loved it and wanted to live there eventually, in a beautiful old château that we could renovate together. It was his dream. Now it will never happen…' Her voice trails off. She feels rage swelling inside her. Outrage and anger like a caged animal. No. It won't. Not for Robert, anyway.

'So, it didn't bother you that he was married?'

Claire is rustling through her cluttered cupboards. They're in dire need of a clear-out but the mere thought of it makes her want to lie down for a week. 'Bother me? Well, I… I… wished he wasn't, if that's what you mean. But he told me that they weren't really *together* together. That they were, you know, what's that word I'm looking for…?'

'Estranged?'

'Yes, that's it, *estranged*. He said from the get-go that he didn't love her and that their marriage was over.'

'Oh, did he? Did he ever mention someone called Kiki?'

The reporter's tone is giving her flutters in her stomach but she's unsure why. 'Kiki? No. Can't say that he did. I knew all about Laurie though.'

'Did he tell you she got pregnant, his wife: *with twins*. His twins?'

Claire is still crashing around in the cupboards, searching through dusty tins of peaches and sweetcorn in a bid to locate those coffee sachets. She knows the bloody things are in there somewhere. And now she's not sure she much likes the direction this conversation is taking. 'Well, yes he did. And believe me I was devastated when I found out.'

'So, he lied to you then, about his wife and their non-existent relationship. Because I'm sure I don't need to tell you this, but it takes two to make a baby, or in this case, babies. So perhaps he wasn't that unhappy after all, Claire, and was just leading you a merry fucking dance. And what would you say if I told you that you weren't the only one. That in fact, you were simply one of very many women he used the same script on time and time again?'

'There they are!' Claire finally locates the sachets underneath an out-of-date jar of piccalilli. 'I'm sorry,' she says. 'What was that you said?' She empties them into mismatching mugs and pours in the boiling water haphazardly, wishing the woman would just fuck off now and let her get some sleep. It was a bad idea to have let her in. She isn't thinking straight.

Handing the reporter the steaming mug she sits opposite her on the battered armchair.

'She had an accident, didn't she? The wife. She was pregnant at the time and lost both the babies. How did that make you feel, Claire? Did you feel sorry for her? Did you feel *guilty*? It was because she discovered the affair, wasn't it, that the accident happened?'

Claire can't be sure but the reporter's tone is beginning to sound accusatory, even slightly menacing. 'I thought you came here to talk about Rob?' she asks, too exhausted to even be angry, though the feeling is there somewhere. She watches the reporter take a sip of her coffee.

'Yes. I'm sorry,' she apologises. 'Forgive me. So, how have you been coping since the tragedy? Who's looking after you? Are you expecting anyone here tonight?' The question is well placed enough not to cause Claire immediate concern.

'My mum was here earlier but she works shifts at the hospital so she can't always be with me. The nightmares… every time I close my eyes I see his face… and imagine all the blood. It's *horrible*. She stabbed him you know, over and over again.'

'Yes, eighteen times. Shocking. So vicious and so tragic… just tragic…'

Claire looks at the woman then, really looks at her properly for the first time. She's got long dark hair and is dressed in a loose-fitting summery dress and ballet slippers. She looks in her mid to late thirties but it's difficult to gauge because she's almost cross-eyed with sleep deprivation. And then it all seems to come to her at once: *how does the reporter know how many times Rob was stabbed?* The police told her it was 'multiple' times but never gave a number and she had definitely not seen anything printed in the news… and why was she asking if she would be home alone tonight?

'Oh my God!' she gasps, but before the terror is able to fully take a hold of her she feels a searing pain as the reporter throws the cup of scalding coffee in her face, catching her completely off guard. Within seconds the woman has pushed her face down onto the sofa and is on top of her. White-hot pain burns into her retinas, rendering her completely blind and paralysed in shock. Her hands are behind her back and they're being tied with something. Terror sweeps through her like fire and she bucks. Something has been put over her head. *Oh no. Noooo!* It's a plastic bag.

Instinctively, she bucks some more, attempting to flip herself up and over, like a fish out of water, but she feels weak against the force of the woman's maniacal grip and is unable to move. Naked fear wraps its tendrils around her now as she struggles to breathe. There's no air and she is completely incapacitated. But her mind is telling her to fight. *Do something! Do something, Claire!*

She feels the sharpness of her assailant's knees digging into the backs of her thighs, pinning her down, and she can't get any purchase on anything, can't move her arms or legs. She must try to breathe. She cannot die like this. *Please dear God, not like this! Matty is asleep. Matty! Oh God! Her baby! Oh God please, no.*

A haze of yellow dots, like tiny stars, comes into her peripheral vision as she feels herself beginning to lose consciousness. But she mustn't, no… she must fight to stay alive, for Matty, for her daughter!

'Stop, please stop, don't do this, pleeeeease… don't kill my baby… pleeeeease, don't kill my baby!' She's not sure if she's screamed the words aloud or if they are just inside her head. She's squirming, twisting her body as hard as she can to push herself up on all fours. If she can just get up on all fours she can kick out. But the woman is a dead weight on top of her, bearing down on her, forcing her further into the sofa. Her lungs feel like they're burning, like someone has set fire to her insides, and all she can see is the yellow markings fading into black in her peripheral vision, like the end of an old video reel.

'I'm sorry, Claire.' The woman's voice sounds faint, like it's coming from afar. Matty is crying… she can hear her baby crying and she wants desperately to comfort her.

'But because of you, you and that bastard child, my life, my future, everything was ruined. So now it's payback time.'

It's the last thing Claire Wright hears.

CHAPTER THIRTY

Call me kinky, but there's something about the sight of Vic Leyton in her scrubs that sort of does it for me. Or perhaps it's just the woman herself? I'm somehow always pleased to see her, even if I know she's the kind of woman who likes nothing more than to be elbow-deep in the guts of the dead.

'Detective Riley,' she greets me cordially with that Mona Lisa smile of hers. It's the kind of smile that suggests she's in on a joke that you don't get, like she knows something you don't, which to be fair, she mostly does. 'Thank you for being so prompt.'

'Well, given your tone of voice on the phone, it sounded quite urgent.'

'Death is always urgent, Detective,' she replies wryly, giving me the once-over. 'You look a little tired, if you don't mind me saying.'

'Your observation skills are second to none, Ms Leyton,' I reply graciously.

'It's *Miss* Leyton, actually,' she corrects me in that enigmatic way of hers as she removes her bloodied latex gloves and goes for a fresh pair, snapping them on to her hands.

I cast my attention to the body on the slab: Robert Mills' body. His white/blue toes are poking out of the end of the green sheet and I can see the hairs on them. *Dead feet*. It still turns my stomach to see a cadaver, no less one with hairy toes. And thank God. It's not something I ever want to get used to.

'Well, Dan,' she says, almost jovially, 'let's start at the beginning.'

'It's as good a place as any.'

Vic pulls back the sheet and I stare down at the corpse on the slab. He's a mass of stitches and wounds, like he's been handmade by a seamstress. The wound on his neck has been stitched shut as best as possible but even after Vic's meticulous attention to detail, you can still detect the brutality of the killer's work on him. The image of his gaping wound flashes up in my mind; the bubbles of yellow sebaceous fat, tissue, bone and gore trying to escape from it. I find myself taking a deep breath.

'The clothes he was wearing, the T-shirt, it showed vertical distribution of blood on it. It was a deep, very deep, obliquely placed, long incision on the front side of the neck. The left end of the injury started below the ear at the upper third of the neck and gradually deepened with the severance of the left carotid artery.'

'His throat was cut,' I say, simplifying it.

Vic gives another enigmatic smile. 'The injury is compatible with a homicidal throat severance made by a right-handed person from behind after restraining the victim's head.'

'Right-handed?'

'Yes. The weapon used was a sharp blade measuring approximately 8 inches long, in keeping with the murder weapon found at the scene.'

I stare at Robert Mills' face. From the neck up he looks perfect, untouched, almost peaceful. He didn't see it coming, did he? I think. It's probably just as well.

'So, the perpetrator sprung him from behind, pulled his head back and sliced his neck open?'

'I'd say so, yes. There are no defensive wounds, no cuts or abrasions to the hands or arms. He didn't try to defend himself, so it's fairly safe to say the killer surprised him. It was fast, and rather brutal. A fair amount of force was used in the moment, but quickly, succinctly. However, he wasn't dead when he fell.'

'No?'

'Dying, yes, but not quite dead.' Vic points to a small wound on Robert Mills' chest, taps it with her finger. 'A stab wound, 2 x 1cm on his chest cavity placed on the front side of the chest near the left anterior auxiliary line downwards, perforating the lower lobe of the left lung and entering the apex of the heart, you see?'

Not got a clue what she's on about. But I nod anyway.

'The lower part of the anterior descending branch of the left coronary artery was severed. I found 2000ml of liquid and clotted blood present in the left thoracic cavity. This is the fatal blow that killed him. Cause of death was haemorrhagic shock.'

'He was stabbed to death, then. Through the heart.'

'Technically yes, although the wound to his neck would have been enough to kill him. It just didn't kill him *first*. The rest of the wounds actually missed most of his vital organs, though this one here punctured his right lung. Judging by the positioning of the wounds the attack was frenzied. Whoever did this wanted to make very sure our friend here was annihilated and never going to get up again.'

'You don't say.'

'So, now we know the cause of death but it's actually the *time* of death that I want to talk about. I think I might have been wrong on my initial examination.'

'You? Wrong? I don't believe you, *Miss* Leyton.'

But Vic isn't interested in my banter anymore. She's fully focused on our friend here.

'Time of death; do you know how it's determined, Detective?'

'Is this a trick question?' I shoot her a sideways glance.

'Isn't every question if you don't know the answer to it?'

Ah, the riddles have begun.

'Rectal thermometer,' Vic says, 'and a temperature reading from the liver.'

'Delightful,' I remark. There's no dignity in death, is there?

'The human body can function for a period of time without oxygen. The brain can survive several minutes without it before the vital organs cease to function completely.'

'Okaaaaay.' As usual, I have no real idea where Vic is headed with this, but I've learned through experience not to press her. I just need to be patient and wait for the punchline.

'As you well know, Detective, it's impossible, unless you're there at the scene, to be completely accurate on actual time of death. And as you also know, I take immense pride in getting as close as I possibly can in determining it.'

'You're nothing if not thorough, Vic,' I say, sensing she might have made a mistake and is cross with herself.

'I did all the preliminaries, photographed the wounds, measured them, sent his clothing off to be examined for fluids and fibres, blood spatter and the rest… I clipped his finger- and toenails and pubic hair—'

I grimace.

Vic smiles evenly. 'Rigor mortis,' she continues. 'It occurs in the face and neck first and then the smaller muscles and works its way down the body. It begins, roughly speaking, two hours after death.'

'So, you got the time of death wrong? Is that what you're saying?'

Vic fixes my eyes with her own and I wonder what she looks like without her glasses on and dressed in her civvies.

'Yes, I think I did,' she says, quickly adding, 'but it was an easy mistake to make.'

'Why is that?' She does like to draw it out, does Vic.

'Normal body temperature is around 98.6 degrees. And our friend here had a body temperature of 81 degrees at the time of death, leading me to establish he had not long been murdered, thus estimating the time of death to be between 8 and 10 p.m.'

'But it wasn't?'

'No,' she says sagely. 'He'd been dead for some time before then. Rigor mortis, the rectal temperature and liver reading suggest he'd suffered the fatal blows a good few hours earlier in fact. Somewhere around 1–2 p.m. more likely.'

I can feel my adrenaline begin to kick into gear. 'Well, well, well. This puts a whole new spin on things.'

'Hmm, I'm sure it does, Detective. Especially since it appears that whoever murdered our Mr Mills here deliberately tried to keep him warm. To make it look like he had been killed later than he had.'

'How do you know this?'

'It can be the only explanation for his body temperature at the scene. Oh, and the fact that the lab came back with some interesting results that seem to support my theory.'

'Which were…?'

'Fibres,' she replies succinctly. 'Blanket fibres.'

'Someone put a blanket over him, to keep him warm?' It's a rhetorical question but Vic nods anyway.

'It certainly would seem that way.'

She raises an eyebrow almost flirtatiously. 'But that's not everything.' Vic's smiling now, enjoying my praise.

'You're killing me, Vic.' I can't stop with the terrible puns; she brings it out in me.

'We found traces of semen on his underwear and his skin. Fresh traces, plus some unknown DNA. Mr Mills here had sex just before he died.'

My adrenaline is off the scale now and I'm shifting from foot to foot.

'So, Detective Riley, I'm pretty sure I don't need to tell *you* this but my money is on the fact that whoever he had the pleasure with in the moment leading up to his death is likely to have been his killer.'

I almost want to kiss her. 'You're a legend, do you know that, Miss Leyton? An actual living, breathing legend.'

She smiles, almost bashfully I think, which tickles me.

'So…' I begin to piece Robert Mills' final moments together. 'Robert Mills arrived at his house earlier in the day, much earlier than we first thought. He had sex at some point, then he was murdered, and his body was deliberately kept warm to make it appear that the time of death was much later.'

I smile to myself. Woods isn't gonna like this. Or Delaney. Because if what Vic is telling me is fact, then Laurie Mills was having her hair blow-dried at the time of her husband's murder.

'You're sure that the time of death was between 1 and 2 p.m. Vic? I mean, *absolutely*?'

Vic sighs as if my questioning offends her. 'I'll go one better, Detective,' she says, 'and say that time of death was in fact 1.39 p.m. exactly.'

'Well, that is exact,' I reply, intrigued. This is what she's been building up to.

'The stage of rigor mortis in the body, the rectal temperature and liver readings… Oh!' she says, as if she's suddenly remembered something. She goes over to a table, picks something up, 'And this.'

It's a watch. A Rolex no less. The face is smashed.

'It was still on his wrist when he died. No doubt the face broke when he fell to the floor. Look at the time on it.'

It reads 1.39 p.m.

I look at Vic Leyton and I can't stop the grin from broadening on my face.

'Now I really *am* going to kiss you!' I say aloud.

CHAPTER THIRTY-ONE

The CCTV from Cedar Close on the day and night of the murder has thrown up the princely sum of sweet FA. Apparently, the Lewises' CCTV wasn't working and those houses where CCTV was operational were positioned in such a way as to be unable to get a direct line of vision to the Millses' property. *Brilliant.* There is, however, a bit of development on the power cut.

'The switch tripped,' the electrician informs me in a throaty cockney accent, seemingly thrilled to be able to impart his expertise and contribute to a murder enquiry. 'Although it's possible it tripped itself out, it's unlikely. Nuffink wrong with the electrics in the gaff – not long been rewired by the looks of it. Someone would've had to have manually gone to the box and flipped the switch.'

'So, there's no way of knowing if it tripped itself or if someone tripped it manually?'

'Sorry, boss,' the sparky says. 'I can't say for sure either way.'

Double brilliant. The results on the knife have come back as suspected, and no doubt in Delaney's case, as hoped. Laurie Mills' dabs were found on it, alongside some of her blood and the victim's.

I impart the good news to Woods after he collars me on my way out. There's only so many times I can limbo past his office and get away with it.

Woods appears happy as I give him the forensic feedback. 'This is good news, isn't it, Riley? That'll be enough to charge the wife now. Motive, fingerprints… Her alibi isn't even watertight. Get her in again, see if you can get a confession and get the job done.'

I haven't told him about Vic Leyton's shocker yet; I've saved the best till last. 'Sir, I think you should know that there's been some new developments.'

'Developments?' Woods looks up from his desk sharply. I can tell he doesn't like the sound of that.

'Time of death,' I explain. 'Initially it was thought that it occurred somewhere between 8 and 10 p.m., given the body temperature at the scene.'

Woods has fixed me with a stoic glare. He knows that I know he isn't going to like this because it will mean that I'm right and that this case is more complex than he'd like it to be. I find it perplexing, almost amusing, that a man with his service history appears to get cross when a case doesn't quite pan out how he wants it to. He wants Laurie Mills to be the killer because that makes things a whole lot easier, for him at least. It wraps things up quickly. It's a fast result. It's numbers on paper. It's good for business. 'Only it transpires that Vic Leyton was mistaken.'

'Vic Leyton doesn't make mistakes,' he snaps dismissively, as if I'm deliberately trying to throw a spanner in the works.

'It was an easy one to make, apparently. Because whoever killed our Mr Mills attempted to keep the body warm. They found blanket fibres on him, sir. After the full autopsy, it was determined that ETD was in fact more like between 1 and 2 p.m. The time on the watch that was found on his body was recorded as 1.39 p.m.'

Woods looks positively vexed now, as if I have really gone and pissed on his fireworks.

'It smashed when he fell, most likely. I'm pretty sure it's safe to assume that's the time it stopped working.'

'So, what does this mean exactly?'

I cough into my fist, clear my throat. 'It means, sir, that at the time of death, Laurie Mills was on her way to a hair appointment at a salon called Harrisons on the high street and that there are witnesses, plus CCTV, to corroborate this.'

'Bloody hell.' He rubs his temples with a thumb and forefinger. 'Are you absolutely sure, Riley?'

I open my palms. 'I'm not the expert, sir. Vic Leyton is and—' I cough again, though largely for effect, adding, 'as you've just said, Vic Leyton doesn't make mistakes.'

Woods' eyes narrow a touch. He looks like he wants to combust. 'Bloody brilliant. I was hoping to give the Super some good news as well.'

'I'm sorry, sir,' I say, adding, 'there's something else.'

'Go on,' Woods sighs.

'Semen.'

'Semen?'

'Yes. They found semen on Mills' body, and some other as-yet-unknown DNA. It's off for testing, sir. Looks like Mr Mills engaged in some kind of sexual activity closely preceding his death.'

'The wife?'

I shrug. 'The results will tell us if it was, sir. But I'm pretty sure that whoever Robert Mills had the pleasure with is the person we're looking for.'

'Definitely a woman then?'

'Most likely,' I say. 'Although it appears Mr Mills was more of a quantity rather than quality kind of man. We're following up all other leads, all lines of enquiry.'

'What other bloody leads are there, Riley?' The veins in Woods' neck are protruding slightly and I feel a flutter of guilt that perhaps somewhat childishly I can't help getting off on his discomfort.

'Robert Mills wasn't the faithful sort,' I say, 'and that's an understatement. There were more aside from the mistress. There's the possibility of a husband, a jealous boyfriend, even a spurned lover… We will be speaking with Laurie Mills again, of course.'

He rubs his chin thoughtfully. 'I still think the wife is in on this somehow, Riley. You're not the only one who possesses this "magical" intuition you know. I can feel it.'

He's upset. Oh dear.

'And I don't want you taking Davis when you speak with the wife. Go with Delaney.'

'But I—'

'You're taking Martin and that's that. He's your number two, Riley – treat him as such. You might find he responds better to you if you do.'

If I was a betting man I'd put money on the fact that Delaney has been in here whingeing to Woods about me. He's just the sort. A snitch.

'Yes, well, he could be helpful, I suppose,' I say, quietly adding, 'especially on understanding the mind of a womaniser.'

The narrow eyes are back. 'What was that, Riley?'

'Nothing. Nothing, sir.'

'Don't let things get personal, Riley. Remember what happened last time.'

'It's okay, sir,' I reassure him. 'Delaney's not my type.'

Woods shoots me a look of contempt. 'You know what I mean, Riley – don't try to be clever.'

'I never try, sir. It just comes naturally.'

'The wife is the key to all of this somehow. So go and unpick some locks.'

Great analogy, I think. But I don't say it. I can see he's not in the mood and respectively I'm in no mood for his sharp side.

'Pick some locks... yes, sir.' I suddenly catch the time on Woods' large wall clock. It's 1.20 p.m. I said I'd meet Fi for a drink in the Hart and I'm already late. *Shit*.

CHAPTER THIRTY-TWO

Kiki – August 1996

'Please, please,' she's begging him as they attempt to pull her into the car, 'don't let them do this, Bertie. Don't let them take me away, please!'

'Get in the car, you little slut!' Her mother attempts to push her into the back of the vehicle but she struggles.

'Fuck you, you fucking bitch!' she screams at her. 'Get your hands off me.'

'You're the devil's work, my girl, from conception, born wicked and evil. Well, you won't be sinning under my roof any longer, you filthy whore! Get in the car!'

But she wouldn't. She wouldn't be sent to some boarding school run by nuns out in the middle of nowhere, hundreds of miles away from the only person she had ever loved, or been loved by.

'You can separate us but you'll never keep us apart! Never!' she spits in her mother's face. She looks up towards the window at Bertie with pleading eyes.

'It's okay, kiddo,' he calls down to her. 'It's all going to be okay.'

He had promised her that he would be back for her, that once the dust had settled he would come and get her out of there, that they would find a place together, be together. 'All the time you're underage, I can't do anything,' he'd said. 'But the day you turn sixteen is the day I will be waiting for you outside that school with the engine of my sports car running.'

Kiki had laughed through her tears. What would she do without her blanket, without Bertie? She'd be alone again and she was scared.

'Promise me,' she screams back. 'Promise me you'll come for me.'

'What on earth is going on out there?' the girl behind him asks, moving towards the window. 'Some kind of domestic?'

'It's nothing,' he explains, playfully pushing her back down onto the bed. 'My mum's going to be gone a while,' he says, raising an eyebrow, which she reciprocates. 'She's taking my sister to her new school… we've got the afternoon to ourselves.'

'Hmm, what will we do?' the girl asks provocatively. Her parents aren't expecting her back for a good few hours. She'd told them she was going to the lido with a group of girlfriends. They'd have had a complete fit if they knew she was here alone, with a boy.

He smirks. 'I'm sure we'll come up with something.'

'She seems upset, your sister—'

He smiles. 'Don't worry about her—'

Kiki calls his name out again as her mother physically forces her inside the vehicle.

'Please! Please! No! Bertie!'

He peers out of the window, watching as she is physically restrained and pushed into the car, fighting and screaming like a tiger. The girl, Justine, peers out of the window to have a look too.

'Don't let them see you!' he hisses at her and she jumps.

'Alright! Keep your wig on, mate!'

He looks down at her from the window, blows her a kiss and mouths the words, 'I love you, Kiki.'

'I love you too,' she mouths back to him as the car screeches away.

CHAPTER THIRTY-THREE

I burst through the doors of the White Hart like I'm Clint Eastwood in a western and scan the pub for Fiona. It's 1.45 p.m. I breathe a sigh of relief when I see her towards the back of the pub. She's standing, gathering her belongings and throwing her bag over her shoulder ready to leave.

'Fi!' I call out to her as I make my way over, my face a mask of apology. At least I hope it is. 'Fi, I am so sorry.' I shake my head. 'Woods collared me just as I was about to leave.'

She wants to look cross but doesn't quite get there.

'Forgive me? Let me get you a drink, please. Glass of red, yeah? Merlot.'

She stalls for a couple of seconds, which feel longer, and then takes her bag off her shoulder. 'Oh, go on then,' she acquiesces, retaking her seat. 'But I haven't got long now.'

I order two large glasses of red from the bar and hurriedly bring them back to the table. Seeing Fi in close proximity again, I wonder what on earth I've been thinking. I must need my head examining. She looks lovely. I think she may have done something new to her hair, although I'm not stupid enough to ask. It's good to see her again.

'I thought I'd been ghosted, Dan,' she says, as I touch the rim of my glass with hers.

'Ghosted? Is that some kind of street-speak I'm not down with?'

She cocks her head to one side. 'I thought you'd disappeared on me. Didn't have you down as the love 'em and leave 'em type.'

I have the good grace to feel ashamed and I take another large sip of red. 'Listen, Fi, it's not…'

'Oh God! Please don't say "it's not you, it's me"! Spare me that, Dan, at least!' She's still smiling.

'No! No… I was going to say…' Actually, I have no idea what I was going to say. I haven't had time to think about it. I decide upon the truth, but even then, I'm not entirely sure what that is now that I'm sitting opposite her. 'Look, I'm sorry I haven't been in touch, okay. After our… after that night together – which was lovely by the way – I just freaked out a bit. It's been a while, you know, since Rachel and… well, I didn't want you to think… I didn't… I don't…' I can hear myself stammering and tripping over my words like a schoolboy and I want to stamp on my own foot. 'Well, look anyway. I'm sorry. I should have contacted you. I was always going to but then the Mills case came up.'

True to her nature I see her ears prick up. I knew that mentioning the case would pique Fi's interest and it was a slightly calculated move on my part. I know, I know, don't judge me. It surprises me when she takes hold of my hand. I get a waft of her perfume as she does; it's a spicy, musky scent indicative of her.

'There's really no need to apologise, Dan,' she says with gentle earnest. Her face is closer to mine now. 'It was a beautiful night, really lovely. I will never forget it. And I was honoured that it was me – you know, the first woman since Rachel. I understand, Dan, honestly. We both know what it was, two friends who needed each other just for the night. I knew you weren't looking for anything more and neither was I. I wasn't waiting on a marriage proposal, but, well, a phone call or a text would've been nice. It's fine, really. I just hope it hasn't spoilt our friendship, that's all.'

Although these are exactly the same sentiments as my own, I suddenly feel a little, well, put out, I suppose, that Fi doesn't seem to want to take anything further, or isn't even interested in a repeat performance by the sounds of things. And there I was, cocky bastard, worrying about what to say, how to say it and trying to work out how I feel, when all the time she had me down as a one-night stand anyway!

'Right… yes… well, I feel the same, exactly.'

Fi pats my hand and takes a sip of wine. 'Well, now we've got that out of the way,' she says, moving swiftly on, 'talk to me about the Mills case.'

I'm a little stunned. Now that she's told me she doesn't want anything more, I kind of feel like maybe I *do*. Or maybe I just want her to want something more and feel a bit rejected. I subconsciously rub my head. I'm not used to all this, second-guessing a woman. It had been so straightforward with Rach, no ambiguity: she liked me, she wanted me; I liked her, I wanted her. The second we slept together it was fireworks and all systems go, no looking back, no discussion. The thought that I may never again feel that way with a woman, nor any woman with me by the sounds of things, makes me feel a bit depressed. But I guess once you've had perfection it's difficult to replicate it. Fiona will never be Rachel. No one will be.

Just one night. Fi's words resound in my head.

'Ah, so that's why you held on for me, is it?'

She gives me a look of mock disapproval. 'C'mon, Dan. You know me better than that.'

Well, I thought I did. But now I'm not sure what I know, or what's what.

'It sounds particularly gruesome,' Fi says, pulling a face. 'There'd be a lot less men in the world if every wife slit their cheating husband's throat. And you're sure the wife's the only one in the frame?'

'Well, this pub would probably be empty for starters,' I say, and she laughs. 'But actually it's not quite as cut and dried as you might think. Pardon the pun.'

'Oh?' Fi's eyes are shining. *Now* she wants to know me. I realise I'm being stupid and childish and I feel cross with myself. She's a journalist. Of course she wants to know.

'Yes, well, you also know *me* better than that, Fiona,' I say. 'I can't give too much away at this stage.'

She looks visibly disappointed. Much more so than she did at the thought of never going to bed with me again.

'We ran the story a couple of days ago,' she says. 'Seemed like a cut and dry to me at first. Cheating husband, jealous wife out for revenge. You released her without charge though? She won't talk to us. Won't say a word. That friend of hers, Monica Lewis, has made sure our lot can't get within ten feet of her.'

'She has a pretty cast-iron alibi at the time of death,' I say, candidly.

'Really, that's interesting.'

'Yes. And it's also not public information. Not yet anyway.'

'Okay. Well, quid pro quo, Detective. You might be interested in speaking to a Leanna George though.'

'The name rings a bell.'

'She came to us after we ran the story and did an interview with the mistress – Claire Wright, is it?'

'Yes, Wright, that's her name.'

Fi smiles. 'Well, we're running Leanna's story tomorrow.'

'Her story? She came to the press?'

'She sure did. Leanna George was another of Robert Mills' mistresses. Or at least she was for a time. He was certainly a busy boy, wasn't he? Well, she has plenty to say about your "victim", put it that way. Seems he wasn't entirely everything he appeared to be.'

I'm intrigued. 'You think she's a potential suspect?'

Fi shrugs. 'Seems unlikely his killer would come directly to us.'

'It's not unheard of,' I say. 'You know that.'

She shakes her head. 'No. This was to set the record straight,' she explains. 'After we ran the initial story, we did a follow-up, got some quotes from various colleagues and friends and whatnot. They painted a picture of Robert Mills as this fun-loving, cool, creative type who everybody thought highly of. You know, a hard-working, easy-going, likeable guy whose life fell apart after his wife lost their babies in a tragic accident and then fell into the arms of another woman to cope with the pain.'

'That's not chronologically correct,' I say. 'His wife lost the babies *when* she discovered he'd fallen into the arms of another woman.'

Fi gives a knowing nod. 'Well, Leanna George puts the cat among the pigeons. The picture she paints is of a serial cheat and pathological liar. She claims Robert Mills was a misogynistic abuser, with a particularly vicious, vengeful streak in him. Reckons he had it coming in spades.'

'Does she now?' This is interesting because in my experience, people don't tend to speak ill of the dead, even if the deceased was a complete bastard when they were living. At least not so soon after they've been savagely murdered, and certainly not publicly, to the press no less. It never reflects well. So Leanna George clearly has a serious cross to bear, one she's prepared to go out on a limb over. I need to speak to her. Urgently.

'You got a number?' I throw back the last of my wine. Fi has hardly touched hers.

'Sure do!' She smiles broadly, retrieving a pen from her handbag. She writes it down on the edge of a beer mat on the sticky pub table and goes to hand it to me, pulling it back last minute. 'You can have it on one condition,' she says.

'Name it.'

'Just make sure you don't lose mine, yeah?' And then she leans forward and kisses me fully and deeply on the mouth.

CHAPTER THIRTY-FOUR

Women – I don't suppose I'll ever fully understand them. With the exception of one maybe. *The only one.*

The words battle, losing and fighting spring to mind, Danny Boy! I hear my dad's voice, full of resignation, in my head. *I spent thirty-odd years trying to understand your mother and never quite got there. She remained forever an enigma.* I smile and remind myself to contact the old boy. It's my birthday in a couple of days' time. Maybe I'll take him out for a drink. I know that, like me, he gets lonely sometimes, not that either of us ever admits as much. *All the lonely people, where do they all come from?*

If I hadn't felt confused about my feelings before my encounter with Fi then I sure as hell do now. The ego is a funny old thing. Mine took a bit of a knock today when she'd said in no uncertain terms that our night of passion wouldn't be repeated. Maybe she doesn't fancy me. Maybe she did fancy me and then we had sex and now she doesn't, which is even worse. Was I a let-down in the sack? Why doesn't she want a repeat performance? Perhaps I was pretending to myself that I didn't really like her as much as I do. I realise now that I've been so consumed with my own thoughts and feelings that actually I hadn't really considered hers much at all. *What a prick.* But then she kissed me full on the mouth, sensually, and told me not to lose her number. Not that I was planning to. And I know she isn't planning to lose mine because I'm a valuable source. Although this time round the relationship – whatever it is – has proved to be mutually beneficial because I'm on my way to pay Leanna George a visit. I've asked Davis to meet me at her address. Woods – and Delaney for that matter – can poke it.

'I was wondering when you lot were going to turn up,' Leanna George greets Davis and I on her doorstep wearing the tiniest pair of shorts I've ever seen and a cropped T-shirt that has 'Not Your Bae' emblazoned across the front.

'That obvious, eh?' I ask.

She smiles, exposing a set of ice-white and no doubt expensive veneers. 'You could say that. Come in.'

Leanna George is, I think, what most red-blooded males would call a complete belter. She's petite, maybe 5ft 2in, with a killer set of curves and long, wavy blonde hair that falls to her tiny waist. A body built for sin springs to mind.

'You'll have to excuse me,' she says in a thick Geordie accent, 'I've just come from the gym.'

Davis and I exchange a look. I've half a mind to ask her which one.

'I'm Detective Riley and this is DS Davis.'

'You're here about the article, aren't you? To talk about *him*?'

'If by him you mean Robert Mills, then yes, Miss George, we are.'

'Better sit down then, pet,' she says. She's the friendly sort. Doesn't seem at all perturbed by our presence, which is quite refreshing. Her apartment is small, compact, but very trendy with white wooden floors and colourful soft furnishings. She has an Andy Warhol picture hanging above a small fireplace and antique mirrors displayed in a collective array on a feature wall, suggesting she's creative.

'I met Rob when I was shooting for a magazine,' Leanna explains. 'I'm a model and actress, well sometimes, you know.'

I wonder what kind of actress she means.

Davis starts taking notes.

'It was when I came down to London from Newcastle, where I'm from, back in 2015 for a photo shoot. It was for a lad's mag called *Geez* – you know it?'

'Can't say I do.'

She gives me the once-over with a half-smile. 'No. Don't suppose you would. Well it's a "tits 'n' arse" title. Glamour dressed up with a bit of low-grade journalism thrown in to make it more palatable.'

Full marks for honesty, I'll give her that.

'But a job's a job, like, and the money was mint if I remember. Though I wish I'd never said yes to it now. No amount of money could compensate for what that motherfucker put me through.'

She smiles unapologetically. 'So, am I a suspect?'

'Well, we've been informed that you were less than complimentary about the deceased. We will need to ask you what you were doing on the day Robert Mills was murdered, Leanna.' Davis says this with just the right amount of authority and friendliness. That's why she's so good at her job.

'Ask away, pet. I was working as an extra all day from 10 a.m. til gone midnight at Shepperton Studios. New Danny Boyle film. There's probably at least 500 people who can corroborate it. I can give you me agent's number. You can check with the production crew. I was there all day and all night.'

She picks her phone up from the low coffee table and scrolls through it, handing it to Davis. 'There's me agent's number. She'll give you the details to check.'

Davis jots the number down.

'So, tell me, Leanna – what was your connection to Robert Mills?'

'I was his on/off girlfriend for nearly four years. We were in a relationship, if you could call it that.' The bitterness in her tone is evident.

Four years.

'I see. How did the relationship begin?'

'Well, like I said to the press, we met in 2015, on a photo shoot, and after that he pursued me relentlessly.'

'He came on to you at a photo shoot?'

Leanna George laughs loudly. It's a raucous laugh. Infectious. 'You could say that! That man set his sights on me. He saw me, he wanted me, he was going to have me – end of story, like. I had a boyfriend at the time too – well, he was me fiancé actually, Rick. Not that this bothered him. In fact, I think it made me even more of a challenge actually.' She drifts off for a second, as if reminiscing. 'He was lovely was Rick, bit boring sometimes, like, but nice and... *normal*.' Leanna sighs.

'What happened, Leanna?'

Her demeanour changes a little then and her wide smile fades. She pulls her feet up underneath her and I try not to be distracted by her slim, tanned bare legs.

'It started off like something out of a romance novel. Honestly, I'd never before in me life met a bloke so... well, amazing I suppose, or someone so into me, someone who "got" me like he did. Or so I thought. It was a match made in heaven... seemed too good to be true. And that's because it was.' She coils a strand of blonde hair around her finger, inspects the ends. 'He was so... attentive. So funny, kind, sexy, caring, talented *and* good-looking. And oh my God, the sex was mind-blowing. I mean, *literally.* He was *very* eager to please, like. Spent hours, you know...' She glances down at her lower body. I get the idea. 'Anyways, he knew how to please a woman, put it that way. Now I realise it was because he'd had a hell of a lot of practice.'

She looks almost nostalgic for a moment. 'He rang me at least five times a day; sometimes we'd be on the phone for hours on end. There were countless texts and pictures. We were in constant contact. I fell for him, for his game, big time; before I knew what was happening, he had me on the hook and he took over me life.

I mean, I've been with a few blokes in me time but this was different. This was the real deal. He was everything I'd been waiting for, you know. He told me he loved me a couple of weeks into our "relationship", which I know now was a huge red flag but it was just so… so intoxicating – *he* was so intoxicating.'

'I was on too much of a high to see what was *really* going on. He said that he'd never felt this way about anyone ever before, reckoned I'd been sent to him by the angels, that I was the woman he'd been waiting for his entire life.' Leanna snorts derisively. 'He wanted to marry me, build a life with me, have a future together. He wanted me to have his babies… I can show you all the messages if you like, all the texts and emails, although maybe not all of the pictures.' She smiles coyly. 'He would text me first thing in the morning, always, telling me I was beautiful, how much he missed me, how he couldn't wait to see me… kisses and hearts and all of that. How he was the luckiest man on the planet, how he was so in love with me… it was' – she pauses, as if searching for the correct word – 'heady stuff. I mean, I've had attention from men all me life. But this was on another level. This was like coming home, you know, finding your soulmate.'

Ah, my Rach.

'Within a month of meeting Rob,' she resumes, a little wearier, as if talking about it takes it out of her, 'he was begging me to leave Rick and come to London and live with him. Start a new life together. And so I did. I upped sticks and went, left me family, left Rick, left me friends and everything I knew, like a lamb to the slaughter.' She looks down at her feet as though she's ashamed. 'Rick was devastated, poor bastard. I just… well, I just fell so hard for Robert's bullshit that I couldn't see the forest for the trees, you know? Greener grass and all of that I suppose. But it was more than that really. I truly loved him, deeply. Well, I thought I loved the fake person he'd created to suck me into his twisted web of deceit and lies. I'd never felt like that before, not with anyone. Do you understand that feeling, Detective, where you love someone so much you literally feel like you're walking on air?'

Leanna looks up at me with these big sad blue eyes and I feel a pang of empathy for her. Even her beauty couldn't save her by the sounds of things.

'Yes,' I say. 'I really do, Leanna.'

She smiles then, wistfully. 'It's a beautiful feeling. A once, if you're lucky, in this lifetime feeling. I wasn't going to let it pass me by, so I grabbed the chance with both hands. I was so lovesick that I missed all the red flags, or maybe I just didn't want to see them because the feeling, the high I was on, was just so intense. But in hindsight they were definitely there, from the very beginning in fact.'

'Go on.'

'Do you mind if I smoke?' she asks, taking a Marlboro from the packet on the coffee table. 'It stresses me out talking about him, makes me want a glass of wine too. Don't suppose you guys can join me in one, can you…?'

I shake my head, regrettably, because something tells me Leanna George is fundamentally a decent person. Beneath her obvious assets and her brash exterior, she appears to be intelligent and sensitive.

She disappears into the kitchen and returns with a glass of something fizzy. 'I know it's a little early in the day, like, but fuck it. People need to know what that man was *really* like.'

I nod, lean forward and light her cigarette for her. 'What was he really like, Leanna?'

She blows smoke through her thick, pursed lips and looks at Davis, almost in solidarity. 'He was a fake, a con man. A cardboard fucking cut-out of a person with no soul whatsoever. It was all lies, right off the bat, like. Not a word of truth came out of that bastard's mouth from the second I met him. I meant nothing to him, let alone being his fucking soulmate. I was an object, not a person. Used, abused then discarded, over and over again. Sent by the angels me arse,' she scoffs, sipping her wine. 'More like straight from the bowels of hell.'

Leanna looks right at me. 'Robert Mills was just a predator, a sexual predator, out for the kill. He got his kicks in the thrill of the chase, by getting women to fall in love with him, change their lives for him, like I did; he persuaded women to sacrifice everything in a bid to bolster his pathetic ego. That man treated me like an appliance and when I became defective, he simply threw me on the scrapheap and went to another one he'd been fine-tuning on the sly.' She gulps back some wine, blows her smoke purposefully through her glossy lips.

'He never told me he was married, of course. Or that he had a mistress, *another* one, or about the baby they had together, or his wife's accident, or about the countless others. Didn't have a clue, like. He told me, when we met, that he was "happily single". Said he'd been divorced for over a year and that his wife was a psycho, that she stalked him and had tried to ruin his life. He said *she* had cheated on *him* and that she was the "lowest of the low". Those were his words. I took him at face value. Why wouldn't I? I had no reason not to believe him – he was so sincere, seemed so genuine. So I got this apartment. Cost me a fortune, like. The rent on this place could get me a four-bed detached house in Gateshead.'

'When did the relationship end?'

She rolls her eyes. 'Never properly did really. Never properly got started either. I *thought* it was a relationship. But it was nothing like a real one, a proper two-way thing. It was push, pull, here today, gone tomorrow, back again, in, out... mind-fuckery off the Richter scale. Almost sent me to the nuthouse after a while, I tell you. But he never quite closed the door. Never gave me that closure, you know. Always left a carrot dangling. He was still sending me the odd text here and there two days before he was murdered, asking me if I was okay, saying he missed me. Complete and utter gash, all of it. He didn't give a shit.'

'Why did you stay, in London I mean? Didn't you think about going back to Newcastle once you found out about the wife, the affairs—'

Leanna stubs her cigarette out in an ashtray that has 'Las Vegas' written on the side in pink letters. 'Well, that's just it, Detective. I only found out about the others when he died, when I read about it in the press. I mean, I had me suspicions – I knew there was something seriously off, but I had no idea he was leading a triple life, at least… Besides, there's more work down here, you know. Rob used that sweetener to lure me down here in the beginning. Said he'd get me on to all these big shoots and that, but it never happened. I had to do it all on me own. He was here a lot of the time though; at one point he was using this place as a shag palace. I had no reason to be mistrustful of him at first. Trust me when I say this man was extremely good at what he did. He was a pathological liar and a master manipulator. I took him on his word because who lies about that stuff? Who lies about loving someone, stands back and watches them uproot themselves, leave a relationship, *change their whole life for them?* Who has a wife and a mistress and another mistress and no doubt many more? Who could be so immoral?'

Robert Mills by the sounds of things.

'Did Robert abuse you, Leanna?' Davis asks gently.

'Psychologically, yes. It happened slowly. In fact, looking back, it was so subtle I didn't realise I was in hell until the flames were already licking me feet, if you know what I mean. His rages came from nowhere. I was shocked the first few times. Devastated and shocked. One minute he was everything I'd ever dreamt of, like, and then the next… he became this vicious monster who I could never please. He was a real Jekyll and Hyde.'

'Was he violent, ever?' Davis looks up from her notepad.

Leanna shakes her head. 'Never physically, although the threat of it was there when he got into one of his rages over nothing.

He was super paranoid. Paranoid *I* was cheating on *him*. He had serious, and I mean *serious*, insecurity and trust issues. Didn't matter how much I tried to convince him otherwise, or told him I loved him and how good-looking he was and how lucky I felt to have met him. It was like trying to fill a bucket with holes in it. I realise now, all the accusations, they were because he was the one doing the cheating and lying.'

'They call it projection.' I nod, adding, 'The psychologists.'

'Well, whatever they fucking call it, like, it's batshit-crazy stuff. I was blindsided by it. Confused, you know. How he could go from being this beautiful man into a raging maniac in such a short space of time?'

'Because he was only ever a monster to begin with,' Davis chips in.

'Exactly,' Leanna shoots back. 'It was like he'd brainwashed me somehow. Turned me into this slave who did everything I could to please him, anything not to upset him. Keep Mr Hyde at bay. I'm no pushover, Detective,' she says and I believe her. 'I might look like a dumb blonde with big tits but I've got a first in English Literature and I'm a member of Mensa. I knew exactly who I was before I met him and where I was going… by the time he'd finished with me I didn't recognise meself.'

'But you didn't leave?' Davis says this carefully, non-accusatory.

Leanna sighs deeply again.

'That's the thing. Eventually, after a while, before I really knew it, he had control of me. He could be a complete angel, like he was at the beginning. That was what kept me there. That magical feeling he'd given me at the start, in that golden honeymoon period that he manufactured to lure his victims in. I was forever working to recapture it, never really knowing just what the fuck I'd done wrong. But just as everything would settle down and I'd start to feel comfortable again, the devil would reappear. That man accused me of all sorts, things I've never been accused of before.

Things I know I'm not. He told me I had jealousy issues, that *I* was paranoid, that *I* had a short temper, that people found me overbearing, that I had mental-health issues… He could create an argument out of fresh air, like… a shower curtain – once he got upset because a few of the hooks came off and…' Leanna closes her eyes tightly.

Reliving these memories is clearly painful for her.

'Everything he'd said he loved about me in the beginning was suddenly everything he despised. And I mean *despised*. I slept with men for money. I danced on tables because I was a whore. I still wanted Rick even though I had left him to be with Robert, and he was long gone. He would question me mercilessly: where was I going, who was I seeing, did I want to fuck other men, did I work out down the gym to attract them, did I dress to get attention from blokes? It was exhausting, always defending meself for no reason, justifying meself; it kept me forever on the back foot, second-guessing meself, working hard to regain his affection, his attention. He'd keep me up all night sometimes, wouldn't let me sleep. If he knew I had an important shoot the next day, he would deliberately start a fight and sabotage it. Yet he was convinced, *convinced* I was the one trying to ruin *his* career. He tortured me emotionally until I didn't know which way was up. I lost meself completely. The same circular argument that could never be resolved, over and over again…'

I feel exhausted just listening to this. But Leanna is helping me to understand. To get a clearer picture of who Robert Mills really was. Someone wanted that man dead. And if she's telling the truth, which I think she is, then it's pretty easy to understand why.

Cut and dry my arse, Woods.

CHAPTER THIRTY-FIVE

'What do you make of that, Gov?' Davis asks as we leave Leanna George's apartment. 'He was certainly spinning a lot of plates in the air at one time. I mean, how does someone do that? Convince all those women… have a wife and at least two other relationships on the go, plus a child and a job and…'

I wonder if now is a good time to ask Davis if she's okay – how things are at home and the other business. But I decide against it. I'm guessing she'll reach out to me again when she's ready.

'I don't think we're dealing with your common or garden philanderer here, Davis. This man was an abuser. Possibly sociopathic, or narcissistic, or both.'

I think about Laurie Mills. If four years on and off with Robert Mills almost destroyed an effervescent, vivacious and intelligent woman like Leanna George, then I can only imagine what almost eighteen years has done to her.

'So, which one of them did him in then, boss?'

'If I knew that, Davis, I wouldn't currently be in Woods' bad books.'

'You're always in Woods' bad books,' she says with a laugh as her phone rings.

I zone out as Davis talks. I need to think. I'm missing something and I don't yet know what it is. No one saw anything on the day of the murder and no one heard anything. There's no CCTV, no witnesses, nothing. The circumstantial evidence all points to Laurie Mills – she has the biggest motive, yet her alibi is sound enough. The blanket, keeping the body warm, the writing on the mirror… This was a calculated murder and Laurie Mills, well, she just doesn't match the profile of a premeditated cold-blooded killer.

I need to pay her therapist a visit, get some background on her state of mind. Murray has given me a name, Dr Wells, a psychotherapist at a clinic in Islington, who specialises in trauma. But first I think I need to talk to Laurie again in person. Much as it galls me to agree with the old git, I think Woods is right about one thing: somehow Laurie Mills is the key to all of this.

'We're heading over to Cedar Close,' I say, dropping down a gear. 'We need to talk to Laurie Mills.'

'Gov…' The gravitas in Davis's voice causes me to take my eyes off the road for a second and glance sideways at her.

'What is it, Davis?' I ask. The look on her face is making me nervous…

'It's Claire Wright, boss.' Her voice sounds tight.

'What about Claire Wright?' I can feel my sphincter muscle contract. This does not sound like it's going to be good. 'Davis… what about her?'

Davis looks at me in horror and puts her hand over her mouth. Then she bursts into tears.

CHAPTER THIRTY-SIX

Laurie wakes with a start, gasping for breath. She can tell by the low light that's seeping through the curtains that it's early and she lies back down onto the pillow, her breathing shallow and laboured. She'd been dreaming of Robert again. Dreaming of seeing him in the en suite, his head practically severed from his neck, the open wound oozing and glistening with blood and bone and tissue matter, like she's taken an axe to him. She sees the look on his face, even when she's asleep. His eyes, those eyes she had looked into a million times before, those beautiful, treacherous, deceitful eyes. They look back at her in shock and terror and surprise. And maybe something else, something else she can't quite put her finger on. What was it? Familiarity… yes, familiarity. *As if he knew.*

They say that your eyes are the windows to your soul and in that moment, the moment she'd awoken and found him there, she'd seen into them as though for the very first time in all the years they had known each other. Robert had sold his soul to the devil long ago, and yet in that moment of his death she felt sure she had seen a glimmer, a last glimpse of the man she had met in the very beginning all those years ago…

Laurie rolls over onto her side. She's unsure if she's dreamt it, but a vision has appeared in her mind. One where she's slumped over the kitchen table, drunk, wasted on vodka and Prosecco and grief. She feels the sensation of being lifted up, carried in someone's arms and taken up the stairs; at one point her shins bash against the bannisters and she thinks she can remember the sharp pain as her thin bones make contact with the wood. It's been bothering her; how she ended up in the guest bedroom. She has no recollection of walking upstairs. What if someone had carried her up there, in her booze- and pill-induced catatonic state? That would explain the bruises too. Is she just imagining it because her brain needs to rationalise it or did it really happen? And who carried her? She knows it wouldn't have been difficult. She weighs next to nothing, the equivalent of a child. Perhaps the intention was to make it appear that she had murdered Robert by placing her at the scene, next to the weapon, and covering her in her husband's blood.

The more she thinks about it, the clearer it becomes and the more convinced she is that this is what actually happened.

Laurie closes her eyes and attempts to focus. She can smell something – what is it? Food? The smell of dinner cooking? No. Something different. Perfume… she can smell perfume. The person who was carrying her was wearing perfume.

Laurie thinks about getting up. She knows she must try. She's been bedridden for almost three days now, relying solely on Monica for her most basic needs. She can barely eat a thing and as a result feels weak and incapable, like she's shutting down inside. Perhaps it would be best if she did. After all, she's a murderer, isn't she? Monica had seen her with a knife in her hand through the window, fighting with Robert. She had been mad as hell. It had all culminated in murder in that moment, the betrayal and the lies and cruelty. So why does she feel sure someone else had been in the house? She could sense that there had been someone else there that evening, and she was sure that someone else had carried her to the crime scene…

The more she thinks about it, the more she feels her memory returning, fragments of it, slow and clunky. But even if she's right, the police will never believe her. They'll think she's making it up to throw them off the scent. Perhaps her mind is playing tricks on her.

She had believed that nothing could ever be worse than losing her two perfectly formed children in the tragic and unnecessary way that she had. But she had been wrong again. *Always wrong, Laurie*.

Despite her adrenal fatigue, Laurie suddenly feels a sense of purpose, a surge of energy course through her frail body. She will confess. She will explain everything to the police. She will tell the truth from the very beginning, that's what she will do. She will tell them about Robert, about the years of abuse and what it has done to her. She will explain about the accident, the aftermath, her depression and the blackouts. She will come clean about the alcohol and drugs too; she will hope that the jury will show her some mercy and compassion; perhaps they will see that in many ways, she has already paid so much; she has paid for the sin of loving a disordered person by becoming disordered herself. She will atone, purge herself and somehow regain herself in the process, the woman she once was – the brilliant, successful, confident, healthy and mentally stable woman she had been before he came along. She will ask to see that detective, the nice one with the kind eyes, and tell him what she remembers.

The truth is non-negotiable, Laurie, she hears her mother's raucous voice inside her cluttered head. She will call her today. She will tell her mother everything. She'd always felt something of a disappointment to her ambitious and outgoing mother. Perhaps that was why her mother had all but abandoned her when she was sixteen years old to go and live in California with her rich lover. Cynthia Harris had always made her daughter feel something of a burden. Once her father had walked out on them soon after her birth, the idea of motherhood had become increasingly less appealing to the free-spirited, twenty-year-old Cynthia. Though she had never neglected her child physically – Laurie was always clean and well presented – she had neglected her emotionally in favour of a revolving line of lovers and her career as a charity-event organiser. They say it begins at home, charity, but that was not the case in the Harris household. As a result, Laurie had become independent at a very young age, while her mother spent increasingly long hours, sometimes days, away from the home they shared. Yet she had instilled some good values in her daughter, despite a lack of her own: integrity, truth, honesty, a hard-work ethic and ambition, though Cynthia had always accused Laurie of being too kind. *People see kindness as weakness, Laurie*, her mother would warn, as if it was a curse to care too much about people. Maybe it was…

Laurie thinks about her father for the first time in years. She had never met him and her mother refused to ever speak of him. He'd been studying medicine at university when he'd met her mother and had, according to Cynthia, begged her to get rid of her unborn child. Laurie wonders if her mother refused as an act of feminist defiance, rather than the desire to keep her, just to be belligerent. Despite the scant and unfavourable information from her mother about the man who was responsible for half of her DNA, she can't help but think that he was a kind person. Somehow she feels this instinctively. Perhaps everything would've been different if she'd known him. *Perhaps*.

She hears voices, a commotion going on downstairs, and groans. The press has been relentless in trying to secure an interview with her. She supposes that eventually she will have to speak to them. But first she will talk to the police, to that detective with kind eyes whose name she cannot remember. She will shower and dress herself, try to look like a human being again, even though she no longer knows how that is supposed to feel. Maybe she was destined for this life: a life of punishment and pain. Like some people are destined for greatness, happiness and success, perhaps others are simply destined for the opposite and there's nothing you can do to change that. Maybe it's all preordained and written by the gods.

Laurie momentarily lapses into inertia, as if asleep again, her thoughts paralysing her physical body. She knows Monica will not want her to confess to killing Robert, but she must. There's no other option, is there? If she's capable of slaughtering her own husband, then she's capable of anything. She'd be better off locked away. And yet somewhere, somewhere deep inside of her, past her shattered, non-existent self-esteem and the quagmire of self-loathing that courses through her every blood cell, she knows – something primal in her *feels* – that somehow she could not possibly be capable of such savagery. No matter how far she had fallen into the vortex of emotional torment, no matter how much alcohol and prescription drugs had altered her state of mind, she cannot accept that she is capable of killing anyone. Not even herself.

Laurie pulls the duvet back from her body. It's an effort in itself and already she feels defeated. But she must try. *Try, Laurie, try.* She swings her frail, tiny body to the edge of the bed and that's when the bedroom door crashes open.

CHAPTER THIRTY-SEVEN

It's part of the nature of being on homicide to have to witness some horror. And over the years I've seen my fair share of it, you know, the stuff of nightmares, the kind of thing that Stephen King would balk at and that would put the willies up Wes Craven. But nothing, *nothing*, could prepare me for what I witness as I walk into Claire Wright's apartment.

I tell Davis to keep back but she's right alongside me, hyper-ventilating loudly.

There's a deathly, eerie silence in the room as forensics set about their grim tasks punctuated by the amplified sound of cameras popping like fireworks.

'The mother found them,' Harding says. She sounds, and looks, choked up. Frankly I'd be worried if she didn't.

'When?'

'About an hour ago. She was on her way to work. She does shifts at the hospital. Says she'd rung her daughter the previous evening twice and got no answer. Said it was unlike her not to pick up, that they spoke most nights. So she came to check on her, on them, and…'

The smell in the apartment is immediately identifiable to my regrettably seasoned nostrils. It's the scent of the onset of decay, of decomposition, of *death*. But there's something else too. Another scent I pick up on. I've got a good nose, metaphorically speaking, and I think I can smell perfume – a faint, underlying sweet scent lingering behind the smell of death.

I walk round to the front of the sofa where her body is resting. She's still wearing the same nightclothes that she had on when Davis and I paid her a visit, a fluffy pink bathrobe and a shorts and T-shirt set with rainbows on them. She's got slippers on, fluffy boot-type ones, and she's lying on her left side in a foetal position. Her chubby legs are pulled almost up to her chest and are blue and mottled in colour, like someone's delicately painted them with watercolours. You might assume at first glance, given the natural positioning of the body, that she was simply asleep on her couch. Until you look at her from the neck upwards that is. Claire Wright's head is encased in a plastic bag. A clear plastic bag that gives her features a ghoulish and distorted appearance, like she's underwater. Her eyes are wide open, her mouth forming an 'O' shape. It's an unnatural sight, surreal, like something from a horror film, something created by someone else's twisted imagination.

'The baby was next to her,' Harding informs me. 'The crying alerted a neighbour who called the mother—'

'And where is she now, the baby – Matilda?'

'At the hospital, Gov. She's critical.'

'Where was she found?'

'Next to the mother, nestled inside her dressing gown, poor thing.'

'Injuries?' I brace myself.

Harding shakes her head. 'Nothing visible. Dehydration. Poor little thing nearly starved to death.'

I shudder inwardly.

Davis looks visibly shaken. I think she may be crying. I think I may be crying. She moves in closer to look at Claire Wright but I put my arm out to prevent her. The three of us are silent for a moment, myself, Davis and Harding, frozen in a triangle, locked into a diabolical moment of disbelief. It's pretty clear how Claire Wright met her end. I can't see any visible markings on her body, no blood, no obvious wounds. It appears that she was suffocated; a horrible, terrifying death, but nowhere near as hideous as starving to death – that would be slow, and ugly.

'Maybe the killer hoped that the baby would be found,' Davis says, but I'm unconvinced. This cold-blooded bastard left a tiny, defenceless baby to starve to death next to her dead mother, and I feel such a rush of contempt that I almost have to sit down.

It's clear to me now that we're dealing with a full-blown psychopath, a mentally disordered killer void of any conscience or empathy whatsoever – someone very dangerous indeed.

I come out of my trance and snap back to the brutal reality in front of me.

'They've found some hair, Gov.' Mitchell appears behind me. 'Forensics.' I didn't even know she was here. 'It's dark, brunette. Doesn't match the deceased's.'

I watch as forensics bag things up and take away the contents of Claire Wright's apartment.

'There were two coffee cups, mugs, on the coffee table,' she tells me. 'It could be that she used them both, but one has faint lipstick marks on it. I think someone was here with her before she died. That she had a guest, or guests.'

'The intercom,' Davis says suddenly. 'There will be CCTV.'

I nod. 'Get hold of it right away and put a rush on the hair, yeah. This is urgent. *Seriously urgent.*'

'Vic Leyton's on her way, boss,' Davis says with her phone to her ear.

I nod again, my brain fizzing and whirring. It hadn't occurred to me that Claire Wright's life may have been in danger, and certainly not her child's. Why? What have I missed? Have I been naïve? Have I been wrong about Laurie Mills all along? Could she have killed her husband before going to the hairdressers and manipulated his watch so it looked as though he'd been murdered later? It would definitely have been cutting things very fine and would've needed a lot of pre-meditation and certainly not much room, if any, for error. Perhaps she's not only capable of savagely slaughtering her husband, but of murdering his mistress and their child too? I feel like I've messed up, like I somehow should, *could*, have prevented this godawful scene in front of me. It's not a nice feeling at all.

As Davis and I are leaving, we see Claire Wright's mother outside in the communal area. She's being comforted by PC Choudhry and a female officer whose name I don't know but probably should. She's standing but is bent almost double, wailing and crying like a wounded animal as they attempt to keep her upright.

I go over to her, stoop down to talk to her. 'Mrs Wright? You're Claire's mother, yes?'

The poor woman manages to look up at me, though it's clear she's in a state of complete shock and unimaginable grief. Whatever memories this woman has of the child she had carried and given birth to, brought up, nurtured and loved, will be contaminated by the truly sickening scene she's been forced to witness today. Every parent's worst, most horrific nightmare realised – her daughter's head encased in a plastic bag, her baby granddaughter dying next to her. I know that the images she's seen will haunt this poor lady until her last breath. People don't get over that kind of stuff. They simply have to find a way to live with it. She's nodding as she cries and wails. Her body cannot keep still; she's twitching and lurching as though the pain is forcing its way into her limbs like a diabolical entity possessing her.

'Please, Mrs Wright.' I can hear the anguish in my own voice as I ask what I must. 'I'm DI Riley, Dan Riley. Can you tell me what time you arrived at your daughter's flat today?'

I don't think she's going to be able to speak, she's so distraught, but admirably she gathers herself.

'Around 10.45ish. I was on my way into work, at the hospital. I called in to check on her after a neighbour called me and said she'd heard Matty crying…' She's breathing heavily, her body flooded by raw anguish and adrenaline. 'She didn't answer my calls last night. I was worried. It's not like her… she's been in a terrible state, about Robert, you know since… Oh God. *My baby. My babies*… This isn't happening. Someone's murdered my girl. Oh God help me, please God help me…'

I blink back tears as Mrs Wright crumbles before me; watch her devastation unfolding in real time. I grip her hands with my own. 'Mrs Wright,' I say, 'look at me, please.'

She struggles to keep her head up but eventually manages some eye contact. I stare into the woman's watery blue eyes and see such pain and horror in them that I want to hurt someone. 'I want to make you a promise that I will personally not rest until I find whoever did this to your daughter and granddaughter, and I will put them away for the rest of their lives. Do you understand that?'

She falls into me then, raw sobs bouncing off my chest. And I hold her; hug her for a moment before letting go. I can't afford to crumble with her.

Davis comes up next to me and I turn to her. 'Let's go and see Mrs Mills at home, shall we?' I say.

'No need, boss,' she replies. 'They've already brought her in.'

CHAPTER THIRTY-EIGHT

The perfume. Laurie remembers now. It's coming back to her in clunky, short, sharp bursts. The smell is familiar, but she doesn't wear it herself. The person who carried her up the stairs, incapacitated like a rag doll, wears it, only she can't remember what it's called; she can smell it in her nostrils as her memory returns in hazy flashes. She knows it… Worse still, she sees the knife: it glints malevolently at her as it hovers over her wrists. They're not her hands holding it, so whose hands are they? She can feel breath on her cheek, someone else's presence near her, their hands on her skin, but she cannot see their face – her mind is refusing to access this last image.

Forgive me. She hears these words in her mind before the blade is dragged across her skin but the voice is unrecognisable, generic. She feels nothing as the blade glides across her wrists and opens her flesh, no pain as she slips in and out of consciousness, eventually losing it altogether. *Oh God.*

Laurie watches from the window of the police car as the colours of the outside world melt into a passing blur. Someone else was in the house on the night of Robert's murder, now she is sure of it. She wants to feel a sense of relief, of euphoria, because this means she didn't kill Robert, doesn't it? And she didn't attempt to kill herself either. But her memory is clouded by a sense of utter hopelessness and despair. No one will believe her. Her DNA is all over the murder weapon; she has motive and opportunity, a history of depression and mental illness, there was no sign of a break-in, no evidence of a third party… She closes her eyes again – they feel dry and gritty and she wonders how this is possible after all the crying she has done. It makes no sense, just like everything else.

'I'll call Marcus Wainwright right away,' Monica had said as they dragged her from her bed. They think she has killed Claire, Robert's lover. Fat, dumpy, mummy Claire: dead apparently.

'What about the little one?' she'd asked as they'd cuffed her and taken her away. 'Is the baby okay?' But they wouldn't answer her. They'll know she didn't kill Claire, surely? How could she have? She was asleep. Monica could, would, vouch for that.

Only when she looks down at her feet, at the ballet slippers she's wearing, she sees dirt on them, spots of muck, and they feel a little damp, like she's worn them.

Laurie swallows hard and exhales deeply as they pull up outside the police station. It's going to be a long night.

CHAPTER THIRTY-NINE

The coffee cup. *Fuck*. She'd drunk from it, hadn't she? *Silly bitch*, what had she been thinking? Or had she? She can't quite remember if she'd taken a sip or not before she'd thrown it in that thick cunt's face. She tries hard to think over the events as they happened. Sitting on the sofa, peering into the crib at the sniffling little bastard while Claire had gone to make the drinks. The coffee had been boiling hot. She could tell it was one of those instant sachet things, not the real stuff, cheap, like Claire herself. Maybe she had just blown on it to cool it down and hadn't got round to taking a sip. *Jesus Christ*, did she or didn't she? She needs to bloody well remember because this was the difference between spending her life behind bars or living the good life in the French Riviera, and that was a no-brainer. Still, at least they'd taken Laurie in: that was something at least. That would keep them busy for a while. She wonders if now is the time to abscond. Just cut her losses and grab her passport and go. She had money in the bank but if she left now it would look suspicious. They might even freeze her assets and that would scupper her plans royally. *No*. She'd just have to sit it out. Wait for them to convict Laurie, for it to be over. If she could just sit tight, soon she'd be free of them all.

Monica recalls the look on Laurie's face as the police had frogmarched her out of the house in handcuffs, her confusion and fear. Poor, pathetic Laurie, forever the victim.

'Now listen, don't you worry, okay. I'll get Marcus onto it straight away. They'll see they've made a big mistake. We'll have you out again in no time. Okay? It's okay, darling… it will be okay,' she'd soothed her friend, smiling at her and kissing her on the cheek briefly as they'd whisked her off. The dishy copper, Martin Delaney he'd said his name was, he'd hung back to ask her some questions. Had Laurie gone out the night before? Had she seen her leave the house? What was her state of mind? Had she been acting suspiciously? Apparently, according to the sexy policeman, who she was sure was flirting with her, a neighbour had thought she'd seen Laurie leave the house around 10.30 p.m. and get into her car… Monica smiles to herself. *Jessica Bartlett.* She'd bet her arse on it. In fact, she'd been relying on her nosy neighbour to do just that.

'I didn't see her go out of the house, no. But then again, I was in bed at 10 p.m. It's been exhausting these past few days, looking after Laurie. She's not been in her right mind, you see. I think it's the drugs she's been taking, and the alcohol… well, she's not been lucid, hasn't been herself since Robert's death, since his murder. She's found it hard to cope, you know—'

'In what way has she not been in her right mind, Mrs Lewis?'

'It's Ms,' she'd said, coyly sighing. 'In every way, really. Rambling, crying one minute, angry the next. Poor thing, it's been awful to see her like this. I think she's suffering from PTSD. Come to think of it, maybe I did hear the door go last night—'

Monica taps her finger against her lips. She'll just have to let things unfold, play themselves out. Laurie is their prime suspect. She's the only one in the frame. She's made sure of it. If she could only remember if she'd taken a sip of that bloody coffee. Even if she had maybe it wouldn't be enough to extract any DNA. And even if it was, she's not on any database anywhere. No one is looking at her. Right now she's just the concerned friend. She's the one who's given Laurie an alibi. She's off the radar.

Monica schleps into the kitchen, makes herself a coffee, grabs the paper and relaxes down onto the sofa. She tries to read but her mind keeps wandering back to Claire and the coffee cup. She flicks through the newspaper, skipping the usual mundane local-interest guff and, oh hang on, what's this? She sits up. There's a piece about Robert's death. The headline screams, 'MURDERED PHOTOGRAPHER WAS DOMESTIC ABUSER'. She frantically scans the article. Leanna George. Who the hell was she? Words jump out at her: '*We were soulmates… together for four years… he pursued me relentlessly… I didn't know he was married… about the mistress…*'

Monica looks at the accompanying photograph and feels bilious hatred and jealousy rise up through her chest, burning her oesophagus like acid. '*Abused: Leanna George, 34, model and actress from Newcastle, claims the deceased, Robert Mills, was "a monster behind closed doors".*'

Model and actress! Who was she trying to kid? So, there had been yet another whore in the background too. This Geordie slut, whoever she was. Monica stares at the article in anger and disbelief. *Four years!* She'd known about Claire, and Laurie, obviously. But this one! Jesus, how many more were there? How many had there been?

She stares at Leanna's picture. It's clearly one of those publicity shots because there's a chintzy backdrop and she's smiling brightly, all teeth and tits. *Fucking bitch!*

She rips the page up in a frenzied rage until it's shredded in a pile. Maybe she'll pay 'abused' Leanna George a visit. *Abused!* That tacky-looking tramp doesn't know the meaning of the word.

Violent thoughts seep into her mind like poison. But she has lost her fall guy now, temporarily at least. As Monica's rage slowly begins to dissipate, she goes into the kitchen for a glass of water and steadies herself against the butler sink. She's still enraged by what she's just read, but she cannot let it cloud her judgement, muddy her thoughts. She needs a calm, cool head on her right now. The next 24 hours are crucial. Only she can't stop the name from resounding in her head. *Leanna George.*

CHAPTER FORTY

The video machine whirs with anticipation. I'm standing behind Mitchell as she runs through it with alacrity, her brow furrowed in deep concentration.

'It's grainy, Gov,' she says, sucking air through her teeth, 'but she's there. Look.'

I lean in, put my glasses on. I find I'm needing them more and more these days. It reminds me, it's my birthday tomorrow. Not that I'm in any mood to celebrate. How could I be when I have a potential baby killer out there? Well, I say out there. Laurie Mills is currently in interview room two right now, waiting. She's been there for at least an hour, stewing. It's a common tactic we use, making a suspect wait. It instils anxiety in them, not knowing when we're going to walk through the door and kick off the fun. Delaney and Davis are going to start proceedings while I tend to some business behind the scenes. I need to speak to Jessica Bartlett and some of the neighbours. I need to visit Laurie Mills' psychotherapist. I need to collate as much evidence as possible so that we can charge her. I know that Delaney will go right for the jugular in the interview room and given the dire circumstances I've currently no qualms with that. I've put Davis in there alongside him as the alkaline to his acid. Any personal baggage between them is currently on hold. We have important work to do.

Mitchell is right about the quality of the footage from outside Claire Wright's apartment block. It's got more grain than a Warburton's factory. Even through my face furniture I can only just about make out the black-and-white figure standing at the entrance. I can see that it's a woman from the hair, the dress, the demeanour. The positioning of the camera is pointing downwards which gives us a pretty fantastic view of the top of her head and shoulders, and that's about it. I don't want to blink in case I miss a second – miss something, *anything*.

'Is that the only angle you've got?' I don't mean this to sound personal, like it's Mitchell's fault that whoever installed the damn thing must've been a 10ft-tall moron. What's the point in having security cameras if you can only see the top of someone's head?

'Just wait a sec, Gov,' Mitchell says. 'There's more.'

I watch, adrenaline ripping through me like a nail bomb, as the figure presses the intercom. I can see the outline of her arm, her finger on the buzzer, the hair, dark, falling past her shoulders. But there's no clear visibility on the face.

'Jesus, shit Christ!' I curse loudly in Mitchell's ear – not intentionally, just through pure frustration. The image is too dark, the quality too poor, to identify who exactly is pressing that damn button. It looks like it *could* be Laurie Mills but that's as good as it gets. The camera gets a great view of her feet though as she pushes the door and enters the building. She's wearing what looks like those ballet-type slippers, the same ones she was wearing when we brought her in the first time.

'Rewind it… please,' I instruct Mitchell and the machine whirs. The entire footage is around thirty seconds long in total.

I watch. The figure is speaking into the intercom, slightly stooped. 'They were discussing something,' I murmur, to myself more than anyone, as I watch it again. 'Claire. She didn't know her; she didn't know this woman… Mitchell, get that footage to Image Analysis as soon as you can, see what they can do with it.'

I ask Mitchell to run through the footage once more and she duly obliges. There's something odd about it. I can't quite explain what, can't pinpoint it, but it's nagging at me like a dull toothache. The figure on screen matches Laurie Mills' description and yet…

Davis pops her head round the door.

'The boss wants to see you, boss.'

I inwardly sigh. 'I'll bet he does.'

'It's seems urgent, Gov,' Davis says, grimacing slightly.

I know what's coming and resign myself to it. 'Tell him I'm on my way.'

CHAPTER FORTY-ONE

Woods is already standing as I enter his office.

'Riley!' He almost trips over himself in his haste to jump out of his seat. He starts pacing the room. 'Where the bloody hell have you been? I've been looking for you all morning.'

'I'm here now, sir.' I hear the door bang shut behind me, like a death knell. I'm expecting Woods to look angrier than he does. Judging by his expression, I'm currently sensing his overriding emotion is worry. Woods looks *worried*. And that's even more worrying than him looking angry.

'We're in the proverbial now, Riley, you do realise this?' he asks, his left eyebrow twitching, the lines on his forehead deepening almost in front of my eyes. 'We had Laurie Mills and we let her go. And now she's gone and murdered another one and attempted a third. One of them a baby! A bloody baby, Riley! We have a psycho baby killer on our hands and *we let her go*! There'll be an independent enquiry over this. My name will be mud with the Super. *I* will have to explain how we missed the fact that Laurie Mills, the *only* suspect in her husband's murder, was released without charge and not monitored closely enough. Why wasn't she monitored round the bloody clock?'

His face crumples, matching his shirt. Even that looks upset somehow. 'The press is going to have a field day with this, Riley, a bloody, fucking feeding frenzy! There's a young mother murdered and her baby clinging to life, attacked in their own home in the most unspeakable way that, on the surface of it, looks as if it could have been preventable, *by us*. They'll want a fall guy, someone to blame. And *I* will be that guy, Riley.' He prods himself in the chest, driving the point home. 'I'll be ripped up for arse paper.'

'You're not at fault, sir,' I say, carefully. *Arse paper*. That's a new one for Woods.

'I know I'm not bloody well at fault, Riley!' he snaps at me, glaring. 'YOU are! *You* allowed this to happen. Laurie Mills is a dangerous psychopath consumed by hatred and revenge and we missed it! YOU missed it. You misjudged her completely. And now Claire Wright is dead and her baby is in intensive care.'

His words cut right through me like an axe to the chest, because I'm beginning to think that maybe he's right. Maybe I *did* misjudge Laurie Mills. Maybe I was – *am* – wrong about her.

'Wouldn't hurt a fly you said! Well, that famous intuition of yours let you down this time, didn't it? And it let Claire and Matilda Wright down too. Now, one of them is lying on a mortuary slab. And if the baby dies, well, I can only imagine how small that coffin will be…'

I close my eyes for a few seconds, let him vent and try not to imagine Matilda's tiny casket as it's carried through a sombre gathering of mourners.

'There wasn't enough evidence to keep her, sir. You know that. She had an alibi. The time of death… We're still waiting on some of the forensics – DNA analysis. That will hopefully give us more to work with. I didn't view her as a potential risk to anyone but herself, sir,' I explain truthfully. 'There was nothing to suggest that she was a danger to anyone. The woman could hardly put one foot in front of the other and—'

Woods walks around his desk. He's running his hands through his thinning hair, which looks as if it's shedding by the second. 'But she is, isn't she, Riley, a bloody danger?' He says this through clenched teeth. 'And in the worst way imaginable. How did you not see this coming? The woman's clearly as mad as a bucket of frogs.'

'It's box, sir,' I say before I can stop myself.

Woods glares at me, rearing back like a snake about to strike. 'Bucket, bag, box, what difference does it fucking well make!'

Woods has used the F word. Screamed it at me in fact. I stay silent.

'They'll have my head for this. And yours, Dan.' His tone has dropped an octave now though, the venom dissipating. He looks concerned again. Concerned mostly, it has to be said, for himself.

'We don't actually know, not for certain, who committed *any* of the murders yet, sir. That's just it. Laurie Mills is our prime suspect, but as I've said, it's largely circumstantial and let's not forget that she has an alibi.'

Woods collapses into his swivel chair and buries his head in his hands. There's a pregnant pause.

'Look, sir, I'm as upset about this as you are,' I say. 'You think I want the death of a baby, or any death for that matter, on my conscience, or on my watch? The team are devastated, sir. *I* am devastated…' I feel my emotions rising and perhaps it shows on my face because Woods' expression visibly softens.

'We've got Laurie Mills downstairs in room two,' I continue.

'And CCTV footage of her going into Claire Wright's apartment?' Woods asks rhetorically.

I shake my head. 'No positive ID, sir. It's too grainy, the angle is wrong. But it looks as if it could be Laurie Mills.'

'For God's sake.' He strokes his clean-shaven chin thoughtfully. 'But a neighbour saw her leave in her car around 10.30 p.m. last night?'

'Allegedly. I'm going to see her now. Jessica Bartlett. Lives next door. Then I'm paying Laurie Mills' psychotherapist a visit. I need an insight into Mills' mind.'

'What we need, Riley, is a bloody conviction. There's no one else in the frame. Focus on gathering evidence. Don't go off on one of your tangents. I mean it, Riley – we cannot afford to cock this up any more than we – than *you* – already have.'

I nod, silent for a moment. 'Seems odd to me that Laurie Mills would brazenly go round to Claire Wright's house and murder her in cold blood knowing she was under suspicion of her husband's murder, knowing that she might be seen, knowing that there would most likely be CCTV at Claire's apartment… It doesn't make any sense, sir. Laurie Mills comes across as a victim, not a psychopathic killer. We're missing something—'

Woods bangs his fist onto his desk, stopping me mid-sentence. 'The woman has mental-health issues. Who knows what the hell goes on in the mind of a psychopath?'

'Psychopaths are cunning, sir. They're smart, they're manipulative, they're… clever. Doesn't seem too clever to me to murder your husband and then brazenly kill the mistress days later while there's so much heat on you…'

Now it's Woods' turn to stay silent, which usually suggests he's starting to second-guess himself. He looks up at me with one of his resigned looks that's generally accompanied by a deep and irritable exhalation of breath.

'Well, Riley,' he says, 'if Laurie Mills isn't the killer, then who the bloody hell is?'

I meet his watery, worried eyes with my own, 'I don't know yet, sir,' I say. 'But I promise you, even if it costs me my badge, I will find out.'

I hear him mutter something as I leave his office. I can't be sure, but I think it went something along the lines of, 'Chance would be a fine thing.'

CHAPTER FORTY-TWO

Jessica Bartlett *looks* nosy. Even before she opens her mouth I can tell. Her narrow eyes dart from side to side as she speaks and she gesticulates in a camp manner that suggests she has a penchant for drama – namely other people's. Still, people like me need the Jessica Bartletts of this world and never more so than now.

'I'm telling you I *saw* her,' she says, 'with my own eyes. It was around 10.30 p.m. I know it was because I'd just finished watching one of my programs. I'd gone to the window because I thought I'd heard someone outside, the sound of a car door opening, and an engine starting up. I thought it might be one of them reporters. There's been press crawling all over the close since… well, since Robert was killed. They've been at my door every day religiously since.'

I'll bet they have. And I bet she welcomed them with open arms. My thoughts drift to Fi then; she's been strangely quiet about this case, aside from the Leanna George tip-off. It makes me think she's avoiding me, which in turn makes me feel a bit shitty. Maybe I'll call her.

'Can I offer you tea? Coffee? How about a latte?' Jessica asks jovially.

She doesn't yet know about the Wright murder. And I'm not about to tell her. She'll find out soon enough.

'I've just bought one of those fancy barista machines. Maggie from number 38 has one. Always raving about it she is, how great her coffee is, so I thought I'd see what all the fuss was about.' She tucks a strand of her dyed blonde bob behind her ear and smiles at me with narrow eyes.

'I'm good, thanks,' I reply, even though I'm tempted. I could do with a hit of something.

'I've lived on this close for almost eighteen years now,' Jessica says. 'We moved here when the boys were little. It was a lovely place to raise kids. Safe, you know. Well, until now obviously.' She snorts a little, rolls her eyes. 'I mean, who'd have thought there would ever be a murder right next door. It's shocking. Truly shocking.'

She looks tickled pink.

'They were always fighting you know, the Millses. I heard them – when he lived there that is. Doors slamming, things banging around. Sometimes I heard her crying in the garden outside. I never interfered though,' Jessica adds, as if this would be the very antithesis of her nature. 'Hardly ever saw the woman. In fact, I've only met her face-to-face once, at the barbecue – the summer barbecue. I suppose you've already heard all about that?'

I nod. 'Yes I have.'

She looks mildly disappointed. 'Dreadful business, that was. She made a right show of herself she did, in front of the entire street as well. Aired all their dirty laundry in public. Drunk as a skunk she was. Still, can't say I didn't feel a little sorry for her. Him cheating on her like that and then that horrendous accident where she lost those babies. Enough to drive most to murder I'm sure. She wasn't the friendly sort, Laurie – kept herself very much to herself. She had a nervous disposition – well, that's how she came across when I met her: jumpy, you know, easily startled. Pretty woman, but a little on the thin side, looked like she needed a decent meal or two; it ages you, it does, being too thin, especially as you get older. She was totally different with a drink inside her though; she wasn't so shy then, let me tell you.' Jessica raises her eyebrows. 'Tore him off a strip she did, publicly outed his affair, and the fact he'd fathered a child with this woman. Never saw her though, the mistress that is. He never brought her to the house – not that I saw anyway.'

I refrain from adding *and I'm sure you would've.*

'Hmm, yes.' I nod cordially. 'Are you absolutely sure it was Laurie Mills you saw last night, Mrs Bartlett?'

She turns from the coffee machine, smooths down the front of her dress in a self-important manner and bristles. 'Well, Detective, it certainly *looked* like her. And she got into her own car. Who else could it have been? Has something happened, Detective? Has something happened to Laurie?'

I refrain from giving her a definitive answer. We've impounded Laurie Mills' Audi. It's with forensics as we speak. I can only hope, pray, that there's some DNA evidence to link Laurie to Claire Wright. The dark hair found at Claire's apartment has yet to be identified.

'It was dark though, wasn't it?' I say.

'Well, yes, it was,' she agrees, suddenly looking as if she might be doubting herself. 'But I definitely knew it was Laurie.'

'How?'

'The dress – I think I've seen her wearing it before. It struck me as summery, for the time of year anyway, you know, floaty and floral. Are you sure something hasn't happened?'

'You'd seen her in that dress before?'

'Yes. It was the same one she wore to the barbecue I think, very boho, sort of Stevie Nicks sty—'

'Did you see her face?' I cut her off mid-sentence. 'Did you get a positive look at her face, Mrs Bartlett?'

'Well, actually…' She glances down at her feet. She's wearing sensible court shoes that look uncomfortable but expensive and a tight-fitting knee-length dress that looks like someone poured her into it. 'Not exactly. I just saw her from a distance. Saw the long dark hair, the clothes and—'

'So you couldn't definitively say it was Laurie Mills then?'

Jessica Bartlett looks a little flustered now. 'Will I need to give evidence in court?' Her eyes light up. I can tell she's planning her outfit already, gearing up for her five minutes in the spotlight.

'Possibly, yes,' I tell her and she practically purrs with impending delight. 'So, can you say for absolute definite that the woman you saw getting into Laurie Mills' Audi last night was Laurie Mills?'

She pauses for a moment, gives me a knowing sideways glance.

'Something happened last night, didn't it? I won't tell anyone, Detective, not even my husband. Not that we do much talking these days.' She laughs, hoping to prompt me into spilling the beans, but I continue with the line of questioning.

'Are you absolutely certain about what and who you saw last night, Mrs Bartlett?'

She sighs in defeat, folds her arms with a sense of purpose and taps her lip with her finger. I've always wondered why people do that; how could it possibly help you to remember?

'Well, I can't say I'm one hundred per cent sure it was her because she was a little way away and it was dark, but I'm fairly certain.'

Fairly certain is not good enough. Not in my book.

'But it had to be Laurie,' she says, offering me a fancy biscuit, which I decline. 'Who else could it have been?'

Harding calls me as I'm making my way over to see Dr Wells, Laurie's psychologist. I swing the car left and put my foot down, think about putting the blue light on in case I hit traffic. Hey, there are some perks to this job.

'This needs to be welcome news, Harding,' I say. And I'm not joking.

'We traced that number, Gov. The one on Robert Mills' phone. The unknown one he made and received calls from on the day of his murder.'

'And?'

'Registered to someone called Kiki Mills, number 253 Rotherham Way, Rochester, Kent.'

Kiki Mills? *Mills…*

'The ping on the day of Robert's murder came from the tower nearest to Cedar Close. Whoever he was speaking to was close by, in the area.'

My brain kicks into overdrive as I change up a gear. 'Okay… and?'

'*And* – she pauses for effect – 'the hair's a match, Gov.' Harding sounds elated. 'The hair found at Claire Wright's apartment. It belongs to Laurie Mills.'

I swallow hard, close my eyes for a nanosecond longer than a blink.

'No fingerprints?'

'Nothing boss. Just the hair. It's enough though, isn't it?' she asks, hopefully. 'We've got her now, boss.'

'We've got her, Harding. Well done. Well done.' I should feel as elated as Harding sounds on the phone but as I hang up, the only thing running through my mind is one name: Kiki Mills.

CHAPTER FORTY-THREE

Kiki – Summer 1996

'God, look at you, you look… incredible.' He takes a step back, admires her, 'You look all grown-up.'

Kiki smiles contentedly. She knows she has blossomed recently, in the last six months in particular; her breasts have become fuller, rounder and more prominent; she has grown taller, slimmer, more streamlined; and she's wearing her hair longer now, in beachy waves past her shoulders. She's begun to turn heads and she likes the omnipotent feeling it gives her. After they discovered she was pregnant and forced her into having an abortion, they'd sent her away to boarding school, left her in the charge of those vicious nuns. They had tried every punishment: solitary confinement, eight hours a day of prayer to repent for her sins, ice-cold baths, even denying her food, but in the eighteen months there they couldn't break her. The daily torture had made her resolve stronger, her desires greater, her determination fiercer. She was seventeen now and they could no longer control her; they couldn't tell her what to do anymore or beat her down mentally and physically. The nuns had had enough of her openly flouting the rules, deliberately antagonising them by wearing stockings and suspenders underneath her uniform, smoking and stealing alcohol from the local town, absconding at night to sleep with strangers she picked up in pubs or by thumbing for lifts. When she'd found herself pregnant again the nuns had expelled her, washing their hands of her. Disgusted and outraged, her mother and father had followed suit.

'We've arranged for you to go and live with a cousin of mine in London. She'll give you free board for a while but not forever. You'll have to go out and earn your keep.' Her mother could barely look at her.

'I'm sure I'll find a way to contribute,' Kiki replied, shaking her breasts provocatively. 'I've been told I have great assets.'

Her mother's stony face is a proper picture.

Get a load of that, bitch.

'You're never to come back here again,' she says stoically. 'You're not welcome here. What you did, what you've done with your brother, and those men, all those other men, it's evil, the work of the devil, against God's will. You stay away from my boy; you will not ruin his life. I will not let you do that.'

Kiki wants to laugh. Her mother knows nothing; it was her precious son who had seduced her in the beginning. It had been her darling boy who had taken Kiki's virginity and introduced her to pleasures of the flesh, and oh such pleasures they were! But it wasn't just carnal lust – they loved each other and they were going to be together, whether her mother liked it or not. She wasn't going to let this bitter old lush stand in the way of true love, of a life of happiness with the man she loved. They would marry and have a family together. That's what he had told her since they were children: their destiny was together, it had been written in the stars by the gods, the real ones, and there was nothing anyone could do about it.

'He's gone away, somewhere you'll never find him. He wants nothing to do with you and your wickedness.'

Kiki laughs out loud now, watches the anger brewing on her mother's haggard features. She's not scared of her anymore. She's no longer that small child frightened of getting a beating and being sent to her room with no food. She's waited for this moment for a long time.

'I'm afraid, Mother, you're wrong. I know exactly where Bertie is and I'm going to live with him, as his lover. Bertie loves me. He wants me – he *needs* me – as much as I need him. We're going to get married and start a family together, a family you'll never see or be part of. There's nothing you can do about it, you or that pathetic old wretch of a "man" you're married to. We're not breaking any laws. He's there, waiting for me now, no doubt hard and ready to make babies—'

Her mother slaps Kiki hard across the face, taking the wind from her. 'You vile little slut! You stay away from my boy! God help me, I will kill you. You should've been drowned at birth. Born to a whore, it was always going to follow that you would become one. Lord knows I tried…' Her mother begins to cry. 'When we couldn't have any more children, I thought I would give an unwanted child a loving and caring home, complete our family, a sister for our boy… You looked so innocent in that crib, lying there like a little angel, but the devil has many disguises, and he was at play that day I went to collect you. You have destroyed our family.'

Kiki rubs her face with one hand while bringing down the hardest slap she can across her mother's cheek, causing her to gasp at the impact.

'That was the last time you'll ever hit me,' she says, resisting the urge to grab a kitchen knife and stab her mother to death there and then. 'Let me tell you something, Mummy Dearest. There is no God. There is no devil either. There is only love and hate, good and bad, light and dark… A loving and caring home you say? Ha!' She throws her head back manically and for the first time she sees fear on her mother's face – the tables have turned. 'I am what I am because of you: starved of affection, starved of love, beaten and abused. You drove me into his arms and into his bed.

You, Mother – you and that sorry excuse of a father. And if there somehow is a God, he must've decided to make you barren for a reason, and that reason is that *you* are evil, Mother – a vicious, cold, alcoholic hypocrite hiding behind religion in a bid to convince yourself you're a good person.'

Her mother is sitting on the kitchen floor shaking, her hand attached to her face where Kiki's slap has left a red mark, unable to speak.

'And because of the wicked evil sinner you are, Mother, you've lost your son, and your daughter too, though I never really was a daughter, was I? Just a punching bag; a reminder of your empty, functionless womb; a smokescreen for the "respectable and caring" woman you portray yourself to be to your churchgoing friends.

'So goodbye, Mother,' Kiki says, turning to leave, taking one last look at the woman on the kitchen floor, a pathetic, drink-sodden harridan. 'And fuck you.'

'I've been waiting for this moment for such a long time,' she says, going to him. He feels warm: her blanket. 'We did it, Bertie. We're free. Now we can be together. You kept your promise – you came back for me.'

'Yes,' he says, 'I came back for you, Kiki, and we can be together, but no one can know. I have to tell Mum and Dad that you're not here, that I've sent you away, that it's over.'

She pulls back from him. 'Fuck them! Fuck what they think! Don't tell me you *care* what they think?'

He drops her embrace, lights them both a cigarette from a packet on the small kitchen table. 'This place costs a fortune,' he says. 'I'm getting more jobs by the day but the rent, well, living in London is expensive.'

'I'll get a job. I'll work day and night and enrol at college, study something so I can earn good money.'

'Mum and Dad are paying the rent on this place, plus my college fees. If they find out you're here they'll stop.'

'Like I said, I'll get a job.' She doesn't like where the conversation seems to be going.

'They said they'll disinherit me if they discover you're any part of my life.'

'What?' Kiki feels the sting of rage as it bubbles up inside her guts. Her parents are wealthy people – not that anyone would especially know it. They certainly weren't flash, but she knew they owned multiple properties and had hundreds of thousands tied up in them.

'I'm set to inherit a little over half a million when I turn twenty-one next year. They've told me I won't see a penny of it if I so much as mention your name again.'

Kiki swallows hard. So they've had the last laugh. 'We should murder them, then we'd get all their money,' she says, only half joking.

He blows smoke heavily from his lips. 'We'd never get away with it.'

'Don't be so sure,' she says and he laughs.

'My bad Kiki… I've missed you.'

She's back in his arms again, their bodies touching.

'You can stay here for a couple of nights, then you'll have to find somewhere else. They'll have tabs on me – you can't be seen here. We'll pretend to people that we're childhood friends, that we went to school together, and we'll meet in secret whenever we can.'

'But—'

'Don't argue with me,' he says, his voice taking a sharp edge, immediately silencing her. 'It's that or nothing.'

'How long for? How long will we have to pretend for? What about marriage and moving to Cannes? What about our babies?

They already made me kill our first.' Kiki feels her anger rising again and steadies her breathing.

'Not long,' he says. 'Just until I get my inheritance.'

She looks at him with wide eyes.

'I promise.'

CHAPTER FORTY-FOUR

Monica Lewis looks down at her hands as the manicurist goes to work on her short, neat nails. There's a hushed silence in the salon and she thinks she notices the other women staring. She doesn't mind the attention. They're not pointing any fingers at her. No one knows anything. The police have been round to search her house this morning. She welcomed them, offered them tea and biscuits in fact. They'll find nothing, nothing to link her to anything anyway. There are, however, Laurie's dress and ballet slippers. They took them away, just as she had expected them to. But she had washed and dried them, just in case, before replacing them back in Laurie's overnight bag. She had been careful. No blood. No fingerprints; she had disposed of the gloves down Claire's toilet, flushing them away before shedding a few strands of hair from Laurie's brush onto the couch, then replacing the brush back inside Laurie's washbag where she'd found it upon her return home.

Laurie is going down for this. She will be held accountable for the deaths of Robert, Claire and that bastard child of theirs. With a bit of luck she'll spend the rest of her life behind bars. Maybe she'll even top herself. Monica supposed she had really believed, hoped even, that after everything, Laurie might have tried to take her own life before now, but she'd been genuinely surprised by her friend's strength and determination, no more so than after the accident that had almost killed her and extinguished the lives of those unborn babies. Laurie had rallied far better than Monica had imagined she ever would've. She'd battled through the grief and depression and had eventually started to come through the other side, though certainly not unscathed. Perhaps, with hindsight, Monica had helped her *too* much and had subsequently helped her recovery. This idea irritates her. Monica had been the one to make sure that Laurie had discovered Robert's affair with Claire in the first place. She had instigated the accident. Laurie, and those twins, were simply collateral damage. Only Laurie had survived.

When Monica thinks about it though, a life behind the door for crimes you didn't commit would be a fate worse than death, wouldn't it? The torment and sense of injustice would eat away at someone like cancer. And, as she languished in a cell, Laurie would feel just as Monica has felt for all these years: helpless, hopeless, bitter and resentful. She smiles softly at the thought of it. It would be the revenge that kept on giving, because out of all of them, even Robert, she hated Laurie the most, despised her in fact, because without Laurie, her life would've been very different indeed.

Everything has thus far worked out, perhaps even better than she had meticulously planned. Monica will, of course, visit her friend in prison, at least once before she takes off for France. She'll do what she's always done and reassure her, sympathise with her and tell her how she will do all she can to help her – how *out of sight will never mean out of mind*. She will remain her truest and most loyal friend, write to her, send her gifts and money to buy basics in prison. Sisters stick together, after all.

Monica looks up at the TV screen on the wall. The sound is muted but the image is a photograph of Claire smiling and holding the bastard. She looks chubby and happy in the photograph, no doubt one that Robert had taken, and she thinks how much the baby really did have his eyes. The ticker underneath reads: '*Young mother murdered in her own home and her eight-month-old baby in a critical condition in hospital. Claire Wright, twenty-nine years old, was brutally murdered last night...*'

She's miffed by the use of the word *brutal*. The press always sensationalises everything. There was nothing brutal about it. In fact, she thought it had been quite a merciful killing all told. There had been no blood and gore. She hadn't opened her up, butchered her like she had Robert. She'd spared her, and herself, that.

'Terrible isn't it,' the manicurist tuts, nodding towards the screen. 'Senseless. Absolutely senseless. I mean, who would try to kill an eight-month-old baby?'

'There's some sick people out there,' Monica says, shaking her head. She notices the other women in the salon are silent, watching her, waiting for her reaction.

'You know her, don't you?' one of them suddenly pipes up, the fat one sitting in the pedicure chair, her cankles just visible above the bubbly water. 'You're the friend, aren't you, of that Laurie Mills woman, the suspect?'

The manicurist's eyes widen although she duly continues filing Monica's nails.

'Yes. Yes, I am. I've known Laurie since we were teenagers.'

'She did her husband in too, didn't she? Cut his throat, I read.' The woman lifts her feet out of the spa and wiggles her chubby toes. 'I turned to the old man the other night and said, "See, this is what'll happen to you, mate, if you ever do the dirty on me!"' She throws her head back and emits a throaty, raucous laugh that makes Monica want to chop off her toes, one by one.

'She's suffered terribly,' Monica murmurs, 'Laurie.' She's not sure if fatso has heard her.

'Fucking nutter, killing that girl and attacking her baby as well. Sick. She needs locking up and the key thrown away.'

The manicurist eyes Monica a little awkwardly as she finishes up.

'Dunno how you can be friends with a loon like that,' the uncouth fat woman remarks with contempt. 'I'd be shit-scared I was next.'

Monica keeps a dignified silence as she pays for her manicure, leaving the therapist a generous tip, which she thanks her for in the form of a large, apologetic smile.

The sun is shining as she exits the salon. It's a crisp autumnal day, superlative really, she observes. The kind she will miss when she moves to France and finally begins life again. Soon she will be reborn, free of the chains that have bound her for the past twenty-four years, free of Dougie, Robert and his mistress and child. Free of Laurie. Free of all of them, forever.

Monica feels good as she struts along the high street. She looks good too. The manicure was the final touch to her fresh blow-dry and nourishing facial. She feels like a femme fatale in a movie – sexy and seductive, invincible, a woman to be reckoned with. She's on the home run now. Laurie is languishing in a police cell, no doubt spiralling into a complete psychotic meltdown, one from which she will hopefully never fully recover.

It's taken over two decades to arrive at this moment and she wants to savour every second. Twenty-four wasted, painful, pitiful years that she will never regain.

As she click-clacks along the pavement in her Louboutin shoes she thinks about what her life will be like once she's on the Riviera. Perhaps she will meet a man? Perhaps she will get married and have a child? But she knows that will never happen now. She can't have children – not anymore anyway. She thinks of her abortions: six in total, or was it seven? She can't remember now. So many.

It's wrong, Kiki. We can't have a child… we mustn't. She hears his voice resonating inside her mind. So they'd been torn from her womb each and every time. But the last one, the last time, there had been complications. An infection. Blood poisoning. It had almost cost her her life. And it had cost her her womb. No more babies for Robert and Kiki. No more babies for anyone.

The sun is harsh as she crosses the street and she places some newly purchased designer shades on her face to shield her eyes. Yes, Monica thinks, the future, finally, looks bright.

CHAPTER FORTY-FIVE

Dr Wells is running late, as doctors are wont to do, and I'm struggling to contain my frustration as I sit in the reception area of this posh North London clinic where people pay a premium to get their heads fixed.

Nothing that a good woman and a holiday can't sort, Danny. That's what my old man would say to me whenever I got a touch of the blues, before I met Rachel that is. I had the good woman, but the holidays, not so much. Now I think about it, I wish we had taken more time off together. We thought we had all the time in the world and that holidays could wait. Now I know that time waits for no man. Or woman. I wish I'd been more spontaneous, whisked her off on a whim every once in a while. *I wish…*

I look around the waiting room of the therapist's practice at the mandatory water cooler and glass table of glossy magazines. God, I hate these places.

'Can you tell Dr Wells that this is important?' I say irritably to the unsmiling receptionist behind the desk. She ignores me for a moment before taking the trouble to look up from her magazine and say, 'She'll be with you shortly.'

Dr Sarah Wells is a very smart, well-dressed, efficient-looking woman in her fifties. She's unquestionably middle class and reeks of expensive perfume, no doubt thanks to the £120 per hour she charges for her services. At £120 an hour I'd need therapy to get over the bill alone.

'Please take a seat, Detective Riley.' She gestures to a comfy-looking, squishy brown-leather chair topped with a large turquoise cushion, as she sits in an identical chair opposite. It makes a satisfying whoosh sound as I sit down.

'So, you want to talk about Laurie Mills, is that correct?' She has an interesting, expressive face: a face that tells a thousand stories. Her bright-red lipstick makes her look cheery. *Cheery*. I really have become my father.

'Yes it is,' I begin. 'And before you say it, Doctor, I appreciate your client-confidentiality agreement, but as I'm pretty sure you're aware by now, this is a very serious murder investigation. Laurie Mills has been arrested on suspicion of the murder of Claire Wright and the attempted murder of Matilda Wright. As yet we cannot charge her for the murder of her husband, Robert Mills, but I would say that this is also imminent.'

She inhales deeply. Shakes her head.

'So, I need to know all you can tell me about Laurie Mills, about her state of mind, if she was mentally stable, anything she may have said during your sessions together that would sound alarm bells… any talk of murder, of suicide, anything.'

Dr Wells nods her understanding, though I notice her dark blonde hair stays statue-still as she does. 'I couldn't believe it when I saw the news,' she says, the incredulity evident in her clipped voice. 'It's knocked me for six, Detective, really it has.'

I can see she's not lying. She glances at the clock. 'I have another client in half an hour, so I'll do my best to tell you as much as I can between then and now, to help in any way I possibly can. Where do you want me to start?'

I give her a cursory smile and open my notebook.

'The only place anyone can,' I reply. 'At the beginning.'

CHAPTER FORTY-SIX

'I specialise in a few things, Detective, grief counselling and PSTD being just two of them. I also focus on personality disorders, namely helping people who've been the victims of those involved with Cluster Bs.'

'Cluster Bs?'

Dr Wells gives an enigmatic smile. 'Bipolar, borderlines, sociopaths, narcissistic personality disorder… Laurie came to see me initially for grief counselling. She was suffering with acute PTSD. I'm taking it that you know about the accident?'

I nod.

'Well, the PTSD was only partly as a result of it. She was experiencing severe symptoms: flashbacks, sweats, heart palpitations, guilt, fear, panic attacks, agoraphobia, shame – the whole works. It wasn't going to be a one-session wonder, put it this way. She had severe depression on top of other symptoms and was on strong antidepressants. She was also developing an alcohol dependency, using it to self-medicate.'

'Due to the accident?'

'Like I said, partly. It was also due to the extremely toxic marriage she was in with Robert. Years of being with a disordered psychological abuser had taken its toll. As it would do.'

'So it would be fair to say that her state of mind was pretty dire. Was she suicidal?'

'Fair to say? Yes, certainly fair, but also certainly not uncommon for people who have suffered very tragic losses, such as the ones she did, plus being involved with a Cluster B.'

'So you think Laurie Mills has a personality disorder?' I begin taking notes and nod at Dr Wells to continue.

'No. No. I don't think that at all, Detective. I think Laurie Mills was *married* to someone who had one.'

I look up at her. She crosses her legs, offers me some water from a plastic jug on the table. I can't help thinking how, for the prices she charges, it should be glass at the very least.

'No. Thank you.'

'I met them, both of them, on' – she does that lip-tapping thing I hate – 'well it was on more than one occasion.'

'And?'

'And, I'd say, from what I recall when speaking to them, that Mr Mills was a covert narcissist, quite far along the spectrum.'

'Did you ever treat him one-to-one? Robert Mills?'

'No. Never. He was a reluctant patient: that was very obvious. I could tell he didn't want to be here, didn't think he needed to be here. His demeanour was quite stand-offish, arrogant, even though he was exceptionally charming with it.' She flashes me a knowing look. 'That's part of the disorder.'

'Being charming?' Delaney pops into my head and I think of him seducing Davis.

'Yes. But also not thinking there's anything wrong with your behaviour. It's highly indicative in fact. People with NPD, well' – she sighs again, more heavily this time – 'it's the kind of disorder where they go untreated while everyone else around them needs therapy.'

'Well, I know that Robert Mills was a womaniser. He was indulging in an extra-marital affair with the victim, Claire Wright, and the baby was his. Another woman has also come forward and there were myriad online flirtations between himself and women he was grooming.'

'Grooming,' she says brightly. 'That's a very accurate word to use, Detective. This is exactly part of the NPD's MO. He, or she, grooms their victims or "supply" as they're referred to in the business. I would say it was highly likely that Robert Mills was involved in some way, shape or form with many other "supplies" on the side too. I knew about Claire – Laurie confided in me, as her therapist obviously.

'Jesus, what's he got that I haven't?'

She laughs a little. 'In a word, Detective, absolutely nothing, other than a personality disorder. You see, those with NPD suffer with something called object constancy.'

I blink at her, blankly I assume because she gives me that slightly pitiful smile again.

'They don't view people as human beings. They view them as objects, as a means to an end. They have impaired empathy. It's what enables them to conduct multiple relationships simultaneously without conscience. To them you are merely a vehicle to extract supply from. Supply being whatever it is they seek from you at that time, namely attention, drama, sex, a place to stay, adoration, an ego boost, financial benefits, a job, kudos... you name it. They're usually highly manipulative predators and users, and their lack of empathy and impaired conscience allows them to dupe and con at will. Those men you read about who pretend to fall in love with women and then scam them out of all their worldly goods? They're narcissists: NPDs. And the women they con are usually highly intelligent, solvent, beautiful, independent, kind and empathetic women, who can't believe they've been stung because these people are extremely good at what they do. They have to be. It's literally their survival. Life and death.'

'The latter in Robert Mills' case,' I remark dryly.

'So it would seem, Detective.'

'How did Laurie feel about Claire? Did she ever voice any feelings of hatred, talk of murder, or taking revenge?'

'No. Never. Not once. Of course, she wanted her to stop having an affair with her husband, naturally. In fact, I think in a way Laurie had empathy for the mistress.'

'Empathy?'

'Oh yes. Laurie Mills is what we call a "super empath", a fixer. She's the perfect supply for the NPD, a reservoir that keeps giving and forgiving, one than never runs dry. She is co-dependent. It stems back to her own childhood, as these things often do. The super empath and the NPD are a match made in heaven, or hell depending on which way you look at it. Both need each other, for very different reasons. They're at opposite ends of the spectrum. The NPD cannot put anyone above himself and his own needs and the co-dependent cannot stop putting others' needs before themselves and their own. The NPD has a need to break others in a bid to feed his or her ego, and the co-dependent has a need to fix others to sustain their own self-worth. They're both feeding off each other, albeit, like I've said, for opposing reasons.'

'So, is someone born with NPD or does it develop?'

'Interesting question.' Dr Wells coughs into her fist lightly, clears her throat. 'Excuse me. Well, that's hotly debated actually. The general consensus is that it develops at a very young age, usually between the ages of two and seven and is a result of the primary caregiver either giving the child too much adoration, or not enough. It's seen in some people who have suffered abuse as small children. It relates to emotional development.'

'But if it's learned behaviour, surely you can unlearn it? Not everyone who's abused goes on to become an abuser?'

'It's incredibly complicated yet simple at the same time,' she says paradoxically. 'I couldn't possibly explain it in detail in half an hour. But needless to say, people high on the spectrum usually share very similar traits, such as pathological lying, poor impulse control, being self-entitled, to name just a few. NPDs need to feel a sense of superiority over others and they support this self-aggrandisement by reducing people to little more than puppets jumping through hoops to please them. Because they lack character they need to keep bolstering their ego to feel anywhere near human. They also lack the ability to feel emotion on a deep level, which in turn doesn't allow them to connect with people very well on a soul level. Paradoxically, underneath they feel incredibly inadequate and insecure. It was a classic case with Laurie and Robert Mills.'

'Classic? In what way?'

'Robert Mills was a manipulator, a sexual predator operating solely from the ego. He was about power and control. He was also a misogynist. But he needed women, much more than they needed him in fact. He could only feel something if he was in full control of any situation and the people in it. He collected women like some people collect stamps and was a bully, an abuser, who played a very typical game of seducing and grooming women using the love-bombing technique, whereby he mirrored back to them everything they had ever wanted in a person. Only it's all a con job, like I mentioned before. He possessed little to none of the qualities he displayed sincerely. Once he'd hooked someone in, he then began to devalue them, tearing them off the pedestal he had first put them on and leaving them wondering just what the hell happened. I suspect his primary caregiver, his mother most likely, overindulged him as a child; she probably placed him on a pedestal, worshipped him. I didn't ever get the feeling he'd been abused.'

I recall the conversation Davis and I had with Leanna George. How she had claimed Robert had gone from being the man of her dreams to a monster pretty much overnight.

'It's a vicious cycle of love bomb, devalue, discard, rinse and repeat. I've seen it go on in relationships that I've counselled for years, literally decades. Once the victim is sufficiently hooked into the cycle, then the dance can go on ad infinitum. But the narcissist is always, *always* Lord of the Dance. The game will go on for eternity until one person stops playing the game. Or dies.'

'Like Robert Mills.' We both say it simultaneously and smile, a little awkwardly.

I shake my head, trying to make sense of it all and I realise now how lucky I was that things were so uncomplicated with me and Rach.

'So, tell me more about Laurie. Could what you've told me, about her years of suffering in this toxic "dance" as you call it, have sent her over the edge and made her capable of murder? Could she just have snapped and taken a knife to him?'

Until one of you dies.

Dr Wells looks thoughtful, as though she's deliberately choosing her words very carefully because she recognises their importance.

'It is absolutely possible that one of the individuals in such a relationship could end up killing the other when one is suffering from such a disorder. We are all of us simply human beings at the end of the day and psychological abuse is perhaps, in my opinion, the most damaging and the most insidious. The scars from physical abuse eventually heal, but emotional scars are much harder to conceal.'

Don't I know it?

'Narcissists don't like the word "no", Detective. And they can be quite dangerous, particularly if they experience a narcissistic injury which threatens their core self. Causing them an injury, such as unmasking them publicly, calling them out on their behaviour, catching them in a lie, challenging them in any way whatsoever, can send them into a rage which could potentially lead to violent behaviour. It's possible that Laurie Mills ran to the end of the rope. Robert made her feel as if she was going mad. He attempted, and I would say on occasions succeeded, in making her believe that she was the unstable one, the unhinged one, the one who needed help. He projected his disorder onto her. Her self-esteem was through the floor when I first started working with her, almost non-existent in fact. He had brought her so low over the years that there was very little left of her. She came to me as a broken shell. Laurie still believed that she loved her husband, despite his undeniable cruelty and infidelities. In reality however, she had become trauma-bonded to him, addicted to the diabolical cycle. This is the ultimate name of the game of a narc however, to keep someone trapped by their own emotions, and tied to them. My job was to begin to unravel it all, to steer her out of the fog and back to herself.

'Are you a spiritual person, Detective?'

The question catches me off guard. 'As opposed to what?'

She smiles, doesn't push it. 'Most cult leaders are narcissists. They brainwash people. It's done by intermittent reinforcement. Let's say you kick a dog then give it a treat. The dog learns that to get the treat it has to first withstand the kick. Gradually the treats decrease while the kicks increase, but by then the dog has been conditioned to associate being kicked with receiving a treat so it will accept the punishment in the vain hope that one day it will get the treat again, just like it did in the beginning, do you follow? Anyway, tell me a little about the murders, Detective, some detail—'

'Well, Robert Mills' throat was savagely cut open. He was stabbed multiple times. It was frenzied, violent and brutal. But there was a different MO for Claire Wright. She was suffocated with a plastic bag and little Matilda, well' – I take a deep breath – 'she was alive but left lying next to her mother's body.'

'I see.' She looks away and pauses for a few seconds, taking my words in. 'Laurie talked about being free of Robert. Deep down, she knew she needed to get away from the relationship. She was well aware that it was toxic, that he was abusing her. She was almost the classic battered wife – emotionally battered I mean. It was going to be a slow and long process, extricating herself from his Svengali-like clutches.'

Dr Wells meets my eyes. 'Laurie was – is, from what I deduced anyway, from the work I've done with her – naturally a gentle, kind soul. I certainly never had her down as someone suffering from overtly vengeful thoughts. The woman was grieving the loss of two almost full-term, unborn babies after being betrayed by her husband, a man she believed she could trust. It was a horrific tragedy, not something one easily navigates emotionally, as you can imagine, I'm sure.'

'Yes. I can,' I say, but decide against mentioning Rachel. She may start charging me and, frankly, I couldn't afford her. 'Do you know if Laurie ever suffered from blackouts? Did she ever mention anything like that? Memory loss?'

Dr Wells sighs. 'Yes. Yes, I'm afraid she did.' She glances at me nervously. 'This is very common for people afflicted with PTSD though. Plus, she was alcohol-dependent, not a full-blown alcoholic but dependent on it, like medication. It's a dangerous combination, together with the PTSD, prescription drugs and alcohol—'

'So you think it's possible that Laurie Mills may have killed her husband, and Claire Wright, and not remembered doing it? Blanked it out.'

She takes a sip of water from the plastic cup. 'Possible, but unlikely, in my professional opinion. I believe we are all capable of murder, Detective, if pushed far enough. I could accept that perhaps Laurie snapped and killed Robert in the heat of the moment. But the murder of the mistress and leaving the baby to potentially die, this is much harder to entertain. Laurie Mills was sad, not bad, or indeed mad. She was actually very focused on making a recovery, on trying to get better. She knew the pain of losing a child – two in fact. Claire's murder was calculated, yes? Pre-planned, thought through? Not a spur of the moment slaying?'

I nod in the affirmative.

Dr Wells shakes her head. 'Rage,' she says. 'Whoever committed these murders is full of rage, Detective. Filled with bitter hatred and thoughts of revenge. Laurie never came across as a vengeful or indeed particularly angry individual. It wasn't revenge she wanted – it was peace of mind. It's difficult to believe she's a cold-blooded killer, a psychopath. Even during a blackout, the violence would be much more spontaneous, much more random – in my professional opinion, of course. What about forensics?'

I can see from Dr Wells' expression that not only does she not believe Laurie Mills is capable of such an unspeakable act, but that she's really hoping there's evidence to support her theory.

'Her fingerprints were on the knife used to kill Robert. They found her DNA in Claire Wright's apartment. There's CCTV footage that would suggest, though not conclusively, that Laurie went to Claire's apartment on the night she was murdered. There's a motive… and a sighting from a neighbour who claims to have seen Laurie getting into her car.'

'I see.' She sighs heavily. 'So it doesn't look good for Laurie?'

It's a rhetorical question that neither of us needs the answer to.

'Laurie Mills is a victim of years of psychological abuse. If, and I say if, Detective, because I am still unconvinced, forensics or otherwise, that she committed these murders, then it's an all-round tragedy.'

'Thanks for your help, Dr Wells,' I say, moving to take my leave. 'If this goes to trial, you may be called upon as a witness, just so you know.'

She nods with a resigned half-smile. 'Of course.'

CHAPTER FORTY-SEVEN

'No. No. NO! You've got this all wrong! This is a mistake. I did not kill Claire or try to harm her baby. I was asleep. I went to bed last night and woke up there this morning. I didn't go anywhere; I didn't see anyone… I just slept… This is a mistake. You've made a mistake.'

Laurie Mills' hands cover her thin face, her fingers touching the hollows of her sunken cheeks. She's shaking her head in disbelief. It feels like she's entered the twilight zone. Like this is all some kind of sick joke or diabolical nightmare. First Robert. Now Claire. They're saying she's killed them both, that she drove to Claire's apartment and suffocated her with a plastic bag and then left the baby next to her.

The male detective starts placing photographs on the table in front of her. His aggression is simmering just beneath the surface. She senses it.

'Look at the photographs, Laurie. It's Claire Wright, your dead husband's mistress. You killed your husband, Laurie. And then you went and killed his lover, didn't you?'

It doesn't sound like a question. It's an accusation. A statement. She's shaking her head.

'You drove to Claire's apartment. You spoke to her on the intercom system and she let you in. Did she know it was you, Laurie? What happened when you went upstairs?'

Laurie is still shaking her head, hugging her knees tightly. She looks to the female detective for some solidarity. Surely she doesn't believe that she could've done this?

'Look at the photographs, Laurie.'

She can't bring herself to. She can see them from her peripheral vision. Claire's body in the foetal position… the baby next to her. She can't look. She doesn't want to.

'We have you on CCTV,' the male detective continues, 'and there's a witness who saw you leaving Monica Lewis's house around 10.30 p.m. last night. Can you explain that, Laurie? Talk us through it, yeah.'

Laurie rubs her gritty eyes. She's groggy from the Valium Monica gave her last night. Groggy and confused as to what's happening, or if it really is happening at all. She knows she didn't get in her car last night: she's sure of it. She wouldn't have been capable of driving, certainly not alone. It scares her. She wouldn't have been capable of killing Claire either and she would never, ever harm a baby. The baby is innocent. She couldn't do such a thing. Never. There's been a mistake, a dreadful, terrible, awful mistake, hasn't there?

'It's not possible. No. No.' She's still shaking her head, like it's about to come free of her neck. 'Monica will tell you. I was asleep. She gave me a Valium to help send me off. Since Robert—'

'Since Robert what?' The male detective leans forward towards her. It feels menacing. She looks at the female detective again, her eyes darting between the two of them simultaneously.

The man sits back into his chair. 'Come on, Laurie. Talk to us. Tell us what happened. You'll feel better once you've told the truth…'

Her head is still shaking, compulsively now. All that's going through it is the word 'no' on repeat, over and over in a loop.

'I want to speak to Detective Riley,' she says. She wants to tell him what she's remembered about the night of Robert's death. About the third person, the smell of perfume, the sensation of being carried up the stairs… If only her memory would give her an image, a face… She had to keep trying, to keep searching inside her mind – it would come to her eventually, wouldn't it?

'I'm afraid Detective Riley is otherwise engaged right now,' Delaney says, dashing her hopes.

'Listen, Laurie,' the woman says; her voice is softer, almost soothing, comparatively. 'We know about the accident. We know what happened, with the car crash, with Milo and Nancy. We know you almost died, Laurie. And we know why it happened. We know how distraught you were when you discovered the affair. It was a terrible thing, Laurie.' She says it with such sincerity that Laurie automatically begins to sob. 'No one could blame you for hating Robert, for hating what he'd done. It's understandable that you felt angry, aggrieved… finding out about the baby, about Matilda. Those children, those babies you lost… it must have been dreadful.'

No, no, no…

'You've suffered, Laurie. Really suffered. We understand that. I understand that – as a woman, I understand. He betrayed you. They both did.'

No.

'You've suffered blackouts before, haven't you? Where you can't remember. Since the accident, you've experienced blackouts where you can't account for moments in time?' the man questions her again. She can't remember his name, though she's sure he's told her.

Laurie's head feels like it's going to explode. This really can't be happening. Only it *is* happening. Perhaps the policewoman is right. She blacked out and killed Robert and now she's done the same with Claire. Only she knows, she *knows* she didn't. She doesn't even know where Claire lives. She looks up at the woman opposite her: young and pretty, fresh-faced, just like she'd been once upon a time. All she can think to say is, 'No.'

CHAPTER FORTY-EIGHT

'She's not talking, boss. Says she was at Monica Lewis's house, asleep. That she'd taken a Valium. Never got into her car. Woke this morning, none the wiser.'

'It's as I thought.'

'Well, Delaney's been going at her for over two hours now and she's not budging. Denies even knowing where Claire Wright's apartment is. What did the shrink say?'

'Is Delaney still with her?' I ask.

'She's back in the cells, Gov. She could hardly string a sentence together by the time we'd finished with her.'

I nod. I can imagine Delaney enjoyed every second.

'So, you've been with her, Davis. What do you think?' I can't help wondering if she's pregnant with that shmuck Delaney's child or not. She hasn't mentioned anything since our candid conversation a few days ago.

'Did the shrink shed any light on the blackouts?'

I sigh. 'Well, she was aware that Laurie's experienced them before.'

'And?'

'And she doesn't think it's likely that she'd become violent, though she can't be sure. In her professional opinion, she doesn't think Laurie is suffering from any kind of personality disorder, or that she's psychopathic, or that she's a murderer.'

Davis looks me in the eyes. 'The hair, boss,' she says. 'Her DNA is there in the apartment. How else would it have got there?'

'That's what I'm trying to work out, Davis,' I reply. 'I suppose it could have been transferred from Robert Mills at some point. Maybe he had some of her hair on his shirt and went over there and it transferred?' I remember the smell of the perfume in Claire's flat. It was the same perfume I smelt on Laurie Mills – a strong, sweet, almost-chocolatey smell, very distinctive.

'I think she's suffering from some kind of disorder where she blacks out and commits these awful murders but has no recollection of it,' Davis surmises.

I make to speak but Delaney enters the room and throws a packet of smokes down onto the desk. 'She's not coughing,' he says. He looks pretty pissed off.

'You will be if you carry on smoking those things.'

He smiles but I think I see a flash of irritation in it.

'Well, we've still got enough to charge her with Claire Wright. Woods is putting it to the CPS as we speak.' He says this with a sense of victory. Men like Delaney make bad coppers. They want to put someone away for a crime, anyone, even if it isn't conclusive, just to show they've got the power, that they get the result. He's all about the finish line.

'She keeps asking to speak to you, boss,' Davis says.

'We're missing something,' I say. 'Something vital, something obvious, something that's staring us in the face.'

'Like the truth, you mean?' Delaney snorts, but no one else joins in and his grin dissipates.

'We've got Laurie Mills for another sixteen hours before we have to charge her,' I say. 'I think we should all get some shut-eye for a few hours. Come back with a fresh outlook. I want to re-examine the CCTV. Let's speak to the neighbours again. And Davis, you and me will head down to Rochester, chase up that address, the one the phone was registered to, the number that Robert Mills called the day he was murdered.'

'The address is registered to an Agnes and Stanley Atkins, boss,' Mitchell says. She's been listening in, paying attention. I like that. She's got potential.

'Well then, we'll pay them a visit.'

'Waste of time,' Delaney mutters underneath his breath. 'Just give me a few hours alone with her. I can break her,' he says. 'Wear her down.'

Like he did with Davis, I imagine.

'No need, Martin,' I reply. 'Laurie Mills is already broken.'

CHAPTER FORTY-NINE

It's unorthodox I know, and if Woods finds out then my neck's for the block, but I want to speak to Laurie Mills off the record, and by all accounts she wants to speak to me too.

She looks like a small child sitting on the edge of the mattress inside the cell: a lost little girl. I have to stop myself from putting an arm around her, remind myself that she's a suspected killer, a double murderer.

'You wanted to speak to me, Laurie?'

She raises her head from the tops of her knees, where it's been resting. She looks exhausted, her face drained of colour and vitality. 'Yes. Thank you for coming.' Her voice sounds frail, a little hoarse.

'Can I get you anything? Water or a cup of tea perhaps?'

'No. No, thank you. I just wanted to tell you that I'd remembered something from the night of Robert's murder.'

'Your memory returned?'

'Not fully, no, just dribs and drabs. It's still sketchy but it's slowly coming back to me.'

'What do you remember, Laurie?'

'Someone else in the house. I felt their presence. I could smell perfume. Not my perfume. And I recognise it but I can't place it, can't remember what it's called. Someone carried me up the stairs. I remember the sensation of being weightless in their arms, of bashing my shins against the bannisters. That's how I got these bruises – see?' She pulls the standard grey joggers up with ease to show me. 'I had no recollection of going upstairs, Detective, because I didn't. Someone took me upstairs and put me in the guest room where Robert was.'

'Can you remember whether it was a man or a woman, Laurie? Please try and think hard.'

She shakes her head with frustration. 'I can't be sure. I can't see their face, but I can feel them, the sensation of being carried up the stairs in their arms. Perhaps it was a man – a man would be able to carry me up the stairs, wouldn't he?'

I'm pretty sure a child could carry Laurie Mills up a flight of stairs.

'But then I could smell perfume, so maybe it was a woman. Somehow I sense it was a woman.'

'Did you tell the other officers this, Laurie? Did you tell them this in interview earlier?'

'No.'

'Why not?'

'Because I didn't think they would believe me. Everyone thinks I did it, that I killed Robert and then Claire.' She wraps her hands around her knees, hugs herself. 'Look, Detective, I need to come clean…'

I swallow dryly. If she confesses now to me off the record, then our impromptu chat is going to be exposed and that neck of mine will be twice for the block and Woods will enjoy every swing of the axe.

'I thought about killing Robert. I even bought some poison, arsenic it was. I couldn't believe how easy it was to purchase. No doubt forensics will find this out once they've gone through my computer so I thought I would tell you, give you a heads-up.' She smiles softly but it has a hopelessness to it, like she knows her goose is cooked. 'I thought about it in a moment of madness, killing him I mean. I just wanted to be free of him, do you understand?'

'Why poison?' It's a very different method of murder than slitting someone's throat and plunging a knife into them.

'Because he was mine,' she says. 'But I couldn't go through with it. It was a ridiculous idea. I didn't know what I was thinking—'

'What did you do with the arsenic, Laurie?'

'Washed it down the sink, threw the bottle away.'

I nod. 'Okay.'

'But there's something else, something Monica said.'

'Monica Lewis, your friend?'

'Yes. She told me she'd seen me that night, the night of Robert's murder. She said that she'd come over to the house to check on me, to see if I was okay. She knew Robert was coming over; I'd told her that morning, when he'd messaged me. It would've been the first time I'd seen him since the day of the barbecue, since I discovered— Well, anyway, she says she looked through the window and saw us arguing in the kitchen, and that I had a knife—'

'She saw you holding a knife in your hand?'

'Yes, and she said that Robert and I were arguing. But I swear to you, Detective Riley' – she looks me directly in the eyes – 'I swear on the souls of my dead children that I don't remember seeing Robert that night, not alive anyway. I recall prepping the food, waiting, drinking at the kitchen table. I fell asleep there, I'm sure of it. But somehow, somehow, when I woke I was upstairs, covered in my husband's blood and Robert was…'

We both know how the story ends.

'Who else knew Robert was coming to see you?'

'No one,' she says, 'just me and Monica, and I guess whoever else Robert told – Claire I'm guessing, maybe his solicitor. I don't know.'

I nod again.

'There was someone else there that night. I know it, Detective. I can feel it. If only I could just see their face in my mind. I didn't kill Robert. I didn't kill Claire. I think I'm being set up.

'Do you believe me, Detective?' she asks, her large brown eyes meeting with mine once again.

I look into them, holding her gaze.

'Yes, Laurie,' I say. 'I do.'

CHAPTER FIFTY

The incident room is buzzing as I walk through the door. I can smell pungent determination mixed with stale sweat and coffee. It's strangely reassuring.

'CCTV, Gov,' Baylis says. 'The geeks have been on it. There's something I think you need to see.'

'I like the sound of that, Baylis,' I say, beckoning Davis over. 'Run it.' I'm feeling hopeful.

'Well,' Baylis begins, 'intelligence has done well. They've enhanced as much as they could and this,' she says, smiling, 'is what they've come up with.'

Davis and I are both standing either side of Baylis, leaning over the desk. I put my glasses on. My heart rate increases as she begins to run the tape. I watch as the shadowy female figure comes into view, begins to start talking into Claire Wright's intercom system. It's obvious she's speaking, even though there's no sound. The image zooms into the top of her head.

'See anything?' Baylis looks chuffed enough to eat herself.

'Run it back,' Davis says, looking as puzzled as I feel.

The machine whirs back and Baylis freezes it.

'What am I supposed to be looking at, Baylis?'

'Hang on! Oh. My. God.' Davis covers her mouth, but it doesn't conceal the smile underneath that's creeping through.

'Davis has got it!' Baylis laughs gently. 'But then again, she *is* a woman.'

I stare at the pair of them simultaneously. 'Well, you'll have to enlighten this *man*,' I say.

'One more try, boss.' She runs the tape forward and then back again to the female figure as she presses the intercom, the camera catching the top of her head, zooming in closely onto it.

'See it. To the left?' Baylis taps the image with the nib of a pen. 'That tiny thing there?'

I squint. 'It looks like the edge of a tag, a label.' I study it, scrutinising the footage with narrow eyes.

'It's only a syrup,' Davis says. 'She's wearing a goddamn wig.'

I feel a rush of blood to my head.

'Well, well, well,' I say. 'Keep running the tape.' I watch the image once more, the woman as she presses the intercom, the top of her head as she speaks into it and then the moment she walks forward to push the door open after Claire Wright has buzzed her in. That's when I notice it. Intelligence has sharpened the image. Her foot. There's something on her foot.

'Go closer in,' I instruct Baylis. 'Get a close-up of her foot.'

She presses the necessary buttons and the woman's foot comes into focus.

'There! See it?' It's small but it's there. There's something on her foot – a mark; a tattoo perhaps. 'Send it back to the geeks,' I say. 'Get them to enhance the foot. We need to see what it is. Davis, ask someone to check Laurie Mills' right foot for any markings, yes?'

'Yes, Gov.'

'And get your coat. We're going to Rochester.'

'You take me to all the best places,' Davis replies, grabbing her coat from the back of her chair.

CHAPTER FIFTY-ONE

Rochester might boast a cathedral, but it's a pretty moribund little town in my opinion, a bit like Canterbury's scruffier, black sheep of a cousin. There's a sense of time stood still here; a sense of faded glory, like a once-beautiful Hollywood starlet who's let herself go.

We pull up outside a large but modest-looking 1930s semi.

'I hope there's someone in, boss. Wasted journey otherwise,' Davis says, stating the obvious. 'Perhaps we should have called first.'

'The element of surprise, Davis.' I turn to her. 'Don't underestimate it. And, Davis, have a little faith, will you? You do realise we're nothing but human transmitters. Whatever you think becomes.'

'In that case I'm a very rich supermodel,' she says. 'Anyway, I hope you're right.'

Luckily, I am. A woman pokes her head round the door. At a glance I'd say she was in her late fifties. She's well presented in smart jeans and a white shirt. Her face is lightly made-up and her hair styled. I imagine she was once extremely attractive. *Faded glamour.*

'Can I help you?' Her expression is blank as she opens the door a fraction wider.

'We're sorry to bother you. I'm Detective Dan Riley and this is DS Lucy Davis. Are you Agnes Atkins?'

'Yes,' she replies, fiddling with her necklace: a cross. 'You're here about Bertie?'

Davis and I glance at each other.

'Bertie?'

'Yes. Robert. Robert Mills. My son.'

Neither of us were expecting her to mention Robert Mills' name.

'Yes,' Davis says quickly. 'Can we come in?'

CHAPTER FIFTY-TWO

'This is Stanley, my husband.' Agnes leads Davis and I into a pristine living room and offers us a seat on a cream corner sofa covered in floral scatter cushions. It smells fresh, like she's just cleaned the place. I spot some sympathy cards on the mantelpiece above the fireplace and a fresh bouquet of lilies in a large glass vase next to them. There's a gilt effigy of Christ on the cross next to the mirror. 'Stanley, this is Detective—'

'Riley,' I say as he stands to shake my hand. 'And this is DS Davis.'

'You took your time,' he says dryly. 'We were wondering when you'd get round to us.'

'You're related to the deceased, Robert Mills?' It's a genuine question. Atkins was the name that came up from the searches, not Mills.

Stanley raises an eyebrow and looks at his wife. 'You could say that. We're his parents. Or were his parents, I should say.'

I hope the shock isn't registering on my face.

'Can I offer you tea? Coffee? A soft drink, maybe?' Agnes smiles at me brightly; the kind of smile that is at odds with someone whose son has just been brutally murdered.

Something isn't quite right here. I can tell Davis senses this too as she's shifting from foot to foot and glancing over at me. We both decline the offer of refreshments.

'I'm sorry for your loss, about Robert,' I say. 'It must've been a terrible shock.'

Agnes glances at her husband as if asking permission to speak. 'Thank you.' Her voice is soft and measured, her body language guarded. 'Yes. Yes, it was. We've been praying for him, haven't we, Stan?'

'Haven't we always, dear?' he mutters his response. I'm not sure whether I was intended to hear the comment or not.

'Agnes, when was the last time you saw your son?'

She folds one leg over the other as she sits down. The husband's face remains expressionless. 'I spoke to him that day. The day of his…' She drops her head. 'The day he died. I hadn't seen him for a while. Weeks, I suppose—'

'More like months, Aggy,' Stanley remarks caustically. 'He never bothered with us much, Detective.'

Agnes shifts a little uncomfortably on the sofa, fiddles with a cushion.

'What did you speak about, Mrs Atkins?'

'General chit-chat, really,' she says, 'nothing unusual. How he was, where he was working, that kind of thing.'

I nod. 'Were you close? Did you get on well with your son?' The question is intended for both of them because I'm sensing some kind of animosity from the husband. 'I notice that Robert doesn't have the same surname as yourselves. Can I ask, is this your second marriage, Mrs Atkins, because the name… Robert's surname was Mills?'

'No. It's not anyone's second marriage, Detective,' Stanley Atkins interjects curtly. 'We're Catholics. We take our vows seriously; forsaking all others til death do us part. We're Robert's biological parents. *He* decided to change his surname.'

'Why was that?' Davis asks.

'Work reasons,' Agnes says quickly. 'He felt Mills had a better ring to it than Atkins. 'That it sounded more… well, I don't know, posher, so he changed it.'

'I see.' Only I don't. Not really. 'Was Robert your only son? Does he have any siblings?' Now I'm on full alert because Agnes's face displays something close to panic and she glances shiftily at her husband.

'He was an only child,' Stanley replies quickly.

'Were you familiar with Claire Wright and Matilda, your grandchild? Once again, we're very sorry for your loss. I can only imagine what a terrible ordeal this is for you both.'

Only it doesn't really seem to be translating as such from where I'm standing. In tragedies such as this there would usually be grief-stricken tears and inconsolable sadness. But Stanley and Agnes appear cold and cool and a little aloof.

'We never met her,' Agnes says, her head dropping again. 'We had hoped to one day. Or at least, I had hoped to…' Her voice trails off. 'Robert promised me he would have her baptised and that when he did we'd be invited.'

'Like I said,' Stanley interjects again. 'He hardly bothered with his mother and I when he was alive. He didn't much care for what we wanted. For what anyone wanted.' His voice is acerbic.

Davis glances at me again.

'Do you know anyone by the name of Kiki Mills? Is she a relative or Robert's, of yourselves?'

I see a look of fresh panic flash across Agnes Atkins' face.

'We don't know anyone by that name,' Stanley Atkins says quickly. 'Do we, Agnes?'

She looks nervously at her husband. 'No,' she replies.

'So you can't explain why a phone has been registered in that name to this address?'

'A phone?' Agnes looks up at me blankly.

'Yes. A phone is registered in that name to this address. The number came up on your son's phone records. There was communication between Robert and the owner of the phone on the day of his murder, and regular contact prior to that day for some time before that. Have you any idea who this Kiki might be?'

'We've just told you: we don't know anyone by that name. It must be a mistake.' Mr Atkins' voice is sharp.

'We can't bury him until they release the body,' Agnes says quietly. 'Our son.' She's fiddling with her cross again, her fingers twitching.

Stanley turns to his wife. 'Don't upset yourself, Aggy. Let the people do their jobs, then we can say our farewells.' He makes to touch his wife's arm but she moves away before he makes contact. I watch the brittle exchange between them. This is not your typical grieving couple.

'Have you any idea who may have wanted your son dead?'

Stanley Atkins doesn't answer.

'We heard that Laurie is in custody,' Agnes says. 'That you think she killed Robert and that Claire girl—'

'Can't say I'd blame the poor woman if she had,' Stanley scoffs underneath his breath, but both Davis and I hear him.

'What makes you say that, Mr Atkins?'

He sighs, mutters something incoherent.

'Don't mind him,' Agnes says dismissively. 'He's just upset. We liked Laurie. She was, she is… well, she put up with a lot over the years.'

'Like what exactly?' Davis asks.

'Well, Robert… Robert wasn't always… I think it was a difficult marriage,' she explains diplomatically.

'Yes, difficult for him to keep his hands to himself,' Stanley adds.

Agnes looks away, embarrassed.

'Those vows meant nothing to someone like Robert.'

'You were fond of Laurie?' I address the question to Agnes.

She smiles faintly. 'Yes, yes I was. We were excited when we found out about the twins. We thought… well, we really thought this might be the chance to be a normal family, didn't we, Stan?'

Stanley Atkins gives his wife a look that immediately silences her.

'It was tragic what happened to Laurie and those babies.' Stanley Atkins' voice is tinged with anger. 'We couldn't condone what Robert had done… the affair with the girl, the one who's dead now.'

'Claire Wright,' I say. 'Her name was Claire Wright.'

'I never had Laurie down as the violent type, Detective,' Agnes suddenly says. 'Laurie wouldn't say boo to a goose. She was a nice girl, decent. She loved Robert. We all did.'

I nod.

'Are you familiar with someone called Monica Lewis? I believe she's a long-standing friend of both Robert and Laurie, is that correct?'

I watch Agnes Atkins' reaction carefully. I'm sure I see fear in her eyes, although she does not look at her husband.

'Yes,' she says measuredly. 'We know who Monica is.'

'She's an old family friend from way back. We haven't seen her in many years though,' Stanley adds.

'Laurie Mills was staying at Monica's house following your son's murder. They seem very close.'

Agnes looks away and I think I hear Stanley make a noise.

'Yes. They were friends; I think they met at school,' he says, his mouth forming a thin, grim line. 'Is there anything else we can help you with, Detective?'

I want to say, *You could start by telling me the truth*, but instead I smile and thank them for their help, apologise for their loss once again and tell them I'll be in touch.

Davis's phone rings as Agnes shows us out and she goes ahead to the car, leaving us standing on the doorstep.

'Thank you for your time, Agnes,' I say, stalling. I feel like she wants to tell me something. I sense it from her body language. There's an urgency behind her eyes. 'If there's anything else… if anything else comes to you, however insignificant you might think it is, please call me.' I hand her my card and she accepts it with shaking fingers. 'Day or night,' I add, making direct eye contact with her.

'Detective,' she says, but Stanley appears at the doorway and she doesn't get to finish the sentence before he closes the door.

CHAPTER FIFTY-THREE

Laurie stares at the smooth white-brick walls and listens to the thudding of her own rapid heartbeat. They've charged her with two counts of murder and one of attempted murder. Her husband, his mistress and their child. She will be vilified and hated, despised by people. *The baby killer*.

She has given in and called her mother, finally. She didn't want her to hear the news via the media. Cynthia would hate being the last to know.

It had been oddly reassuring to hear her mother's voice on the telephone. It's different to how she remembers it as a child; it has a slight nasal US twang to it now that doesn't really suit her. She imagines her mother as she has become today, bohemian and pseudo-intellectual, stuck in the 1960s, a cereal-box feminist who'd secretly always needed a man by her side to feel complete, and sometimes more than one. She lived near Venice Beach somewhere in California. Laurie has seen photographs of her condo surrounded by cacti and vintage metal signs. It has a small porch with one of those swinging chairs that American homes always have on TV shows, but she has never been there. Her mother has never invited her.

Robert had never liked Cynthia. And the feeling had always been mutual. Laurie's mother had been a reluctant guest at their wedding, leaving as soon as it was safe enough not to raise eyebrows.

He may be easy on the eye, Laurie, but mark my words that man has secrets… He's bad news. That's what Cynthia had said to her on their wedding day. Laurie had wondered why her mother could never just be happy for her. Nothing and no one had ever been good enough, or even simply enough. When Laurie had told her she was pregnant with twins her mother's response was to say, 'Two! That'll put years on you! That man will leave you to do all the work, you know. You'll be left holding the babies while he's off doing goodness knows what with goodness knows who…' Her words had always stung, even though Cynthia had been right.

'Oh, Laurie… what a mess.' Her mother's strained voice displayed a mix of worry tinged with, she thought, disappointment. 'It's those meds you're taking isn't it, with the booze… Look, we'll get you a good brief. *I* will get you a good brief, pay for the best there is. Maybe if you plead insanity you'll get a lenient sentence—'

'But I'm not insane, Cynthia!' Laurie had said, incredulous that her mother could be so blasé about it. 'I didn't kill them! I didn't kill Claire or try to kill the baby… and I don't think I killed Robert.' But she hardly had any energy left to protest. It was an effort just to raise her voice.

Her mother had remained quiet for a moment as the line crackled and Laurie had felt compelled to fill the silence.

'They tell me I blacked out. That the PTSD causes me to experience these moments where I don't remember things…' She'd looked down at her shaking hands and wondered if they belonged to a murderer, if there was blood on them. *But there was a third person* – she's absolutely sure of it.

'I'll get a plane over as soon as I can, Laurie.' Her mother's voice sounded weary now, resigned, like it used to when she was a child and she needed something from her. Laurie had always felt like a burden and that Cynthia found her presence an irritation.

'I always knew that man would be your downfall,' she'd added before hanging up.

Laurie thinks of the images the detective had shown her of Claire, blue and mottled and dead on the sofa, a plastic bag over her face, and starts to cry. She'd had a pretty face really, Claire. It wasn't her fault. None of it was, or Matilda's. Robert, he was responsible for all of this; he was to blame. But now she will take the fall. Somehow, even in his death, he was still managing to punish her. She wonders if she can speak to that detective again, the one with the kind eyes: Detective Riley. He had believed her when she'd told him about being carried up the stairs by someone – she could see it in his eyes, his body language. He believed she was telling the truth. Someone has set her up, but who and why remained a mystery.

She will be able to prove this, won't she? They claim she was seen by a neighbour. That Jessica Bartlett woman from next door. She told the police that she had seen Laurie leaving and getting into her car, alone, and driving off on the night of Claire's murder. But she knows she would never get into a car alone. That she *can't*. Not anymore. Not since the accident. There's DNA and CCTV footage too, so the male detective had said; hair belonging to her was recovered at the scene and there were images of her buzzing Claire's intercom and entering her apartment building. They had grilled her for what felt like hours, until she wasn't sure which way was up. They've told her she's calculated, a cold-blooded killer; a mad, bad, possessed woman, consumed with rage and hell-bent on revenge; a *baby killer*.

Laurie shakes her head as a guard opens the hatch and places a small, white plastic dish filled with something that she assumes is food but that does not look identifiable, let alone edible. She can't eat. She can't accept what they're trying to tell her she's done and what that makes her. She's tired but lucid, the Valium having long since worn off. Perhaps Monica will slip her some more in when she visits: *mother's little helpers*. Monica. Surely Mon would've heard her coming and going the night of Claire's murder? She was sleeping in the next room. She would have heard her get up and go downstairs, get into her car, the engine starting up… And then something comes back to her, startling her so much that she bolts upright with a gasp.

CHAPTER FIFTY-FOUR

'Now *that* was *not* normal,' Davis comments as she buckles up. 'They're definitely hiding something.'

'Your powers of deduction are second to none, Ms Davis. You'd make an excellent copper, do you know that?'

Davis shoots me a snarky grin.

'So, what do you reckon then? What's the story?' I want Davis's take on things. Sometimes she sees nuances I miss.

'Well, for starters they didn't seem too upset about the fact their only son has just been savagely murdered.'

'Hmm, they didn't, did they? But why?'

Davis shrugs. 'Family feud? Not exactly uncommon, is it?'

'It's more than that,' I say. 'I think they know who Kiki Mills is. Agnes's reaction – she recognised the name.

'But Mills wasn't Robert's real surname, was it? He changed it by deed poll from Atkins.'

'So, do you think it could be an alias for Laurie, or a coincidence maybe?'

I shake my head. 'It would seem odd to use your married name as an alias, but too much of a coincidence to be a coincidence, if that makes sense. Anyway, I think Agnes wanted to tell me something but stopped short when Stanley appeared.'

'That was Murray on the phone by the way,' Davis says.

'And…?' What is it with women? They all seem to enjoy playing guessing games.

Laurie Mills doesn't have any marking on her foot. She doesn't have any tattoos – nothing at all.'

I nod. *I knew it.*

'And the other DNA they found on Robert Mills, it's not a match for Laurie's. It belongs to someone else. There's nothing on the database though. They've run it through.'

I can't help smiling. Woods is going to go spare. And Delaney is going to look like a right chump. 'She's not our killer, Davis,' I say with confidence.

'You've said as much from the beginning, boss. But if Laurie Mills isn't our woman, then who is?'

'Kiki Mills,' I say.

'Yes, but who the hell is Kiki Mills? The Atkinses deny knowing anyone of that name and nothing has come up on the database either.'

'That's because it's not her real name,' I say.

Davis looks sideways at me. 'So what is?' she asks.

Two can play at guessing games. I stay silent for a moment.

'Come on, Gov, tell me who you think our killer is.'

I grin at her. I can't help it. 'I'll do better than tell you, Davis,' I say, cocksure now. 'I'll show you.'

CHAPTER FIFTY-FIVE

Monica turns the radio up as she makes her way along the M23 towards Gatwick and hums along to Alanis Morissette's 'Ironic'. She likes this song. She glances at the expensive handbag next to her; her passport pokes out of the top. She's booked on a 5 p.m. flight to Cannes where she'll check into the Hotel Roberto. Now that *is* ironic, don't you think? She almost laughs out loud. Everyone has been dealt with now: Dougie, Robert, Claire, Laurie… The child had been a different matter; she had planned to smother little Matilda, send her off to join her parents so they could all live happily ever after in death. Only the baby had begun to coo at her, kicking her little legs up in the air and grabbing her toes. She had found herself watching the child for some time, lying there next to her dead mother on the sofa, transfixed by her. She had fantasised about being her mother, imagined bringing her up as her own daughter, the child she had never had by the man she had spent a lifetime loving and waiting for. All those abortions, all those dead babies, *their* babies, murdered by the doctors who had ripped them from her womb until her womb had stopped working…

Next year, Kiki, I promise. We'll have a baby next year, be a proper family, just like I've always said… Robert's voice resonates inside her mind like he's standing next to her. She had thought about taking the baby with her, the last connection she had to Bertie, but common sense told her not to. Killing Claire was one thing, but snatching a baby? They would close the borders – they'd be looking for a woman with a child and she'd be conspicuous. So instead she had left her untouched, half of her hoping that the little mite would starve to death and half of her hoping she would survive and be saved, go on to lead a happy, healthy normal life. She really did have her daddy's eyes…

Monica had tied up the loose ends. The estate agents would be putting her house on the market ASAP. She's not left any forwarding address and she's insisted on cash buyers only. She doesn't want a sign outside alerting those nosy neighbours of her intentions. She'll be long since gone by then. When it's sold, she'll get them to transfer the money into a French bank account, one she plans to open in her real name. They might try to find her, subpoena her when it comes to Laurie's trial. Perhaps it will even be okay for her to attend, but she will have to play that one by ear.

She lights a cigarette and opens the electric window a crack to let the smoke out. They might want to know why she's left the country. She'll tell them she is simply on holiday, having a well-earned break after all the dreadful business of the last few months. She'll keep her mobile alive for a week or two then dispose of it. She has a new passport, a new identity and a new life to lead. All her ducks are in order now.

Only there's one thing, or rather one person, who's bothering her, a loose end that needs tying up: Leanna George. She would never have known about Leanna George if the silly bitch hadn't gone whingeing to the press. The ones she didn't know about, they didn't matter – what Monica didn't know couldn't hurt her – but now that she knew about this woman, well, that was a game changer.

Leanna's image flashes up in her mind; the picture of her from the newspaper, all tits and teeth and bouncy blonde hair, calling herself an actress and model. She'd been incensed by it: *brazen slut*. Who did she think she was? She was no one, nothing, just another slag in Robert's harem of whores. She had thought she was special, just like they all had. Only they weren't. None of them. Not one. Not even Laurie, in fact – especially not Laurie. Laurie may have lasted the longest, been given the privilege of marriage, but that was simply because she provided the best decoy and had been the greatest ruse. Monica had even selected her for him. She'd told them as much as well, Agnes and Stan, pair of treacherous bastards that they were.

'You can't keep us apart!' she'd whispered in her mother's ear at the wedding. 'It's all a facade. It will always be me… it will always be us! You can't stop it!' It had been the very last thing she had ever said to them. They had tried to drive a wedge between them by threatening to disinherit Bertie, tried to keep them apart, but nothing and no one could. They thought they'd been the ones calling the shots, ostracising her, banishing her and cutting her off as they had. They despised her, and what they believed she'd done to their son. They had called her evil, said that she was Satan's work, all the while protecting their darling boy. But they had betrayed her, just as Robert had. She wishes she could've killed them both too. Only that would have been too easy. This way they suffered in silence. Hiding behind their religious beliefs and middle-class aspirations.

And now their only son was dead because of their refusal to accept what was meant to be. Now they had no one but each other to wallow in their collective misery with, guilt-stricken, filled with remorse and regret. They blamed her. They always had. Robert could do no wrong in their eyes. She had been the temptress, Eve to his Adam. They could not, would not accept it any other way. And so now they'd paid the price. They'd all paid for what they'd done to her: Agnes and Stanley; Robert, Claire and their bastard offspring; Laurie and those unborn twins…

She thinks about Leanna George again then, the tits and teeth, and feels a familiar rage spreading up through her diaphragm, burning through her chest like poison. She wants to silence her, to punish her, punish them all. She weighs up the risks. Her fall guy is in custody so she can't pin anything on Laurie, not this time. But Leanna strikes her as the kind of woman with a murky past, one which would take a bit of investigating. Ex-boyfriends, disgruntled wives of men she'd slept with, no doubt plenty of people in the running who may want to cause her harm. Putting herself out there in the press like that was practically inviting old skeletons to come out of the closet, not to mention stalkers –that's where they'd be looking first, not at her. She had no connection to Leanna George; she wasn't a suspect in any of this and there were no links back to her. If she was quick, she could get the job done and be out of there.

'Fuck it!' Monica says aloud, indicating to come off at the next turning. She had to turn back and finish this. She would get a later flight.

CHAPTER FIFTY-SIX

'Why are we here, boss?' Davis looks up at the house on Cedar Close.

'DNA,' I say. 'And a blanket.'

'But forensics already have everything.'

'From the Millses' house, yes,' I say cryptically. 'It's Monica Lewis I want to speak to.'

'Monica Lewis?'

I ring the doorbell. We wait.

'No one's home, boss. And it looks like her car is gone too.'

'Uh-huh.' I covertly glance to my left and then to my right. 'Cover me, Davis.' I say, only half-joking as I boot the front door in.

'Woods is going to have your guts for garters, you know that?'

'What's new?' We walk through the hallway.

'Can you at least tell me what we're looking for?'

I don't answer because the truth is, I don't really know myself. But something, that instinct of mine, is telling me that the missing link has been staring me in the face the whole time. Monica Lewis. Mon-ik-ca. *Kiki.* It came to me in the car, the lizard tattoo. I finally remembered where I'd seen it – on Monica Lewis's foot.

'Monica Lewis killed Claire Wright. I think she killed Robert too.'

'She did? Why? How do you know?'

'The tattoo,' I say. 'Did you know that Monica Lewis has a tattoo of a lizard on her right foot?'

'Jesus. She does?'

'You need to stop answering a question with a question, Davis,' I playfully berate her. 'It's very… American.'

'It is?' she replies in a bad American accent.

I somehow manage a smile.

The house is still and quiet. No sign of life. Davis checks downstairs while I go upstairs. There's nothing of note in the bedroom, nothing out of place. I rifle through a few drawers – they're practically full and her toothbrush is still in the en suite.

'Well, her stuff looks like it's still here,' I say to Davis as she joins me in the bedroom. Yet something tells me Monica Lewis is already long gone.

Davis looks at me, bewildered. 'Why would Monica Lewis want to kill Robert and Claire and then frame Laurie for it? Do you think she was having an affair with him?'

'Yes, but it's more than that. Did you find anything downstairs?'

Davis shakes her head. 'Nothing, Gov. Maybe she's just gone out on an errand somewhere, visiting a friend or something.'

I shake my head. 'Kiki Mills. Monica Lewis is Kiki Mills. She set Laurie up. She killed Robert, provided Laurie with a false alibi—'

'But why? If she wanted to frame her, why give her an alibi?'

'Because she gave herself an alibi in the process and threw us off the scent at the same time. She deliberately kept the body warm to make it look like the murder had taken place later in the evening. He was already dead when Laurie came back to the house from the shops. Then she impersonated her, used her clothes, wore a wig, made sure she was seen by the neighbour getting into Laurie's car—'

'And then went to Claire's apartment—'

'… killed her and planted Laurie's DNA at the scene. She framed her friend.'

'But what's the motive, boss? Jealousy? Pretty extreme lengths to go to—'

'Did you catch Agnes's expression? There was fear on that woman's face. They know who Monica Lewis is, and they know that she and Kiki Mills are the same person.'

'So who is she then? They said she was an old family friend—'

'Family being the operative word, Davis.'

Davis looks at me, perplexed. 'I'm not sure I follow you, Gov.'

'Well, you need to follow me now, Davis,' I say, making my way to the front door. 'I've just had the most terrible feeling, and if my instincts are correct, we haven't got much time.'

CHAPTER FIFTY-SEVEN

Leanna George checks her make-up in the mirror and listens out for the front door. She's buzzing with adrenaline, so much so that it's proving tricky to apply her third coat of lip gloss. The producer on the phone had said that she'd got her number from a journalist at the *Gazette* and that she was interested in casting her for a new reality TV show. And now she was on her way to her house to meet her in person!

You'd be perfect for it. Those were the actual words she'd used. *You're incredibly photogenic and you came across so well in interview.* Leanna replays the conversation over in her head, basking in the glow of such complimentary feedback. She supposed she had hoped that by coming forward with her story it might get her noticed in some way and potentially lead to her getting booked for more work, but she could never have envisaged this. A reality TV show was exactly what she needed to take her career to the next level. Those reality TV stars, some of them had gone on to become properly famous, not to mention ridiculously rich. The possibilities were endless if you managed to capture the public's heart. Endorsements, fitness videos, diet books, photo shoots, presenting jobs. Some had even ended up doing stints in soap operas and films. This really could be the big break she'd needed and been looking for. She wasn't getting any younger and it was tough competing with girls half her age.

Leanna smiles at her reflection, hopeful. Maybe all that shite she'd had to endure with that bastard Robert was going to have been worth it.

'Every cloud, eh, pet?' she says aloud to herself, brushing through her tonged hair once more until it shone. If she managed to seduce the producer well enough she was guaranteed an 'in'. The woman had sounded so keen to meet her that she'd insisted on coming over to speak to her directly that morning. Usually, she would have asked her to go through her agent but the woman, Kiki Miller, she'd said her name was, couldn't wait and needed to see her immediately.

She shudders and giggles at the same time, brimming with anticipation and self-confidence.

Leanna's already fantasising about becoming a household name and being interviewed by Phillip Schofield when she hears the doorbell ring.

CHAPTER FIFTY-EIGHT

'Leanna George?' The woman cocks her head to one side and gives a convincing, friendly smile.

'Kiki Miller, the producer I spoke with earlier, yes?'

'That's right. Gosh, you're even more perfect in the flesh.' She looks her up and down over-appreciatively and watches as Leanna's ice-white smile widens. 'Seriously, you really are going to be perfect for my new show.'

'Please, come in,' Leanna says, trying to contain her ego rush. 'I've been really looking forward to meeting you; this is so exciting.'

Monica follows her inside, sizing the place up for CCTV. There isn't any. *Happy days.* 'Beautiful apartment,' she says. 'A woman with taste as well. I like it.'

'Thank you so much. Please, please, sit down. Let me get you something to drink. What would you like? Tea, coffee, juice… something stronger? Some wine perhaps?'

She doesn't hesitate. 'I'd love a vodka, if you have any.'

'Vodka! Ah, a woman after my own heart.' Leanna is tickled pink.

It's just as Monica thought: Leanna is a lush. She's undoubt-edly a pretty face, of course, Robert was always a sucker for one of those, but she can see the hard edges creeping in as she studies her. Years of boozing and whoring always takes its toll in the end.

'Tonic or orange? I'll join you in one.'

'Orange please. Absolutely, and why not? We're celebrating, after all.'

Leanna disappears from the room to fix the drinks, giving Monica the opportunity to check on the bottle of sulphuric acid she's just bought from the hardware store where she'd stopped off en route. She'd told the man behind the counter that she'd needed 'the strongest they had, as she had a severe blockage'. It wasn't entirely untrue when she thought about it: Leanna George was the last 'blockage' that needed to be dealt with. She hadn't even had to strong-arm her into having a drink with her like she'd anticipated. *Bloody pisshead.*

'As soon as I saw your story in the local paper I felt I had to get in touch,' Monica calls out to her from the living room. 'It really… resonated.' She pauses thoughtfully. 'I think it's important that women speak out about domestic abuse, especially beautiful women like yourself. It debunks the myth that it only happens to doormats and plain Janes.'

Leanna returns with the drinks and hands her one. She would put money on them being double measures. 'Cheers,' she says, chinking her glass to Leanna's with some purpose.

'Cheers. Here's to a successful meeting and working together in the future.'

Leanna's wide, gormless grin sickens Monica. Women like Leanna can't get enough of an ego stroke. *No wonder she ended up in Robert's bed. No effort required.*

'Oh yes, I'll drink to that. I couldn't believe it when you called me,' Leanna gushes. 'I can't tell you how long I've been waiting for an opportunity like this to come along. I'm just so glad I went to the press now. That I came out and told the truth about my ex.'

The words 'my ex' set Monica's teeth on edge and it's all she can do to swallow back the mouthful of vodka and orange she's just taken.

'Your "ex" met a rather unpleasant end, didn't he? Although reading your story, some might say he had it coming to him.'

'Aye.' Leanna nods, taking a swig of her drink. 'It was still awful, like. I mean, I hated what he did, but him being murdered like that... I never wished him dead. Whatever he did, he didn't deserve to die like that. No one does, do they?'

Monica smiles. 'Yes, well, not everyone is as empathetic and kind as you, Leanna. He betrayed you, didn't he? Had a wife, and a mistress with a love child. He told you that you were the only one, didn't he?'

Leanna shifts in her seat. Monica can see she's not interested in talking about Robert anymore. *She never really loved him, not like* she *did. She just wants to cut to the chase now. The TV show, that's all she's really interested in. Fame. Fortune. Just another gold-digging, glory-seeking whore. She doesn't care about domestic abuse, or its victims. It's all just an excuse to further her career opportunities.*

'Aye, I had no idea the man was married. Never knew about the mistress, or the kid – none of it.' Leanna sighs. 'That man led more than one life, yet accused me non-stop of being the cheat. I changed me whole life for him too, like, did everything I could to convince him and please him, jumped through flaming hoops for that lying piece of shit. He was mugging me off the whole time. Not to mention the others too.'

Leanna's eyes look like they're filling up with tears now. *Not a bad little actress really. Bitch would probably do well on some third-rate reality show.*

'They're saying, the police, that the wife lost the plot and killed him. I think I would've too if I'd spent all them years married to a treacherous bastard like that. He nearly sent me off me head in two years, so I can only imagine what he did to that poor woman he was wed to.'

Monica looks at her closely. She studies Leanna's lips as she speaks, imagines them wrapped around Robert's dick, and no doubt countless others, as she rests her hand gently against the flap of her handbag, the outline of the bottle palpable inside. She almost feels sorry for her; another of Bertie's victims, sucked in by his inimitable charm only to be fooled and used, duped and confused. He would never have loved a girl like Leanna – not truly.

'Well, you're going to make a great poster girl for abused women the world over. Women who have suffered domestic abuse and survived it. It's a great hook. I mean, professionally speaking, it helps if viewers can relate to human-interest stories. You come across as a down-to-earth woman, which is always a hit.'

Leanna looks like she wants to lick herself. 'So, tell me a little about this show then,' she says brightly. 'It's one of them reality things? Like *Love Island* for grown-ups?'

'Yes, that's it… But the contestants have all faced adversity at some stage during their lives. We want real people, you know, people who've lived, experienced a bit of life… People like yourself. We're hoping to start shooting by Christmas. The concept is pretty straightforward and… oh God!' Monica deliberately misses the low glass coffee table as she attempts to place her vodka and orange down onto it. She watches in mock horror as it spills over the floor, and all over Leanna's pristine cow-print rug. 'I'm *so* sorry!'

Leanna jumps up. 'It's no bother at all, pet. Not to worry. I'll get a cloth. Shall I make you another one?'

Monica pretends to look embarrassed. Leanna's accent is grating on her. She wishes she'd brought a knife now. Stabbed the bitch through the heart. 'Oh, would you?' she says apologetically. 'I'm such a klutz. I'm really sorry.'

'No bother, pet.' Leanna is still beaming that ridiculous smile as she leaves the room.

She waits a moment for her to return with a cloth and watches as she dabs at the stain on the rug.

'There. No harm done. Let me get you another.'

'Thank you, Leanna.' As soon as she leaves the room again, Monica takes the bottle from her handbag and pours the contents into the half-empty glass, giving it a quick swirl around to mix the liquid before replacing it.

Leanna returns moments later with a refreshed glass.

'Right then. Sorry about that,' Monica apologises once more. 'How about let's do that toast again. Down in one, yes?'

Leanna laughs at the suggestion but needs no encouragement. 'Are you sure you're not from Newcastle?' she says with a laugh, picking her glass up and throwing the remainder of the contents down her neck.

CHAPTER FIFTY-NINE

'I need to speak to the detective – the one with the kind eyes, Detective Riley!' Laurie has been pounding on the door of her cell until her fists feel like they're about to crumble. 'Will someone listen to me! It's important! It's about my friend, Monica Lewis. Please, someone… anyone… I need to speak to that detective.'

My friend. Monica flashes up in her mind. Her face so familiar, yet suddenly a total stranger's. She'd remembered. *Finally.* The night of Robert's murder, she had opened her eyes and seen her. It was Monica carrying her up the stairs. And the night of Claire's murder, she remembers now that she'd woken up and gone to the window and seen Monica getting into her car. *She'd seen her.* She'd been wearing her dress, and her ballet pumps and a long dark wig. Laurie had thought she'd dreamt it. She'd truly *believed* that she had. Only it wasn't a dream at all. It had been real and she'd seen it.

Laurie attempts to remember as much detail as possible – anything, however small, to help corroborate her memory. The old woman from across the road, the blind one, Mrs Foster, the one whose foot she had trodden on at the ill-fated barbecue, she had seen her sitting at her window looking out.

With her new-found clarity, Laurie realises that Monica has been pumping her full of pills ever since the accident. It had been Monica who'd suggested she start on the antidepressants, then the Valium. Now she really thought about it, Monica hadn't been helping with her recovery at all but enabling her descent into addiction. Instead of steering her away from the prescription drugs and alcohol she was fast becoming dependent upon, she'd been gently guiding her ever closer towards them. Just like Robert, it had been a slow and insidious process, so covert that she'd not noticed it was happening. But now, now that she could remember... now it all made some kind of diabolical sense, a hideous, ugly jigsaw that fitted together. Monica had given her Valium to put her to sleep that night so that she could pretend to be Laurie: frame her for Claire's murder.

But why on earth would she do that? Why would her best friend of almost two decades want to frame her for something she didn't do?

Monica had told her that she had seen her arguing with Robert on the night of his death. But what if she hadn't really? What if she was trying to get her to believe that she was the killer, when really it had been Monica herself? Why had she provided her with an alibi? During Laurie's interview, the detectives had accused her of trying to outsmart them by keeping Robert's body warm to make the time of death look later than it actually was; they said that he was most likely killed around 1 p.m., just before she left for the hairdressers. Had Monica done this deliberately in some kind of calculated double bluff?

An assault course of questions hijack Laurie's brain until it's a spaghetti junction of unanswered whys. No. It wasn't possible, was it? Monica was like a sister, the closest she's ever been to another human being on the planet, her own mother included. Monica had been there her entire life, practically. She'd been her rock and her confidante, caring for her like family in the absence of her own.

Monica had introduced her to Robert when they were just eighteen years old. Robert was a friend of the family's, she'd said. *I think you're going to love him.* And she had been right, because Monica was always right. She had been there, stoic and solid, since she could remember. She'd been there on her wedding day; she'd been there as a shoulder to cry on throughout her toxic marriage to Robert. She'd been there before the accident and after it too, weeping at the graves of her unborn babies, holding her up as their tiny caskets disappeared behind the velvet curtain...

She thought about how strong Monica was as a person. How well she had coped when poor Dougie had passed away so suddenly. Good and bad, ups and down, highs and lows. They had shared them all, like sisters do and... Oh God! *Dougie*. It hits Laurie like an out-of-control freight train and she feels the force of the sudden realisation crushing her chest and restricting her breathing.

'Please!' She begins to bang on the cell door again, as hard as she can this time. 'Pleeeeease, someone! I need to speak to Detective Riley.'

CHAPTER SIXTY

We are too late.

Leanna George is being stretchered out of her apartment as we arrive. She is screaming out in agony. 'The pain… God help me the pain!' She looks like she's drifting in and out of consciousness as the paramedics attempt to get an IV into her. I run up to the stretcher.

'Leanna, Leanna! What happened? Tell me, what happened?'

'Looks like she's swallowed something,' the paramedic informs me. 'Probably some kind of acid.' He gives me a look that suggests it's not looking great for Leanna George, though you don't need to have gone through the training to work that one out, judging by the poor girl's moans and cries of agony.

'Goddamn it! Leanna!' I'm shouting now, my emotions getting the better of me. Her pretty eyes stare up blankly at me and I see the pain in them. 'Tell me, Leanna,' I say. 'Tell me who did this to you.'

Davis is holding my arm, horror plastered all over her face. Leanna is gurgling, making a horrendous, inhuman rasping noise that can only be described as the onset of an impending, agonising death as her vital organs burn inside her.

'Tell me, Leanna!' My voice is a high-pitched plea. 'Tell me, darling, who did this to you?' I look down at her, at the vibrant, ambitious woman who Davis and I had spoken to just a few days ago. A woman who'd fallen foul to the likes of Robert Mills and who had changed her life for what she believed would be the love of hers.

'Was it a woman? Who was it? Please, Leanna, don't die on me… You're strong, Leanna, strong. You'll get through this… it'll be okay. Tell me – tell me their name.'

I can see she's attempting to speak. I can see her Adam's apple moving furiously inside of her throat as she struggles to breathe through the searing agony that is tearing through her insides, shutting down her vital organs, killing her slowly. I think I might be crying because my vision is suddenly blurry.

'I will get whoever did this to you, Leanna. God help me, I swear I will find them and I will make sure they rot behind the door til their miserable death.'

I can see her slipping away in front of my eyes; her petite body writhing and twisting on the stretcher, even as they begin to pump it full of morphine. She's dying like an animal, a torturous, agonising, undignified and most of all unnecessary death.

I turn to Davis. 'Get Woods on the phone. We need to secure the borders. I won't let that bitch leave this country. Send out descriptions and photos of Monica Lewis. We need to find her before she gets on a plane and disappears. Do it, Davis – do it now.' But she's already on the phone before I can finish.

I look down at Leanna. She's still writhing on the stretcher, her body twitching; her pretty face is deathly pale, eyes bulging from their sockets as she stares back at me.

'It was her, wasn't it, Leanna? She did this to you.'

Suddenly she seizes my hand, almost like an involuntary spasm, grasping at me with claw-like fingers. 'K… K… K… Ki… Ki…' she says before finally, mercifully, passing out.

CHAPTER SIXTY-ONE

Monica is perusing a selection of make-up at the Clarins counter in duty-free under the attentive eye of the commission-based, over-made-up sales assistant.

She can't remember the name of the foundation she usually uses. *Is it the wheat or the honey wheat?* She pumps a little of each onto the back of her hand and rubs it in. *The wheat. Yes, definitely.* The honey is too yellow for her complexion. She's more of a red tone. Or so the assistant observes, looking at her like she's a rare work of art.

Monica purchases the make-up, plus some of her favourite Coco Mademoiselle perfume, after liberally spraying herself with the tester. It reminds her of Robert. He'd loved it and had bought her a bottle of it ever since she could remember, for birthdays and Christmases mostly, but sometimes just because he wanted to.

Taking her purchases, she heads through the departure lounge and into the women's toilets. It's busy of course; it's an airport. Usually, so many bodies in a small space would irritate her but today she is glad of the sweaty, hassled-looking strangers and their ugly luggage.

Locking herself in a cubicle, she opens her flight case and takes a small mirror out of a washbag, placing it on top of the cistern. Securing her hair back, she fixes the wig onto her head before tying a headscarf around it. Quickly she changes out of her jeans and blouse. There's no room for them in the carry case so she stuffs them into the sanitary bin. Shame really. The blouse was Zadig et Voltaire and cost a small fortune. Never mind, she consoles herself – plenty more of that in Cannes.

Slipping into a plain white shift dress, she struggles a little with the zip, eventually pulling it all the way to the top, just as he had done for her all those years ago for the first time.

Monica checks her reflection in the small mirror and adjusts her headscarf; it makes her look Parisian, like Audrey Hepburn, not least when she puts her dark, cat's-eye Chanel sunglasses on as a final touch. No one will recognise her. No one is looking for her. She doubts anyone will discover Leanna George for a while. Days, maybe even weeks perhaps. By then she will be a putrefying corpse, with only those tits and teeth left.

She is smiling to herself as she exits the cubicle.

CHAPTER SIXTY-TWO

'She won't be here. I know it,' I say as I ring the bell, conscious I am being watched by pairs of eyes from neighbouring houses.

Davis raises an eyebrow. 'I thought we were all just transmitters, Gov, and that whatever we think, we—'

'I'd ask you to boot the door in yourself, Davis, but I figure maybe not in your, well, in your *condition*.'

'False alarm, boss,' she says without missing a heartbeat. And I think she probably sees the relief on my face because she grins at me and does that thing where she cocks her head to one side. 'Besides, it's still open from the last time we did a Bruce Lee on it.'

I peer through the letter box.

'Monica? Monica Lewis? It's Detective Riley. Dan Riley. I need to speak with you urgently…'

'Jesus Christ,' Davis says, turning on her heels and holding her head. 'Do you think we've really lost her?'

I stop for a moment. Try to think. Think what Monica Lewis would do. Where she would go. She believes she isn't under any suspicion; she doesn't think anyone is looking at her. This is a good thing. It means she won't be too heavily on her guard, might even make a reappearance of her own volition.

'You think she's done a bunk, boss? It didn't look like she's taken much if she has.'

'Does a psychopath need much?' I reply, tapping my lip with my finger, despite how much it irritates me when other people do it. I was right. It doesn't help you think any clearer at all.

'If Monica doesn't think we're looking at her as our girl then she's bound to come back home, isn't she? Makes sense, doesn't it? She's not going to put heat on herself.'

'Nothing makes sense to a psychopath, Davis,' I lament. 'I don't think Leanna George was part of the original plan. She's taken a chance. The others… the others she could try to pin on Laurie, but not Leanna. Laurie is in custody. Not even Delaney can argue with that alibi.'

Davis turns away at the mention of his name.

'We've both made mistakes, Davis,' I say. 'We've both been looking in the wrong places the whole time. Sometimes the truth is so close that you can't see it staring you in the face. But I can see clearly now.'

'You're not going to start singing are you?' She smiles and strangely I feel like hugging her.

'Leanna George was an afterthought. Not part of the plan. She was impulsive. So, where would you head if you'd just spontaneously attempted to murder someone?'

Davis makes to speak but I cut her off when I see an old lady standing in the doorway of the house next door. She looks like she's watching us.

Davis waves her hand, dismissively. 'The blind lady, Mrs Foster. She won't have *seen* anything, obviously.'

I go over there anyway. I think I see Davis's eyes rolling as she reluctantly follows me.

'Mrs Foster?' I say, walking up to her front door. 'I'm Detective Riley, Dan Riley, and this is—'

'DS Davis,' the old woman finishes my sentence and I detect a strange twang to her voice. 'I've been expecting you. You'll have to speak very slowly,' she says, pulling the door open and gesturing for us to come through.

CHAPTER SIXTY-THREE

'Can I get you tea? Coffee? I'm having a brandy. I need one.' The old lady speaks in odd, muted, clipped tones.

'We haven't got much time, Mrs Foster,' I say, harried. 'We need to ask you a few questions.'

'Slowly. Please,' she repeats herself. 'And it's Miss.'

I glance at Davis, prompting her to speak. 'We'd like to talk to you about—'

'The murder, yes,' she cuts Davis off mid-sentence. 'That sonofabitch from over the road. Good riddance to bad rubbish if you ask me.'

I look at her properly. I can't gauge her age. Late seventies, perhaps early eighties. She's thin and her skin is papery, yet I detect a strength in her that defies her years.

'I used to be a dancer,' she says, as though reading my thoughts. Women seem quite adept at doing this, whatever their age. 'A long time ago now though… Ballet,' she continues, melancholy heavy in her strange voice. 'I travelled the world, Detective. We were all young and beautiful once upon a time.' She sips her brandy regally. Savours it. 'She trod on my foot you know.'

'Who did?' My eyes scan the room quickly, taking the contents in. It's clean and neat but very old-fashioned, as you might expect. I spot some old black-and-white photographs on an upright piano of a stunningly beautiful young woman wearing a leotard and tutu, striking a dance pose with an equally fit young man with slicked-back hair. For some reason I think of Rachel, and I have a vision of us in our dotage together, old and infirm, looking back at photographs and memories of times when we were in our prime. *Look at how we were, darling.* I wonder what Rach would have looked like as an old woman. I know she would still have been beautiful, at least to me anyway.

Perhaps the old lady senses my own melancholy because she says, 'When you get to my age, all you really have left are memories.' She glances at the photograph and gives a wan smile. 'Love is a strange thing, isn't it, Detective?'

'Yes... it is.' I nod and smile, caught up in the moment with her.

'That poor girl, Laurie, isn't it? The wife. You have her in custody, don't you?'

'Yes. Have you seen Monica Lewis? The lady who lives next door. Have you seen her today?'

The old lady smiles then. And Davis looks at me, mouthing the words, 'She's blind, Gov!'

'Terrible thing, getting old,' she says. 'You'll have to speak slower, Detective. My eyes aren't what they used to be.'

'Of course.' I nod apologetically and try, for a second or two, to imagine what her life must be like. Old, alone, blind. Left with only faded memories of a glorious yesteryear.

'Ms Lewis, your neighbour—'

'Ah... the Lewis woman. Oh yes. Are you sure you can't join me in a drink?'

Davis is almost dancing on the spot she's so agitated.

'Why not,' I say, nodding harshly at Davis and silently mouthing, 'It's my birthday.'

The old lady moves slowly to the drinks cabinet situated to the back of the dated room; every step appears laboured, and Davis and I watch her as she pours us both a small brandy in cut-crystal tumblers with papery, blue-veined hands. I notice her nails are clean and neat and buffed to perfection, and for some reason this makes me feel sad.

'Laurie trod on my foot, the day of the barbecue. Poor thing. She apologised profusely. As women like her always do.'

'Women like her?' Davis interjects gently, taking the smallest sip of her drink and toasting me silently, mouthing, 'Happy Birthday, Gov.'

'Abused women, always the first to say sorry. Oh, and Happy Birthday, Detective.'

I shoot Davis a confused look. Perhaps the woman has psychic powers. They say that when you lose one of your primary senses, such as sight, that the others become even more heightened as a result.

'Anyway' – Miss Foster takes another sip of her drink – 'Monica. Not so much a friend as a wolf in sheep's clothing. I saw what she did.'

'Meaning?'

'Slower, please. It's difficult for me to keep up.'

I shake my head. Roll my eyes at Davis. 'Miss Foster, we don't have much time.' I speak slowly. 'Monica Lewis. You said you *saw* what she did?'

The old lady looks in no hurry to accommodate us. 'Yes. I saw her today, and the day before. Getting into Laurie's car.'

I almost choke on my drink. 'Getting into Laurie Mills' car?'

'Yes. Dressed as her. Slower, please, Detective, slower. She flipped me the middle finger. Terribly rude.'

I glance sideways at Davis. 'Flipped you the finger?'

'You know…' She demonstrates. 'I'd have thought your profession would be the first to know what that meant. Anyway. She took her car. I saw Laurie at the window, poor little wretch. I think she may have seen me too. Anyway. I often saw her – Laurie, that is. I saw her on the day he was murdered. You know, the husband.' She sips the last of her brandy and pours another. It's Courvoisier, the good stuff. 'I saw what was going on. I saw Monica get into her car dressed as her, all very strange. But then again, life is, isn't it, Detective?'

I stare at her confused, holding the glass in my hand. She keeps saying the word *saw*. 'You saw? But… but I thought you were blind, Miss Foster?'

She laughs then, a funny sound, almost ugly. 'Oh, I'm not *blind*, Detective… I'm deaf. Have been since 1997, not long after I moved here. But blind? No, no. No, no. Whoever told you that?'

I look at Davis and she looks back with wide eyes, shrugs.

'But… but I thought – we thought—'

'Well you thought wrong, dear! I see *everything*. People have made the mistake of thinking I'm blind because of the dark glasses and the fact I walk with a stick. It's rather good fun really. I let people believe what they like. When people think you're blind they invariably show you much more of themselves. Anyway, I saw him too, Robert Mills. The day he was murdered.'

'You *saw* him?'

This conversation is almost becoming a comedy sketch.

'Yes!' the old lady says. 'I just told you, I saw him go into his house, about 1ish. Then I watched as she followed around ten minutes later.'

'As who followed? Laurie?'

'No!' She looks slightly agitated now. 'Monica Lewis. She went into the house after him at around 1.15 p.m. I knew it was 1.15 p.m. because I was expecting a parcel to be delivered and kept checking my watch.

'Did you see her come out again. Did you see Monica leaving the house?'

She finishes her brandy, delicately replacing the glass next to the crystal decanter.

'I'm afraid not, Detective. I take an afternoon nap around 2 p.m. every day, just half an hour to recharge my old batteries. I was asleep on the chaise longue in the conservatory. I did, however, see Laurie coming home around 3 p.m. Monica must've left before that because I saw her pop back over for half an hour or so before

Laurie left again. I saw her coming back around 4.30 p.m. – from the shops I think. She was carrying what looked like heavy bags, struggling with them, I thought. Well, she's a tiny thing isn't she? She has a car but never uses it. I've only ever seen her drive with that Monica woman next to her. Not really a surprise when you think about it, is it? After such a tragic accident…' she says, her odd voice trailing off. 'Tragedy, it happens to us all at some point in our lives.' She looks at me knowingly, as though she can sense I've had my share of it too.

I'm dumbfounded. All along there had been a witness, an *eye*witness to Monica Lewis following Robert Mills into his house. How had we missed it? Someone's head is for the chopping block. And I have a feeling it could be my own.

'Why didn't you tell us, Miss Foster?' Davis asks gently. 'Why didn't you come forward and tell us what you'd seen?'

The old woman smiles at her politely and pours herself another small brandy.

'Because, my dear,' she says, bringing the glass to her thin lips, 'no one asked me.'

CHAPTER SIXTY-FOUR

Delaney is pacing as Davis and I charge into the incident room.

'Where have you two been? Laurie Mills has been banging the door down asking for you.'

'Have you released her yet?'

'Released her? What for?'

I turn round, head for the door.

'Gov? Look, is someone going to tell me what the fuck's going on here? You two have been God knows where, doing God knows what this morning while I'm stuck here waiting on your instructions with a serial killer who will only talk to you calling the shots. I'm supposed to be your number two on this, Gov, not her.' He points, casting Davis a derogatory look. 'Just tell me what's going on!'

'She's not our killer, Martin. Laurie Mills is not our woman. She never was.'

'So if she's not our killer, despite all the forensic evidence and practically an admission of guilt, then who the hell is?'

'Monica Lewis is,' I say, 'or should I say Monica *Mills*.'

Delaney opens his hands, brow furrowed in confusion. 'The neighbour? And you know this how?'

'Eyewitness from next door saw her going into the Millses' place ten minutes after Robert arrived at the address on the day of his murder. She also saw her getting into Laurie's car the night of the Wright murder dressed as Laurie, wearing her clothes and a wig. Monica Mills planted DNA at the scene and convinced Laurie she'd blacked out and murdered Robert. On the CCTV from Claire's apartment, you can see a lizard tattoo on the murderer's right foot. Laurie doesn't have any tattoos but Monica Mills does – incidentally, on her right foot. And just a few hours ago she attempted to murder Leanna George by getting her to drink sulphuric acid. Now I think she's on the run. And we need to find her. Fast. I need to talk to Laurie.'

'Yeah, well, she's been screaming for you all bloody morning, banging on the door until her fists started bleeding. Complete nutter.'

'Let's go, Davis.' I turn to Delaney over my shoulder. 'Oh, and Martin. I'll tell you how else I knew Laurie Mills wasn't our girl…'

He stares at me with a defeated look on his face.

'Intuition,' I say as the door swings shut behind me.

CHAPTER SIXTY-FIVE

'Oh God, thank God!' Relief floods through Laurie's nervous system like a burst river as the detective opens the door of her cell. It takes all the strength she has left in her emaciated body to stand. She feels weak but knows she has to find the strength from somewhere.

'Detective Riley.' Her voice is laced with panic. 'I need to speak to you. It's about Monica…my friend – the one who lives opposite my house. The one who gave me an alibi, remember?' She doesn't give him a chance to answer. 'Well, I've remembered something from the nights of Robert's and Claire's murders… Oh God… I… Monica, I think she killed them; I think she murdered Robert and Claire and then tried to frame me.'

Saying the words aloud causes tears to flow as the full horror and confusion of Laurie's words hit home. She knows how it must sound, like she's concocted some absurd cock and bull story in a bid to save herself.

'I think she pretended to be me that night. Took my clothes and shoes and drove my car to Claire's. She must've planted my DNA in the apartment because I've never been there before; I don't even know where Claire lives. She killed them both and made it look like I had done it. Look, I know… I know how this sounds, Detective, but you've got to believe me. You've got to believe me, please.' Laurie crumples back onto the cell bed like a piece of paper, exhausted.

'It's okay, Laurie.' The detective places his hands on her shoulders. 'I do. I do believe you,' he says and embraces her, pulling her into him. She feels weightless in his arms, like she's made of dust. His voice is soft and, despite what he's telling her, gently reassuring. 'You didn't kill your husband, Laurie. She did. Monica.'

'Oh God,' she says. 'Oh God. Oh God. Monica. Why would she do this? *Why?*' A dozen or so more 'Oh Gods' follow.

'I was hoping you might be able to help us with the answer to that, Laurie.'

Her whole body is shaking, vibrating uncontrollably, awash with adrenaline, a familiar feeling that tells her she's going into shock. The relief of knowing that she's not a murderer is muted by the horror that her closest and most trusted friend is, and that not only is she a psychopath capable of killing two people in cold blood, but that she'd set out to frame Laurie for it: all of it.

'I trusted her, Detective,' she says, not bothering to wipe away the tears that are dripping from her face. There's no point anymore; there'll only be more. She feels as if she hasn't stopped crying in years. Perhaps she never will.

The detective takes a handkerchief from the inside pocket of his jacket and dabs at her face with it, a caring gesture that only threatens to undo her more.

'She was my *friend*.'

'I know the shock must be terrible right now, Laurie. Someone you loved betraying you so badly—'

'Betrayal.' She says the word aloud, unable to process the scale of it. First Robert and now Monica, who had always been there for her, *always*. She thinks of all the memories they've shared; the life they've experienced together. Monica was the one person she could count upon in a crisis: her confidante; her rock; her bridesmaid and nursemaid; her personal stylist and relationship counsellor. Monica, who loved to watch old black-and-white

1950s films, curled up on the sofa together, sharing a bottle of Chardonnay; the woman whose infectious laugh and acerbic wit always brought a smile to her face. Monica was the girl who did a great impression of Phoebe from *Friends*; the girl she'd shared carefree holidays with in her twenties, flirting with guys around the pool and getting glammed up with in the evening. Normal, nice, salt-of-the-earth Mon, who knew what was what and who was always on hand with a box of tissues and a bottle of wine to help mop up Laurie's tears over the years.

It's not possible, is it, that this person, this clever, funny, reliable, kind woman she had felt she'd known so intimately, so completely, is capable of slaughtering two people – that she's a cold-hearted monster who's orchestrated it for Laurie to carry the can for her wickedness.

The thought is too much to bear, too much to contemplate or accept. It undoes the fabric of everything Laurie has ever believed in; it's like discovering your parents aren't your real parents. Robert and Monica. She had loved them both deeply and they had both betrayed her. And she thinks she might die right there and then rather than live with this knowledge. All these years Monica had been pretending. They both had.

Detective Riley sits down on the thin, hard cell bed next to her and puts his hands on his knees. He smells good. Clean and fresh like soap.

Was she having an affair with Robert? There can be no other explanation for any of this.

'All these years,' Laurie says. 'All these years…' The pain stings like salt in an open wound and she places her hand over her heart, wondering if it's possible for a heart that's been shattered so many times to be pieced back together again.

'I'm so sorry, Laurie, truly; I am so, so sorry.' She can tell he means it. 'You've suffered so much at the hands of those who were supposed to love you and care about you.'

Laurie pulls her knees up to her chin like a child and hugs herself. She is all she has now. All she has left. 'How is this possible?' she asks herself the question out loud. 'How did I not see it?'

The detective sighs, a deep sad sound. 'Psychopaths are very convincing people, Laurie. They fool everyone. Monica is a very dangerous woman. She's a fraud. That's why we need your help to stop her.'

'But if this was about Robert, if she loved Robert and they'd been having an affair, then why did she kill him? Why not kill me instead? Get me out of the picture. It doesn't make any sense.' None of it did.

'Did you know Monica's parents, Laurie? Did you ever meet them?'

She shakes her head. 'She wasn't living with them when we met. Said her parents had kicked her out and wanted nothing more to do with her. She hardly ever spoke about them, and when she did it was always with complete contempt.'

'What about siblings?'

'No. At least none I'm aware of. She was an only child. Or a "lonely" child as she used to say.'

The detective nods. 'We think she attempted to kill a woman called Leanna George, a woman Robert had had an affair with for some years.'

Laurie closes her eyes: *so many women*. She doubts she will ever know how many there really were. It doesn't matter now.

'She went to her address and put sulphuric acid in her drink.'

Laurie gasps, covers her face with her thin hands. 'Oh God. No. No… Is she dead?'

Detective Riley's head drops, a display of inevitable resignation. 'It's not looking good.'

'So she's punishing his women: Claire, this Leanna girl… and me… punishing me by trying to frame me?'

'Yes, I think that's right, Laurie. But there's something missing. Something more… but I don't yet know what for sure.'

Laurie looks up at his face and suddenly realises how handsome he is, those kind eyes…

'We need to find Monica, Laurie. We need to catch her and put her away for a very long time.'

Icy fear travels the length of Laurie's spine. So now Monica is missing. She'd left her to rot in a police cell, stripped of her liberty, labelled a monster, mad and bad. Killing her would have been kinder, but she had chosen a fate worse than death for her best friend instead. *Why?*

'Have you any idea where she might be? Somewhere she may have mentioned before, friends she might visit to lie low for a while…?'

Laurie is overcome with emotions as she tightens her grip around her knees. She can't think straight. She doesn't want to think at all. Part of her wishes she could end up in a mental asylum where they'd lobotomise her and erase her memory.

'It's possible that she may have decided to leave the country.' The detective has shifted to face her now; his expression is earnest and grave. 'If she was to leave the country, where do you think she would go? Look, you knew her best. Or at least you thought you knew her best. Psychopaths don't come with it written on their foreheads, Laurie. They come as your friend, as your lover, as your saviour; you have nothing, *nothing* to reproach yourself for. Did she ever mention a place, any places she'd like to visit, had connections to, anything…'

Laurie pauses for a moment. '*Paris When it Sizzles*,' she says quietly, her voice barely above a whisper now.

'Paris? You think she's gone to Paris?'

'Audrey Hepburn. She starred in the film. It was one of Mon's favourites. I can't remember the name of the leading man now… it's escaped me.'

The detective shakes his head. 'Me neither.'

'It was set in Paris but parts of it were shot in the French Riviera. Monica loved Audrey Hepburn and the French Riviera. She always said she wanted to live there one day.'

'Where, Laurie? Where in particular in the French Riviera?'

'Cannes,' she says, 'where all the film stars go.'

The detective stands abruptly but she doesn't follow suit. Her limbs won't allow it.

'I'm sending an officer down now to collect you, Laurie. Take you somewhere safe. And once this is all over I'll come to see you, okay? I'm sorry, Laurie.'

She looks at him and sees that his eyes are watery and blue, like a clear sea. She watches as he begins to walk away and then he suddenly stops short of the cell door and turns round.

'William Holden,' he says, with a smile that's almost as sad as her own.

CHAPTER SIXTY-SIX

'Check every single flight that's leaving today for Cannes,' I direct Murray as I march into the incident room. 'Find out if they've got a Monica Lewis or Monica or Kiki Mills travelling with them. Every airport in London, Murray.'

She nods efficiently.

'Listen up, everyone. We're letting Laurie Mills go. She's not our murderer. Our suspect is Monica Lewis, friend and neighbour of the Millses. She may also go by the name Monica or Kiki Mills…' I tell them about Leanna George, and about our surprise witness, Miss Foster.

'We missed Miss Foster. I need to know why and how this happened. Who did the initial house-to-house?'

The team all look at each other shiftily.

'Me and Baylis spoke to some of them.' Harding takes her notebook out, flips back through it. 'We talked to the Bartletts, and numbers 73–115, all covered, boss.'

'Who was responsible for the rest?'

There's silence among the team. I think I hear a few sniffs, the shuffle of papers.

'Right, well, if we'd been doing our jobs properly then Laurie Mills wouldn't be wasting away down in the cells and Leanna George wouldn't be in intensive care with her organs disintegrating, so come on—'

'I did the other numbers, Gov,' Delaney says measuredly. 'They're all listed here. Statements from all of them.'

'All of them except Miss Foster.'

'She's blind, Gov. She wouldn't have *seen* anything.'

I look over at him in his flashy, pristine suit, his hair perfectly styled. He does look good, granted, but there's a slight smirk on that handsome face of his. One I'm going to relish wiping off.

'So, you didn't speak to the old lady because she's blind? Is that what you're telling me, Martin?'

'Like I said, boss, she wouldn't have seen anything.' He's almost grinning now, looking at me like I'm the village idiot.

'Who told you she was blind, Delaney? Did she tell you that herself?'

'No. No. It was Monica Lewis who told me. She said she'd seen her on the day of Robert's murder, staring out of the window when she'd gone over to the Millses' place to have coffee with the suspect – with Laurie Mills I mean.'

'Did she?' I ask rhetorically. 'Only she was wrong, Delaney. Monica Lewis got it wrong. She thought the woman was blind because of her dark glasses and walking stick. But she's not blind, not at all. You were misinformed.'

Delaney's expression goes from cocksure to panic in a split second and I can't say it doesn't give me a small rush of satisfaction.

'Schoolboy error, Martin,' I berate him. 'Always double-check the facts. It's page one, as well you should know. You can't just believe what someone tells you, or make assumptions. Stone-cold facts. You should've spoken with Miss Foster yourself. Instead you took a murderer's word for it. Monica Lewis fucked up royally too. Like you, she simply assumed. She judged a book by its cover and as a result she shot herself in the foot and provided us with a star witness.'

I think I see Davis turn away, hiding the smile on her face by pretending to drink from an empty paper cup.

The team are staring at Delaney now. Waiting for some kind of response, an explanation. But he doesn't give one. He doesn't have one. He fucked up big time and he knows it, only men like Martin Delaney are too arrogant to admit it. It's why he's such a lousy team player, and it's the reason Leanna George is lying in a hospital bed right now and our killer is on her way to Cannes.

'I'll deal with this later,' I say to him, his suit looking less sharp by the second.

'Gov?' Baylis puts the phone down. 'There's someone downstairs to see you. Says it's urgent. Says her name is Agnes. And she says that you'll know what it's about.'

Davis and I exchange a wide-eyed glance.

'Tell her I'm on my way.'

'No one called Monica Lewis booked on any flights to Cannes, Gov,' Murray tells me.

'Mills? How about Monica Mills?'

'Nope.' She shakes her head, scrolling down her computer screen. 'But there is someone called Monica on a 6.40 p.m. flight to Cannes this evening. A Monica Atkins. Flying from Gatwick Terminal One with Air France… she's already checked in. Could that be her, Gov?'

I look at my watch. It's 4.17 p.m.

'Get onto them, Murray. Make sure that plane does not leave the runway. And tell them to reserve the two seats next to her.'

Davis looks at me. 'Two seats?' she asks and I nod at her slowly. 'Great!' She smiles. 'I've always wanted to go to Cannes.'

CHAPTER SIXTY-SEVEN

'Agnes.' I greet her in the interview room with a handshake. 'You remembered something?'

She shifts on the plastic chair, looks like a fish out of water. I ask her if she wants any refreshments and she politely declines.

'Stanley can't know I'm here,' she says nervously. 'You won't tell him, will you?'

'No, Agnes, of course not – this conversation can be just between us if you like. What is it you want to tell me? I'm sorry to press you but there was another attempted murder this morning and I'm pretty pushed for time.'

'Another one? By the same killer?'

'We think so, yes.'

'Good God.' She shakes her head, buries it in her palms and mumbles something. 'She's mad. God help us, she is truly mad and it's my fault.'

'Who's mad, Agnes?'

But she turns away from me, can't look me in the eye.

'Do you have children, Detective Riley?'

I struggle with how to answer this question. Technically I don't. But then I think about how Rach and I had created another life, one that was just getting started inside of her when she was taken from me.

'Almost.' I answer.

'Sometimes I wish I had never had them. Children I mean. The heartache and shame it's brought me… and Stanley. You're sure you won't tell him I'm here. He'll go spare.'

'I promise,' I say. 'But you need to tell me why you *are* here, Agnes. If you've something important to say, please say it. Like I said, I don't have much time.'

She pauses for a moment, as though she's unsure where to begin. 'We loved Robert, Detective, perhaps too much. He was our first-born. Bonnie little chap he was, all gurgles and smiles. After the birth I suffered with severe post-natal depression. I wasn't well... I developed a bit of a...' She pauses, lowers her eyes. 'A drinking problem. Ironically, I thought that having another baby might help – ridiculous when I think back on it now, but at the time... Anyway, it turned out that I couldn't have more children: polycystic ovaries... I should have accepted it as God's wish, should have left well alone and been happy just with my Bertie, but I wanted a little girl, a little sister for him to complete our family.'

I stay silent: I let her tell her story.

'The shame has been the worst thing, Detective. We're Catholics you see, God-loving people. The church has always been integral to our lives: mine and Stan's. The Lord is my shepherd, I shall not want... We tried to stop it – believe me, we tried. We prayed and prayed and prayed...'

'What did you try to stop, Agnes?'

She doesn't answer me. Not directly anyway.

'You must meet a lot of bad people in your line of work. Tell me, do you think they're born that way or created?'

I blow air through my lips. 'I think it's a mix of both, Agnes.' It's the simplest answer I can give to such a complex question. And the shortest.

'Stan thinks she was born with the devil in her. From the moment she came into the world. But I know I neglected her; I abused that child... I can't tell you why. I have no excuses, only that I was sick; I was an alcoholic suffering with depression at the time. I blamed her for it; she became my scapegoat. I felt like I'd chosen her for a reason.'

'Chosen her? Who did you choose Agnes?'

'Kiki,' she says, 'Monica. We adopted her when she was just six weeks old. I *tried* to love her. But right from the moment we took her on I sensed she was a bad seed.'

I nod.

'I never bonded with her, not like I did with our Bertie... she wasn't my blood. I should have given her up – maybe she would've had a better chance then. The guilt I feel, Detective... I was a different person back then, do you understand?'

'Are you telling me that Monica is your daughter? That she's Robert's *sister*?'

Agnes can't look at me. I see shame and humiliation burning in her eyes like fire.

'Adopted daughter, yes.'

'So, they were having an incestuous relationship, Robert and Monica?'

The word 'incest' causes her to visibly flinch.

'I never bonded with Kiki but Bertie did. They were so close as children. He doted on her from the moment she entered our home; he never let her out of his sight. They would spend all their time together as children, playing in the tree house in the garden, picking apples, playing in the park... They were best friends. I suppose I was jealous, that I resented her in some ways...' Her voice trails off. 'We could only hope that the Lord would forgive them, forgive us. We prayed and prayed and prayed, Detective...'

I feel my heart rate increase; pulsing loudly in my ears with the powerful surge of adrenaline that's rushing through my system. *Brother and sister.*

'When we found out, we did everything we could, *everything* we could to stop it. We sent her away to a boarding school in a bid to keep them apart. She was pregnant—'

'Pregnant?'

'At fourteen.'

'And the child was Bertie's – Robert's?'

She nods quickly, wipes the rims of her eyes with a finger. 'Yes. I'm afraid it was. We dealt with it, got her seen to, but there was no stopping Kiki. That girl had an unstoppable force inside of her, Detective… the nuns threw her out in the end.'

'And Robert? Bertie?'

'Well, he wasn't blameless either, not like Stan would have it. I see it all much more clearly now, now that I'm clean and sober. He was promiscuous from a very young age. Obsessed by pleasures of the flesh, Detective. And nothing, *nothing* we did could prevent them from finding a way back to each other. In the end, they couldn't hide their… *feelings* for each other, right under our noses, under our roof.' Agnes lowers her eyes in disgust. 'We knew what was going on. It made us sick. Stanley, well, he had a breakdown in the end. Had to go away himself for a while.'

This is the missing piece. This is the piece of the puzzle I've been looking for. *Brother and sister.*

'We washed our hands of her, disowned her. Told her to leave and never come back. We, Stan and I, tried to put an end to it by threatening to disinherit Bertie, write him out of our will. We're not poor people, Detective. He stood to lose a great deal.'

'It's okay, Agnes,' I say, nodding. 'I understand this must be extremely difficult for you.'

She exhales loudly. 'We cut her off completely, made her go and live with a distant cousin of mine in London. But she found a way back to him; they found a way back to each other.' She's crying now, and I see the guilt and shame and regret in each tear that falls. 'I am to blame, Detective. I was a monster back then; I was sick. I should never have been allowed to adopt a child. I wasn't fit. I'm a different person now, and I spend every single day repenting my sins and praying for Kiki, for her damaged soul.'

I nod again. I'm trying to understand, to make sense of it. 'What about Robert? You said you remained in contact with him when we last spoke.'

'Briefly, yes – sporadically. When he married Laurie, we were ecstatic. Equally when we learned that not long afterwards Kiki had married too. We were hopeful, Stan and I, that this was the end of it. That we could put it all behind us, blame it all on teenage hormones and feel satisfied that God had heard our pleas and answered our prayers. But they couldn't keep away... whatever it was between them, that pull, that diabolical connection...'

Her voice catches and she takes a breath, composes herself. 'After Laurie's accident, they moved into the house opposite Kiki, the one on Cedar Close. Stan would never speak of her, but secretly I kept tabs on her; I couldn't help it. I begged Robert not to do it, to move there; I begged him to stay away from her. I wanted to believe that it was all her: to believe that Kiki was the seductress who had lured my son away and into the devil's clutches, but it was just as much him; this bond between them, they had a hold over each other, a truly diabolical hold. The others – Laurie, Dougie – they were all simply collateral damage; their marriages were smokescreens for what was really going on underneath. Robert hoped we wouldn't find out. He didn't want to be disinherited. I kept it quiet from Stanley when I discovered that they lived opposite each other. But when that baby came, baby Matilda, Robert changed. Something in him shifted. He wanted to be a dad to that little girl; he wanted to do right by her, be a proper family.

'The moment we found out about Robert's murder, I wondered if it was her who had killed him, deep down. Only I didn't want to believe it; I denied it to myself... There's still part of me that refuses to believe she could ever do such a wicked thing—'

'So, you think she killed Robert because she couldn't have him? That they couldn't be open about their love?'

Agnes flinches again.

'There was something between them, Detective, something evil, a force so strong that it obliterated any good that came near it. Whatever it was, they destroyed each other's lives, and the lives of many more… Love should never hurt, Detective. Love is the antithesis of pain and suffering. Love is everything that's good in this world. What they had wasn't love, not love as I – and I'm sure you – know it to be. It was something twisted and dark, something deviant.'

'I need to find your daughter, Agnes,' I say gently and she nods with the inevitability of what she knows will follow: their family secret exposed; shame, blame and sensationalism; her own skeletons yanked from the closet. Monica Atkins will be written about – she will have notoriety and fame, an incestuous serial killer who murdered her lover brother and his mistress, and attempted to poison another mistress while setting up her best friend to take the rap. It's got Hollywood movie written all over it. I realise what courage and strength it has taken Agnes Atkins to come here today and I sense the dark cloud of sadness that seems to hover over her oppressively. I can sense sadness in a person now, like cadaver dogs can smell death.

'Will you find her, Detective?' She stands up and collects herself; I wonder if she feels a lightness for having unburdened the truth at last. 'You must find her.'

I nod. 'I will, Agnes. I will.'

CHAPTER SIXTY-EIGHT

'Will all passengers for flight Air France 447 to Cannes please make your way to gate 67.'

Monica moves through the airport crowds at a carefree pace, wheeling her Burberry travel case behind her. Her mood is buoyant as she thinks about her duty-free purchases: some Crème de la Mer moisturiser and a Chanel lipstick in Rouge Noir. She'd gone back after donning her disguise; she had some time to kill before her flight.

'It's so your colour, Madam,' the young Arabic girl in the headscarf had remarked, smiling at her. 'It offsets your eyes.'

She'd purchased the nail polish as well, plus a kohl pencil, but the pièce de résistance had been an Asprey handbag that had caught her eye. It was peach leather, very 1950s, very retro, and as soft as butter to touch. It had been an impulse buy, but then she was an impulsive kind of woman. It felt good to spend Dougie's life-insurance money. He'd never once bought her a gift she'd genuinely liked throughout their sham of a marriage. Still, he'd made up for it in the last hour or so, *God rest his tortured soul*. Poor old useless, sexless, insipid Dougie; he was in a better place now, just as she soon would be.

Monica summarises her emotions as she struts past the departure gates. She knows she's catching people's attention in her white shift dress, headscarf and oversized Audrey Hepburn-style sunglasses. She looks like a film star, a rich, successful woman who men want to fuck and women want to be. She can't wait to reinvent herself once she arrives in Cannes. The beautiful, rich widow from the UK, mysterious and alluring, someone with an intriguing past and a sensational wardrobe. Finally she's going to lead the life that she was meant to; the life he had always promised her she would have. She will no longer be a dirty secret, shunned and betrayed and rejected by her own family, by the one and only person she has ever loved. She can start anew with a clean slate. Everyone gets what they deserve, in the end, don't they?

Grabbing a copy of the *Evening Standard* from the complimentary news stand – something to read with the large gin and tonic she's planning to order once they've taken off – she makes her way to gate 67. Monica's not a seasoned flier and she feels a flutter of nerves hit her digestive system.

She passes through boarding without issue, smiling at the heavily made-up woman behind the counter who checks her passport, and waits in the queue as her fellow passengers begin the slow and laborious process of boarding. The man opposite her is reading the free newspaper and the headline sends a jolt of adrenaline through her like an electric shock. 'ACID ATTACK: MODEL IN CRITICAL CONDITION.'

A jolt of adrenaline hits her solar plexus like a fist, almost taking the wind from her. *Critical condition?* There's a photograph of Leanna George, that publicity shot that had accompanied the interview she'd given about Robert, the one that had sent her into a furious rage. Next to it, inset, is a smaller photograph. One she recognises. It was taken on the day of the street barbecue, the day she had found out about Matilda, and discovered Robert's plan to abandon her for fatherhood and a life with Claire.

'*Police are looking to interview this woman, Monica Lewis, although she may also be using the aliases Monica Mills or Kiki Mills.*'

Monica freezes, momentarily stunned. How was it possible that Leanna George was still alive? She had left her incapacitated and in agony and had been sure to dispose of her mobile phone so that she would be unable to call for help even if she was capable of it. She'd ingested sulphuric acid and should've been dead within ten minutes at the very most: a mercifully swift death, albeit an agonising one. Monica had banked on her being a putrefied corpse before she was discovered. But someone had got to her in time and saved her.

Had someone second-guessed her intentions? Had Leanna been able to tell them who she was? The panic that's engulfed her is swiftly followed by acute paranoia. Her picture is in the newspaper. Suddenly she sees it everywhere she looks, hundreds of passengers holding or reading their free copies of the *Evening Standard*, her face staring back at her from the front page. *Jesus fucking Christ!* Someone will recognise her. *Damn it!*

Automatically she lowers her head, grateful that she's chosen to wear a headscarf and glasses, although now she's wondering if this will afford her more attention.

That wretched slut Leanna George – she'd been a big mistake. It had been an impulsive decision to kill her and now it looked as though it would be her undoing. *How could she not be dead? How had they got to her in time?*

The realisation dawns on Monica that she is now a wanted woman, a suspected murderer. The police will be looking for her. She needs to board this aircraft, lively. Once she's up in the air she'll be safe, won't she? She got through security without event, French customs won't know who she is. They won't be looking for her. They don't know where she's headed. No one does. She has a new identity waiting for her in France. She'll have plastic surgery, change her eye colour, reinvent her whole history if she has to. They'll never find her.

Monica is shaking as she opens the newspaper and covers her face while pretending to read it. Is the man opposite staring at her? *Stay calm, Kiki*, she tells herself. *Just stay calm.* She almost loses control of her bladder as finally the queue begins to move and she steps onto the aircraft.

CHAPTER SIXTY-NINE

The plan was always to let her board the plane. It's difficult to abscond from a plane once the doors are shut and I wasn't prepared to take any chances of Monica Atkins making a break for it. The French borders have been alerted though, just in case.

I board flight Air France 447 with Davis about five people deep behind me. We're both incognito. I doubt Monica will recognise Davis but there is a chance she could recognise me. Never underestimate the cunning of a psychopathic killer, so I've prepared for the worst-case scenario. If she manages to get past me, which is unlikely, then Davis is there as back-up, plus the team of armed police who are on alert at Gatwick, should we royally screw it up.

I watch her from behind the newspaper that I'm pretending to read; she's looking at a copy too and I wonder if she's seen the headline yet. I'd given Fi a heads-up and told her to talk to her contacts at *ES*, which she gratefully did. I needed Monica's mugshot on the front page of that paper. Besides, it's not every day you get the scoop on a serial killer at large. That said, the usually tenacious Fi has been uncharacteristically quiet throughout this investigation; I hadn't heard a peep out of her since our last encounter in the pub, and the Leanna George tip-off.

'It has to make the late edition, Fi, *has to*.'

'Don't worry, Dan. It will – you have my word.'

That was good enough for me. And she hadn't let me down.

'Actually, I'm glad you called me, Dan,' she'd said, hesitating. I sensed she wanted to tell me something. 'I need to see you, to talk to you.'

I didn't have time to ask why, so when she said she'd come to my apartment later that night, I agreed and hung up, momentarily perplexed. Whatever the reason, for now it had to wait. I had a killer to catch. One who thought she'd outsmarted me and everyone else. I suppose she had, for a time. One who thought she was going to get away with it, pin her crimes on someone else, someone who had trusted her and called her a friend. Arrogance: I've seen it be the undoing of so many.

Psychopaths are known for remaining calm in situations that would cause most people to freak out, largely because of emotional detachment and lack of conscience, yet still I wonder what's going through Monica Atkins' mind as she boards the aircraft. If she's panicking on the inside then she's doing a stellar job of holding it together on the outside. It's unfathomable to the rational mind how a human being can just a few hours earlier have attempted to murder a virtual stranger by tricking them into ingesting acid, leaving them to die in excruciating agony, then simply carry on about their day like nothing happened. I attempt to imagine the level of hatred a person must have to feel to enable them to carry out such an abhorrent crime, but I can't. Revenge, they say, is like swallowing poison and expecting the other person to die. Only it was Leanna George who swallowed that poison. Now it was time for Monica Atkins to receive a taste of her own bitter medicine.

Perhaps Agnes Akins was right and Monica was simply born bad. Just as there are geniuses in this world, lauded for their supreme intellect and goodness, their altruism and selfless dedication to the good of others, there are also those who are inherently evil and for whom no amount of love and care would ever have changed that fact. It's a depressing thought.

An image of Claire Wright flashes up inside my head, of her chubby, mottled legs pulled up to her chest on that milk-stained sofa, the expression of horror on her face, distorted through the plastic bag, and baby Matilda, deathly pale and barely breathing as she nestled beside her mother. It's an image I'll live with for the rest of my life. Crimes of passion, however brutal and frenzied, are more commonplace than people think. Jealousy, sex, passion, infidelity, the need to be in control… all these things are potential driving forces behind a mentally sound person who flips. But the Monica Atkinses of the world, they're a different kind of creature altogether.

Part of me is glad Robert Mills is dead. I don't condone his murder, but perhaps the world will be a better place without him in it. And I definitely know it will be once I've dealt with Monica Atkins. I owe it to Claire Wright's grieving mother; I owe it to Leanna George. And perhaps, above all people, I owe it to Laurie Mills.

She looks unruffled as she takes her window seat and buckles up. I tilt my straw trilby as I sit down next to her, hoping it and the dark Ray-Bans are going to be enough, for long enough.

CHAPTER SEVENTY

Monica scans the article, rereading each line twice before she can take in the words.

> '*Leanna George, a model and actress who lives in London, is currently in a critical condition in St Thomas's hospital after allegedly ingesting what doctors believe to be sulphuric acid. Ms George, 32, originally from Newcastle, was rushed to hospital this morning after she was found collapsed and screaming in agony on the floor of her apartment in West London...*'

Thirty-two my arse, Monica inwardly scoffs as she stuffs the newspaper into the seat pocket angrily, silently praying, *hoping*, that Leanna doesn't pull through. Bitch won't be able to talk anyway, not with a burnt-out throat. She curses herself. She'd covered her tracks well before Leanna George, had everything worked out. There were no witnesses, nothing that could lead the police to her. She had made sure that everything pointed to Laurie, had set it all up so that there was no one else in the frame. Leanna George, if she survived, had the potential to undo everything. She wishes she'd slit the silly bitch's throat now, left no room for error.

Monica tells herself to calm down. They'll be taking off imminently and she'll be home and dry. No one has recognised her. The headscarf she'd chosen to wear had been a godsend and for a moment she wonders if someone, some higher power, is looking out for her.

She exhales, a flutter of nerves gently resting on her stomach. She's always like this before take-off. She's not big on flying, but this is a necessary journey. Anyway, it's a short hop really. She'll have a couple of gin and tonics to ameliorate the butterflies; maybe she'll listen to some Chopin on her iPod – that always cheers her up. Chopin was Robert's favourite. Stanley used to play it to them when they were kids on that old record player from the 1970s that he no doubt still has; it was his favourite too. They had made love often, her and Robert, with Chopin playing in the background, and Piano Concerto No. 1 had been their wedding-day music. She thinks of it then, that day they had married in secret. It had been the single happiest moment of her entire life. She'd been wearing the dress she has on now, a beautiful white dress she'd found in one of those vintage shops in Portobello, original 1950s with a lace overlay.

'You look like a blonde Audrey Hepburn,' he'd told her as he kissed her lips.

'Don't!' she'd berated him. 'You'll ruin my lipstick for the photographs.'

But there hadn't been any of those. Robert wouldn't allow any to be taken. 'You know why, Kiki,' he'd said. And as always she hadn't challenged him.

He had led her to believe, following the wedding, that they would start a life together as man and wife, move away to a place where no one knew them or who they really were. But it had always been 'soon'. Only 'soon' never came. Robert wanted their relationship to remain nothing more than a dirty secret. And then, just a couple of years after they'd tied the knot in secret, he had dropped the bombshell that he wanted them both to marry other people, live behind a facade of respectability to please Stan and Agnes.

'If they see that we're leading normal lives, I'll inherit their estate, the house, the cars, the jewellery… then we'll be set up for life, Kiki. We'll just have to bide our time. You know they'll fight us as long as they're alive—'

'If they're alive,' she'd said. 'We could always just kill them. They're over halfway dead already. Besides, they're always banging on about being closer to God.'

He had laughed at her. 'My bad, bad, Kiki…'

But she'd been serious.

Watching him marry Laurie had been one of the hardest things she'd ever had to endure in her life – her husband betrothing himself to another woman, albeit a woman she had chosen for him. Robert marrying her best friend meant that she could keep a very close eye on them both. She had never viewed Laurie as a threat. Nice, normal, unassuming Laurie who had followed her like a lamb, forever in her shadow and easy to manipulate. Soon after, she'd married Dougie and she'd been secretly pleased to witness the jealousy Robert had displayed on their wedding day.

'You'll always be mine, Kiki,' he'd whispered in her ear after she had said her vows. 'No matter who comes and goes… when you fuck him you'll be thinking of me. You know it and so do I.'

He'd been right of course, though largely she had starved Dougie of attention and intimacy throughout their marriage, tortured him mentally, slowly, until the poor thing had gone and had a heart attack.

By then, Laurie had become something of an issue. She had blossomed into a striking, successful young woman who was turning heads and earning well. Luckily, she remained as insipid and prissy as ever and Robert had soon grown tired and irritated by her. So, over the years, Monica had learned to wait. She recalls the lazy stolen afternoons together, when Dougie was working, or

Laurie was away. They would make love in their respective houses, sometimes hotels, wherever they could.

'When the time is right, we'll abandon them both, Dougie and Laurie, and we'll have a child of our own, Kiki,' he'd told her. 'We'll go somewhere far away, somewhere no one will ever find us. Just you and I and our baby. You know that's what I want, Kiki, what I've always wanted. We just need to be patient…'

But patience wasn't one of her strongest attributes. If it was money they needed then she had a better plan. The life-insurance policy she'd taken out on Dougie and the equity in the house would set them up for a life together, screw Agnes and Stanley and their money. That just left Laurie to deal with, and those bastard twins she had growing inside of her. And fate had sorted that out too. Only Laurie had gone and survived the crash – she had been stronger than Monica had given her credit for, and she had fought hard.

Initially, she had believed Claire to be simply another mistress, a plaything to taunt Laurie with and send her plummeting further into psychosis, a favourite pastime of Robert's and one she understood. She knew he didn't love Claire, fat, dopey, dumpy Claire with her lack of intellect.

But she hadn't known about the baby. The baby had been a complete shock. She'd only discovered it on the day of the barbecue, when Laurie had gone into public meltdown in front of the neighbours.

The baby had changed everything… it had changed Robert. Something had happened inside him, something human and real. He had felt love for the child, had wanted to see her, be with her, watch her grow. Perhaps, she wondered, he wasn't really like her at all. Robert had been planning to leave and start a new life with his daughter and that ignorant fat slut for months behind her back. He had betrayed her, after everything she had done for him, every sacrifice she had made for him, *for them*. She had done everything he had ever asked of her. And she had waited so long. All he had promised her, the dream he had sold her of marriage and a family together, of a life in Cannes, it had all been a lie that he'd strung out for years. There could be no forgiveness for what Robert had done, robbing her of the chance of a normal life, of a family, to hold her own flesh and blood in her arms; he had sold her a fantasy, a dream of somewhere over the rainbow without the crock of gold at the end of it. Robert didn't really love her: he never had. He simply saw her as his possession. And the eventual and brutal realisation of this had caused her to mete out her own justice. She had righted the wrongs, evened the score. Now she could be whole again.

Only now that her rage and anger have waned she feels a terrible sense of loss. Not for Claire, not for Dougie or Laurie or that slut Leanna George, but for Bertie. She would spend the rest of her days missing him, the cruel, selfish bastard that he was. He had made her kill him. Loving him had made her do all of it.

The plane is filling up now and the seat next to her has been taken. Suddenly she's aware of the man next to her, a man wearing a straw trilby hat and sunglasses who smells good. She likes men who smell good.

A steward in an unflattering brown and orange uniform struts down the aisle towards her and she calls him over with a wave of her hand.

'Is it too early for a gin and tonic?'

CHAPTER SEVENTY-ONE

She shifts naturally in her seat as I take mine, tucking her elbow in politely. She smells of perfume, expensive and strong, and she's wearing a white 1950s dress and a headscarf. It's difficult, when I look at her, to believe that this woman has killed two people, and attempted to murder a third in such brutal and callous cold blood. She looks like she's just stepped off a film set.

'Beautiful day for flying,' I remark without turning my head fully to look at her. I see the small lizard tattoo on her right foot in my peripheral vision.

'I guess it is, yes,' she concedes. 'I hope they hurry up. I'm not the best flier. I get terribly nervous before take-off.'

'I'm the same,' I say, as Davis takes the seat next to me. 'Get the jitters. I find a little livener helps.' I take a small flask out of my inside pocket and offer it to her. She briefly looks at me and takes it, manages a swig of the Jack Daniels it contains.

'You're a whisky man?'

'Bourbon,' I correct her.

She smiles provocatively. 'What takes you to Cannes?'

'The promise of fame and fortune,' I say, careful not to face her full on. She laughs. 'And you?'

She clears her throat a little then, as though buying herself some time to think. 'I'm going to meet my husband,' she says, 'Robert. We're emigrating. He's set us up in a beautiful chateau on the Côte d'Azur. He's been waiting for me to come but I had some business to attend to before I could manage to get away.'

'Business?' *The murderous kind.*

'Family business,' she explains. 'You know how it is.' She smiles but it doesn't reach her eyes.

'Your family, will they be visiting you and… Robert you say? Your husband.'

She looks a little nervous now, uncomfortable. 'I doubt it – they never really approved of our relationship.'

I chuckle. 'Really. Bit of a bad boy, is he?'

She gives a wry smile. 'Something like that, although actually, it was his parents who disapproved of me.'

'Why? Are you a bad girl?'

She looks directly at me. 'Are you flirting with me?' she asks, delighted. 'I'm a married woman!'

'All the best ones are,' I say.

She laughs, enjoying herself. 'Are you married?'

'No,' I reply. 'I'm holding out for someone.'

'Really?' she says, intrigued. 'Someone unobtainable?'

'Something like that. Her name is Rachel. She's very beautiful.'

'Lucky Rachel,' she says.

'I was the lucky one,' I say. 'Sadly, she's already been taken.'

Her smile fades a little. 'Well, that is sad.' She pauses for a moment. 'You know, there's plenty more fish in the sea. You never know who you're going to meet.' She's blatantly flirting with me now, taken the bait hook, line and sinker. 'Or sit next to on a plane.'

'You're so right.' I grin at her, tap my nose with my finger and she grins back.

'It's nice to meet you… er…' Monica extends her hand, the hand of a killer.

'Daniel,' I say, taking my hat and glasses off. 'Daniel Riley. I think we've met before.'

CHAPTER SEVENTY-TWO

Laurie looks at the prison guard and then across the white Formica table at Monica. 'Thank you for agreeing to see me,' she says.

'I'm glad you came,' Monica replies, 'but then I always knew you would.'

Laurie fights with her conflicting emotions, battling between sadness and revulsion. Even behind the make-up, she observes how terrible her friend looks. Her face is bloated and her skin is pasty and grey, her once lustrous hair now shorter and darker. She wants to feel some satisfaction at her obvious demise but strangely all she can feel is pity.

'So, did you come here to gloat? To tell me what an evil, sick person I am and how much I've betrayed you, how much you hate me and how you're glad I'll have to spend the rest of my life in here?'

Laurie tries not to react, not to show any emotion. She had expected this, been told to. Monica had pleaded not guilty at trial, and her brief had gone for the defence of diminished responsibility, painting Robert as a twisted, evil sexual predator who had groomed her from a young age and manipulated her into becoming a murderer, a psychological abuser who had systematically broken her down so that she was no longer sound of mind. The most tragic part of it all was that Laurie knew that some of it was probably true. Robert had done the same to her, the same to everyone. Only she hadn't become a killer, and that was the difference.

Despite her protestations, the evidence presented in court was overwhelming. Monica's DNA found on Robert's body, the eyewitnesses, Leanna George's statement, the phone records, the CCTV footage and the tattoo… and then of course there was the revelation that Monica and Robert were brother and sister, and how their incestuous relationship had begun when Monica had been just thirteen years old… It had drawn gasps in court, but not from Laurie. Somehow it all made disturbing sense. All those years she had simply been a pawn in a game. Used and abused, betrayed and blamed. It was difficult to put into words how she felt. Even now, all these months later, she struggled to comprehend how two people she'd thought she'd known so well, and had loved and trusted, could have kept such twisted secrets and deceived her on such an abhorrent level. Robert, the man she had spent her life loving, her husband, had been nothing but a stranger, a Jekyll and Hyde character, a perverse bigamist who had stolen and violated her life, along with his diabolical lover and adoptive sister: a psychopathic killer who had masqueraded as her friend so convincingly for so many years. *How could it all have been a lie?* It was almost impossible to reconcile the Monica she had known for so many years with the stranger sitting in front of her now, and Laurie wonders if she will ever be able to trust another living soul again. Despite everything that's happened, it is perhaps this that hurts her most of all.

'Yes, I received your letters,' she says measuredly. 'And no, that's not why I came.'

'Then why are you here, Laurie?' Monica blinks at her.

'I came to ask you a question.'

'A question?'

'Yes.'

'One you couldn't ask in a letter?'

'I needed to see your face, look into your eyes.'

Monica holds her gaze.

'The twins,' she says, 'the day of the accident. The reason I was in the car in the first place was because you alerted me about Robert's affair with Claire. You knew I would be shocked and hysterical, that I would be devastated. I was almost eight months pregnant. You convinced me to have it out with him, told me to get in my car and go and confront him… Was it deliberate, Mon? Did you intend for me to crash, for me and the twins to die in a car crash?' Laurie isn't sure but she thinks she can detect the faintest hint of a smile on Monica's bloated face.

'You always were so trusting, Lolly.'

'You wanted me to die, me and the twins – you wanted us eliminated. We were in the way of what you wanted. What you'd always wanted.' Laurie struggles to remain calm; the horror and the pain are still too raw. She'd thought she was ready for this but now she realises that she isn't, that perhaps she never will be. 'You helped nurse me back to health, you pretended to care when really… And when I survived, you found another use for me, didn't you?'

'We all had our uses, Laurie, every one of us. We were all Bertie's puppets in one way or another.'

'Tell me one thing, Monica.' Laurie moves closer towards her across the table, looks her dead in the eyes. 'Did Robert know? Did he know about the accident – that you planned to kill me and our babies?'

She knows it's a gamble, her coming here today. Detective Riley and her therapist had both told her that they doubted Monica would be forthcoming with answers. They said that she would relish leaving them unanswered in a bid to keep some form of control over her, leave her wanting. It's all she has left now that she's rotting away in a 10 x 12 cell.

Monica sits back, affording Laurie a brief glimpse of her burgeoning stomach – fat, bloated Monica who had always taken such care of her figure. She's silent for a long moment as she looks at Laurie with her cold, dead eyes. Had they always been like that and Laurie had never noticed before? She vows always, from now on, to look more closely at people's eyes.

'We're all victims, Laurie. Loving Bertie, loving Robert, it destroyed us all—'

'You led me to him, like a lamb to the slaughter. You let me marry him, your brother, your lover… why, Mon? *Why*? What did I do to you? What did I ever do?'

Monica tucks a piece of her hair behind her ear in that typical way of hers. 'It was never personal, Lolly,' she says. 'It was never about you.'

Laurie shakes her head. *Nothing personal.* 'I shouldn't have come,' she says, standing.

'I'm glad you did.' Monica looks up at her and for a second she sees her as she always had, like she's leaving after a coffee and a chat together, like they always used to do.

'All those years, Mon. All those memories – a lifetime of them. All that love and trust, all that friendship, all those firsts… Tell me – tell me you weren't faking all of it, that it meant something, that it was real…' Laurie hears the urgency in her voice, feels the tears coming, tears she had promised herself she wouldn't cry, not another single one.

Monica's face is expressionless, void of any emotion, and she knows – in that moment she knows the answer to the question.

'We'll always be sisters,' Monica says after a long pause, her voice almost a whisper, 'forever.'

Laurie shakes her head, stands to leave. The exchange has drained her; she feels exhausted. 'Goodbye, Monica.'

'Monsters are real, Laurie,' Monica calls out to her as she walks away. 'And ghosts too. Sometimes they live inside of us. And sometimes they win.'

EPILOGUE

The trial lasted three weeks. Despite the mountain of evidence, the DNA, the phone records, the CCTV footage and the tattoo, Miss Foster's eyewitness testimony plus Leanna George's statement, Monica Atkins pleaded not guilty. But psychopaths usually do. They relish their moment in the spotlight; it's their opportunity to continue causing hurt and pain by putting their victims and their relatives through more agony.

It all came out in court: the incest, the secret marriage between brother and sister, the abortions and the false promises made. It takes a fair bit to shock me nowadays, after the things I've seen, but the web of deceit and betrayal in this sordid story managed to. Robert and Monica Atkins had been leading double lives and keeping a dreadful secret that took the lives of two people and damaged countless others.

Leanna George survived but Douglas Lewis didn't. She couldn't be tried for his murder because there was no evidence left to convict her, but I think it's pretty safe to say she was behind her husband's untimely demise. It was challenging having to listen to the evidence of how she murdered Claire Wright and left baby Matilda to fight for her life, a life that was fortunately saved, thanks to the doctors.

There were tears and gasps of horror from the gallery, from the family and friends who had come to see justice done. Leanna George had to give evidence through a vocoder. Her larynx was all but destroyed by the lethal cocktail administered by Monica, who sat, for the most part, expressionless, as the evidence was presented in court. When the judge sentenced her to two concurrent life sentences, the gallery erupted and I think I fist-pumped the air. I'd told Claire Wright's distraught mother that I wouldn't rest until the culprit was behind bars and I'd meant it. But most of all, I had promised Laurie Mills that I would try in some small way to make right the many wrongs that had been done to her.

Laurie suspected that Monica was behind the car accident that had killed her unborn twins and subsequently sent her spiralling into alcoholism and depression but she couldn't prove it. The evil inflicted upon one woman by Robert and Monica Atkins was, at times, almost unbearable to hear. I had gone to see Laurie after the trial to talk to her and offer my support, and I discovered that she was planning to visit Monica in prison to try to find out if she and Robert had planned to murder her and their babies. I tried to talk her out of it, advised her not to. Monica would never be released and I didn't want Laurie to put herself through the pain of having to face that woman ever again. But she was adamant. I guess we all have our own ways of needing closure.

I hope, in some way, that it gives Laurie Mills some sort of peace.

Woods was ecstatic at the trial's verdict when the judge praised myself and my team for the work we put into catching Monica Atkins. One less murderer on the streets now.

'The press has gone wild for this story, Riley, and we come off looking like the winners.'

Winners. I don't see any of those in this story, but I let him have his moment of glee. That's what Woods really cares about: looking good, his reputation intact – reflective glory.

'We're lucky Laurie Mills isn't suing us,' I said, killing his buzz. 'Or that she hasn't gone to the press and bad-mouthed us.'

Woods' euphoria evaporated fast. 'Yes, well, I suppose we have you to thank for that, Riley,' he said, though I could tell it hurt him to say it.

'That sounds suspiciously like a compliment, sir,' I remarked dryly.

'Don't push it,' he said.

'I knew right from the very beginning that Laurie Mills wasn't our killer. Do you remember, sir? Do you remember me saying and that you kept saying—'

'Yes, yes, alright, Riley. You were right. I was wrong. There. Happy now?'

I smile. 'I think so, sir,' I replied.

As I made to leave, he stopped me, looked me square in the face. 'Oh, and Dan, that intuition of yours – keep it up, won't you?'

'I'll do my very best, sir,' I said as I closed the door behind me.

The media went mad for the Millses' story. I suppose, looking at it from their point of view it has everything a sensational story needs. Incest, love, betrayal, murder, abuse, religion, psychopaths, passion, jealousy, an explosive trial… and babies – dead babies. There can be nothing more emotive than dead babies. In fact, babies had featured heavily in one way or another throughout this case. Milo and Nancy, Matilda and Davis's pregnancy scare… perhaps, in some strange way, the cosmos was trying to tell me something.

Later that night, after Monica's arrest on the plane, I eventually returned home, elated but exhausted. It was still my birthday, but only just. Fi was waiting outside my apartment door. She was holding a balloon with 'Happy Birthday' written on it and a bottle of wine. I had no idea how long she must have been there.

'You remembered!' I said, genuinely surprised. I don't recall ever telling her when my birthday was.

'I'm a journalist,' she replied. 'We're known for our research skills.'

I took the balloon and the wine and invited her in.

'You got the killer then?' she said, sitting on the couch.

'Don't I always?' I replied, opening the wine and pouring two glasses. She looked radiant sitting there, her skin glowing and that spicy scent of hers filling the air.

'You look well, Fi,' I said, handing her a glass.

'Not for me,' Fi replied and I pulled my chin into my neck.

'That's not like you, Fiona,' I remarked, taking a deep gulp of my wine. I remembered then that she'd said there was something she needed to tell me.

'Yes, well. I won't be drinking for the next nine months at least.'

'Really? Why is that?' I ask, the penny not having yet dropped. I've always been a bit slow on the uptake where women are concerned. Rachel used to laugh at me, said it was 'endearing'.

'Because I'm pregnant, Dan,' she said, looking at me with her deep brown, almond-shaped eyes. 'And please don't even ask me, because the answer is yes, it *is* yours.'

I can't quite remember what exactly I did in those few seconds after she told me, but when I came to I was sitting down next to her. I think I was holding her hand.

'You're going to be a father, Daniel Riley,' Fi said.

I took another large gulp of my wine and said, 'Happy birthday to me.'

A LETTER FROM ANNA-LOU

Dearest Reader,

I am so grateful and thankful that you chose *The Couple on Cedar Close* as an addition to your reading list. I do so hope you'll enjoy the complex characters I've created and the dark twists and turns their lives, and the story, takes. I've loved every minute of writing this novel and hope it shows. In this book I have touched upon the subject of emotional and domestic abuse – an important issue close to my heart and one I hope I have done justice to – let me know what you think, and if you fell a little bit in love with Dan Riley like I have!

Your comments, feedback and reviews mean everything to me, so I'd be thrilled to know what you thought of *The Couple on Cedar Close* and if it was everything you hoped it might be. So, if you enjoyed *The Couple on Cedar Close* it would mean a lot to me if you would take the time to leave a review and let me, and other readers know why. I'm always recommending books to friends and family and vice versa, so if it encourages others to read one of my novels and enjoy the ride then I cannot thank you enough. – it makes it all worth it.

I'm busy beginning my next novel, something slightly different but once again with a chilling, dark and intriguing edge with a cast of complex and flawed characters. I don't want to give too much away at this stage so you'll just have to wait and see! I will keep you posted…

Much love, Anna-Lou xx

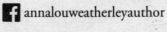

 annalouweatherleyauthor

 @annaloulondon

ACKNOWLEDGEMENTS

With special thanks to my wonderful editor and mentor, Claire Bord and all the amazing people at Bookouture who have helped bring this book to life and to the inimitable Kim Nash. Thanks to my fabulous agent, Madeleine Milburn and to Hayley Steed and all at the MM agency, my inspirational friend Kelly (and the girls) and to my beautiful sister and mummy – my life support – and my boys, Louie and Felix. And to my best boy ever, David. The summer of 2018 changed my life forever. I will never forget it. The gods put us together and I love you more than all the words I could ever write in a lifetime.